Praise for M
OTHER ARMS R

M000111280

"From the swamps of Georgia to the shores of the Guadalquivir River, from Flannery O'Connor to Walt Whitman, these stories demonstrate the extraordinary range of Michael Bishop's talent. Like O'Connor, he traffics in the southern gothic. Like Whitman, he preaches the freedom of the human spirit. But his voice is all his own. You will not soon forget the stories in this book. They cleave to the heart, and stick to the soul. They reaffirm Michael Bishop's mastery of his craft."
    —Dale Bailey, author of *The End of the End of Everything*

"It's time for the world to know what I've known for decades: Michael Bishop is our finest storyteller—bold, warm, wise, and incisively funny."
    —Kelly Robson, Aurora Award-winning author of "A Human Stain"

"My favorite things to find as a reader: intelligence, invention, surprise, wit, and wisdom. Michael Bishop's work is a master class in all of the above. This collection is a joy and did I mention funny? Bishop is so often so very funny. Here is a wonderful opportunity to discover or rediscover an extraordinary writer. Let's do it together!"
    —Karen Joy Fowler, author of *We Are All Completely Beside Ourselves*

"Strange, humane, cunning and clear-eyed, these are the short stories of a master of the form. Let me sing the praises of Michael Bishop."
    —Kelly Link, author of *Pretty Monsters*

"In his *Other Arms Reach Out to Me: Georgia Stories*, Michael Bishop accomplishes something all writers strive for, yet few achieve: near perfection in the literary arts. His handling of setting, character, language, and pacing is the work of a master artist, a writer reminiscent of O'Connor and Faulkner. I cannot remember such an engaging reading adventure in many years. This collection will surely secure Bishop's place among significant Southern writers."
    —Terry Kay, author of *The King Who Made Paper Flowers*

"I love these stories. They are as poignant, funny, sad, and tender as life. This is reality distilled and intensified, inventive and inevitable at the same time. Bishop's endings are both satisfying and subtle, a most difficult combination. These stories may be set mostly in Georgia, but they are stories for the world. And this may seem overdone, but it's how I feel: For anyone who says we'll never see another Chekhov, I have news. In Michael Bishop, the spirit of dear old Anton has returned to earth in a land of red hills, kudzu, decorative laundry, and Yellow Jackets. One more time: I love these stories."
    —Bruce Holland Rogers, author of *Thirteen Ways to Water*

"I first encountered Michael Bishop when I was in college and fell in love with "Dogs' Lives" in the *Best American Short Stories* of 1985, and I had to read everything he wrote! A long time has passed since then, but I'm still astonished by this man's work, and deeply excited—and grateful—for this new book!"
    —Dan Chaon, author of *Ill Will*

OTHER
ARMS
REACH
OUT TO ME

GEORGIA STORIES

Other Fairwood Press /
Kudzu Planet Productions novels
by Michael Bishop

Brittle Innings

Ancient of Days

Who Made Stevie Crye?

Count Geiger's Blues

A Funeral for the Eyes of Fire

Philip K. Dick is Dead, Alas

Joel-Brock the Brave and the Valorous Smalls

OTHER ARMS REACH OUT TO ME

GEORGIA STORIES

Michael Bishop

MICHAEL BISHOP

Pine Mountain,
Georgia
August 7, 2018

KUDZU PLANET
· PRODUCTIONS ·
BONNEY LAKE WA

OTHER ARMS REACH OUT TO ME GEORGIA STORIES
A Fairwood Press/Kudzu Planet Productions Book
June 2017

First Edition

PUBLICATION CREDITS:
"Andalusian Triptych, 1962," "Baby Love," and "The Road Leads Back" first appeared
in *Polyphony*. | "Unlikely Friends" first appeared in *Ellery Queen's Mystery Magazine*.
| "Crazy about Each Other," "The Russian Agent," and "Free" first appeared in *The
Chattahoochee Review*. | "Her Smoke Rose Up Forever" (under original title "Cutouts")
first appeared in *The Georgia Review*. | "How Beautiful with Banners" and "Doggedly
Wooing Madonna" first appeared in *Century*. | "Change of Life" first appeared in *New
York Stories*. | "Unfit for Eden" first appeared in *Postscripts*. | "Rattlesnakes and Men" first
appeared in *Asimov's Science Fiction*. | "Other Arms Reach Out to Me" and "No Picnic" are
wholly original to this collection.

Fairwood Press
21528 104th Street Court East
Bonney Lake, WA   98391
www.fairwoodpress.com

Cover image © Getty Images

Cover and book design by
Patrick Swenson

Kudzu Planet Productions
an imprint of Fairwood Press

ISBN13: 978-1-933846-65-1
First Fairwood/Kudzu Planet Productions Edition: June 2017
Printed in the United States of America

AUTHOR'S NOTE

About

two

years ago, I tried to persuade Patrick Swenson that this collection of mostly realistic (as opposed to fantasy- or SF-oriented) stories deserved to come out under the Kudzu Planet Productions imprint at his own fantasy-and-SF-oriented Fairwood Press. I gave him several reasons why he should accede to this idea, including the fact that the collection would start with a fantasy-tinged Flannery O'Connor *hommage* and conclude with a Georgia-based story set in the near future of an alternate timeline. I gave each reason an ordinal lead-in: "First," "Second," down to "Fifth" and maybe "Sixth." Patrick quickly emailed me back: "You had me at 'First.'" Therefore, Patrick, accept these heartfelt thanks.

For this book, as for my recent book for young people, *Joel-Brock the Brave and the Valorous Smalls*, Brad Strickland provided an additional close textual reading that resulted in the correction of many humbling factual goofs and stylistic infelicities. Brad, you indisputably warrant both credit and gratitude, and you indisputably have mine.

I also owe thanks to friend, colleague, editor, constructive critic, front-line proofreader, and all-around supporter Michael Hutchins, who long ago built a website for my work consisting of a bibliographical catalogue of my novels, story collections, short fiction, nonfiction pieces, poetry, even writings *about* my work. Without Michael's *Primary and Secondary Bibliography*, I would not have easily compiled this volume's Publications Credits. Also, after I revised "No Picnic" for a reading commissioned by Reinhardt University's low-residency MFA program, Michael asked to do a final proof of *Other Arms* . . . and found several more subtle points in need of addressing. Thank you, Eagle-Eye Hutchins.

Let me also earnestly thank the editors who published or gave direction to the stories just listed: Deborah Layne and the late Jay Lake at *Polyphony*; Hugh Ruppersburg for "The Road Leads Back" in *After O'Connor* and T. R. Hummer and Stephen Corey at *The Georgia Review* for having earlier made suggestions to improve the story; the late Eleanor Sullivan at *Ellery Queen's Mystery Magazine*; the late Lamar York at *The Chattahoochee Review* for "Crazy about Each Other," his successor Lawrence Hetrick for "The Russian Agent," and Hetrick's successor Marc Fitten for "Free," and managing editor Jo Ann Yeager Adkins, who provided direction during all three of these men's editorships; Dean Wesley Smith at *Pulphouse*; the late Stanley W. Lindberg at *The Georgia Review*; Robert K. J. Killheffer at *Century*; Daniel Caplice Lynch at *New York Stories*; Michele Colonna at *Driftwood*; Peter Crowther and Nick Gevers at *Postscripts*; and the always supportive Sheila Williams at *Asimov's Science Fiction*. Each reprinted story appears in a purposely different form than it did in its earlier place, or places, of publication.

Finally, these stories were written over many years, the earliest publication occurring in November 1982 ("Unlikely Friends") and the latest in February 2015 ("Rattlesnakes and Men"). Over all this time, as well as many years before and after these dates, the chief constant in my life, affording me food, drink, money, nerve, counsel, solace, and unconditional love, has been my wife, Jeri, without whom I would never have written these stories, for I might never have spent most of my adult life here in Georgia.

Jeri, this book is for you, as is the following dedication, which assertion may seem a contradiction. However, we both know it's anything but.

Pine Mountain, Georgia
July 23, 2016

for
Jamie
(November 9, 1971 – April 16, 2007)

≈

"Unable are the Loved to die
For Love is Immortality . . ."
                              —Dickinson

TABLE OF CONTENTS

Introduction by Hugh Ruppersburg   13

The Road Leads Back   17

Unfit for Eden   33

Andalusian Triptych, 1962   51

Unlikely Friends   62

Crazy about Each Other   77

Her Smoke Rose Up Forever   90

Other Arms Reach Out to Me   104

How Beautiful with Banners   117

The Russian Agent   131

Doggedly Wooing Madonna   147

Baby Love   160

Change of Life   174

No Picnic   187

Free   194

Rattlesnakes and Men   207

INTRODUCTION: BEYOND REGIONALISM
by Hugh Ruppersburg

The

stories

in Other Arms Reach Out to Me *take place in the American South,* most of them in Georgia. An exception is "Andalusian Triptych, 1962," about a Georgia-born man living in Spain. Ironically, their author, Michael Bishop, hasn't made his name as a regional writer. He's widely known as an award-winning writer of science fiction and fantasy, with two Nebula awards and other accolades to his credit. Yet several of his SF novels have Southern settings. His 1983 novel *Ancient of Days* explores what happens when a prehistoric human is discovered living in West Central Georgia. *Brittle Innings*, his wonderful 1994 baseball novel, takes place in a fictional South Georgia town whose farm club has a first baseman straight out of a famous tale by Mary Shelley. Bishop's deep familiarity with baseball as well as with the habits and ways of small-town Southern life during World War II—heat, eccentric characters, racism, humor, sex—enables him to provide a rich array of carefully observed details that evoke a rich sense of Southern place.

The same is true of *Other Arms Reach Out to Me.* These stories are steeped in the Southern landscape, culture, and character. They are grounded in a geographical place, a cultural milieu, that helps bring alive his characters and their situations. Their Southern ambience feels neither forced nor artificial. But I am hesitant to describe them as "regional," a word that might seem limiting. What most stands out for me in these stories is their emphasis on human individuals and dilemmas: children chafing against parents, parents distraught over lost children, teenage love, desire, marriage, old men in nursing homes, grief and depression, death. These are the topics and themes of the world's great literature. As richly evoked as the Southern setting may be, I could imagine most of these stories set in other parts of the world. The people and situations they describe are fundamental to human life.

Even so, it's important to consider the role of the American South in this collection. The literature of the South has offered since its early days a rich assortment of eccentric and unusual human characters. We saw them in the early writings of the southwestern humorists—for example, A. B. Longstreet's *Georgia Scenes* (1835) and George Washington Harris's *Sut Lovingood: Yarns Spun by a Nat'ral Born Durn'd Fool* (1867). Samuel Clemens (Mark Twain) was their successor.

A Southern writer of the twentieth century who continued to develop this tradition, and who made comic and grotesque characters a distinctive mark of her work, was Flannery O'Connor. Her most memorable characters are a strange fusion of the humorous and the malevolent. Mr. Shiftlet in "The Life You Save May Be Your Own" and Manley Pointer in "Good Country People" come immediately to mind. O'Connor's manner of characterization, her penchant for portraying grotesque characters and situations, are clear influences in many of the stories in *Other Arms Reach Out to Me*.

O'Connor's influence is especially evident in the first story: "The Road Leads Back," where a famous writer named Flora Marie Craft (based on O'Connor), at the urging of her friend Hettie Bestwick (an avatar of O'Connor's real-life friend Betty Hester) seeks a miraculous healing of her lupus in an Alabama monastery. A tale that might have ended in a stirring moment of spiritual healing or of disappointment instead goes awry in a fantastic and comical way. The story's whimsical humor, along with Bishop's compassionate portrayal of the ailing writer, makes it one of the best in the collection. It works as both homage and parody.

Other Arms Reach Out to Me offers many of its own eccentric and comical characters: in the bear-hunting father of "Unfit for Eden," the unprincipled detective-narrator of "Unlikely Friends," the institutionalized lovers in "Crazy about Each Other," the cerebral young man who proposes to a celebrity by mail in "Doggedly Wooing Madonna," and so on. The behavior and speech of Bishop's characters are often hilarious, but he portrays them with sensitivity. Rarely does he ridicule them. Usually, with a few notable exceptions, he displays more compassion toward his suffering characters than does either Twain or O'Connor. Distinctively drawn characters are a major element of the Southern atmosphere of Bishop's stories, and a means by which he speaks to the larger concerns of human experience.

One of the most traditional "Southern" stories here is "Unfit for Eden," told by a boy who grows up near the Okefenokee Swamp. After his father, a self-reliant bear hunter, dies in prison, neither the boy nor his mother can escape his legacy. The stepfather who replaces him is a truck-driving, wife-beating religious fanatic. The boy's entire background will seem strange to anyone who did not grow up in the swamps, for the tale's atmosphere grows out of its peculiar details: bear skulls, hidden copies of *Leaves of Grass*, sex in a cemetery. Everyone will recognize the conflict at its heart (a boy rebelling against a stepfather who denies his every interest and inclination), but the distinctiveness of this story stems from its deeply Southern milieu.

More often, Bishop takes an unusual, unexpected approach to traditional situations. Two of the stories are set in nursing homes. The title story "Other Arms Reach Out to Me" pits a cantankerous old man against a violinist who plays for residents of the home. He takes advantage of her need as a single mother for money, and in general there's not much likeable about him. A pathetically lonely figure, he describes himself as a "dying old fart who's buried four wives and gone ornery to boot." The story's ending is perhaps the grimmest in the volume, leaving us uncertain as to who the real villain is. In a second nursing home story, "No Picnic," a black attendant cares for an old man who harbors a personal resentment against him. He finally discovers a disturbing explanation for this attitude. Even if it does not lead to reconciliation, it at least allows a measure of understanding of the role that each man plays in the other's life. Both stories are notable for their ambiguous resolutions, as if Bishop intentionally leaves to the reader the burden of deciphering the moral and ethical questions they raise. These questions both unsettle and move the reader.

Bishop's stories are impressively diverse in style, voice, and content. Often humorous and/or satirical, they are never shallow, and comedy never overshadows the darker realities of men and women struggling with their lives, with what one of Bishop's characters calls "a series of ever more outlandish shocks." In "Baby Love," a man deals with grief and loneliness over his wife's death by devoting himself so obsessively to his infant daughter that he denies himself connections with others. In the poignantly humorous "Change of Life," a woman struggles with her love for a younger man obsessed with frogs. In "How Beautiful with Banners," an aging man who has lost his wife tries to prove his worth by "laundry bannering," competing with his neighbors in creatively hanging out clothes, old linens, dish rags, and assorted other items.

The most wickedly satirical story, "Rattlesnakes and Men," takes aim at the American mania with guns and the Second Amendment: instead of guns, however, the citizens of a small Georgia town must, by law, own rattlesnakes. The story, which Bishop himself has described as a "Georgia-based story set in the near future of an alternate timeline," has a grounding in fact: in Georgia, in 1982, the city of Kennesaw became the first of a number of towns to require citizens to own guns. Also, the small North Georgia town of Nelson recently passed its own mandatory ownership ordinance. In this day of alternative facts, "Rattlesnakes and Men" hardly over-stretches truth. Like George Saunders in *Tenth of December* or *CivilWarLand in Bad Decline*, the author portrays a recognizable world just askew from the one we know.

Michael Bishop works in the tradition of Erskine Caldwell, Flannery O'Connor, Harry Crews, Larry Brown, Janisse Ray, and other writers of the modern American South. The wealth of details in his descriptions of Georgia locations invests his stories with an authentic, palpable sense of place. But it is his skill in portraying distinctively individual characters that most strongly marks this collection. Because they reflect his deep empathy for the general human condition, the stories in *Other Arms Reach Out to Me* transcend regional limitations.

In the end, they are redemptive and life-affirming.

Hugh Ruppersburg is University Professor Emeritus of English and retired Senior Associate Dean of Arts and Sciences at the University of Georgia. He has written books on William Faulkner and Robert Penn Warren and edited five anthologies of work by and about Georgia writers, including *After O'Connor: Stories from Contemporary Georgia*, as well as a collection of essays about the writer Don DeLillo. He has received the Governor's Award in the Humanities in Georgia, Georgia Author of the Year award, and the Albert Christ Janer Creative Research Award at the University of Georgia.

THE
ROAD
LEADS
BACK

"I am really only interested in a fiction of miracles." —Flannery O'Connor

Flora
    Marie
        did not want to visit the Benedictine monastery in Alabama. Back in April, at the insistence of her aunt Claire, who had paid for the pilgrimage, she'd made a fatiguing round-trip journey by air to Lourdes. Aunt Claire had believed that a reverent dip in the shrine's waters would enable Flora Marie to throw away her crutches and live again as a "normal person."

Today, viewing herself in the rippled mirror on her bedroom door, Flora Marie still wore her crutches like jai alai baskets, their metal armlets pinching her biceps, her fingers clutching the padded grips. She wanted to pivot about and stump over to the paper-strewn desk visible in the murky glass—to settle in and work for an hour—but her unflagging encourager from Atlanta, Hetty Bestwick, had slain that option a week ago. Peeved, Flora Marie tried to resign herself to a long, dusty car ride in the bludgeoning July heat. It was plaguesome. If her mother and her aunt had had a nit's worth of sense, they would have sent her to Cullman, Alabama, two hundred miles away, *before* flying her to France and the overcrowded shrine of St. Bernadette.

Flora Marie closed her eyes. She knew what she looked like. "Not a beauty," her mama said. "Not even groundhog cute. But you have this quirk—almost a dignity—that may rescue you from spinsterhood."

But Flora Marie did not expect or even desire rescue from spinsterhood. She hoped instead for rescue from the inherited disease—systemic lupus erythematosus—gnawing at her connective tissue and periodically adorning her face with a rash like small red butterflies basking in the sun. This morning one such butterfly had alit in the valley between her nose and her left eye socket. It did not pain or even tickle her, but it seemed a malign rather than a healthy omen. Shoo enough of these critters into the morning and they would whelm the eye of day with blood . . . .

Flora Marie opened her eyes and her bedroom door and stumped into the gloomy hallway. This damned trip to the abbey was interrupting her writing, and who knew how long she had left, for writing or anything else? Seventeen years ago, her daddy, still a young man, had died of lupus.

In the hall, Mama Craft grabbed her by the shoulders, tugged at a pleat, grimaced at her hair. Flora Marie bore the insult. After all, she did not look like a woman to whom miracles happen. Sparse henna bangs stuck to her brow, while the rest of her hair stood out in frowzy Bozo-the-Clown tufts. Pressing them down had no effect; they sprang out again, like packets of cotton batting or fiberglass insulation. A dress of blue polyester with a strand of pearls at the neck, almost a choker, rescued her—that word again—from utter risibility . . . or, going by Mama Craft's sour grimace, maybe not. Who but a lupus patient or a hypothermia victim wore long sleeves in July?

From the parlor Bestwick shouted, "Come on, Rima! Unless you want to spend an extra night in a motel, we need to hit the road!"

"Rima?" Mama Craft said in a stage whisper.

"It's one of Bestwick's jokes, Mama. You call me Flit, she calls me Rima."

"I don't get it."

"*Green Mansions* by W. H. Hudson. I'm the bird-girl."

"I still don't get it."

Frowning, Flora Marie kissed her mother on the forehead. "Bless you. And never, never change."

"I don't get that either."

"Innocence becomes you. So does your total absence of irony."

"Oh." Mama Craft frowned just like her thirty-some-odd daughter, who clanked into the parlor like a tipsy Frankenstein monster.

Bestwick strode forward in a loud floral-patterned skirt and a blouse of such sheer white muslin that her bra showed through like a Mafioso's hidden heat. She kissed Flora Marie on the forehead, as Flora Marie had kissed Mama Craft. Her lips tarried, though, as if distilling nectar from the other woman's sweat.

"Hey, Rima, you look tiptop. I mean it. You'll come back ready to knock out a thousand pages."

"I look like a wounded pterodactyl. Half a page knocks *me* out." She leaned back from Bestwick's kiss. The red in the parlor thermometer, with ceramic hummingbirds on either side of the stalk-like tube, rose a quarter-inch.

"You ready? You look ready."

"My death on the road is on your shoulders, Bestwick. Find an old Negro man to dig me a hole and dump me into it. Then tamp down enough red clay to keep the hounds from clawing me back out."

Mama Craft took Bestwick's arm. "Forgive her. Flora Marie's always preferred sarcasm to sentiment, crassness to courtesy."

"Plain talk to alliteration. What's happened to you today, Mama? Did you drip vinegar into your egg-poaching water?"

"See? If Flit does die on the road, she'll slide straight to hell—with no layover in purgatory."

Flora Marie said, "With Mama around, God need never send me demons."

"You two." Bestwick seized the lumpy suitcase near the door, a TWA tag still on its handle, and swung it outside to her ivory, post-war Packard—in Flora Marie's eyes the automotive equivalent of a dromedary. Three peahens scratched in the driveway dust, and a black-and-white cow with enormous eyes ogled the house, its lips scrubbing each other like suede castanets.

Refusing help, Flora Marie slapped on a wide straw hat with a green plastic window in its brim and made her way outside to the Packard. She shoved her crutches through the back window and assumed the shotgun post with a gaze of stoic martyrdom. Let's get this over with, she thought. Once she had, no one—not even Bestwick—would impose again on either her fear or her tractability.

Driving northwest on Georgia 212, Hetty Bestwick steered as if the edges of the blacktop kept shifting, as if each dip in the road had the depth of a gulch. She sang torch songs like "Stormy Weather," "The Man Who Got Away," and "Some Other Spring," not kiddy crap like "This Old Man" or "She'll Be Comin' Round the Mountain." For this blessing, Flora Marie lifted thanks to the archangel Raphael, the Magi, St. Christopher, Saint Nick, and Anthony of Padua.

She and Hetty Bestwick had met in person only twice before this road trip to the Ave Maria Grotto at St. Bernard Abbey—once at the Crafts' homeplace, Blue Peacock Pastures, and once in Atlanta during a week that Flora Marie spent in Piedmont Hospital. Otherwise the two knew each other only through correspondence, which Bestwick had initiated by writing a letter, at once approving and critical, about a story of Flora Marie's, "The Feast of Perpetua," in an issue of *The Okefinokee Quarterly*. Not many people read the literary journals in which Flora Marie published under the pseudonym *F. M. Throne*, and fewer wrote letters to their contributors. The letters that did come sounded like either the praise of doting parents or the ravings of psychopaths.

Hetty Bestwick had written, *"Did you have Wm. Faulkner's* The Town *in mind when you wrote this story? Not as a model, of course, or even as an anti-model, but as a satiric riposte to its romantic satire of idiot country lust. If so, Mr. Throne, you probably should have made Perpetua a little more self-aware."*

The critique went on—intelligently—for three more single-spaced typed pages. Flora Marie replied as earnestly as Bestwick had addressed her, confessing her true identity and divulging her real name. Soon, they were avid typewriter-pals, discussing—debating, in fact—everything from the writings of Dietrich Bonhoeffer to the novels of Iris Murdoch to the probability of miracles in a secular age. Flora Marie did not care to imagine the vast hole that would open in her life if Bestwick—cheerleader, kibitzer, and pest—ever withdrew from their friendship.

"Roll up your window, Rima," Bestwick said as they bumped past a tumbledown strip mall on Atlanta's outskirts.

"Why? You figger to get rich off your otter-graphed F. M. Throne first editions if I die of heat stroke?"

"Come on," Bestwick said. "Roll it up."

Flora Marie cranked the handle. Squeaking, a pane of glass hitched upward in the opening. Like the visor in her hat brim, this pane must have originated in a factory in the Emerald City of Oz. It filtered the world into her vision in kaleidoscopic shades of green, as if through the bottom of a Co' Cola bottle, bathing her in fake forest coolness.

"Criminy," Flora Marie said.

"I meant to have green in every window, but couldn't afford it. So I put it there." Bestwick shrugged.

"Thanks." A doctor had told Mama Craft that Flora Marie's sensitivity to light, a feature of her lupus, required special measures—a hat, stockings, and long sleeves in summer. They should also put tinted glass in their car windows. Taking these measures made every trip outdoors a complex safari.

"For a two-day trip, Bestwick, you shouldn't have bothered."

"Sue me."

"For what? Signed copies of my own books?"

"And of a hundred other, even better, writers'."

Bestwick had a library, all right. She wrote reviews for the Atlanta newspapers and a Catholic publication, *The Bulletin,* to which "F. M. Throne" also contributed. She spent most of the money she made as a civilian office grub at Dobbins Air Force Base on novels, biographies, philosophy texts, and periodicals. According to her letters, books insulated her sitting-room apartment. They held up tabletops, spilled from her closet, smoldered on stove eyes. She slept on them. She traded them for others and used them as barter bait. The clothes she wore today she had swapped for a review copy of a new book by a notorious Southern female novelist.

"You sure made out on that deal," Flora Marie said.

"Amen." Bestwick guffawed, and the Packard chugged along with three of its windows open, like a blast furnace on Firestones. Soon they hit U.S. 278, which angled up to Cedartown, down to Piedmont, Alabama, up again to Gadsden, and up and across to Cullman, their destination. Despite the Andrew Marvell shade of her green window, Flora Marie's dress stuck to the upholstery. Sweat pooled in the toes of her low-heeled pumps. Her joints burned like sulfur pits.

Still, they halted only for fuel and bathroom breaks. Motoring westward, they ate Mama Craft's tomato-and-mayo sandwiches, guzzled ice water from cheesecloth-draped Ball jars, and wrangled like sisters. Why couldn't they have waited for cooler weather? Lourdes hadn't really had time to kick in yet.

Bestwick said, "Some folks have bosses and can't pick their vacation times."

Flora Marie said, "Anyway, St. Bernard Abbey has no *reputation* for healing the blind and crippled. It's a monastery with a bunch of tiny buildings as a tourist attraction. I might as well dip in Lake Sinclair."

Bestwick said that a "woman of faith"—this was a dig, for Bestwick seemed always about to jettison her faith like a prolapsed girdle—could turn a cathouse into a hospital. A monastery clearly offered better source material for a positive transformation than a bordello.

"But *you* don't credit miracles," Flora Marie said. "You thought my pilgrimage to Lourdes a 'superstitious farce.' That's a quote, Bestwick."

"Yes, but I have more faith in you than in God, and more love for you than for Yahweh in his Cosmic Bully guise." When Flora Marie flinched, Bestwick said, "Easy. God won't chunk a thunderbolt through our engine block."

Ahead of them, an Alabama State Trooper in a fawn-colored uniform, a Smokey Bear hat, and glossy boots stood in the highway, his hand extended like a halfback stiff-arming a defender. An eight- or nine-year-old boy in blue jeans, sneakers, and a T-shirt with a big zigzag across it—like Charlie Brown's in the *Atlanta Constitution* funnies—squatted on the shoulder, his eyes on the ground.

Bestwick cried, "Holy Jeez!" and hit the brakes. Envisioning a collision, Flora Marie shut her eyes. The Packard screeched to a shuddering stop.

Thankfully, they had *not* steamrollered the trooper, who squinted at them out of a horsy face twitching madly. He reminded Flora Marie of a cowboy actor over whom she had once swooned in serials at the Pix Theater downtown.

"What did I *do*?" Bestwick said. Despite her skeptical adult conversion to the Catholic Church, she had an ineradicable streak of guilty Calvinism in her makeup. That streak sometimes mixed with a severe blue nihilist tendency that caused her to pale about the dewlaps, as she had now.

"Howdy, ladies," the trooper said. "I need to borrow your car."

"Where's yours?" Bestwick asked.

"A fella playing possum right there," nodding toward the boy, "tricked me into playing Good Samaritan. Then the sneaky sumbitch—pardon my Esperanto—grabbed my pistol and stole my patrol car."

"That *child* grabbed your gun?"

"Nome," said the trooper. "That's my boy Wallace. A perpetrator unknown hoodwinked us. If you won't give up your Packard, ma'am, I'll have to expropriate it."

The boy piped, "He didn't hoodwink me! That red-checkered rag over his face told me straight off he was a sneaky sumbitch!"

"Watch your language, Wallace," the trooper said.

Bestwick told Officer Stagger that he and Wallace could ride with them to Hokes Bluff or the nearest Alabama patrol station, but she had no intention of giving her car to anybody without legal title to it. Officer Stagger could try to make her, but lacking a gun, he would have to compel two law-abiding women—one on crutches—with his fists or his wits, and Bestwick doubted the efficacy of the latter.

"We'll ride." Officer Stagger beckoned the boy over, and they climbed into the backseat. The trooper's knees rose up behind Flora Marie like stony peaks.

Wallace hugged his door and refused to look at his daddy. He mumbled, "This is fer shit." Officer Stagger flushed like a Baptist at a beatnik poetry festival. Flora Marie feared that he would lean over and strangle his son.

"Sir," Bestwick said, "why'd you bring Wallace out here with you?"

"For two months he begged me to. This morning, I truckled and did it."

"I never figgered *this*'d happen," Wallace said.

Flora Marie said, "Is it legal for troopers to take kids on patrol?"

"Nome. I broke the rules for the ungrateful little squeak. I may've lost my job." His he-man voice had a tremolo in it.

"Why don't I drop you at the next phone?" Bestwick said. "We'll carry Wallace home while you get right with your bosses. No need at all to mention the boy rode with you this morning."

"I appreciate that," the trooper said. "I still may get canned, but I appreciate that an almighty lot."

Wallace snorted.

They did what Bestwick had suggested, dropping Stagger at a farmhouse to use the telephone and then transporting Wallace to a wood-frame bungalow outside Gadsden. Their good deed did not divert them from their own route even so much as a mile. But as he got out, Wallace told them that because his mama worked, he would have to spend the afternoon alone, watching sunlight crawl across a pine-plank floor.

"Do something useful for your folks," Bestwick said. "Wash some dishes. Make a bed. Get dinner ready."

"Read a book," Flora Marie said to his back.

On the front porch Wallace, who had an impressive dearth of charm, turned and shouted, "Think I'll haul ass to Alaska!" He jumped off the porch and darted into a bleak copse of sycamores.

"He's running away," Flora Marie said mildly.

"The little heathen's snapping your garters. Don't worry about him. It's time you worried about yourself."

They drove on past pines and blackjack oaks, past cow pastures and huge tree-festooning veils of kudzu.

*

By the time they reached Cullman, Flora Marie could not even think about visiting its outlying monastery. The torrid backblasts of eighteen-wheelers had rocked a hot ache into her bones and scoured her of strength. Their whole on-the-road adventure had set a lupine beast loose inside her, and the beast was rampaging, tearing up the place. Aloud, she confessed only to travel fatigue.

Bestwick found a motel, Osterreider's Slumber Shacks, a village of twelve log cabins with blinding white seams, as if someone had caulked them from giant toothpaste tubes. The Shacks sat two miles from St. Bernard Abbey, in a pine glade, with a totem pole before each cabin and a placard on the pole to name the cabin: Sequoyah, Black Elk, Pontiac. Both women chortled when Mr. Osterreider assigned them to cabin Rain-in-the-Face.

The shower in Rain-in-the-Face barely worked. Water leaked from it in echoey drips. There was a clock radio but no television set, and every station—as they searched for an accurate time report—had a gargling announcer wailing Gospel songs or a rushing avalanche of static. Silverfish infested the wallpaper. Palmetto bugs scuttled from the radiator to the shade of their spavined double bed. Without warning, Flora Marie stabbed one of the critters with a crutch tip.

"I know why your mama calls you Flit," Bestwick said.

Flora Marie sat down on the bed. "You do, do you?"

"Because you're lethal to insects."

"Actually, Bestwick, she calls me Flit because I don't. It's her only gallop into facetiousness."

"You don't what?"

"Flit about. I stay the course. I have the patience of Job. Except when I get to thinking that pretty darn soon I might cease to be—here, anyway—and leave an irksome lot of work undone."

"So why not get good and Catholic and pray?"

"I ain't a good prayer, Bestwick. My type of spirituality is almost totally shut-mouth."

Like ten-year-olds in a summer-camp cabin, they talked long after darkness had fallen. They traded gibes, secrets, jokes, philosophies, literary likes and dislikes, and chunks of family history. Flora Marie learned that, from the age of ten, Hetty Bestwick had stayed her own course as an orphan.

"I saw my mother hang herself," Bestwick said. "When I came in the front door, she kicked over the stool she'd climbed and began to strangle. I grabbed her feet to pull her down, but that just made it worse."

"Oh honey."

"Do you suppose she went to Hell?"

"For killing herself?"

"For letting me see her do it."

Flora Marie had no answer for that. She had no answer for a lot of things. She understood the impetus to apostasy, though. Prostrate, she had crawled to its brink once a week for the past eight years.

"I don't think Lourdes worked," she said. "I'm afraid this won't either."

"Hey, Flit, maybe you haven't given Lourdes enough time. Put on the patience of Job. Some miracles have to gestate."

"If you believed that, why'd you bring me here? It steps all over the miracle that Aunt Claire tried to give me."

"Insurance," Bestwick said.

Flora Marie stayed mute. She did not consider faith insurance but a response to love. It wavered only when you saw no clear evidence of the love that had triggered it. Disease, betrayal, and suicide could strike you with spiritual cataracts more surely, and much more quickly, than could either age or rationalism.

"What's the matter?" Bestwick said. "Didn't you pay your premiums?"

"Probably not. It ain't my policy."

Bestwick walked over to Flora Marie, lifted her pointed chin, and kissed her on the mouth. Flora Marie stared at her in frank perplexity.

On Tuesday morning, the ivory Packard cruised onto the grounds of St. Bernard Abbey, past the small monastic cemetery and into the parking area near the entrance to Little Jerusalem and Ave Maria Grotto. They had come so early that they had first choice of the tourist slots, so Bestwick parked in front of the gift shop by which visitors stepped down into Brother Joseph Zoettl's one-of-a-kind garden of miniature basilicas, churches, and statues, "The Scenic Shrine of the South."

A man in a coarse white habit—the monks in the distance wore *black* robes—met them at the car. Construction noises issued from the deeper grounds, methodical work on a huge stone abbey. Wielding her crutches, Flora Marie saw them as flying buttresses—the architecture of man versus the architecture of God. Obviously, the new church would last longer.

"Pardon," the monk in white said, "but no one may enter the garden until noon." Brother Joseph, he added, was installing a new replica, and the abbot wanted no mishaps as the old man pursued his special calling.

Bestwick protested. She recounted all their reasons for visiting and catalogued their travel hardships. "This is F. M. Throne," she said, nodding at Flora Marie. "For eight straight days her mother has recited novenas to heal her of her lupus. At nine a.m. today, Mrs. Throne will recite the final novena as her daughter genuflects before the Virgin in Ave Maria Grotto. Miss Throne's cure, her mother believes, hinges on the simultaneity of these two faith events."

The white-clad monk did not even blink.

A regular stele of salt, Flora Marie thought.

"Miss Throne writes reviews for *The Bulletin*," Bestwick said. "Her story 'The Feast of Perpetua' appeared in last fall's issue of *The Okefinokee Quarterly*."

The monk turned to Flora Marie. "I've *read* that story." His pupils contracted. "It was wonderful—excellent, in fact. Come." He led them around the gift shop, so that Flora Marie would not have to negotiate the stairs, and introduced them into the garden by a gate reserved for monks and postulants. Then he vanished.

"Our first miracle," Bestwick said.

"Yeah. A monk who reads *The Okefinokee Quarterly*."

Flora Marie looked about. An asphalt path made a circuit among the garden's trees. On each side Lilliputian structures arose, entire cityscapes alternating with isolated caves, towers, and statues. You could not help feeling like a clumsy ogre here, especially if you lurched past the displays on crutches. I'm King Kong in a Disneyland for kobolds and leprechauns, Flora Marie told herself.

Still no sign of Brother Joseph, the hunchback Benedictine who had created the miniatures and laid out the garden showcasing them. The women strained to see farther down the path, to hear some noise betraying Brother Joseph's work at a site beyond the main grotto and the hillside Holy Land replicas. Despite the patchy shade, heat seethed from the path and from the stones of the low retaining walls.

"My God," Bestwick said. "This place is bizarre."

Brother Joseph had based his models of the Statue of Liberty, St. Peter's Basilica, the Alamo, the Hanging Gardens of Babylon, Noah's ark, and every other structure on postcard images. He had shaped them from marbles, sea-shells, cold cream jars, green-glass fishing-net floats, birdcages, broken glass, paste jewelry, sequins, and concrete. For the twin domes of the Immaculate Conception Cathedral in Mobile, he had used old toilet-bowl floats. Every structure had something cockeyed or askew about it because Brother Joseph had gathered his materials at random and guessed at the architectural features not visible on his postcards. This asymmetry, along with a childlike disregard for scale, blessed the whole garden with the waking irreality of a fever dream. Except for the sincerity, it all hinted at something akin to satire.

"I like it," Flora Marie said. She approved of distortion. Abstraction, on the other hand, always got her goat.

"You would," Bestwick said.

They hiked past a Roman aqueduct, the Coliseum, the Leaning Tower of Pisa, and an effigy of St. Frances Cabrini. At the Ave Marie Grotto they halted so that Flora Marie could hang her head—in worship or shame?—before a standing Virgin Mary, baby Jesus in her arms, at the center of a cave at least thirty feet tall. They did this for the white-clad monk's sake, in case he was spying on them from a gift-shop window.

Bestwick whispered, "Feeling any stronger?"

Flora Marie lifted her gaze to the Virgin's chalky face then turned it on Bestwick. "I'm ready to go, Hetty."

"You only call me Hetty when you're irritated."

"I'm ready to go, Bestwick."

Bestwick's upper lip glistened with sweat. "You're the one who buys into this miracle stuff. Work with me a little." She nodded at the Virgin Mary among the shell-encrusted stalactites. "Work with *her*.

"It doesn't want work. It wants submission."

"Then sub*mit*, goddamn it. I didn't drive across parts of two states just for you to tighten your jaw."

Flora Marie looked down the path, which, just beyond the hillside of Holy Land miniatures, circled back to the gift shop. She clanked off toward those scenes.

"Work *does* enter into it," Bestwick said, following her. "*Ora et labora*—work and prayer. That's the Benedictine motto."

"I work better at home."

"You're deliberately misconstruing me."

Around the Holy Land diorama, clanking *up*hill for a change, Flora Marie spotted the creator of the miniatures. Near the end of the path, Brother Joseph Zoettl, a miniature himself, stooped over a fairy-tale structure with a central bell tower and independent flanking turrets. He wore the black Benedictine habit, which stressed rather than softened his hunchback, and probed with a putty knife at the tiny steps climbing to the model's turret level. Beside him, a fidgety weasel of a man in overalls and ragged tennis shoes held out a palette of soupy cement.

"Hold still, Norbert," Brother Joseph said.

"Finally," Bestwick said. "Behold the miracle worker. He looks less than godlike to me."

"He's an artist, not a miracle worker," Flora Marie said. "You only get them mixed up if you mistake talent and craft for omnipotence."

Bestwick sucked her teeth. "Let's cut the sniping, Marie, and see what the little bugger can do for you."

Brother Joseph looked up, squinting out of a thin gnomish face. His putty knife sliced the air anxiously. He smiled with puzzling tentativeness. The man whom he had called Norbert scowled as if his belly hurt and stared at the approaching women with obvious distaste. Neither man had expected visitors.

Bestwick took charge. She escorted Flora Marie up to Brother Joseph and told him the same story—minus the novena business—that she had laid on the monk in white. She said that the white-robed monk had let them into the garden so that Brother Joseph could speak an intercessory prayer for Miss Throne and heal her once and for all of her potentially fatal disease. Flora Marie turned tomato red, but *not* from a rash of epidermal butterflies.

"I make little buildings." Brother Joseph tapped his current project. "For healing prayers you should go to Abbot Luibel or Brother Rotkopf." The skin on Flora Marie's arms began to itch. Brother Joseph's project was a model of the basilica-shrine at Lourdes. An image of the original shrine flickered in her mind's eye atop this detailed but imperfect copy. "Oh," Brother Joseph said, nodding at the ferret-faced fellow beside him. "Meet Norbert Grimes, postulancy candidate. Only yesterday he came—again. Already I have put him to work."

Norbert Grimes seethed like a boiling kettle. "Hullo." A glob of cement plopped on one of his sneakers.

"So you hope to find God here, Mr. Grimes?" Bestwick said.

"I'd planned to get lost from whole damned herds of hell-bound women."

"Norbert," Brother Joseph gently chided him.

"Until y'all take me in, call me Ishmael," Grimes said. "Why? 'Cause my mama kicked me out, my grandma dumped me onto no-account strangers, and three ungrateful bitches divorced my ass." He laid his palette of cement aside, pulled a red-checkered rag from his pocket, and wiped his angry face.

"Maybe they didn't like the way you talked," Bestwick said.

"So far as my blood kin goes, I doubt it," Grimes said. "They unloaded me 'fore I'd said word one, much less pea-turkey. My exes I won't assume to speak for."

"Good for you," Flora Marie said, registering the hate in his eyes and seeing his handkerchief with a tingle akin to recognition.

Bestwick turned from Grimes. "We believe in *you*," she told Brother Joseph. "And in God, of course, and we've driven two hundred miles. You must pray for Flora Marie, you must lift the curse of her lupus."

Brother Joseph shook his head.

"How hard is it to say an intercessory prayer? It can't be as hard as making these buildings."

"I am better with my hands than with words, Miss Bestwick."

"How old are you?"

"Eighty—eighty this year."

"Miss Throne is thirty-three and an artist like you. Do you want her life snuffed out before she can complete even *half* her life's work?"

"Don't blackmail the poor man," Flora Marie said.

Brother Joseph shook his head again, but seized Flora Marie's left arm and laid his other hand on his Lourdes replica. "Can you stand without your crutches, young woman?" Flora Marie nodded. "Then hand them to Norbert."

Grimes took them as if receiving a pair of aluminized rattlesnakes.

"O Raphael," the old man said, "lead this woman to the country of transfiguration. Heal her so that she may not be as a stranger in the province of joy. Remember her, you who are strong, you whose home lies beyond the region of thunder."

He neglected to say *"Amen,"* but Flora Marie, who intuited that Brother Joseph had never spoken so many words at one time in his life, felt a charge in her blood, a fresh elasticity in her joints. When he released her arm, she half

believed that she could walk unassisted back around the Ave Maria Grotto
to the garden gate and Bestwick's car. She resolved to try.

Grimes's arms leapt unexpectedly into the air. "What the hell!" he
shouted.

Flora Marie's crutches broke free of his hands and stepped out onto the
path *by themselves.* They scissors-hiked in mechanical cahoots along the route
that she had just contemplated. Looking at once snake-bit and spite-driven,
Grimes dragged a pistol from his bib pocket and blasted away at them hap-
hazardly. His shots reverberated like sonic booms. Even the blue jays fell
silent.

"Damnation!" Grimes cried in fury.

Flora Marie's legs failed her, and she dropped amid her skirts like a cut-
loose marionette. Brother Joseph crouched beneath his lopsided hunch, leaning away from his fake Lourdes and grasping his head like a well-schooled
student during a Civil Defense drill.

Bestwick said, "Holy Jeez," and knelt beside Flora Marie. "Dear God,
Marie, are you okay?" She glared at Grimes as Flora Marie imagined she
would at a rowdy library patron.

"Please don't fret. I'm fine—no different than before."

"No thanks to Ishmael there." Bestwick stood and faced the alleged pos-
tulant. "You crazy bastard. It's no damned mystery why all your women cast
you out."

"Shut up," Grimes said. He turned his pistol on the miniature Lourdes
and blew away a turret. Concrete shrapnel jumped into the air, striking both
Brother Joseph and Bestwick, and grazing the brim of Flora Marie's hat. "If I
want comments from a high-horse lezbo, I'll ask for 'em." He leveled the barrel at Bestwick. Its bore reminded Flora Marie of a ravenous open manhole.

"Take him at his word," Flora Marie advised Bestwick.

Bestwick put her hands on her hips. "Like you'd *really* shoot, you two-bit
make-believe gangster." Cuts on her forearm oozed flamboyant red freckles.

Flora Marie cringed. Grimes thrust the pistol forward and squeezed the
trigger, which *click-click-clicked* like the switch on a dead car battery. Bestwick
assumed a stooped knock-kneed stance, crossed her arms over her bosoms,
and screamed in terror. From everywhere around the grotto, monks came
running, including the dignified monk in white, all lifting their skirts like
belles at a cotillion. "You lucky bitch!" Grimes cried and threw his gun at
Bestwick's feet. Then he zigzagged up the slope on which Brother Joseph had

built his Lourdes, vaulted a wrought-iron picket fence, and ran like sixty. His red-checkered rag fluttered atop the turret fragments on the shrine's upper court.

The white-robed monk shouted, "Norbert, you can't just keep coming and going! Eventually, you'll have to make your profession! One day you'll have to *stick!*" Grimes yelled an obscenity over his shoulder. Some young Benedictines pursued him out of sight, hearing, and bounds—whereupon Flora Marie's crutches scissored back around the pathway, climbed the slope, leapt the fence, and, clanking almost melodically, joined the implausible chase.

Bestwick recovered her wits. She seized fistfuls of Brother Joseph's habit and twisted them cruelly. "I didn't want you to make the *crutches* walk! You were supposed to help *Flora Marie!* Can't you even do a simple miracle right?"

"Stop it," Flora Marie said.

Brother Joseph had gone as white as a bleached camisole. He put his hands on Bestwick's and leaned away from her frenzy. "I tink everyting I try comes out a little crooked," he said, his old Bavarian accent resurrected. "Maybe you haff come to the wrong man."

"No," Flora Marie said. "You did fine. You certainly knocked the props out from under *me*. The real miracle is, you kept us from getting killed."

"Poppycock!" Bestwick blurted. *"Poppycock!"*

The white-clad monk helped Flora Marie up. Brother Joseph approached his shattered facsimile of Lourdes and knelt before it as a penitent. He sifted turret fragments through his fingers. With corrugated brow, he appeared to ponder the task of renovating what Grimes had ruined. Allowing Brother Joseph's superior to support her, Flora Marie regarded the old man with clinical rue. It wasn't every day you witnessed a miracle, even a splendidly bungled one.

Bestwick turned on the monk in white. "That man stole a state trooper's pistol and car!" She flung her hand after the fleeing culprit. "He shot up that toy building. He nigh-on to murdered *me*, and you're worried about him making a *profession of faith?*"

The white-robed monk thought a moment. "Well, even if the brothers fail to catch him, he'll be back. He shows up here three or four times a year. When next he does, we'll give him over to the proper authorities, the unhappy fellow."

Bestwick raged at this offhand expression of sympathy. How many innocents would Grimes maim or kill before he returned to St. Bernard Abbey?

Flora Marie dialed this rant out. Grimes longed for commerce with humanity, solace in the company of men. His inability to stick surely had something to do with the fact that these men wore habiliments reminiscent of the raiment of women. Flora Marie felt woozy again. How long would her crutches run before they collapsed and would they ever return to buttress the rest of her problematic walk?

A month later Hetty Bestwick telephoned Flora Marie from Atlanta to announce—as a courtesy to Flora Marie, given her sisterly interest in her soul—that she had decided to leave the church. The events at the abbey had forced her to an irrefutable conclusion, that the patriarchal God who had effected the "miracle" of the crutches would rather play the fool than the physician.

Distressed, Flora Marie said, "What about the fact that Grimes's pistol jammed when he tried to shoot you?"

"That was no miracle," Bestwick said. "That was shoddy firearm manufacture." Anyway, she no longer believed in a God who would pull such a pair of grotesque stunts. She would certainly never renounce her painstakingly arrived-at disavowal of an antique communal superstition.

"I ache for you," Flora Marie said.

"Rejoice for me," Bestwick said, and soon rang off.

Two days later Flora Marie posted a letter in which she harangued her apostate friend: *"Faith is a gift but the will has a great deal to do with it . . . . Subtlety is the curse of man. It is not found in the deity."*

Their friendship endured for several years, but nothing Flora Marie ever wrote or said turned Bestwick back. And when Flora Marie died at age thirty-nine, devastating Mama Craft, Hetty Bestwick, and a vast cloud of admirers, butterflies rose from Blue Peacock Pastures and whelmed the eye of day with blood.

UNFIT
FOR
EDEN

I

began

life as a trespasser and a squatter. Against the laws of state and nation,
Cynthia Thrash Colter bore me in a cane-syrup shed on Colters Hammock.
I saw my first light at first light on May 27, 1946, on a swamp-pent island on
the southeastern boundary of the Okefinokee[1]. It was hot, but summer had
not yet fully infested the longleaf pine barrens or the cypress bays.

My birth certificate—which Miss Cynthia picked up at the courthouse
some months on—gives my birthplace as Fosterville, but I emerged from her
womb a bona fide swamper, the scion of two old families of swamp squatters,
the Colters and the Thrashes. Both go back four generations to the arguable
beginnings of the Okefinokee settlement. Mama didn't squeeze me out in
that syrup shed because her own house had no attraction, but because her almost hormonal sense of tradition drove her to this foot-shaped island where
the Colters had grubbed a living for eighty-odd years. She had no one to help
her. If my head had banged her pubic bone, or my butt had presented first,
we'd have died on that half-mile-long hammock, a scimitar of peat mats in a
sluice of neverwets and purple bladderworts.

Where was my daddy? Well, Ezra Colter had got life in prison for killing a man in a ranger-op station between Colters Hammock and Fosterville.
Late in 1937, the feds declared most of the Okefinokee a national wildlife
refuge—a fine thing, unless you'd been baptized in swamp tannin and spent
your boyhood gossiping with gators, Lord-God woodpeckers, wildcats, and
such.

---

[1] Dictionaries spell it *Okefenokee*, but early settlers preferred *Okefinokee*, and I use
the latter because, as a descendant of those settlers, I am a swamp thing, a spawn of
that primal stew.

As newlyweds, Daddy Ezra and Miss Cynthia withdrew from Colters Hammock to a patch of palmettos and sand as near to the Oke as they could legally get. They left behind a syrup shed (my future nativity site), a grinding sweep, a smokehouse, a corncrib, and a graveyard that the feds kept their promise to protect—by girdling it with a chain-link fence. Daddy Ezra might have fared better if he had cajoled them into giving him a bale of chain-link to encincture his new homestead.

Actually, he did have a fence there—a picket fence with a cypress gate from the Colters Hammock farm. But this fence only walled off the dooryard from the palmetto scrub, leaving the livestock (a few Herefords, some razorbacks, a mule) to the mercy of marauding black cassena bears. What made that fence infamous, though, was that Daddy Ezra adorned its stakes with the skulls of bears he'd shot. Each long white skull reminded him of a particular skirmish in his campaign to save his pigs from predation. Although he admired those bears' appetites, he despised them for lusting after bacon, *his* bacon, and sixteen skulls on sixteen palings told everybody just how much he hated them and how unrelentingly he fought.

A neighbor—a cousin of Miss Cynthia's, a veteran of the Okinawa campaign, and a wildlife ranger—warned Ezra against shooting the "casseniyie bears." As denizens of a federal refuge, they had a right to kill whatever they stumbled on as prey. Ezra loved the bears he hated, but never regarded them as holier than his livestock. He hung stone deaf to the warnings of Myron Thrash, the ranger in question, and broke out his 12-gauge to defend his animals.

Despite his combat ribbons and Purple Heart, Thrash dreaded every face-to-face with Daddy Ezra. He did have balls enough to sneak over on moonless nights and snatch a couple of skulls from their palings. He never stole more than two at a time, though, so it took Ezra three of these moonlight trips to wise up and set out a trap for the skulljacker. If he'd shot Thrash in the act, no jury would have convicted him, but Thrash caught wind of Ezra's stratagem and skulked low. Sadly, he told the head ranger in Waycross about Ezra Colter's war on the bears, and word of this betrayal by a kinsman flew falcon-quick back to Ezra.

Thrash made a second mistake, or let circumstances conducive to his undoing arise in his own house. One morning his nine-year-old son trekked across the palmetto scrub with a dilapidated garden cart, figuring to bask in the glory of Colter's legend by handing over three sun-bleached skulls. He hoped Daddy Ezra would mount them on his fence alongside his other grue-some trophies.

"Where'd you get these?" Ezra asked young Chad.

"Offn the back seat of our car."

"Did your daddy get them from somebody else, or did he just happen on them on his own?"

"That last," Chad said. "Said he had some skulls pretty enough for your hurrah fence, so I brung them over."

"You've a good heart, boy. Reckon where you got it?"

The next day Ezra poled a pirogue out to Sturgis Island where Thrash did most of his rangering. He tracked him to the operation shed, denounced him as a Judas, and then, with one trigger squeeze, sent Thrash slamming into the wall. Before anyone could seize him, Ezra stalked out, stepped in his pirogue, and stobbed as far toward home as the tea bogs would allow. He crooned old swamp ballads one after another—from "The Rabbit Song" to "My Pretty Mohee." He hoped to escape, but if he didn't, he sure wouldn't lie to anybody about what he'd done.

That evening, the law came to the door with Chad as guide, arrested him, and took him to Waycross. At trial, Daddy Ezra wore shoes for one of the few times in his life, and convicted himself by answering every question straight up.

Daddy Ezra died in prison. He refused to kowtow to inmate bullies, one of whom knifed him on the exercise yard. Ezra bit off the nose of his killer, who screamed twenty minutes after my old man passed.

With state and federal permission, the Colters—and a few forgiving Thrashes—buried Daddy Ezra in the Colters Hammock cemetery. Mama laid a black-bear skull from our picket fence on his grave. Jimmy Day, a hard-shell preacher, pled for God's mercy, but promised nothing. Miss Cynthia held me on her hip, a counterweight to the skull until it came time for her to lay it.

Mama had me christened *Dwight David* after the supreme commander of the Allies, Dwight David Eisenhower, who took the German surrender at Rheims. Ezra disliked this name—it had no antecedents among swampers—and, in one of his letters to Miss Cynthia, told her to re-christen me *Job*, for with a daddy behind bars I would dog-for-sure suffer other calamities.

In the summer of 1948, Miss Cynthia remarried. A man named Traskell Higgins came to Fosterville from God knows where to pay her court. He didn't care that her first husband had slain a man or that she'd borne this killer a gallberry child named Dwight David. Miss Cynthia still had her looks, title to a house, land near the swamp, livestock, and a Philco that broadcast *Fibber McGee and Molly* into the loblolly bays.

I was maybe two, but I recall my first sight of Higgins. He swaggered toward Mama and me out of Burt Bros. General Merchandise over the raised sidewalk. He doffed his fedora, disclosing a head of spun-gold hair, and asked Miss Cynthia directions to the hiring office of Vickery Timber & Turpentine Co. He had a smile like the cotton lining of a pocket in a pair of work pants. His beauty impressed me even then, and he persisted in his courtship in spite of in-law opposition.

The family's objections stemmed mostly from loyalty to Daddy Ezra's memory. Others arose from Higgins's affiliation with a Christian sect little known in Fosterville, the Jehovah's Witnesses. He did not merely court Miss Cynthia, he bombarded her with Bible Student doctrine from the 1920s and '30s. He held that Christmas, Easter, and birthdays were pagan holidays. He rejected the notion of the Trinity. He pounded her with his offbeat scriptural literal-mindedness and his heroic looks. When Miss Cynthia and Higgins eloped, they became not only former in-laws but also outlaws and enemies. The wedding took place in Waycross, in a Kingdom Hall where a local elder instructed them in the proper behavior of married Witnesses.

"I, Cynthia Thrash Colter, take you, Traskell Horace Higgins, to be my wedded husband," said my mother in that hot cinderblock building, "to love, cherish, and deeply respect, in accordance with divine law as set forth in the Holy Scriptures for Christian wives, for as long as we both shall live on earth according to God's marital arrangement." Higgins had already said like words to Miss Cynthia, omitting—as Witness men did—the phrase "deeply respect."

After a two-day honeymoon in Waycross, they returned to Ezra Colter's house in the pinewoods, where Higgins gave Miss Cynthia a life comparable to that she'd known as my old man's wife, but with a standard of abuse totally alien to her. Higgins scolded Mama for her "sins," i.e., doting on me, misreading the Book, and unduly "prettifying" the dresses she made. If she backtalked Higgins, he hit her, often within my view, and justified such attacks by citing their wedding vows and applicable passages of scripture (Ephesians 5:23). He never quoted verses calling on husbands to "love their own wives as they love their own bodies" (Ephesians 5:28). Thus, Miss Cynthia ran into many phantom doorposts and cabinet doors, and when Higgins hit her for wearing a light-pink lip-gloss, she brushed on makeup to *disguise* any signs of violence.

Higgins prospered as a turpentiner, logger, and truck driver. On the outskirts of Fosterville, he remodeled an old concrete garage into a Kingdom Hall and held meetings in it for those he recruited as potential converts. Miss Cynthia carried me to these studies, where Higgins rebuked her for my inattention and told her to rap my noggin or pinch my arm to straighten my kinks.

When these techniques failed, I was hauled outside—away from the drone of Witness dogma, which included the evil of blood transfusions, the idolatry of saluting a flag, and the restriction to 144,000 souls of all human beings eligible for heaven. (The rest of the *redeemed* Witnesses would live in new bodies on an evergreen planet Earth.) "How long you been in the Truth?" Witnesses around the swamp asked one another. I had no vocabulary of contradiction beyond "No!" and my Pavlovian wails, but even then I knew my stepfather's Truth made me miserable—unhappier than huddling naked in pelting hail. Not yet, though, did Miss Cynthia countenance either flight or divorce.

As Higgins grew richer as a warrant of Jehovah's favor, he loosened up at home, if not at the Kingdom Hall. He joked, drank, and pranced about. He attended a frolic to which some Colters on speaking terms with Miss Cynthia invited us. Some Thrashes, LeFlores, and Millsapses—swamp clans enjoying post-war prosperity—also showed up. Higgins sang "Daniel Spikes" and "My Pretty Mohee." Miss Cynthia loved him again. Even I warmed up, for he took me camping on Colters Hammock, and briefly, gaping helplessly at his near-seraphic face, I came to idolize my stepdaddy.

Few others felt like me. Higgins had avoided military service by registering with the Tampa draft board as a minister—a *pioneer* of his faith—and thereby winning his exemption. Around the nation, though, half of draft-age Witnesses applying for the 4-D classification were denied; they got jail time both for resisting induction and for refusing alternative civilian work. Doing such work might have squared them with Americans who saw the war as a crusade against earthly Evil, but Witnesses believed that *Jehovah* would soon eliminate that Evil at Armageddon and usher in a New System of everlasting righteousness.

"I'll fight at Armageddon," Higgins told detractors, "but not until."

At a frolic after a grave cleaning on Colters Hammock, a veteran of the Italian campaign asked Higgins how any man with clangers could sit out the war with a loon like Hitler threatening Civilization itself.

"Did that loon succeed?" Higgins asked.

"No. But no thanks to yellowbellies like you," said Del Colter, a cousin of Daddy Ezra's.

"Of course not. All thanks go to Jehovah."

Del said, "How can you sing 'Daniel Spikes' after using your religion to sidestep the army?" ("Daniel Spikes" is about a man who slips into the Oke to keep from donning rebel gray.) Higgins knocked Del Colter down. Del's friends rushed up to help, but Miss Cynthia started shouting for them to show Higgins mercy, and Del, still angry, waved his allies off.

After that, Higgins attended no more frolics. If he hadn't been driving for the turpentine company, hauling materials all over the Southeast, Miss Cynthia *might* have risked disfellowshipping and divorced him. But Higgins's absences made her heart more forbearant, if not fonder, and she stayed. By age eight, I didn't tingle quite so much to his enigmatic beauty. Besides, he often told me to shut up, to curtail my questions of Miss Cynthia, questions that nipped at the hem of Witness teachings. We stopped camping and fishing, not because his travels wore him out, but because a key Witness elder reminded him of the satanic allure of Evil. He needed to bring to heel family members bewitched by the insidious trap of *play*.

On his rare days at home, Higgins took me and some retired Witness— he always called his partners "brother"—to canvas Fosterville with copies of *The Watchtower, Awake!*, and the New World Translation of the New Testament. (This translation renders "cross" as "torture stake" and "Christ crucified" as "Christ impaled.") We peddled this junk, along with our hokey after-death message, door to door. Higgins always began by offering to share a little of the Word of God, and, often, the people of Fosterville asked us in. Then he'd say, "How'd you like to pass on to a world where women and men, blacks and whites, and all God's other critters live in harmony forever?"

"Even gators and brush pigs?" a doubtful householder once replied.

I loathed these pamphlet-peddling trips. I trudged along beset by rage and shame, my earlobes radiation red. Some amateur shrinks say, "No wonder you can't pray: Your daddy hit your mama and withheld affection as a disciplinary tool. Of course you've got a distorted view of faith. For you, believing in a loving God is like crediting tenderness to a turkey vulture."

I don't concede the point.

When Higgins went on the road, Miss Cynthia's bachelor uncle, Samuel Thrash, sometimes took me on outings—often to Wednesday-evening prayer at the Philadelphia Baptist Fellowship. There I met "lightard knot" believers who sang Sacred Harp music and moved more like happy animals than judgmental robots. At one communion, Samuel insisted on my taking a crust of unleavened bread and a thimbleful of muscadine wine. He didn't insist to *me*, but to a deacon fearful that my partaking would violate not only Baptist regulations but also my Witness upbringing.

Samuel said, "Do you want this boy to collect what Jesus did for him or not?"

On another Wednesday, Samuel shepherded me to the altar platform and sat me on a ladderback chair. Behind me glowed a stained-glass window of the Christ holding a lamb. Samuel scrolled up my overall cuffs, removed my tennis shoes, and bathed my feet in a basin of lukewarm water. Then he patted them dry with a fluffy white towel and took me back to his pew. My heart warmed. Such a sensation of peace and arousal visited me that I had an odd foretaste of orgasm. I loved both the man who'd taken me to that footwashing and the little wooden church hosting it.

The next year, in March 1955, the swamp caught fire, as it had twenty-two years earlier, when many families still had homesteads there. Higgins stayed gone most of that month, and Mama fretted that the fires, visible from any tiny height in Fosterville, would leap to Colters Hammock and rampage through the Colter cemetery. She envisioned them melting the fence, charring tombstones, and effacing family names and dates.

Late one night, she came to my bed and laid her hand so gently to my brow that I awoke smiling. "Daddy Ezra came in a dream. He wants us on the Hammock, to stand as a charm against his graveyard's ruin."

We set off, the stench of smoke in our noses and lungs like gunpowder batting. I clenched the largest of Daddy Ezra's bear skulls under my arm. Impervious to the smoke and the purple bruise of sky behind the magnolias, Miss Cynthia poled a cypress canoe to the hammock, and we crept through its underbrush to the cemetery.

Flames jumped like blazing squirrels from the beards on water oaks. A wall of scorching heat—Shadrach in his furnace could not have felt any hotter—pressed upon us. The cemetery palings shone red and silver. Trees crashed down. Air sucked itself away, and a grim ammonia stench filled in behind it.

"Stand there," Miss Cynthia said. "Lift that animal's head bone."

I obeyed. She braced me from behind. My bear skull grinned at the toppling trees and at the stars shining through livid fire.

"Great God," Mama prayed, "don't let this burning take us."

For over two hours we withstood its raging heat. So did the graveyard. Only when certain that we had accomplished Daddy Ezra's dream charge did we leave the island and pole ourselves home, our faces as greasy with sweat and char as any jungle commando's. Our canoe sank—yes, *sank*—and we stumbled to land. I recall a like thirst from only one other time in my life . . . on patrol in Vietnam. Mama squeezed out lemonade, with which we irrigated the limitless deserts of our thirst.

"You held that fire off, Dwight," she said, "just like Daddy Ezra prophesied."

Stepfather Higgins would not have agreed. He would have said that a *demon* had invaded Mama's sleep. But he was gone so much that she no longer thought herself truly espoused. Besides, he treated me shabbily and denied her the solace of a half-sibling for me. He thought the imminent end of this wicked system turned the making of a baby into an act of selfishness, even cruelty. How would a child ever understand the holy tenor of the horrors attending Armageddon? Better to withhold life than to subject an innocent to the gory cleansings of this Final War. Of course, Mama believed that Higgins dreaded even more the prospect of diapers and feedings, and that he had less pity and rue for the living than for the unborn.

As for me, I hated almost everything about our practice as Witnesses.

When other kids rose to pledge allegiance, I sat tight. Fights about my lack of patriotism continually broke out—from wrestling matches to barefisted playground bouts, from slapping contests to scary chases through back alleys and side streets. Also, we never celebrated birthdays. And we could not observe Halloween, Armistice Day, Christmas, Valentine's, St. Patrick's, or

Easter, a pagan bacchanal embraced by Papists and Protestants. In the 1950s and early 1960s we did get away with Thanksgiving, but only because so few fellow believers lived locally and we ate our turkey in hiding. And, finally, Higgins wanted me reading nothing but *The Watchtower*, which served as history, scriptural commentary, and daily guidebook, and *Awake!*, a pious poor person's *Reader's Digest*, minus "Life in These United States" and "Humor in Uniform."

We owned a squat Motorola television, but only for news, sporting events, and Westerns, which Higgins approved as edifying *allegories* of the ongoing battle between God and the devil. Luckily, TV offered Westerns out its cathode-ray cornucopia: *Wagon Train, Gunsmoke, Have Gun, Will Travel, The Life and Legend of Wyatt Earp, Wanted: Dead or Alive*, etc. Higgins liked *any* Western. He preferred me sprawled out watching *Death Valley Days* than holed up in my bedroom with a "dissolute" movie-monster magazine.

One day in 1959, before school let out, Miss Cynthia and I looked up at the sound of a loud centrifuging sigh, like a flying saucer landing. From our screen door we saw the hood of a gigantic red truck push into view beyond the cypress gate, as if it had plowed through swamp and over sandy plain to dock beside our fence, for this vehicle—a brand-new Peterbilt cab—did resemble a submarine's conning tower. Higgins opened its driver-side door and shouted, "Hey, get your sorry selves out here!"

Vickery Timber had bought the truck cab and a trailer, too, but just to show off Higgins had driven this one up from Florida after a weeklong haul in another cab. Now, to amuse us, he set it bucking down an asphalted lane, and we had a rollicking two hours. We phlooged the air horn at some crackers in a pickup, roared past a codger in a Lincoln Continental, and cruised back to the farm, where Higgins said I could bunk in the cab's sleeping box. His generosity surely stemmed from long-haul horniness, not an upsurge of fatherly affection, but I leapt to the bait anyway.

I did not sleep much. Stripped to my briefs, I pretended to *drive* the Peterbilt. I yanked its wheel, jobbed its gear knob, and pumped its pedals. Starlight glided over the windshield, a magnolia painted its shadow across the rig, and a mosquito droned like a speedboat on a faraway lake. Twice, I padded from the truck to the house to pee. Weird moans and heavy-duty furniture scraping came from my parents' bedroom, but they were making whoopee, not mayhem, and I paid little heed. Back in the cab, I lay on Higgins's plaid-lined sleeping bag, pedaling the air or lurching side to side like a rolling pin.

As an energy release, I jerked off, repressing with my thumb the milky bolts that had just begun to conclude this secret ritual. Then I slept.

At dawn I sat up. Poking around under the sleeping box, I found some issues of a well-thumbed magazine, *Fit for Eden*, which touted the benefits of fresh air and nudism. Its photographs showed naked people of all ages at poolside, in badminton or volleyball games, or on strolls through the woods. I gawked with more curiosity than lust. These folks did not resemble sexy libertines so much as they did churchgoers, sans clothes, at a Sunday potluck.

Eventually, I hit upon a centerfold of a man in a Charles Atlas body-building pose. Like a sun-tanned Greek, he flexed his biceps and blithely dangled his participle, but his photo did not so much re-arouse me as alert me to a feeling of wordless longing. Had my stepdaddy felt something akin? Some truckers, I later learned, asked harlots into their sleeping boxes. Higgins, though, had found the lineaments of semi-gratified desire in these pricey "fitness and health" publications.

"Give me that!" Miss Cynthia said, snatching the magazine.

I had not even heard the door open. Recovering, I protested that all the magazines around me had been aboard *before* my ascension into the truck. Miss Cynthia scrutinized Mr. Nude Greek American briefly and hurled the issue aside.

At breakfast she brooded.

Higgins never noticed. He sopped cathead biscuits in the sunny outflow of his over-easy eggs.

But that evening Mama slapped him with a *Fit for Eden* baton and called him a hypocrite who had undermined my innocence. I prepared for the backlash of Higgins's rage, the crack of Mama's body hitting the wall.

Instead, he said, "Those magazines don't mean what you suppose. *Fit for Eden*—that means these folks have a head start on us, practicing the harmony of life on Paradise Earth after Armageddon. They walk in our after-Judgment garden just like Adam and Eve walked in Eden."

Miss Cynthia replied that he had fried corn for brains.

"You wait," he said. "We'll all go nekkid, and nobody on Jehovah's New Earth will think a thing about it."

"*I* might."

"*You* won't get there. Your lack of faith will strand you like Lot's wife on the plains of destruction."

"Get out of my house."

"It's yours and a murderer's." He left, though, and slammed the door, going.

How had Higgins turned copies of *Fit for Eden*—paeans to middle-class nudity—into an indictment of Mama and an eschatological blow at Daddy Ezra? (I still bore the Colter surname because he had never given even a mayfly thought to adopting me.) That night, the question had no answer. Higgins drove away in his new truck not to offload his magazines but to punish Miss Cynthia with his absence.

Higgins's prohibitions on my reading did not extend to my homework: He and Mama wanted me to excel—not so much to "increase in learning and wisdom" as to prove that a Witness was as smart as, or even brighter than, anybody else. I only had to remember to despise what I learned as contingent upon our current corrupt order and as ephemeral as burning pine straw. So I read like a junkie: dog stories, mysteries, science fiction, and sea tales by writers like Melville, London, Sabatini, and Herman Wouk. If he had kept track, Higgins would have condemned it all as literary street smack.

Contact with the Colters and those Thrashes who hadn't disowned my mama and me often meant contact with the swamp. Samuel Thrash took me to study gravesites on Colters Hammock, to machete-chop perch by torchlight, and to gaze raptly at the herons, kingfishers, goshawks, and Lord-God woodpeckers in the bay stands.

One night on Pine Island I caught a puny *scritch*, or screech owl, and sneaked it home hoping to raise it. I figured the owlet for an orphan and brought it in during one of Higgins's absences. It hopped across the floor, or squatted on our icebox turret like a frumpy midget god. As soon as Higgins got home, he threw it out. Civilized people didn't keep owls in their houses. So I nailed a cigar box to a tree in our yard and waterproofed it with a coat of Elmer's Glue: free housing if the scritch chose to stay. Predictably, it flew off or fell victim to a weasel. Anyway, something knocked the cigar box askew and a sad gray feather stuck to my ankle when I shinnied up the water oak to straighten it.

Cousin Samuel said you could quiet an owl's cries by turning your pants pockets inside out, or by hooking your index fingers and pulling, hard, *without* snapping them apart. So I kept my pockets inside in and spent my days hooking, pulling, and *breaking* the stipulated finger link . . . all to no avail.

More than anything, I wanted an owl cry to prophesy *Higgins's* death. He stayed gone a lot, but always came back. Usually he and Miss Cynthia celebrated the first night of his return. I never slept in the truck cab anymore, though. He kept it locked, a sign to me that he had preserved his *Fit for Eden* library. I greedily recalled the face and form of the bodybuilder whose photo Miss Cynthia had caught me ogling, as well as the faces and physiques of a dozen other men, but the women I could conjure only fuzzily, and this last fact, for reasons not altogether obscure, scared me.

After their homecoming parties, my folks settled in for a Bible study to prepare for Sunday at the Kingdom Hall, but also for Christ's Second Coming. On Monday, if Higgins had not already left, he would find a fault for which Mama needed correcting—and correct her, almost always by hand. If I objected, he swung me down and sat on me, knowing that if he ever struck me, Mama would wreak havoc.

At fifteen, I stopped needing her protection. I was still a few inches shorter than Higgins, but I weighed more. In the summer of 1961, just after my birthday, I stopped one of his assaults on Mama by seizing his belt from behind and flinging him into a door so that the knob gouged him in the back. As he fell, the knob spun up his spine like a gyroscope and conked the base of his skull. With a black eye and a cut lip, Miss Cynthia knelt over him glaring as if I'd just taken an ax to her china cabinet. But Higgins declared a recess on spousal abuse, settling for threats, strutting, and fake indifference. Even when I was away, he laid off, knowing that if he hurt Mama, I'd retaliate. He could have killed me, I guess, but he knew my daddy's story and may have feared the likely consequences.

Even before the doorknob episode, I had begun to assert myself. I had let my hair grow—not in the shaggy way of the Beatles a couple of years later. Like Elvis and the Everlys, I flaunted a pompadour, sideburns, a ducktail. I used Higgins's absences and an assortment of hats to hide this do. When Higgins finally saw it, he called me a juvenile delinquent. I thought this cool, but one night, as I slept my hard teenage sleep, he gave me a humiliating buzz cut. With Mama's permission, I laid out of school a week. When I returned, girls and boys alike snickered, but several of my classmates dug my new look. The weirdo Witness had done it again. In their eyes, I looked romantically dangerous, maybe even romantically criminal.

A year later, I caught Higgins whaling on Miss Cynthia again. I jacked him into the fridge, hurled him to the base of the sink, and bounced a pickle jar off his shoulder for punctuation. After that, I let my hair grow back, stopped going to services, brought home paperback crime novels (Mickey Spillane, Carter Brown), and retreated to the swamp, where I read, fished, and tracked deer. Often I stripped naked and edged around eating huckleberries and possum haws, like a deer myself. Neither sun nor thorns nor stinging bugs kept me from emulating the middle-class nudists that Higgins imagined would one day populate Paradise Earth.

I had no real friends in Fosterville. In the early 1960s, my local kin—Colters, Thrashes, and Millsapses—had no kids my age to act as allies. Once, my Witness ties had estranged me from my classmates, but now my defiance of those ties and my rebel outfits—a fake leather jacket, white socks, black loafers—stranded me without backup. Our town's God-fearing folks could not make room for a God-mocking fifteen-year-old with a chip—no, a cinderblock—on his shoulder.

Blacks might have accepted me, but they had schools and circles all their own. Besides, the only blacks I really knew were Witness converts to whom, in my apostasy, I had become anathema. Still, a couple of these women, seeing me in town, asked me back to the Kingdom Hall. Their affection flowed from a spring that Witness theology had not yet filled with stones. If nothing else, my stepfather's religion had taught me the vileness of racism. For that reason alone, I never used the n-word, an omission that led a few of my classmates to see me as a holier-than-thou commie race-mixer.

As a junior, I drew Mr. Pettis for English, the only male on our faculty other than coaches. A tall balding newcomer, whose wife taught in the elementary school, he saw *I, the Jury* in my book bag and asked what else I liked to read. I cited a raft of poets, from Geoffrey Chaucer to Walt Whitman, because their names would impress him and because I had actually begun to read Whitman in a volume from our school library.

"I like him too," Mr. Pettis said, "but who'd ever guess, even if I can bench-press three times my own weight?" His poker face never altered. "Of course, a hundred and twenty pounds won't set any records." (I almost didn't get the self-parody.) Mr. Pettis smiled. "I'll remember that you like Whitman."

He did. Passing me in the hall, he recited, *"I am larger, better than I thought, I did not know I had so much goodness."* In class, after someone made an inane or even an astute remark, he'd ask, "Dwight, is wisdom finally tested in schools?"

I'd say, "No: '*Wisdom cannot be passed from one having it to another not having it, Wisdom is of the soul, is not susceptible of proof, is its own proof.*'"

To which Mr. Pettis would reply, "'*Camerado, I give you my hand,*'" making me blush because I knew that that poem ends, "'*Will you give me yourself, will you come travel with me? Shall we stick by each other as long as we live?*'" Well, no. Mr. Pettis never propositioned or flirted, as wicked non-Witnesses understand those terms. He had a wife. He lived for her love and for nineteenth-century American literature. He liked me because I too liked Walt Whitman.

At Christmas, a pagan holiday, Mr. Pettis gave me a copy of *Leaves of Grass*, one allegedly incorporating all the separate volumes of *Leaves* that Whitman ever published. I hid it in a plastic bag under a plank in my bedroom. I read it on the sly, amazed that every line sets out a refutation of, and a rebuke to, the tight self-righteousness that recommends itself to so many as religion. I embraced it as Higgins did *The New World Translation of Holy Scriptures* and the tracts telling him how to parse the Word and why apostasy meant eternal death.

With Whitman as a counterweight to Witness dogmatism, I felt *free*. I loved my mama, but mourned her surrender to the tyrannical sect defining and delimiting Higgins, who hoped to live forever on Paradise Earth because he had abandoned all hope of living authentically on *this* earth. Ditto Miss Cynthia.

And yet Whitman, singing of himself, wrote, "*I have said the soul is no more than the body, And I have said that the body is not more than the soul, And nothing, not God, is greater than one's self is, And whoever walks a furlong without sympathy walks to his own funeral in his shroud.*" This last line seemed an indictment of Higgins, whose sympathy enwrapped only fellow Witnesses and likely converts.

The year after Mr. Pettis gave me *Leaves of Grass*, I dated girls. They liked me even if I didn't play varsity sports—maybe because I wasn't an all-out nerd. Everybody at school realized that I'd fallen out with my parents. I no longer went with them to the Kingdom Hall. Sometimes I saluted the flag or told a classmate happy birthday, and my rebellion against my folks won me points, probably for implying an endorsement of the town's prevailing mores.

I was also acquiring a reputation as an outdoorsman and an informal historian of the Okefinokee—a forerunner, I suppose, to my later role as an ecological educator. My knowledge of wildlife, my ability to navigate the swamp, and a broad aura of eccentricity lent me a mystique that I worked to cultivate. I also owned a black '54 Ford I had bought with money from my jobs as a carryout at Phelps's Food Market and as a hunting-and-fishing guide for hire.[2]

Anyway, in the fall of 1963, I lost my virginity to a young woman a year older than me—a senior to my junior—one Saturday evening on Colters Hammock. We had repaired there with a lightard torch (for drama), a flashlight (for reliable illumination), a can of insect repellant, a picnic hamper, and a blanket smelling vaguely of mineral spirits. At the Colter cemetery we spread this blanket just outside the metal fence surrounding, and the bronze plaque commemorating, all the folks who had once lived on the island. In the amber-honey moonlight, I pointed out the weatherworn bear skull that my mother had placed on Daddy Ezra's grave.

"Boy, can you romance a gal," said Erica, unbuttoning my shirt.

I quoted Whitman, *"If anything is sacred, the human body is sacred,"* and she, bless her, did not laugh aloud, but dragged down my jeans and pulled her yellow jersey over her head. And so, if I wasn't a man before, I *became a man*, although maybe not the one that my biology decreed. I worked, but only as a stamp press or a desktop stapler does—mechanically, soullessly.

After our tryst on the Hammock, I dreamed that I took Erica out there again, but when she reached to embrace me, she changed, sinuously, into Traskell Higgins, and our ensuing argument over my mean spirit spun into a wrestling match that ended only when he tore flesh from my arm and I awoke, highly agitated, sick in both gut and soul.

"The love of the body of man or woman balks account," I thought in the darkness. *"That of the male is perfect, and that of the female is perfect."*

If Armageddon came tomorrow, I would die in the first onslaught; the seraphim of its transitional strife, according to Higgins, must not suffer

---

[2] Once I took three clients on a quest for the alleged giant swamp owl, *Ornimegalonyx okefinokoi*, a near-extinct member of the *Strigidae* family with a wingspan of 13 feet and a beak like a steel hatchet. None of my clients accused me of lying, but such a bird would have tattered its wings plunging through the refuge's treetops. Having seen a good-sized gator instead, they went home happy, and I made $100.

monsters to live. He also often said, *"And this world passes away, and with it the lustful; but he who does God's will abides forever."* I lusted, although in which direction I did not fully know. In any event, I, Dwight David Colter, would *not* abide forever—not even in Daddy Ezra's house, for my rejection of JW dogmas and social protocols had given Higgins grounds to evict me, and other Fosterville elders adjudged me right on the edge of disfellowshipping.

Miss Cynthia informed Higgins that if he tried to evict me, she would divorce him on the grounds of his own immorality, as evidenced by the magazines he still obsessively bought. No one on the committee reviewing his behavior would countenance his reading of Witness doctrine as presaging eternal nakedness for Armageddon's virtuous survivors, and *she* would emerge the only Higgins-Colter still in good with her faith. Besides, he was gone so much that if he tossed me out, she would prowl from room to room without company or solace.

But I kept Mama company as little as Higgins. I ate breakfast with her because she fixed it, but seldom came home for dinner. Phelps's Food Market tied me up from four to eight p.m. every day, after which I hopped into my Ford and drove—to Waycross, Fargo, Homerville, or one of the little zoos-*cum*-peanut-brittle-emporia that then cropped up amid the pines—crooning high Roy Orbison arias.

In mid-October I got intercom instructions to report to Mr. Pettis during second-hour planning period. I found Higgins pacing in a fresh khaki jumpsuit in front of my former teacher's desk. He swung a lumpy burlap bag in one hand while jabbing an index finger as if to perforate Mr. Pettis's bemused equanimity.

"'*Be. Not. Curious. About. God,*'" he said. "'*Be. Not. Curious. About. God.*'" Each word got a finger poke. Then he added, "'*And the threat of what is called hell is nothing to me,*'" misquoting. "'*And the lure of what is called heaven is nothing to me.*'"

"Please, Mr. Higgins, sit down."

"Have you *any* notion how hard it is to raise up godly issue, Mr. Pettis?"

"Maybe not. My wife and I have no children."

Higgins stopped pacing. "Well, that's *one* thing you all may've got right." He set his bag on the desk and turned to me. His voice a singsong—"Here,

Dwight David"—he thrust at me the copy of *Leaves of Grass* I had hidden since Christmas. Over the summer I'd transferred it from its hole in the floor to the front seat of my Ford. Yesterday Higgins had borrowed that car to run an errand, and now he had come to Mr. Pettis because of the flyleaf inscription in the Whitman volume.

When I reached for the book, Higgins drew it back and shook it over Mr. Pettis's desk. Several pages sifted out, like leaves. Then he chunked the book into a trashcan that toppled and rolled.

I wanted to choke him, but Mr. Pettis stood there, an obstacle to murder he'd no doubt counted on. He picked up some of the signature units and tore them into strips. I tried to stop him, but he sidestepped me and kept ripping.

"Dwight, this garbage must *not* stand proxy for the Word of God." He dropped more pages and booted the trashcan toward some oaken lockers. Several leaves lifted and swirled. Then he pulled from the burlap bag a pitted, discolored skull, which he furiously thrust into my hands.

"Let this be your Bible and *memento mori*. Let it warn you away from sin." And he marched from the room an aggrieved Christian soldier.

I followed him into the hall holding the skull. Higgins whirled and poked me in the chest. Sneeringly, he said, "*I'm* your father, not 'Daddy' Ezra, not that murderer your mama first wed. *I'm* your father."

"What?"

"What I said, boy: *I* sired you. You sprang from my loins. And that book you love so all-fired much only goes to prove it."

I could only gape. "You lie."

He shoved me in the chest, hard enough to knock me backward a step. "The lie is seventeen years of silence, you blind pup. I'm not the world's kindest man, as your mama knows, but for all the pain I've given her, I never spoke truth to you till now."

I tried to answer, but had no words.

"You're heading down a soul-sick way." Higgins shook his head in disgust. "Get on over to the Damascus Road and straighten out whilst you can."

He pivoted and walked down the hall to the door, which he eased through with a weariness I could feel where I stood. When it clicked shut, I hurled Daddy Ezra's bear skull after him. It clattered when it struck the tiles and caromed to a wobbly standstill just shy of the door.

"Dwight," Mr. Pettis said.

I turned.

Apologetically, Mr. Pettis clasped my wrist and took me back into his classroom, where we salvaged what we could of Whitman's lifework, neither of us speaking and the silence between us no silence at all.

ANDALUSIAN TRIPTYCH, 1962

The Cabby: Juaquín's Story

I

rouse

next to Hermelinda and study her closely, a rare pleasure. Usually her back pain keeps her awake, and my gaze annoys her. But this morning she slumbers, her silvering hair spread across our pillow. She resembles a bride, not the brooding crone to whom I have not made love since our son died in childbirth sixteen years ago.

After touching Hermelinda's hair, I creep from the broken altar of our bed. In the kitchen—bread and tea. Hermelinda's sister Evarista will look in later. Alone together, they will speak ill of me for leaving my poetry paperbacks atop the toilet, and for making too little money to hire a maid. To perdition with Evarista. She looks like the Mexican comic Cantinflas, even down to her silly moustache.

I drive my cab to Alejo's barbershop. Alejo has a dream for which he enjoys working: to fly to America and to open a Hollywood salon. (A salon, *not* a shop. I see Alejo in this place wearing a beret and powder-blue Italian shoes.) He wants to cut the hair of James Stewart and Rock Hudson. To increase profits, he often takes clients even during siesta.

"Good day, Juaquín," Alejo says. "I admire a man who doesn't neglect his appearance." A tall man, Alejo must stoop while cutting my hair. "Look, you're thinning here." He touches my crown. "In school you had thicker hair than anyone."

A paperboy runs in. I ask him for a paper. The boy tosses it into my lap and scurries back out into the street.

Alejo says, "It wouldn't hurt you to consider a dye. Many older men ask for touchups."

"No time today." But the idea plucks at me. What would Hermelinda say if I came home looking like a handsome flamenco dancer?

"Or maybe you'd like a flattop." Alejo uses an unfamiliar English word. "An American airman lives nearby. When he comes in, I give him a flattop." Alejo presses his hands against his own hair as if to demonstrate this haircut. "You know, like an astronaut. Even if Colonel John Glenn walked in, I could cut his hair."

"If he did, I would go somewhere else." I thumb through the newspaper, making the pages snap.

Alejo seizes my wrist. The page before me has photographs from the Oscar awards in California. Handsome men in tuxedos. Swanlike women half-naked in shiny foil gowns. Marilyn Monroe gleaming larger and blonder than any of the other swans. Even newsprint discloses to us her sexiness.

"What a grand soft chest." Alejo giggles. "Hips as lovely as a heifer's." Why this act? He has never cared for women as most men do.

I rattle the pages shut. "Finish. I must go to work."

I drive a thin middle-aged woman to the Hotel Cristina and a fat man back to the Calle de Sierpes. All morning I have many fares—to the Giralda, to a high-rise beyond the Guadalquivir, and so on. One fare spills most of a cylinder of ripe cherries onto the floor, and I must stop, kneel at my back door, and drop them one by one into the curbside gutter. Like a fresh scab, one cherry lies mashed on my floor mat.

At two, I go home to find Hermelinda listening to flamenco music wailing from the radio. Evarista has already left, but Hermelinda has not set out any food, not even gazpacho. Still, she smiles, even in her eyes, when she sees me. I turn down the radio, nuzzle her neck, and place a hand on the cliff of her chest.

Hermelinda does not object. "My sister wants me to go to Cadíz with her and Hector in May. You don't mind, do you, Juaquín? This rainy weather has sickened me."

"Why would I mind?" I spread my fingers downward.

My wife takes them. "You've visited Alejo. I can smell the tonic." She lets go of my fingers and struggles to rise. "I must call Evarista."

That evening I drive past midnight. My fares include an American airman who speaks bad Spanish without relent. I drop him at Exportadora, the American commissary enclave on the southeast side of Seville.

Later I cruise toward Exportadora looking for a final evening fare. The Americans swagger down our streets like soldiers, even when they wear no uniforms. Sevillanos selling fried squid or lottery tickets, people whose ancestors built the cathedral Giralda, exist for them only to photograph. Even their children act as if they own the city—not the small ones, but the almost-grown boys with Elvis Presley hair and the budding girls in dresses that would shame a whore. In the bistros on Calle Sierpes, I have seen them flash their peseta notes so that even senior bartenders preen and fetch for them.

On a far boulevard, a hacienda glows like a citadel among sprawling gardens. Noisy rock and roll pours forth. My headlamps light the silhouette of a figure beckoning me to stop. This figure and a more graceful one stoop into my cab: a tuxedoed boy, with wavy hair and a large Adam's apple, and a girl—no, a young woman—in a silver-black gown. They link arms in my back seat. In faultless Spanish the young woman directs me to a bar downtown and promptly turns back to her sweetheart.

I drive, and drive carefully, but cannot help watching this privileged couple in my mirror. Their faces meet. Their lips touch and cling. Hardly breathing, the boy and his wench cannibalize each other. God himself blushes. If either of these children belonged to me, I would slap their mouths and lock them away from each other in dark closets. The devouring—the moaning—goes on. The boy sees my face in the mirror, smirks, and applies his own face even more defiantly to the girl's. I cannot look away. Do Americans never employ chaperones? Do they teach wantonness and harlotry in their schools?

The boy's hand strokes and plunges. It spider-walks and kneads. The female, who may have a tattered remnant of shame, grabs his wrist and holds it without ceasing to kiss him. She sees me watching. Her eye white resembles a growing quarter moon. Both of us startle.

My taxi vaults a curb and strikes a metal gate. I bump my forehead.

My hood flies up. A geyser spouts from the radiator. The young woman's hand appears on my seat back. The boy, crumpled on the floor, moans—from pain rather than lust.

Bleeding from the brow, I leap out and yank the shameless boy from my cab. "Son of a whore!" I fling him against my geysering taxi. When he falls, I kick him in the haunch. The young woman pushes me away. Standing between me and her sweetheart, she rapidly explains that tonight the older students at their school have attended a special spring dance, a *promenada*. At such events, the dancers take special liberties, just as we Sevillanos do during the Fair after Holy Week.

I still want to kill the boy, but the young woman calms me as a good wine calms. I make a fist at him but do not kick him again. She puts her hands on my neck and kisses my brow, taking with her some of the red lip-ice of my blood. Her ghoulish tenderness astonishes me.

My taxi company keeps me on, but owing to the repairs that I must pay for, Hermelinda cannot go to Cadíz. As bitter as a bad olive, she places an old wooden stool across my half of our bed.

On first seeing it, I grab it up and splinter it on a coal grate. Hermelinda wires it together and again lays it in my sleeping place. For weeks, I must pass my nights on our sofa or in my battered cab.

In August, a little before Hermelinda relents, the movie star Marilyn Monroe overdoses on sleeping tablets. Alejo predicts worldwide grief, the composing of poems and songs, the founding of a cult.

I tell Alejo, "Let her fare straight to Hell. Satan rejoices to welcome each new American slut."

Alejo shuts up. He likes my money as well as anyone's, and he still harbors his ignorant dream.

The Cherry Thrower: Lisa's Story

In the spring of 1962 I stand eyeing the cathedral tower in Sevilla—as the people call their city—when a small round object strikes my jaw. This object skitters across the roof toward a concrete wash basin.

Another cherry loops up from the street and hits my bare ankle. I pick it up and pop it into my mouth. A sizzle like red licorice and *vino rojo* electrifies my taste buds. A bombardment of cherries follows. I hurry to the roof's parapet to see who or what has launched this barrage.

"Sonny!" cries a voice from Calle Leoncillos.

Diego Fernandez squints up clutching a paper funnel of cherries. A U.S. airman of Puerto Rican descent, he looks ready to fling every cherry in his cone.

"Daddy's napping," I shout down at him. "Go away."

"Wake him up, Lisa! Diego's come!"

Diego has a pretty-boy face, sleepy spaniel eyes, and hips like a coy matador's. I don't like him. He visits only when he needs something. Daddy—Tech Sergeant Sonny Walker—gives it to him because Diego teaches him Spanish and makes him feel eighteen again. And Joy, my stepmother, dislikes Diego even more than I do because he cadges money and leads Daddy into drinking binges and get-rich-quick boondoggles.

"*¡Guapa! ¡Novia!*" Diego cries. "Let me in!"

Looker! Sweetheart! For the whole street to hear. I spit my cherry pit four stories down. When it ricochets off Diego's nose I grin as helplessly as a shark.

"*¡Puta! ¡Bruja!* Open your friggin door!"

Whore! Witch! How can a girl resist?

I pelt down to the first landing to hit the button springing the foyer's security grate, and Diego hops up the stairs to our second-story flat. Joy meets us both at the door.

"What in hell do *you* want?" Joy asks Diego. She wears lime-green shorts and an ivory blouse. A Marlboro dangles from her lips, a Nero Wolfe mystery from her yellow fingers.

"Friendship!" says Diego. "Amusement! Life!"

"Money," Joy says.

"Let me talk to Sergeant Sonny." Diego lays a hand on my stepmother's arm.

Joy shrugs it off. "There he snores. Go to it."

Diego rubs the blood speck that the cherry pit left on his nose and tiptoes into the bedroom. My father sprawls in his off-white boxers, a compact statue of flesh and hair. Sometimes his boxers gap, and he twitches like an old dreaming dog.

Joy leads me into our living room. We hear Diego and Sonny talking. The upshot is that Diego borrows Daddy's '54 Chevrolet soft-top, a red and white gunship on wheels, as conspicuous on Sevilla's streets as a Rose Bowl float.

Joy rages. What if *we* need the Chevy? What if Diego plunges it into the river? What if the leather-hatted Guardia Civil jail him and come after us?

In the end, Diego keeps the soft-top three days and returns it with scorched upholstery and the overall stench of an empty oil drum.

"Fool," Joy scolds my father. "Big-shot patsy."

On Monday Daddy rides the Bluebird shuttle to the SAC base at Morón de la Frontera. He spends the night on a World War II era cot in a tight corner of the personnel office.

In Sevilla Joy pulls curtains across our enormous balcony windows and paces about the apartment in her panties, finger-painting with cigarette smoke and spieling nonstop about this field-grade British officer who jilted her in Scotland. After school that evening I sense her at my shoulder as I fix our dinner.

"Never trust a cherry thrower," she tells me, her boobs as small and pink as twin dips of strawberry. "They throw them because they want to catch them. Do you follow me, Lisa?"

Without my asking, she puts on one of Daddy's shirts to eat her BLT. Then she fingers out its strips of bacon and feeds them to herself like so many blistered worms. I watch in amazement.

Joy Scott Walker wants me for an ally, but she has never trusted Sonny so how can she trust me, even if I come to her from Waycross, Georgia, ignorant and female? Besides, she resents my youth and my gangly body, which might one day prove a bigger man-draw than hers—even though I often glance sidelong at *her* body, liking it more than I do mine. Joy's mind also unsettles me. It darts about like a tiny dog on amphetamines. A chihuahua, maybe.

"Lisa, which do you prefer, *The Sun Also Rises* or *Lie Down in Darkness*?"

A teacher back home in Georgia, learning of my departure for Spain, gave me a copy of Hemingway's *The Sun Also Rises*. But I have never heard of the other novel or of its author, William Styron. I confess my ignorance.

"Go with Styron. Hemingway runs on swagger and bull gravy just like—"

"Just like Daddy?" I interrupt her.

"I meant like Diego," Joy lies. "Stuck-up Latin lover boys. At least Sonny has a tender feeling or two."

*

After the Chevy incident, Daddy does other stuff for Diego. Holds a cheap ring for collateral for a fifty-buck loan. Introduces him to the Spanish secretary in his office. Mails a large package to Puerto Rico. Confirms Diego's excuse when Diego cuts work on the flight line. Daddy tells me these stories because he cannot tell Joy and he likes me to see him playing the impresario. Diego has snowed Daddy so deep frost glazes Daddy's eyeballs.

On Calle Leoncillos Joy drinks, smokes, reads, fumes. She cannot drive and has never learned very much Spanish. With Daddy and me gone all day, her apartment-pent time must feel more like solitary confinement than a party. And when a Red Alert keeps everyone out at the base for five straight days, Joy says Daddy's absence is a result of his tomcatting and growls at me as if I have two-timed her myself.

Lonnie Jarvis, a boy I like, visits one evening during the alert. Joy treats him like a Polish count, setting out candles, pouring wine, flirting a little. When Lonnie kisses me goodnight by his motorcycle on Leoncillos, I easily spy Joy spying on us from one of our shadowy balconies.

The day after Daddy returns, Joy overdoses on aspirin and sprawls across their bed. While I sleep, Daddy slings her over his shoulder, dumps her into the Chevy, and drives her to the San Pablo infirmary. Air Force medics pump her stomach. Joy stays three days and vents to a military shrink. Daddy gets compassionate leave. I keep going to school, but on the third day hitch a ride to San Pablo with Lonnie, meet Daddy at the unit canteen, and visit Joy. Lonnie rides over to the library to study.

In the infirmary Diego sits at the foot of Joy's bed while Joy perches atop the coverlet in shorts and a purple-and-white polka-dot shirt. Diego cradles a funnel of *cerezas*, or cherries, and Joy holds a dish of them in her lap. Seeing Daddy and me, she waves us in.

Daddy beams. Everybody talks. Everybody eats cherries. Diego banks three or four of them off a medicine-cabinet mirror into a trashcan. Joy applauds. Diego laughs. I cry, "*¡Viva!*" Only a few days ago, Joy loathed Diego Fernandez and even made a sloppy effort to kill herself.

Eventually Lonnie calls me into the hall to say that he must go. Pecking me goodbye, he tastes Diego's bloody cherries on my lips. He smiles, relishing the flavor, and saunters out.

Diego finds me in the hall. "First guy you ever kiss?"

"Mind your own business, Zorro."

"Kissing is a big part of my business." He executes a fancy step that puts me between him and the wall. His odd wine-and-cherry smell leans into me. I shove him away. His chest—and the nipple under his khaki 1505 shirt—shoves back. Then Diego vanishes, as if an invisible rope has yanked him from the corridor.

Refocusing, I see him lying on the floor—curled up, his hands on his head, my daddy crouching above him. Daddy attacks with a barrage of words that Diego does not try to deflect. He balls tighter. Daddy gouges him in the kidney with a knuckle and, like a belligerent weekend drunk, dares him to fight.

Joy comes into the hall. "You've never done anything like that for me," she says in a low-key voice.

Daddy looks between Joy and me with almost pleading eyes. He does not know how to tell Joy that what he has just done for me, he has done a billion times for her in his mind. His tongue-tied anger hangs over all three of us even after Diego has uncoiled and slipped out of the building.

At the end of August, I fly home to Georgia. On seeing me again, my mother looks into my face and dissolves into tears.

The Malingerer: Sonny's Story

Alejo Reyes has a one-chair shop near our apartment at 15 Leoncillos. I call him *El barbero de Sevilla*—the barber of Seville—until he politely asks me to stop.

The guy likes Americans, though. He gives honest-to-God butch cuts and flattops, styles that most Spaniards despise. When I bring him a U. S. Air Force poster featuring front, back, and side views of four approved military haircuts, he hangs it on his wall next to pictures of Natalie Wood, Jimmy Stewart, and other Hollywood stars. Once he asked me if I'd ever met Marilyn Monroe, and when she died that summer, Alejo tied black ribbons to her eight-by-ten glossy.

In October I say that I won't see him for a while and ask for a *short* flat-top.

"Why? You going on holiday?"

I laugh. "If only. I have to help save the world from nuclear destruction."

"Then I will give you the best flattop ever." Which he does. "It wouldn't hurt to consider a dye, Sargento Walker. Many older men ask for touchups."

I hate to leave Joy alone in our apartment. This latest Red Alert will glue every serviceman to base for days. And, back in May, Joy tried to beat Marilyn to the punch—with Bayer aspirin instead of sleeping pills. Right after that, my daughter Lisa graduated from the dependent high school in Santa Clara and flew back to the States for college. Joy smoked like Bethlehem Steel and mainlined Carter Brown, Rex Stout, and Richard Prather mysteries.

I urge her, if she gets low, to go shopping or to visit our landlords, the Zuritas.

"We always use hands signs," Joy says. "I come back upstairs feeling stupid."

"Take my dictionary along."

Whoops. In twenty months overseas Joy has learned possibly fifteen words of Spanish. She doesn't lack brains, just a foreign-language knack. She accuses me of learning only enough "Yollie" to sweet-talk the local B-girls. I have to grab her to keep her in the room.

"Don't start popping aspirin, Joy."

"Up yours, Dr. Berlitz."

"You don't have to kill yourself. The Rooskies plan to do all of us that favor."

Joy laughs, but my words scare me. The bombs that hit our base at Morón de la Frontera will also fall on Lisa, now at school in Washington, D.C., capital of the Free World and Major Commie Target. I imagine her vanishing in a gigantic white flash.

On the ride to Morón, the twisty shadows of orange and olive trees slide across our bus's grimy windows. Local support people—secretaries, maintenance men, clerks—crowd the seats, but Diego Fernandez, the Puerto Rican two-striper, lounges next to me. He helps load bombs into

B-47s and B-52s and sees himself as a walking firewall against the advancing Soviet threat.

At San Pablo, after Joy's botched suicide, Diego put a stupid move on Lisa. I've forgiven him, sort of, but I no longer loan him money or my car. Now he runs his scams on younger airmen from the States and gullible Spanish women. Joy rags me mercilessly about my past naïve fuckups with him and other moochers.

"We will all die this month," Diego says. "Nothing for it but beer and poontang."

"No way that happens," I tell him doubtfully.

"Ten bucks. Triple or nothing. Give me a ten. If we make it to Thanksgiving, you'll get thirty."

"But if we don't, you go up a ten spot."

Diego makes sarcastic saucer eyes at me. "Right. Up to heaven. Come on, Sonny Man, bet your optimism."

I give Diego a ten, which he sticks in a fatigue pocket. A chill slinks into my lungs. Rather than pay me, Diego will pray for the world to end.

Khrushchev has sent missiles to Cuba. Kennedy has blockaded Cuba. Every Strategic Air Command base in the world has placed its people on highest vigilance. Pilots sleep in flight suits. Even recreation specialists work overtime.

Nobody at Morón but bigwigs can call out. The news flowing in, along with the aircraft whining overhead, hints that at any second mushroom clouds will skip around the globe in a gaudy doomsday fandango.

I want to comfort Joy and get Lisa out of Washington, but type until my fingertips have dimples and my eyeballs smoke like joss sticks. Even when Major Chatto directs me to a cot in the personnel pool, I can't sleep.

During the fourth day I decide to rest. No breakdown or crackup overcomes me, I just *decide* to rest. When the bell on my carriage return dings for the blue-zillioneth time, I clutch my head and shout, *"I've gone blind! Help me!"*

Major Chatto and Airman Schrambling rush over. Briefly the room actually dims. Ghosts in uniforms ease me down and whisper over my clocking eyeballs. I wave an arm around like a big pink squid tentacle.

"Rubbers in a Catholic country," I tell them. "A fly in a whiskey glass.

Don't swat the flies. They'll take away your *tapas*. A few crazy fools like it hot."

Major Chatto says, "Jesus. Get him to the infirmary."

I lie in bed gibbering. The missile crisis continues. A doctor labels my condition hysterical blindness and asks the major in a clumsy stage whisper if I have any history of malingering.

"He once lost a stripe for insubordination."

"I'm not surprised," the doctor says. "Watch him."

They watch me. And listen. I shovel them crap loads about Soviet tractor repair, Doris Day's freckles, and Generalissimo Franco's secret fallout shelter in the Prado. I pine for JFK's missing fidelity gene. I impersonate Jimmy Rodgers singing "The Sloop John B." The more shame I feel the more crazy bunk I spew.

Every man in my office and two secretaries visit, but Diego never shows. He remembers how I manhandled him in the infirmary when he got fresh with Lisa and how Joy scolded me for never busting his butt for her. Instead of visiting he pulls multiple flight-line shifts, instructing bomber pilots in all the latest radiation-decontamination techniques.

Khrushchev agrees to withdraw Soviet missiles if Kennedy pledges not to invade Cuba. The crisis winds down. I began fantasizing about Joy in nothing but her birthday suit and a nice cologne. Airman Schrambling brings me a deck of dirty playing cards and deals me a hand.

"Schrambling," I say, "you have restored my sight."

Two days before Halloween, I ride the bus back to Seville. Joy greets me at the door wearing a bottle-green satin sarong and a furry black sleep mask. Later, straddling me with the mask atop her head like a weird little beret, she cannot stop kissing me. Her passion makes me feel like DiMaggio must have early in his famous marriage.

At last Joy breaks off and roughly massages my scalp. "O my shaggy man. How fast your hair grows when the world's about to end."

Outside, several young Sevillano males bop along the sidewalk caterwauling the Spanish lyrics of an American pop song, "Speedy Gonzalez."

UNLIKELY
FRIENDS

You
    had
            to wonder about them, Sheila said. It wasn't natural, their relationship.
And so she *had* telephoned, synapsing the gap between her trailer court in
Mountboro and my brownstone in wicked old Hotlanta. I had to *do* something—namely, make sure that Paul's life didn't go monkey-mash sour before
his twentieth birthday. I figured I owed him that much.

"Listen, Sheila, I'm on a case, and it doesn't sound so godawful serious as
all that. My rent falls due—"

"You're Paul's daddy,' Sheila reminded me, although I hadn't forgotten.
She insisted that something fishy was going on. It scared her, for Paul, but
she couldn't do anything because she didn't move in the circles this high-
tone old geezer named Samuel Halterman moved in. Besides, Paul hadn't
spoken to her since catching her *in flagrante interdicto* with a Man Not Her
Husband while still the Lawful Wedded Wife of Jack Whitman, Paul's most
recent stepfather. At chance meetings downtown—the bank, the post office,
Foster's Barbecue Hut—her own son cut her dead. Made her feel lower than
Pekinese puke.

"He's not any fonder of me, La."

"Fonder? Jimmy Bevilacqua, he hates your ugly face."

"Right. Perfect reason for me to butt in. What a break for Paulie, you
ringing me up like this."

As in the Old Days, La and I went back and forth. Eventually she hit
me with a shopping list of my fatherly faults, failures, and copouts. Her voice
quavered through the line the way a record sitting crooked on a turntable
wobbles the music coming out. When I finally tossed in the towel— "Okay,

okay, I'll look into it" —she whooped in triumph, then nigh on to splintered my ear bones cradling her receiver.

Collect call. What else?

Just what I needed, another nonpaying case. (Put "case" in quotes.) Plus a chance to rub raw the sensitivities of some of the skeptical citizens of Mountboro who Knew Me When, to open lots of old wounds with my ex, and to rile a hostile teen who remembered me, chiefly, for hurling beer cans and pounding on walls.

Not to mention the chance to meet this Halterman character, a retired architectural muck-a-muck from Noo Yawk Noo Yawk. Upon him, according to La, Paulie had fixed the spillover of his grateful-puppy affections. Or something. Anyway, they'd become an every-evening item around Mountboro, as common as cornbread and collards.

I drove down early Tuesday in my twice-repossessed-and-reclaimed Trans Am and stopped three miles outside of town at the Ocmulgee Pulpwood Company, where Paulie worked. The fastest way to lay La's overimaginative worries to rest, I figured, was to talk to the boy. If I could catch him alone for twenty minutes, I could probably get a handle on his business with Halterman, reassure my ex by telephone, and scoot back to Atlanta without ever putting leather to a Mountboro sidewalk.

The Ocmulgee Pulpwood Company looked like a military installation. A chain-link fence surrounded a pine copse cleared to reveal a prefabricated office building, a warehouse, and an elevated conveyor belt for dropping aromatic wood chips into open railroad flatcars. You had to stop at the gate to tell the guard what business you had.

The guard manning the booth was Chaz Seeley, a hefty-bellied bubba from my senior class at Mountboro High. In intramural scrimmages twenty years ago, he had lined up against me in the defensive-end position, from which, with Good Old Boy affability, he had taunted me for my failures to slip around him for a pass. A couple of weeks into the season, as Chaz sashayed back to the bench after coating my nose with quicklime for the third time in as many plays, I bounced my helmet off his skull and got suspended from the team. Today, though, my shades, beard, and motoring cap concealed my identity from old Crazy Legs—right up to the moment I opened my mouth and asked him to let me talk to Paul.

"Paul don't want to see you, Jimmy," Chaz told me gently. "Ain't you got some other reason I should let you through?"

"I'm his daddy. That ought to suffice."

Grudgingly, Chaz told me where to find Paul—moving wood chips from an asphalt lot into one of the warehouse bays—and passed me inside.

I parked in front of the corrugated office building and walked between it and the conveyor-belt tower to the chip lot. Engine noise led me right to Paul. Periodically wiping his forehead with his sleeve, he drove a dirty yellow tractor with a dented lift-scoop. He had had his hair cut so short his blond temples looked naked. Eighteen years old? Hell, an elongated twelve was more like it. Watching him do a man's work filled me with a paradoxical mixture of shame and pride.

"Paul!" I shouted, waving my cap.

When he saw me, his face changed, an expression of concentration giving way to one of mad-dog meanness and intractability. He wheeled his tractor around and drove it grumbling and popping straight at Dear Old Dad. I retreated through a narrow corridor between the fence and the warehouse. Paulie kept coming. When he had approached as near as I meant for him to, he dumped a scoop of wood chips at my feet, spilling them out like the sawdust guts of a disemboweled Trojan Horse.

"You can't get past my defenses with a wave and a shout!" he cried because, well, eight years ago I had deserted his mother and him, and the times I'd returned with cash, toys, and funny stories hadn't squared our accounts, not by any reckoning that he wanted to consider. Well, I had known that, but I'd never expected him to try to bury me under a pile of miniature pine shakes.

Paul backed his machine away and went contemptuously back to work. I tagged along behind struggling to make myself heard over the noise, but with so little success that I began to feel like an invisible, and inaudible, man. I had dwindled in his estimation from daddy to stranger to haint to impalpable ectoplasm. In fact, his hatred wiped me out of existence.

At which point it occurred to me that Sheila had got Samuel Halterman's latter-day role in our boy's life all wrong. He wasn't a pederast or a leech, this dude from Up East, no. He was an attractive paternal substitute for Jimmy Bevilacqua. Yeah. The old coot had filched from me the magical cloak of Father Figure. As soon as this thought hit me, I stopped trying to make Paul acknowledge my presence and fled the prison yard of the pulpwood company.

As I drove through the gate on my way to the River View Trailer Court, Chaz Seeley touched the brim of his hat, not quite sarcastically.

"That's bull, Jimmy. Halterman ain't no father figure to Paulie. You've been reading too many *Psychology Today* articles."

"Tell me, La, just why is it bull?"

"Paul's already got a father. You don't need a father figure if you've already got a father."

"Me?"

"Like hell."

"Who, then—Jack?"

"Who else? Paul loves that man. They used to hunt, fish, everything. Why you suppose he took me messing around with Gene Darby so hard?"

"But Jack's hardly ever here." No truer words. Jack Whitman worked oil rigs off the Louisiana coast, and his duty tours sometimes kept him on a platform for as many as ninety days on end. These protracted absences had led La into temptation (just about the only place a man could ever hope to point her with her full compliance). "That's why you had to telephone Hubby Numero Uno, remember?"

"You just want to weasel out of this and hightail it back to Atlanta."

"Sure I do. It looks pretty innocent to me."

"Nothing looks innocent to you."

"Sheila-love, what the hell do you *want*?"

"Talk to this Halterman fella. I'm afraid to. Talk to him, check him out, see if you can find out what's happening to Paulie."

I felt it a bona fide mercy to escape Sheila's doublewide, which reeked of dirty diapers and day-old bacon grease. I headed through town to the resort where Halterman spent alternate afternoons working as a starter on the golf links. Orange spider lilies and smoky-blue hydrangeas lined the marshy ground behind the first tee. Coming down the path from the clubhouse, I soon caught sight of my prey.

Halterman stood chatting with a man in a mixed foursome. He wore gray plaid trousers with a discreet yellow stripe, perforated loafers with tassels, and a short-sleeved yellow jersey with gray piping. His face was long and deeply creased, his hair silver and plentiful. He reminded me of a wartless Honest Abe, if Abe had cleverly contrived to jog past his assassination and into the fullness of Senior Citizenhood. I liked his features, but not the way he slapped scapula, tilted his head back, and cracked jokes through the shiny off-white baleen of his dentures.

Dapperness, I thought, but no dignity.

Two groups went off before I could get up the grit to approach Halterman, and even then I didn't know how to play my hand. I didn't want to waste time on transparent ploys, but I didn't feel easy just introducing myself as Paul's daddy and taking it from there. My son, no doubt, had already set out rat poison around my reputation. So I flashed a phony ID under Halterman's nose and told him I was a Georgia Bureau of Investigation agent looking into illicit drug operations in predominantly rural counties.

"They told me in town, Mr. Halterman, that you know a little something about the young people hereabouts."

"Really? Who told you that?"

"I can't divulge my sources. Is it true?"

"Actually, I'm afraid it isn't."

"You know Paul Whitman, don't you?" I'd almost said Bevilacqua for Whitman. But three years ago Jack Whitman had legally adopted Paul, and my son had forfeited his beautiful Italian moniker for an Anglo-Saxon whicker and gulp.

"He's one of my closest friends in Mountboro." The way Halterman said this put me off. "You don't suspect *Paul* of buying or selling drugs, do you?"

"Should I?"

"Hell, no. Considering his background, he's about as up-and-up a soul as you can find today—what my generation called a straight arrow. Doesn't smoke, doesn't drink, wears his hair just the way Dwight D. Eisenhower would've liked."

"I understand you two spend a lot of time together."

"Who told you that?"

"Why did you deny knowing something about the kids in this community?"

"I didn't deny knowing Paul. I just don't lump him with your faceless herd of 'kids in this community,' that's all."

"Why not?" My anger had freshened like a midnight wind, and I was pressing too hard. Another foursome moseyed down from the clubhouse and eavesdropped on our talk from the edge of the waterlogged putting green. Halterman's eyebrows shot up. When they lowered again, he began chuckling like a munitions manufacturer after a declaration of war. "Oh, my goodness. If you look closely, a real family resemblance emerges. It's the mouth, I think."

I glanced at the people waiting on the putting green. No help from that quarter. No help from anywhere.

"You've no legitimate business with me," Halterman said, "and Paul wouldn't want me talking to you without his consent."

"I'm looking out for Paul's best interests."

"Better late than never," Halterman said, not unkindly.

"You're a grown man," I pressed. "Why would you need a boy's consent to talk to me?"

Halterman looked me straight in the eye. "You'd better go before I call the course manager down here." He made this sound like a suggestion rather than a threat. "I've got another foursome to start."

Bravado opens doors that timidity stubs its toe against. In the clubhouse I wangled Halterman's address from the burly manager he'd just threatened to have bounce me off the links. I told this orangutan that I was the son of one of Halterman's old cronies in the architectural business. Said I hoped to surprise him when he got home that evening. Said I had a case of his favorite wine in the trunk of my car and an orchid for his wife. It was dot-to-dot easy, my impromptu scam.

Two minutes later I was cruising out Alabama Road to the Mountboro Chalets, a pseudo-Swiss village in a forty-acre glade of loblollies. Leaving my car, I felt I should be wearing Tyrolean shorts, brocaded suspenders, and a pointed cap with a feather in its band. The chalets were A-frames with curlicue cutouts in the gingerbread trim, and they all had dappled sundecks overlooking a weedy black tarn that didn't much resemble Lake Geneva.

I climbed to the boxy front porch of Chalet No. 73 and introduced myself to Mrs. Halterman's daytime nurse as an insurance investigator checking out the credentials of a policy applicant by the name of Paul Whitman. The nurse, a middle-aged black woman in rubber-soled shoes, led me through the house to the sundeck. Here, Neva Halterman sat in a wheelchair knitting, or crocheting, or whatever old crippled ladies do with colorful balls of yarn on afternoons stretching out before them like the wastes of the Mojave.

"Sammy could tell you more about Paul than I can, Mr.—"

"Waters. I came straight out from town. Didn't know your husband wouldn't be here. Maybe you could answer a couple of questions to keep me from wasting the trip."

Mrs. Halterman juked through this opening like a tailback cutting for daylight. She said Sammy—Mr. Halterman—had met Paul at the Ocmulgee Pulpwood Company when her husband had driven a neighbor's truck out there to fetch home a load of wood chips as mulch for her flowerbeds. Then, it having been near quitting time, Paul rode back with Sammy to help him shovel out the load—an offer that Paul had made unbidden, possibly because he doubted Sammy's ability to do the job alone. As a paltry reward for the kind young man's help, Mrs. Halterman had popped another frozen dinner into the oven, and, eating together, the three of them had discussed history, politics, architecture, literature, music, and religion.

"Heavy," I said. "Did the kid bring along his note cards?"

"He's a bright young man, Mr. Waters, but we talked about practical matters too. He told us about working at the pulpwood company and the difficult circumstances under which he grew up. He has a lot of residual hostility toward his parents, I'm afraid, but as he matures he'll likely unload it. 'A good man,' said John Dewey, 'is someone trying to be better.' That's what Sammy and I liked about Paul, even more than his courtesy or his intellect or his industry—this directed struggle to release the butterfly in the chrysalis of his own youth." Mrs. Halterman stared mistily off over Little Lake Geneva, as I thought about Paul trying to plant me up to my neck in a heap of pine chips.

Some butterfly. Some chrysalis.

"So you and Mr. Halterman have become stand-in parents? Substitutes for the ones he doesn't get along with?"

"No. He's too independent for that. We treat him as an equal. In fact, we asked him to stop calling us Mr. and Mrs. Halterman and to use our first names."

"He must spend a lot of time here."

"Not really. He's probably visited us only four or five times. Sammy sees a great deal of him downtown, but I go to bed early and they're able to talk more comfortably at the place Paul's renting in Mountboro. Paul's been very good for Sammy."

"'Good for him'?"

Neva Halterman fixed me with a frank stare. "I was paralyzed in an accident two years ago, Mr. Waters, on a hike in the North Georgia mountains. I tumbled down some carven steps. Sammy had to abandon me for an hour to summon help. I survived, as you see, but for months on end my husband was a changed man, listless and very negative in his feelings about himself. He became a kind of zombie, an entirely different person."

"He's all right now?"

"Paul revitalized him. I had to nag Sammy to drive out to the pulpwood company for those wood chips, but that trip turned him around. After meeting Paul, Sammy took his job as a starter at the golf course. It was really a miracle, and I'm grateful to Paul for performing it."

Answering another question of mine, Mrs. Halterman said that after learning that Sammy had grown up in the Bronx and served in World War II, Paul had researched the histories of all the New York boroughs and both military units to which her husband had belonged. He'd also done some genealogical work on her and Sammy's family names. In her view, Paul had undertaken these researches to supply himself a fund of "artificial memories" to coincide with the Haltermans' real ones.

"What was the point?" I asked.

Mrs. Halterman put a dunce cap on me with her eyes. "Why, to get closer to us. To earn—in his *own* mind—the status of equal that we'd bestowed on him by insisting he call us Neva and Sam. An elder person can seldom be a really good friend with a younger person—a post-adolescent, I mean—because of the enormous disparity in their funds of experience, but Paul worked to close this gap."

A good deal of time had passed. All I needed was for "Sammy" to arrive while my buttocks dimpled the canvas of one of his recherché deck chairs. When he did come home, his wife would tell him about her visitor, and he'd quickly deduce my identity. By that time, I intended to have Paulie's house staked out in a last-ditch effort to determine Halterman's unsettling interest in him. His wife's confinement to a wheelchair—which Sheila had not even mentioned—had begun to worry me. And I was tired of listening to Neva Halterman's focused patter.

I stood. "So you think this kid's a good insurance risk?"

"I know nothing of his driving record, but I don't regard him as your stereotypical teenager. Say, don't you want to wait for Sammy? He should be here soon."

"No, no, you've helped me a lot, Mrs. Halterman."

She propelled her chair toward the patio doors, conspicuously sur-
mounted by an abstract stained-glass window of weird angular diamonds
that glowed indigo, amber, and lemon in the afternoon sunlight. I had paid
scant attention to this window earlier, but now I gaped at it raptly, like a kid
watching a Roadrunner cartoon.

"Paul made that," Mrs. Halterman said.

"You're kidding." My own surprise surprised me.

"He's exhibited and sold some of his work at crafts fairs. Within a year or
two he hopes to quit his current job and do stained glass fulltime. He's hugely
talented, don't you think?"

"Very classy." I liked the window—but its cruel angularity made me
shiver.

"He's teaching Sammy how to do it too."

She crossed the threshold into the chalet without my help or her nurse's.
Then she wheeled about before a cabinet filled with stand-up photos of Halterman children and grandchildren. In two, her husband wore a soldier suit
and balanced curly-headed tykes on both knees. Thirty years ago, the photographs revealed, Neva Halterman had been a looker. Even in her wheelchair,
she was still a handsome woman.

"Must be hard for you," I said, "not being able to be a proper wife."

Her eyes caught fire. "Sammy was never one to want a proper wife, Mr.
Waters."

I stood there vainly seeking a handle on this remark.

"Sophistication can be a bigger trap than innocence, sir. Worldly people
outsmart themselves with cynicism at least as often as rubes sabotage themselves with ignorance."

"Thank you for your help, Mrs. Halterman." I got out of the Mountboro
Chalets pronto. On the drive back into town, I passed Samuel Halterman's
red Datsun heading jauntily toward them.

I didn't know what to tell her, so I didn't report back to Sheila. Her suspicions about Paul's spiraling down into some sort of weird dependency on
Halterman had begun to niggle at me. Neva Halterman had characterized
my son as a self-sufficient, mature eighteen-year-old, but I considered her
testimony on that point worthless. She had talked with Paulie only four or

five times, and she had not seen him in action that morning at the Ocumul-
gee Pulpwood Company. Most of what she knew about him she had cribbed
from her husband.

I got to thinking about the stained glass over the sliding doors to the
Haltermans' sundeck. The irony of the whole screwed-up situation was that
Neva Halterman probably had as much cause to regard Paul with suspicion
as Sheila had to regard the architect with a skeptical eye. What if our kid was
playing the affection-starved old man for a nest egg to finance his handicraft
ambitions? Or if Halterman had made his payments contingent upon Paul's
coming across physically? Being country-shrewd and church-mouse poor,
Paul might well tiptoe out of this imbroglio unscathed, but Halterman had
placed himself in a hair-trigger blackmail trap. Whoever jostled the spring,
or threatened to, would stand to bleed the old guy dry.

This last thought was worth a private smile. I kept it between the rear-
view mirror and myself.

After two pork sandwiches, a side order of Brunswick stew, and a cup of
gritty black coffee at Foster's Barbecue Hut, I got a to-go cup of coffee and
set forth to my stakeout. Paul lived alone in a one-story frame house on a
narrow street angling off the Atlanta highway. I parked my Trans Am in the
rear lot of Cooksie's Texaco station, which overlooked an unmowed meadow
comprising Paul's corner of the neighborhood. The shell of an ancient school
bus and a mound of discarded tires effectively concealed my car from the
house. Although I made my coffee last until sunset, the last few drops went
down like cold linseed oil.

Forty minutes later, Halterman drove up and parked parallel to the house
under the cork elms drooping over the front porch. The porch light burned
whitely, and the old man paused before knocking to peer up and down the
street. He looked directly up at Cooksie's for a second, but his gaze didn't
tarry and I exhaled in a nervous burst. Neither Paul nor Halterman knew
the make of my car (unless Chaz or Mrs. Halterman's nurse had passed the
information on), but, clearly, Halterman had been looking for someone—
namely Jimmy Bevilacqua. Semis and pickups rumbled by on the highway,
and a gaggle of pubescent black kids made their way up Paulie's street from
the shantytown everyone called Pearl Harbor to the convenience store across
from Cooksie's. Otherwise, a spooky quiet hung over the town.

I got out of my car and scampered down the slope behind the service station into the meadow beside the house. I had a small recorder on my hip and a camera that could operate in the dark without a flash. After creeping around to the back, I climbed onto the rickety screened porch, eased my way through the unlatched door, and stepped up onto an old railway bench to see what I could through the panes of the casement window. Pink Floyd's *The Wall* was vibrating the floorboards, muffling the telltale bumps and creaks of my maneuvering on the bench.

Inside, Paul and Halterman had bent over a worktable on which glazing tools, lead cames, and pieces of carefully cut stained glass lay atop a complicated paper pattern. The pattern appeared to reproduce a gothic window big enough to turn a K-Mart's into a cathedral.

My timing had not quite clicked. Paul had his shirt off, but his eyes shone with purpose. He pointed at various parts of the design, explaining what they had to do yet, and Halterman paid almost obsequious heed. He put his hand on Paul's shoulder and laughed about the shape of a piece of glass that hadn't come out quite right. Studying the layout, they struck me as giddily cozy. The music rendered my recording unit useless. I shot a couple of photographs and stepped down from the bench. And just as Pink Floyd took a between-cuts breather, a slat dropped out of the back of the bench and clattered into an empty metal basin under it.

I hopped through the door and down the dilapidated rear steps. The moon rolled out from behind a cloud to spotlight my getaway. To avoid revealing my car's location, I veered toward a drainage ditch, not Cooksie's, and crouched low in the grass. Paul and Halterman burst out onto the porch and clomped down the exterior steps into the dew-soaked meadow. "Leave us alone!" Paul shouted. "Leave us *alone!*" Halterman touched Paul's elbow, talked to him quietly, and inveigled him back to the porch. I stayed put for a long time. Eventually, the old man's Datsun pulled away from the house and glided through Mountboro toward the turn-off to the retirement village. My watch put the time at 11:42. More than likely, I had sent Halterman packing early. The lights in Paulie's windows snapped off one by one. After all, tomorrow was a workday.

Relieved, I crept out of the drainage ditch and made a wide circuit through the meadow to Cooksie's. Then I climbed into my car, leaned my head back, and promptly fell asleep.

*

A crash awoke me. In my windshield, fissures spidered in an expanding network. My car began bouncing up and down, and beyond the glistening fissures Paulie, dressed for work, loomed into the high dawn like a gigantic hood ornament. He had just thrown a small cinderblock into the windshield, and now he shifted his weight from side to side to set up a rocking motion in my Trans Am. I kicked the door open and jumped out, right into a hill of threadbare tires. Flinging out my arms, I managed to retain my balance and to face him square on.

"I'll whip your butt, boy!"

His face gleamed as bright and hard as a hubcap. "God, I hate you."

"Any idea why?"

My question made him blink. "You're the only living soul I know who can make me carry on like this."

"I'm your friend, Paulie. I'm trying to look out for you."

"So you told Sam. But you lied through your teeth to Neva. And you've got no business subjecting her to such mickeymouse."

"She's got a stake in this too."

"In *what*, Daddy? In what?"

First time he'd called me Daddy in eight years. A slip-up or outright mockery? "In this fishy do-si-do between Halterman and you." Paulie just stared. "I'm here to get to the bottom of it."

"Hey, you've reached the bottom. You always do. Stop fretting your evil mind and you might figure everything out."

"I already have."

"I'll just bet you have." Paul jumped down from the hood and paced along the slope that fell away behind the filling station.

"What about my windshield?"

"It's cracked, Daddy, like your opinion of my life." Paul trotted down the slope, then stalked off through the bejeweled morning grass toward his own automobile, a beat-up VW bug with oversized tires and a custom-made grille.

"I'll have your wages garnisheed!" I called after him.

He whirled and pointed a finger at me. "Stay away from my friends and stay away from the pulpwood company. You're in real danger if you keep this up—I swear to God, Daddy, you're in real danger."

*

"His life is ruined."

"That's the small-town view, La. How many kids Paulie's age have a steady job, their own car, and a house to rent?"

"Halterman's ruined him."

"Circumstantial stuff, Sheila-love. Nothing hard. Besides, you'll find thousands of well-adjusted people in Atlanta like Paulie."

"Mountboro ain't Atlanta, and those other people ain't Paulie."

"What do you want me to do? I've got about as much influence with the kid as the Man in the Moon."

"Stop Halterman, Jimmy. Get him out of Paul's life."

"You putting out a contract, La?"

"I don't mean knock him off. Just scare him off. You can do that."

"Why the hell *should* I?"

"Mama!" a child cried. *"Mama!"*

Kimberly, Sheila's two-year-old daughter, making her presence known. Right at the beginning of *Captain Kangaroo*, Sheila had sat her in a high chair in the living room with a couple of squeeze toys and a big box of Honey Bran cereal.

"I mean, I'm not making any money here. Nothing I do is really going to change anything."

"Paul's your son, I'm his mother, and you owe us."

"But it won't make any difference."

"It will to me. It's the least you can do."

"Mama!"

"Coming, darling!"

An hour later I stumbled from Sheila's trailer into the sunlight and found myself smack against the flank of a red Datsun. The passenger door swung open, and Halterman asked me to get in.

"What for?"

"To talk to you, Mr. Bevilacqua. Yesterday you *wanted* me to."

Wearily, I ducked into the car, which accelerated, nearly struck a mailbox at the end of the trailer court, and careered off down Fry's Mill Road at a furious clip. As if I were a space creature doing a shabby impersonation of a human being, Halterman kept glancing at me sidelong. When I returned the favor, staring hard, he paid more attention to the shanty-lined road.

"Paul phoned from work this morning. He told me what he'd done to your car."

"Don't sweat it. I mean to make him pay for it."

Halterman turned on an access road leading up into the state park, tourist territory. Autumn haze threaded the meadows and pine copses like cannon smoke, the aftermath of a ghostly Civil War engagement. I liked this country much better than I liked Atlanta and environs, but unless you were a mill hand, a pulpwooder, or a knick-knack merchant, you couldn't make a living here.

"Mr. Bevilacqua, I'm an architect. I know something about building complicated structures from the ground up. If you lay your foundation on quicksand, you can't even begin to build. Do you know what I'm telling you?"

"I learned about metaphors in high school. Catching onto when folks talked down to me I picked up a lot earlier."

"Touché." With stiff hands and a cowcatcher chin, Halterman negotiated the curved and steepening road. "What I'm trying to tell you is that you've misjudged this thing between your son and me."

"'Misjudged'?"

"Paul and I are friends. Very good friends. That's the extent of it, the whole truth and nothing but."

"Seventy-year-old men and eighteen-year-old boys ain't 'friends,' Sammy. The world doesn't work that way."

"The world doesn't, but sometimes people do." He yanked the Datsun into a semicircle of gravel overlooking the matchbox landscape of pastures and churches in the valley and unfolded himself from the automobile, leaving the door open, and walked to the edge of the turnout with his hands in his pockets. Maybe a minute later, I followed him, watching the smoke from my cigarette laze into the autumn air.

"Mr. Bevilacqua, I want you to get out of Mountboro and stay out. There's not a thing to keep you here—absolutely nothing."

"I grew up here."

Halterman approached as if to grab my lapels and fling me over the guard rail into the valley. Instead he thrust a check from his shirt pocket at me. Tilting my head, I could see that he'd made it out to me for a thousand dollars.

"My, my, what could this be for?"

"Don't assume it hush money. Part's to repair your broken windshield. The rest's an inducement for you to save at least two lives, maybe more, by returning to Atlanta."

I refused to touch the check.

"The lives are yours and Paul's," he went on. "I fear what he may do if you stick around any longer. So does he. He'll make a fine man, one of talent and accomplishment, if he can outlast this urge to prove himself by doing you some terrible bodily harm."

"I came down here to help him."

"You can do that—and help yourself, too—by taking my check and leaving."

I told Halterman his motives were transparent. He feared the impact of exposure on his frail and trusting wife. Besides, a grand was an insulting drop of chlorophyll in the immense evergreen forest of his bank account.

Halterman seethed. In fact, he got heart-attack angry and threatened to report me to the GBI for impersonating first one of its own agents and then an insurance-company detective. For an old guy, he put on a rousing show, pacing the edge of the overlook just as Paul had paced the slope behind the service station after fracturing my windshield. At length, though, he remembered his Up East manners and simmered down enough to paint me a picture of "provoking Paul further"—an appeal to my better nature and an empty threat, nice and fatherly.

"Come on, Jimmy, take the check."

Not a bad two days' work for a between-jobs detective on a pleasure jaunt into the sticks. After all, how often does a man get paid for preventing his own murder?

As I drove, the faceted countryside gave way to shards of skyscraper and splinters of concrete overpass. It was delicious to be shut of Sheila and the shackles of small-town domesticity.

Because a man's friends, I had decided, are nobody's business but his own.

CRAZY
ABOUT
EACH
OTHER

Twenty-
seven's
      tardy to go schizo, but it happens. Cotton-mouthed and blurry-eyed, I came off a night of hard drinking and lurched into Mr. Billy's Chevron station to replace the alternator belt on a Dodge 400, its pebbly vinyl roof the same refrigerator-white as its body metal. Mr. Billy had driven his tow truck forty-some miles, round trip, to fetch the 400 back, and I was supposed to get her running by noon.

Under the hood, my fingers felt like jumbo franks. Soon, caked with carburetor grease, they *looked* like charred jumbo franks. In my mind's eye, they'd grown so big that my entire body seemed to be nothing but the sunburned tip of my nose pointing into the engine well and ten enormous fingers bunged up on the fan blades, the radiator cap, the dipstick. They wouldn't do anything I wanted them to do. Instead of replacing an alternator belt, I might as well have been defusing a terrorist's bomb.

"Gordo, you're totally worthless today," Mr. Billy said. "Get on out there and wait on that fella."

I pulled my blimp-sized fingers out of the engine and floated from the garage to the pumps. It was one weird journey, a dreamy oozing. I crept up on the guy the way a garden slug creeps from one end of a sun porch to the other. My shoes left—or *seemed* to leave—sticky silver prints on the asphalt.

"Fill 'er up," the guy in this ghost vehicle tells me. I say ghost vehicle because I can't remember what he drove. It could have been a pickup, a Greyhound bus, a Subaru, a tin outhouse turned on a mechanic's slide. It had doors, windows, tires—that was all I noted or cared about it.

"Fill her up," the doofus said. "Reglar unleaded. Get a move on, skinny."

His passenger window stood open. I unfolded the regular-unleaded snake from the pump, stuck its evil snout through the guy's window, and started milking the sucker. Its flow had a dangerous stench, like high-grade lighter fluid.

Pretty damned quick, the son of a bitch in the driver's seat yelled like a madman, leapt out of his wheels, and scurried away to a strip of neon-green grass between Hwy 27 and the gas-pump island.

"You idjit! You crazy damn fool!"

He'd been smoking, merrily puffing along. Now he was grinding out the butt in the grass, frantically twisting his shoe on it. Through the passenger's window, through the driver's window, I watched the bozo twisting away. Meanwhile, I kept the venom flowing in a good-faith effort to fill up his car—at least until Mr. Billy and Gene Hastings sprinted up and wrestled the snake out of my hands.

That's how I came to be in the Quiet Harbor Psychiatric Center, a private hospital for crazies, druggies, and sex freaks. (I'm a crazy.) The insurance Mr. Billy carries on his mechanics, along with him being buddies with a QHPC social worker from his wife's stay in the center six years ago, got me in. Else I would have wound up sleeping behind a Dumpster and ineptly cadging quarters from lampposts.

Dr. Emmett Vogan installed me in a room with a white-collar alkie named Trent Brodwin, then ordered my unruly brain pickled in about a million ounces of Thorazine a day. Someone's always shoving a paper thimble of schizo medicine at me, telling me to get up, eat, or sit down, or asking me to discuss—usually in an embarrassing group gab—all the weird acts and feelings that unloaded me here.

One crucial thing, though—in group gab, I met Karen Cleveland, Mrs. Obsessive-Compulsive 1982. If that's so, and I suppose it is, I'm Mr. Inappropriate Affect 1982. I cackle at Karen's agonies. I pound the wall over her narrow sudden-death triumphs. I admire her for her gross-out efforts to uglify herself and her unsubtle attempts to run me off. You see, Karen and I are crazy about each other. We're in passionate, out-of-our-gourds, sexual-emotional-spiritual love. Swear to God.

Karen Cleveland is two, three, maybe five years older than me. She's hitched and has two kids. Her old man's this roofer for a big southeastern construction company that sent him to Birmingham two months back. When Derek accepted this move and drove off to Alabama with little Keivano and even littler LaKeisha, Karen stayed on at Quiet Harbor. In case her kids' names didn't tip you, Karen's a black lady—chocolate-brown, in fact, like bittersweet cooking squares melted smooth in a double boiler.

Three other goofballs, not counting Dr. Vogan, attended the group-gab session where I met Karen Cleveland: my rummy roommate, Trent Brodwin; a coke dope named Fred; and a middle-aged guy, Charlie S—, with depression. (What really depressed me about Charlie involved finding out that, with only the moody blues, nothing else, the guy believed he *belonged* in a hospital.) Me, I was in a haze. The Thorazine had shot to my gut. It had washed into my blood like waves of liquid blotting paper, blotting up feeling and what the shrinks here call vividity.

I saw Karen, though. She leapt into my eyes and siphoned that Thorazine blotting paper right out of my system. I sat up. I drew a bead on her black-olive eyes and uptight beauty. She wore a white linen dress that fell to her ankles. Her linen headscarf made her look like a Tanzanian nun—something eye-blitzing, something special.

In comparison, the other crazies at group gab were nobodies, absolute nobodies, even my bloated hangdog roomy, a guy I'd annoyed one night by sitting at his bedside and talking to him for a couple of hours about such stark truths as the unnaturalness of automatic transmissions and the super-reliability of antifreeze as a dog poison. As I filled him in on these *issues*, he had glared as if he disagreed or didn't enjoy reminders of such sobering facts after lights-out.

"What issue's foremost in your mind, Gordon," Dr. Vogan asked. "Tell us."

Group gab was a time for issues. Everybody had to have one. A patient without an issue was "not cooperating." I mumbled some crap. I didn't feel at home yet. I was antsy. I was shy. Besides, if Karen thought whatever stupid boring issue I brought up was stupid and boring, I'd never be anything to her but a whitebread moron, a schizo grease monkey from the boonies. What the bother did she know, though? What the hell did Dr. Vogan? A radio broadcast from my dead mama—her soul had a broadcasting booth in one of my underside cranial lobes—told me to ignore wily old Dr. Vogan, to bite my fantasy-addled tongue.

But he crossed me up by saying that my reluctance to talk was under-

standable. I was new to Quiet Harbor. Maybe, today, I'd do better to sit back
and observe, just to get an overall feel for the group-therapy approach.

"What about you, Karen?" he said. "What issue's most urgent with you?"

"My chirren."

"They're fine," Dr. Vogan said. "And it won't be long before you join your
family in Birmingham."

"They think I'm crazy. And I am. I *am* crazy—a blithering female fool."

"You have a behavioral disorder, Karen."

"I'm crazy!" she shouted. "Full-out crackers!"

"So am I," I piped up. All of group gab gaped at me. I didn't feel shy
anymore. I said, "My brain was a stick shift. So that was the shift I automatically shifted. Now it's an automatic transmission. It automatically transmits
this pilot disease. You could call it craziness, but it most likely wouldn't come.
Come or not, I'm crazy. I concur with Mrs. Cleveland. It's the unavoidable
automatic conclusion, the only one that flies, on-shift or off-." Some of what
I said that morning was Mama's doing, but some was just gear slips of the
tongue.

"If I ain't crazy," Karen said, looking at Dr. Vogan, "why am I here with
the likes of him?"

I smiled at her, inside. Karen sneered. Her black-olive eyes—or their pupils, at least—began to spin. The pupils whirled inside the black outer rings,
the outer rings spun counterclockwise about the pupils. But a more upsetting
thing about Karen Cleveland was that she had no eyebrows, just a shelf of
bone where her eyebrows would have been if she'd had any.

"Forget, for now, the condition that brought you here," Dr. Vogan said.
"Put it out of your mind."

"It is out of my mind. *I'm* out of my mind."

"Don't play word games with me, Karen. If you can't forget what brought
you here, show us. Show Gordon, anyway—*he* doesn't understand."

Karen gave me a snotty chin-up look, then pinched a corner of her
scarf—it was only a sheet or pillowcase—and yanked it off her head. Her
skull shone like a gleaming chocolate globe. Here and there across it ran
patches of nappy black hair, nearly invisible strips of fuzz. It was ugly, her
splotchy baldness. In a way, though, it was also beautiful. Trent Brodwin,
Fred, and Charlie, my fellow goofball nobodies, looked away, but Dr. Vogan
and I stared. For me, the ugliness of Karen's head just grew lovelier and lovelier, gradually. In fact, my dead mama's radio voice whispered that the Karen

Cleveland look was "no pun intended, a head of its time." Karen, not hearing Mama, made claws of her hands, held them to her temples, and cried, her face a damp pretzel.

"It's nothing to be ashamed of," Dr. Vogan said, reaching over to touch her arm. "The only shame is in not seeking treatment, in giving up."

"I *want* to give up," Karen said.

"No, you don't, Karen. No, you don't."

"I love you, Karen," I said. "It's my automatic deduction. I think you're pretty—beautiful, even, just the way you are."

Mrs. Obsessive-Compulsive 1982. What Karen did was pluck out the hairs on her head and body with her fingernails, or tweezers, or round-nosed grooming scissors. She had something weirdly out of kilter in her brain chemistry that drove her to do it, almost all the time. Except for the therapy aides on the ward, two or three nurses, and a visiting psychologist, Karen Cleveland was the only black person at Quiet Harbor. The therapy aides threw her sidelong looks. They'd seen crazy white folks, mostly female, suffer the pain, shame, and heartbreak of her Plucking Sickness, but never one of their own. Crazy black women usually couldn't afford Quiet Harbor. They had no insurance because they had no money, and, broke, you just couldn't dock at Dr. Emmett Vogan's sanitarium for well-heeled crazies. Karen had got in only because Derek's construction firm had a high-minded employee insurance plan. Karen and I were birds of a feather, sort of.

My heart went out to her. I mean, when I told her I loved her at that first group gab—a session Dr. Vogan put a stop to, right then—I meant that I loved her as a parent, a pastor, or God the Creator would.

Agape love. Grace. Love at first sight is storybook nonsense, run-amok hormones or rosy-tinged nearsightedness. You can't trust it to go the distance. Besides, I couldn't fall for a bald pluck-head, even a truly foxy mama, without learning a few things about her first.

I began visiting Karen in the women's wing. If you weren't a gibbering yahoo, someone in need of constant restraint or an occasional electrobuzz, which I wasn't—at least during the day—you could walk around the hospital. True, I heard voices. I saw my body parts mutate into papier-mâché piñatas or the limbs and torsos of department-store dummies, even red plastic birds. I also figured out the *real* intentions behind the falsely random parking patterns of Quiet Harbor's staff members and patients. You see, vehicles of primary colors alternated with cars of off-shades and pastels to relay to Japanese spy satellites tips about the hottest American stocks.

I wasn't dangerous, mind. I was just a schizz, of the "tentative undifferentiated" variety. Even so, Karen's roommate, Janna Maxman, a manic depressive wife who liked to telephone world leaders long-distance with her plans for reforesting India, Pakistan, and the Middle East, always walked out when I came in. She didn't trust me. She feared one of my piñata appendages would explode and shoot hundreds of licorice jaw breakers and bite-sized Tootsie Rolls through her and the hospital walls.

"It must hurt," I told Karen one morning after Mrs. Maxman had hustled away. "Pulling all those hairs out."

"It does," she said. "It really does. More than it would a sick whitey. Silk's easy to tug free, Afroturf's lots tougher. You gotta be a dummy to try to pluck Afroturf. You gotta be tough. You gotta have stick-to-it-ivity. Dumb, tough, and *pre*sistent—that's what you gotta be."

This was a lament, not a brag. Karen clutched her own arms, clawing down.

"I started plucking when I was thirteen, bout the time I got my monthlies. It hit me like horse hits a needle-man, hard. I'd pick, pluck, tug. I got into hair harvesting big-time. Round bout sixteen, I let up on it and grew back some hair. Then, who digs why, the urge tapered off and Derek Cleveland started in to call.

"We get married. We have a baby, then another one, and I'm all to once at my eyebrows and skull rug again, pinching and plucking. I can't help it. I do it all the time, then hide what I've done with a eyebrow pencil and a scarf. Derek, he finally finds out. That did it for him—I was the maddest woman in good old Columbus, G. A. Who wants a gal who hides out to tweeze herself? Who wants a bald-head wife?"

That was just how she talked. She mowed herself down. She shamed herself. She was proud of being tough, but embarrassed by what she was doing—what she couldn't *help* doing—to show it off. She missed Derek dingbat, her husband, and little Keivano and even littler LaKeisha, and knew that Derek had surrendered to his company's plan to transfer him to Birmingham because her hair plucking—Dr. Vogan called it a long word, *trichotillomania*, which I can spell because Karen had a banner with the word on it taped to her mirror—well, because her hair plucking had freaked out their kids. Derek had moved to get his *chirren* away from her, either for a little while or forever. "Whichever come first," Karen said.

She had no tweezers in her room. No fingernail clippers. No sewing scissors. No grooming scissors. Of course, I didn't either, and neither did any other crazy in Quiet Harbor, but not having them hacked Karen off. She said she was tired of having the "sisters"—our therapy aides—cut her fingernails; tired of the humiliating lack of trust, just flat-out tired of being crazy.

"Don't they give you Thorazine?" I asked.

"That's for schizos, Gordon. They're trying to reprogram my behavior. It don't work, though. I get a urge, I pinch out a eyelash. I get on a roll, I mow down a whole field of Afroturf. I pluck it without tweezers. Shee-it, I do it with hardly no fingernails."

"They should dope you," I said. "It's not fair they don't dope you."

"They give me tranquilizers, all right—relaxers. But these drugs that really work, clomipramine and something else just as funny sounding, they're not licensed here. You got to be a European to get em, a European *living in Europe*. Or you got to be a member of a special treatment program. Over here, though, we just got to suffer."

At first, Karen didn't like me much. My hands were dirty, not black. And I'd sometimes correct her grammar, which, as both a white guy and a big reader, I had this advantage over her on. She hated that. And she didn't care for it much when I asked her why she'd stuck handles like Keivano and LaKeisha on her innocent kids.

"What's wrong with those names, Gordo? They're pretty."

"God, Karen, they're"—I had to think a minute—"showoffy."

"Showoffy? What *do* you mean?" I saw her neck stiffening, her chin coming forward.

"You ever hear about this Afro-American couple—Mr. and Mrs. Brown—who found out the missus was expecting?"

Karen sort of paused, like a cobra considering whether to bite or not. "No. What about them?"

"They were first-timers, and when their doctor told them they might have triplets or somesuch, they started thinking about some highfalutin names to go with Brown. One day, Mrs. Brown was in a pharmacy store to fill a prescription for morning-sickness and found herself on the headache-, cold-, and allergy-medicine aisle. That gave her an idea. When her bouncing boys were born, she and her husband would baptize them Tylenol, Benadryl, and Robitussin Brown." When I helplessly started to laugh, Karen reared back and smacked me silly. You could hear it all over the ward.

"Criminy!" I cried, grabbing my face with both hands. "What the hell!"

"You're a honky bigot, Gordon Sweat." I tried to buy her off by saying I'd heard that story from an *Afro-American* comic on late-night TV, but she said, "And you think that excuses you for being a two-legged pile of crap in cheap-ass tennis shoes?"

"Because it frets me you've burdened your kids with godawful names?"

"What's so fine about Gordon? It means fatty in Spanish!"

"It means Wonderful Counselor," I shot back. I have no clue what Gordon means, but I wasn't about to let a hair-plucking female tell me it means fatty in Spanish, even if it does. Besides, I was being a wonderful counselor to her, wasn't I, talking to her when nobody else but hired staff would. I always told her she looked beautiful, even minus the standard allotment of eyebrows and head hair.

I'm no honky bigot. A crazy son of a bitch, maybe, but no wild-eyed Archie Bunker type or idiot Ku Klux Klansman. I've shouted some ugly names in my time, I guess, and I'm not proud of it, but I've never firebombed a church, at least not one with anybody in it. (That's a *joke*, okay?)

Two weeks went by, and I stabilized. Dr. Vogan praised me for my "encouraging progress." My voices, even Mama's, sounded farther and farther away, if they sounded at all, like a radio in another room. My fingers didn't balloon up like cartoon-character blimps in a Thanksgiving Day parade anymore. My belly didn't split open at night to give birth to creatures like crosses between baby rats and piranhas. My ears and nose and pecker didn't detach themselves and flutter off like red plastic birds. That was such a relief you wouldn't believe. . . .

Anyway, I was stabilizing. The Thorazine still tasted rank, but it helped. Having a cottony mouth and not being able to dump my bowels every morning after wakeup were small prices to pay for body parts that stayed put.

Karen, though, she wasn't doing so good. She couldn't get the dope she needed—clomipramine—and old Dr. Vogan's depth-psychology behavioral therapy left her feeling stupid and out of it. Dumb, she said. Inadequate.

Late at night, while her roommate Janna Maxman dreamt her insane reforestation schemes, Karen plucked—a hair from this side, one from the exact same spot on the other side of her skull; an eyelash from the right, an eyelash from the left. Her eyebrows had long since gone, squoze out with steady cunning, so she didn't have to work on them—but she hunted every other hint of fuzz above her neck, as if a starring part in a follow-up to Spielberg's *E.T.* was on the line.

These developments did not please Dr. Vogan. If anything, they pissed off and alarmed Dr. Vogan.

Me, I tried to help Karen. I visited the women's wing every day to provide her wonderful counsel and generally behave like the Christian gentleman Mama wanted me to be before she realized I was a foul-mouthed carouser and gave up. (While she was still alive, at least.) Janna Maxman was seldom around because she watched game shows and soaps—pretty obsessive-compulsive about it, really—and padded off to the dayroom to see them with all the other TV-hypnotized loons. Which gave Karen Cleveland and me talk time and privacy. Amazingly, Karen didn't run me off. She liked me to annoy her. If she knew I was practicing my Christian gentleman act, she assumed—and she was right—I was doing it sincerely. She kept a headscarf on when I showed up, true, but she didn't try to disguise the fact that in the days since our first meeting, she'd plucked herself to global nakedness. She admitted it.

"Why?" I said.

"I have to," Karen said. "That's about the dumbest thing you've ever asked me."

"But why?"

"Answer that and you can have you Dr. Vogan's job. And *he* can go pump gas."

And she cried, just like in our first group gab. Only today, sitting on her bed, she didn't put clawhammer fingers to her temples or wipe away the wetness with a Kleenex. She let her agony flow.

"Derek," she said. "My chirren. I haven't heard a goddamn thing from them for ten or eleven days. I used to get letters, a phone call, something. But now that no-'count, low-down—" She broke off, ugly sobs almost strangling her.

"Karen," I said. "Karen, *what?*"

"I know what he's doing, Gordon Sweat. He's . . . he's trying to wean them from me, taking the babies of my womb off the mama's milk of my love."

"Then he's a real shit," I was about to applaud myself for that little masterpiece of comfort when the sobs stole on her again and she turned her head away.

"Shut that door, Gordon."

Against the rules—shutting the door when a patient of the opposite gender was in your room, but, hey, I shut the door. I wouldn't want every whacko that strolled by seeing me cry like that, either.

"What am I going to do?" Karen said.

"Treatment," I told her. "Treatment and—"

"I mean about my chirren, fool. Treatment's got diddly to do with it. How am I going to let them know I'm still alive? That I still love em? That I'm not so crazy I flat-out forgot them?" She dabbed one eye and looked at me as if expecting me to spit out a big-time brilliant solution, Dear Abby style.

"You could send them a lock of hair."

Karen's bottom lip pooched out. She was ready to unload on me with the kind of mindless fury that I'd poured unleaded regular into the front seat of one of Mr. Billy's customers' cars. Instead, glory be, she laughed.

"You honky bigot b-b-bastard," she sputtered and laughed again—laughing and crying at once. When she reached her long arms to me, I slid forward. We rocked on the edge of her bed, then on the bed itself. A voice, from two or twenty brain coves down, said I wasn't behaving in the grand tradition of courtly Southern white gentlemanliness, but I figured—going by its fretful tone and the wide range of skin shades among latter-day "black" folk—that this voice shamelessly lied.

Several of my later visits to Karen's room, while Mrs. Maxman was watching *The Price Is Hyped* and *All My Lovers* and such, ended the same way. Not in tears—not every time, anyway—but in bed. And never believe I didn't enjoy lying with Derek's lovely woman, either—*cuckolding* him, to use the correct dirty Shakespearean term. He deserved it—for not behaving in the best tradition of Southern *human* gentlemanliness, if I may quote, sort of, my departed but still broadcasting mama.

But one afternoon the odds went against Karen and me. Mrs. Maxman stumbled in while we were *sessioning*, to use the semicorrect nonprofane psychiatric argle-bargle, and reported her "shock and disappointment" to Quiet Harbor's staff. Dr. Vogan hailed Karen and me to a private meeting in his office and scolded us—deservedly, I suppose—for "surrendering to the lures of unmonitored propinquity and unbridled libido."

"I beg your pardon," Karen said.

Dr. Vogan reexplained, in layman's terms—to which I replied that he might have had a point if I was a psychiatrist using my father-figure status to take advantage, but I was a peer of the opposite sex, a fellow loon, and Karen and I were adults. He should butt out PDQ, our private sessioning was none of his bee's-wax.

"Everything at Quiet Harbor is my business," Dr. Vogan argued. "Gordon, no good can come of this—for either of you. Karen's married. She has children." Karen began to cry. "And she's afflicted with trichotillomania. As for you, Gordon, you're a borderline schizophrenic Good Old Boy beneath Karen's level of sensitivity but certain you're better than her because she's black. It's impossible. You need to stay away from her, Gordon. She needs to stay away from you."

"We're crazy," Karen said, wiping her eyes. "We ain't dead or desexed."

"Don't say ain't, Karen."

"Hush, you stuck-up peckerwood! Sometimes you say it yourself." To Dr. Vogan she said, "I haven't spayed myself, whatever else of me I've plucked away, and Gordo's no castrato." Pleased with herself, she winked at me.

"Great, Mrs. Cleveland. What a forceful defense of adultery and fornication." Dr. Vogan looked a little ashamed. "Forget that. Here and now, it's inappropriately priggish. My point is, well, you may be hurting each other, more than you know."

"I'm helping me," Karen said. "And Gordo's not exactly suffering."

"Then for God's sake, people, be discreet," Dr. Vogan said.

I guess we were—more discreet, anyway. But Dr. Vogan's own boss, the director of the center, heard the buzz about our relationship through the loon-and-goon grapevine, patients and therapy aides rumormongering and semifibbing, and there was a minor stink foul enough to put me in a security lockdown and Karen hovered over by QHPC's ebony counterpart to Big Nurse in *One Flew Over the Cuckoo's Nest*. If that was curing us, if that was helping, why not give flood victims a scuba-diving vacation without any use of aqualungs. At the time, I didn't know what Karen got from this treatment.

Me, I got a major depression, the Moby Dick of all Moody Blues.

Nobody visited me. My daddy took a sixteen-wheeler out of town when I was eleven and never came back. Mama, as already noted, was dead. A Big C of the ovarian variety carried her off half a year before my psychotic snap at the Chevron station, about three months before Cynthia Jane Hogarth threw me over for Steve Creed, a Hothlepoya County LP gas man. I was an only kid, with aunts, uncles, and cousins God knows where, so who could possibly visit me? Who?

Mr. Billy, that's who—him and Gene Hastings.

Gene came a week or two after Dr. Vogan admitted me and never again, but Mr. Billy on and off across my whole stay, usually to drop off an old Louis L'Amour novel, a wrestling magazine, or a box or two of Milk Duds. He said my job was open until I got back and to just get well. Then he came to see me in security lockdown upstairs because he's an all-around good guy.

"Dr. Vogan says you're about ready to come home," Mr. Billy told me. "Long as you don't get off your What's-a-zine, that's about the worst you could do, he says, go off your medicine."

"Yeah," I said.

"Your insurance runs out next week, anyway. Next week, Tuesday or so, they'll let you out." Mr. Billy scratched his fuzzy white head, which—no surprise at all if you think about it—put me in mind of Karen Cleveland. "I'll be here to pick you up, Gordo. Meanwhile, behave. And be ready."

He left. I wasn't comforted. Quiet Harbor was okay. It was almost home. Besides which, in case you've got the memory of a gerbil, Karen was there—the bald and lovely, the plucked and ravishing, dark lady of my heart.

"I've got nothing left to tug," Karen said.

"Shhhhhh."

"Not a eyelash. Not a eyebrow. Not a head hair. Not a—"

"Shhhhhh."

It was one o'clock a.m. Janna Maxman had gone home with her brother and her sister-in-law. I had sneaked through a ward barricade with a key pick-pocketed from a careless therapy aide. I was being bad, contributing to the propinquity of a naughty pair of loons. I was sitting on the edge of Karen's bed. She perched on her knees behind me, her long hands clawing down tenderly on my shoulders.

"I got a postcard from Derek," Karen said. "It said that Keivano and LaKeisha are doing fine. It said that they're always asking about me."

"That's what happens when you send your young uns a lock of your hair."

"There's no more to pluck," she said, more or less ignoring me. I could tell by the way her strong brown fingers moved on my shoulders that she was in the grip of a strong, out-of-skew, deep-down emotion. Hurting. Really hurting.

"Do me," I said.

After a while, she began using her quick-cut fingernails to pluck first a hair over one ear and then a hair over the other. It hurt like crazy, but I never flinched. She kept it up, grooming and pinching, tweezing and pulling, until what she was doing began to feel better than sex, purer than love, wiser and warmer than your own mama's voice. She kept it up, slow but steady, and minute by sweet, pain-filled minute, I grew closer and closer to Karen, closer than I'd ever felt before.

HER SMOKE ROSE UP FOREVER

What
    first
        drew me to Merle Jean Draper was smoke. She threw off a charcoal haze that untangled beyond the curls of her hair. I don't mean that as a put-down. Her *smoke* gave her mystery. Even when she was doodling with a pencil or scratching her elbow, Merle's haze would fan out across the room and niggle at you, until—in my case, at least—your eyes were close to tearing.

It wasn't sex. Or not only. No "Hey, Rogers, ain't old Merle a looker?" or "That baby could really sizzle your Simmons, couldn't she, Rodge?" The smoke Merle threw off was more than the product of internal combustion, of her brain at work. Her real feelings, pent by adult rules and other kids' ideas of what was cool, flickered just under the skin, behind her eyes.

I wasn't a goody-goody in those days. (And I don't think I'm one now, but a Calling marks you, like a brand.) I smoked. I drank some. I honky-tonked with rowdies who, after high school, had hired on with Georgia-Pacific as cutters, with the mills as loom operators, with local contractors as bricklayers and drywall men. But even if no walking saint, I never qualified as a total rakehell either.

One long-ago October, I turned away from a homecoming bonfire to duck the smoke gusting off it. When I did, I stumbled straight into a pocket given shape by Merle Jean Draper's smoke. She was goofing with some girl-friends, all of them so much more with it than me that I covered my redneck clumsiness by lipping a cigarette James Dean-style and mumbling, "Anybody got a light?"

"Try the bonfire," one of Merle's friends said. But Merle, who had an old Zippo, lit me up, her eyes sliding off me as if I'd been greased. I stood wind-whipped beside her and her smirking friends under the pale stadium lights, talking trash in the hope that she might fix on me.

Cheerleaders were leading cheers, letter-jacketed players were boasting how they were going to cream Central (or whoever), a dunce with a cowbell and an ooga horn was serenading everybody. All of it together was irritating and silly. All of it was magic. I talked my trash even harder. I pressed. Merle focused. Soon the various smokes at our rally knit into a bowl-wide haze that still veils that week's game, the postgame dance, the whole year.

I was at sea, but Merle clearly began to fancy me—me, Rogers Tilghmon—right back.

What happens first is you figure ways of earning your rent money, and then you get married. I went to work in the weave shop at Milliken. And when my foreman griped to a higher-up that I'd back-sassed him, I skipped to West Point Pepperell. (For years I yo-yoed between the two companies, until sticking at Pepperell.) Merle landed a job right out of high school in the jewelry and cosmetics department at Gayfer's in West Georgia Commons Mall. These positions were enough to convince our folks—I had Mama, Merle her mama and stepdad—not to oppose our wedding. They didn't, finally, and Merle and I drove up into Cherokee National Forest on the Tennessee side of the Unicoi Mountains for a honeymooon, where we canoed, rode horses, and inner-tubed.

By rights, I should have been drafted and sent to Vietnam. I was a working-class cracker with a high school sheepskin, no record to speak of (a speeding ticket, a night in the Troup County stockade for disorderly conduct), a back strong enough to hump the boonies with all the other shit-for-luck draftees, and a gut conviction that Uncle Ho Chi Minh wasn't really kinfolk and needed his tail kicked.

But I didn't get drafted, and I didn't go over. My mother wrote and called our Congressional representatives, noting that I was her sole surviving son (my older brother, Jake, hadn't been killed in war, but in a motorcycle crash on his fourteenth birthday). I oughtn't to be called up, she said, unless the Viet Cong rowed attack rafts at our Gulf Coast beaches. I knew Mama was doing this, and I knew Merle's stepdad, Mr. Pugmire, was working on a save-my-son-in-law's-heinie campaign of his own. Well, so what? I didn't see President Nixon as bloodthirsty scum, the way some hippie college kids did, but I'd've been a fool—I thought, and so did Merle—to *volunteer*. In the end, Mama's and Mr. Pugmire's string pulling got me, well, permanently deferred.

*

Merle and I did okay. We rented a trailer in a shabby court between Toc-queville and Mountboro, bought shutters, slapped paint about, dug up some sprawling nandinas and crape myrtles. Then Merle got pregnant, but come its time, the baby stuck. Merle's doctor had to do a C-section: a slap, but no cry. Richland—Merle called the boy by her daddy's name—had no lungs. We had a funeral, a quick one. You can't say much about the dead in such cases, so the minister, unless he's a dolt, uses his skills to comfort. It's not easy. Even a guy who ain't a pious jerk can end up mouthing watery oatmeal and sounding like one. Scientific explanations don't help, and all the religious ones mostly just soak your heart in wormwood.

Still, Merle and I came through okay. Not that we didn't hurt, not that it wasn't bad for months on end, but there's your work, and people to palaver with, and funny surprises to bump against. You creep by all the worst parts on hands and knees before coming erect the way those evolutionists theorize. (But it's an emotional evolution I'm talking, not a phony biological one, and by the time you're upright, the terrain around you doesn't look so bombed out and smoke swept. There's a clean blue spreading, a dazzle on the joints and leaves of sycamores.) So we hobbled ahead, me at the mill, Merle with her necklaces, Isotoner gloves, and face creams. In less than a year, the smoke gusting from her had to do with sex again—the tumbly sort—and we made another baby. No one had told us not to and it only seemed right to try.

This was when we were happiest at home with each other. But it was also when I was having troubles with my boss—half the words breaking his gul-let were curses—and getting genuinely sick news through the mails from Ev Cromartie, my high school buddy who'd signed up and gone to Nam.

Ev's every letter was a casualty list of guys from his company or a revela-tion of small atrocities, given or taken, that he couldn't gear up to share with his mama. In a school sense, Ev was not much of a writer, but what he did manage to say—misspelled, comma free, erasure smudged—made me quea-sier, quicker, than any evening edition of Cronkite. I hated hearing from Ev, but I always wrote him back, right up to the day Mrs. Cromartie told me I didn't need to anymore.

By then Holly, our kid, was soccer-kicking Merle's taut belly from the inside out. We didn't know Holly's sex or name yet, but Merle was doing fine—the morning ralphs, then no appetite at all, then oddball hankerings after raspberry sherbet and raw onions, frozen yogurt and fried shrimp. In fact, Merle'd been eating good again when Ev's mama hit us with *her* evening news.

One night later, dreaming our new baby lungless, cradled in the blood-streaked arms of a doctor in battle fatigues, I had my conversion experience. *"Save her, Rogers,"* the camo-wearing doctor said. *"Save everybody else too."*

Then he turned and hung our dead baby on the wall—she stuck, as if to a patch of Velcro—just like she'd been spread-eagled by centurions.

My heart clenched, my feet felt clammy as two caught bass. I raised up from bed expecting to see the baby and her haint doctor, raised up sweating through my soul.

Not just a conversion. A Call.

A Voice mimicking Ev's or maybe my daddy's—who'd skedaddled when Jacob was six and I in diapers—had called me, but I knew it for Who it in truth was. (Your skin prickles, your arms buoy up like water wings.) Granted, as a teenager I'd been dunked and spoken over, but suddenly, what with Richland and Ev dead and our unnamed womb-daughter in peril, this Voice sledgehammered me—to new life, though, not to terror and nothingness. I prayed, and Merle, still sleep-fuddled, held me.

I couldn't quit a job to preach. I hadn't been to seminary and would not have gone even if I'd been asked to. But I started toting everywhere, and reading, the King James Study Bible Mama had given us when Merle and I married. I pored over it. To keep our new baby from ending like Richland, I had to do that—study and pray.

Same time, though, I worked my looms, watched TV, treated Merle at Hardee's, and dug around our trailer. You can't go around acting like a God-spooked fool. I wasn't then and I'm not now, which you can't get over to folks who think you should visit a shrink if your religion sends down roots.

Even Merle, who believes or says she does, got her back up. "I don't want a born-again, Rogers. They're holy snoops."

"I'm not," I told her. "Honest."

We edged past it. Besides, my being a born-again isn't the point here. You have to live beyond the mountaintop event, for not much that follows provides you, in any sense, a glimpse of the Kingdom.

"And we're not calling this baby after some Bible character," Merle said. "A boy isn't Abraham or even Peter. A girl isn't Naomi or Mary. You hear me?"

"Yessum," I said.

She listed her boys' names, including Rogers, and said any girl would be called Holly. I said okay. There aren't any Rogerses in the Book, and the closest you'll get to Holly is Asher's wife Helah in First Chronicles.

I met some part-time preachers. I studied and wrote. Pretty soon I was visiting-preaching two Sundays every month at little backroads churches called the Full Gospel Holiness Congregation, Disciples of the Pentecost, the Scepter-out-of-Israel Temple, and so on. Some were black churches, but I didn't care. I preached, they *amen*'d God's Word, and many a Sunday eve, as a bonus to my outreach, I went home with thirty to fifty bucks more than I had started out with. It helped. Every congregation met with, every sermon delivered, every love offering banked or spent on family, slipped another stone into the foundation of my Calling.

When Holly came, nobody ever had any doubt about *her* lungs. She had them. To take care of her, Merle had to leave Gayfer's again. At home, she threw off a glittering smoke-halo that wreathed Holly too, turning their sprung Goodwill chair into a kind of throne. But after three months, Merle hopped off it and hurried back to work. She took a job clerking at a gift shop in Mountboro, eight miles from our trailer. The manager didn't shout or huff around if Merle brought Holly in a car seat or folded out her playpen next to the register. She had the perfect job, actually, and because I was still yo-yoing between Milliken and West Point, with no guarantees of a pulpit to preach from come Sunday, it also proved a grace and a blessing.

The days shuttled. We crept home hangdog from Vietnam, which made Ev's death seem like all the others—a dumb joke, never mind the patriotic English you put on any eulogy. If God had been with Ev on that last patrol, how to explain the *thinness* of his presence to Mrs. Cromartie, or even harder, to a vet who'd lost an eye, a foot, his whole clan-binding faith.

Holly grew, bless her. And our boys—Cecil and Bernal, names not Biblical that pleased Merle for that reason and for others that escape me—entered the world a year apart in the early seventies. They grew too. Merle quit the gift shop then found us this clapboard house north of Mountboro with a metal outbuilding and a carport to rent and remodel.

She'd learned some things from her gift-shop work, namely, that tourists will blow honest cash on clutter a junkman wouldn't hoard—plywood ducks, T-shirts with cottonballs glued on for bunny tails, mugs glazed and fired to look like melted pizzas. She'd also discovered that she had a talent for designing and overseeing the crafting of such shiny rubbish.

Mr. Pugmire gave Merle a start-up grant, and she opened a mail-order business out of our new place: *Merle's Mountain Works.* She hired some black women to sew Raggedy Anns, potholders, and dishtowels, and a retired cop to run the table saw. At the same time, she kept an eye on the kids, thought up new products, and helped her workers as they made their gewgaws or filled the mail orders that tumbled in from all over. From day one, Merle's Mountain Works throve.

Merle started carrying MMW items to weekend crafts fairs around the state; later, the Southeast. She became an exhibitor in loose association with antique dealers, artists, cloggers, rosin-potato vendors, pony-ride operators, clowns, and blacksmiths. I could go with her on Saturdays, if the Pugmires would baby-sit our kids, but Sundays were out because by then I'd become the only pastor of the Living Bread Tabernacle on a spur of Lower Butts Mill Road.

The Living Bread Tabernacle had twenty-two members, seventeen active. Their welfare meant more to me than selling another funny ceramic pig or a dozen lacquered peanut-shell necklaces. Merle understood, but if I didn't go to the crafts fairs with her, she had to hire someone to help her pack, drive, and unload. Once, she didn't get home until Monday night, after a steamy sprint through west Alabama farmland pagodaed with kudzu.

For the first time in our lives, Merle and I had extra money. She employed seven people who weren't even family members and repaid DeWayne Pugmire's loan—money he didn't want, swearing it had been a stand, free and clear—and rented three classrooms in the old primary school. These rooms became a new Mountain Works production plant. MMW had outgrown our house, the carport, the metal storage building. I wasn't sorry. It was sweet to get back our house. Paint, lumber, and ribbon spools, among other fixings, had been stored in it for way too long.

One day, an old couple came in to Merle's Mountain Works to look

around. We learned they were New Yorkers who'd retired down here. The
woman wore a weird sort of paisley turban and a kind of roomy overgown,
her husband some gaudy maroon slacks and a bright yellow shirt. They had
handsome faces, even if they sagged a little at the jowls and throat, and I
recall their visit because MMW is really a manufacturing plant, not a whole-
sale outlet. Also, the wife fell in love with Merle's coping-sawed ducks and
forest animals, bought three or four ducks, and asked a load of questions.

"We feel like prodigals who have finally come home," she said as her husband stood by beaming. "This is where we've always belonged." She smiled.
"And your work, Mrs. Tilghmon, is delightful."

They didn't look or sound like they belonged in Georgia, but I guess
they felt they did—retirees self-separated from the run-amok go-getters in
Manhattan. By the time they left, I had already pigeonholed them in one
of my mental file drawers as a pair of friendly Jews. The wife's talking about
herself and her husband as "prodigals" had struck me as maybe heartfelt but
definitely shrewd—a good example of the funny things folks'll do to cut
themselves in.

Our kids had long since started school. Merle kept busy, and I did too. If
we were lucky, we'd say grace together every third night. Even Saturday was
no sure bet because of crafts fairs. I'd prepare a roast or bake a chicken, and
we'd eat it in gulping silence. Holly excused herself, and then the boys, eager
to escape the musk of fatherly piety I'd given off ever since toting them to
my church that morning. (*My* church was as foreign to them, despite their
weekly attendance, as a day on the New York Stock Exchange would have
been—a "total drag.") My offers to play pepper or head up a trail hike got
scoffed at. So I'd retreat to my office, and the kids would busy themselves, by
themselves, for themselves, Sunday afternoons without end.

Two years ago, Holly ran away. She wasn't kidnapped, or slain, or the
victim of a freak accident—she left a note and took a quarter of her wardrobe
with her, most likely in an old duffel bag that I still haven't found.

Holly's note went, *"Dear Mama, Dear Daddy, Im cutting out. Dont worry
and please dont look for me. Ill be alright. Love, H."* She'd stuck it to her cork-
board with a pin. We just about didn't see it because it hung amidst 4-H
ribbons, theater ticket stubs, and rock star posters.

We told the Mountboro police, the highway patrol, and the GBI, but nothing has happened. Holly may have fled to Seattle, about as far away as anyone can get inside the continental US. She could be living with a pack of runaways and courting AIDS. (You see such stories on TV. It's a commonplace.) I should fly out there and see—a good shepherd rescuing his lost sheep—but it's a needle-in-a-haystack deal and, Calling aside, I admit to being scared.

"I think I know what it is," Merle told me soon afterward. "It's a slap in the face, but my face, Rogers, not yours."

Maybe. I could see some reasons. But it felt, and still does, like a slap in my face too. Because I won't fly to hunt her down, I spend a lot of time on the phone and scads of money faxing photos to search agencies and big-city police departments. (Networks *do* exist. A break could occur any time.) Both Merle and I believe that Holly's still out there, alive. We have to.

The boys were thirteen and fourteen when Holly cut out. They acted at first as if a world-sundering catastrophe had befallen our family—apocalypse, Armageddon. (It had, I guess.) In just a few months, though, they behaved as if Holly'd only gone on a hiking trip up the Appalachian Trail, or maybe off to college somewhere. They were always out skateboarding, or in their room plugged into razzle-dazzle video battles, or in a creek bed tossing rocks at crayfish. They even began wondering aloud why they couldn't divvy up the stuff Holly had left behind. *Loot,* they called it.

Merle stayed busy at Merle's Mountain Works. I pulled third shifts at the mill and took care of pastoral duties for my Living Bread congregants. The work was there. Not to have done it would have pulled our thoughts like dowsing rods toward Holly's absence. And there was balm in the supplications I made while watching the looms, or that Merle managed while deciding how to tie up a potpourri sachet or to coping-saw a raccoon. We also had the boys to worry about.

Cecil was the instigator, Bernal his fetcher and dupe. It was Bernal—you called him Bernie only if you fancied Merle down your throat in hipboots—who crept into our room one predawn, the sun not even a promise, to demand a motorized three-wheeler, a sport vehicle he and Cecil could ride on the ball field or in the nearby dunes: something to do when we had to work, a pastime that would keep them, in Bernal's words, "out of miss-shev." Other kids had them. Their bikes—Cecil poking his head in, self-cued— were wrecks.

Mangled spokes, flat tires, slipped chains. In this way, Cecil and his Big Bro'
stayed after us until Merle and I, guilt-strapped, gave in to the boogers.

Two weeks later?—something like that—I came home to find Merle
standing in the driveway in a raincoat, surrounded by DeWayne Pugmire,
two neighbors, and Terry McGowan, our police chief. Merle eyed me sidelong, through my pickup's windshield, from an absence of smoke (a vacuum)
that sucked the wind from me. Why a *rain*coat? It was sunny, almost New
Mexico-ish.

"Go with Terry," Merle gesturing into the dunes over the ridge behind
our house, "and see about the boys."

I already knew what I'd find—I'd overheard Mr. Pugmire telling Vivian
Ludy that the county coroner was en route—but Terry led me out there, as
Merle had directed, and I found my young sons dead. Their squatty three-
wheeler had failed to reach the crest of a sixty-five-degree incline. In loose,
gravelly dirt, it had flipped on them, crushing Cecil's rib cage, shooting carti-
lage splinters into lungs and heart. Bernal, although thrown clear, had landed
on his neck, snapping it. They lay only three or four feet apart at the bottom
of the dune—closer than they'd ever been, their ravine-jockeying aside, but
who could take solace from that?

"If Bernal'd had a helmet, he might've been okay," Terry McGowan said.
I gave him, not on purpose, a look that made him flush and plunge his hands
into his pockets.

Like my lost daddy's decamping, like Holly's flight—and, now that I
thought of it, like my brother Jake's crackup on a borrowed Harley—our
sons' accident seemed a fated thing: a rebuke, a judgment, a test, a lesson. It
struck Merle about the same way, except that—raincoated indoors and out
until the morning of the funeral, as if readying herself for tears that never
came—she seemed too distracted by making arrangements, notifying kith
and kin, and tidying up to ponder the lesson. She prepared for the burial as
she would have for a dinner party, dipping and floating.

I didn't do the funeral. Maybe another daddy could've, but I wasn't that
daddy. Merle called in Ricky Tyree, her favorite pastor at the church she'd
been raised in, who drove down from his latest Methodist assignment, up on
the Tennessee line, to preside. Tyree made a sweet, easy job of it, which was
all the harder on us, I think, for being so tenderly gentle.

*

The concrete time that follows hard on any wrapped-up ceremony fell upon us. To Merle, who smoked cigarettes without herself smoking, I'd read passages of solace: *"And not only so, but we glory in tribulations also: knowing that tribulation worketh patience; and patience, experience; and experience, hope."*

Or: *"We are troubled on every side, yet not distressed; we are perplexed, but not in despair; persecuted, but not forsaken; cast down, but not destroyed."*

Merle, smoking, heard me, but her eyes said I might as well have been reciting census forms. Once, then, I closed the Book, went to her, hugged her. She let me, but the glints in her pupils looked like nicotine flares.

"Never talk to me about Job," she warned. "If you *ever* bring up that son of a bitch, I'll take off faster than Holly."

Later, Merle did some things to stare down her grief. She had baby Richland's casket disinterred from its plot in a LaGrange cemetery and moved to the Living Bread Tabernacle churchyard where the boys are buried. She started designing plywood figures, two-dimensional cutouts, to stand by the graves already in our family plot. She had me use the table saw—Ferrel Peck, the former cop she'd hired to run it, had retired shortly after the funeral—to free her silhouettes from the wood. And, finally, Merle showed me where to anchor her figures when it was time, as she calculates it, to replace an old cutout with a new one.

They show fine from Lower Butts Mill Road, but because the churchyard is set back a way, and because we've put up a metal fence to discourage vandals, you have to look fast and sharp to glimpse them as you breeze by in a car.

In one sense, the painted figures are just more plywood ducks for the tourist trade, more coping-sawed cows with long eyelashes and big udders the color of uncooked hot dogs. Merle tries to make her churchyard figures seasonal, but her motives are hard to read. She won't talk about the memorials, she just does them. (Once, a *Ledger-Enquirer* reporter saw one and phoned to ask if he could write a story about us. "No way," Merle said.) There's a boy in a baseball uniform for baseball season, one in football gear for the fall, a boy flying a kite for the early spring, complete with a reinforced kite that I wire to a pecan-tree bough overarching our plot. Every few weeks, Merle trades out figures or works up a batch of fresh ones for installation later. She also does cutouts meant as nothing but backdrop ornament—Walt Disney chipmunks, smiley-faced sunflowers, a lopsided bicycle-built-for-two.

It has no sacred overtones, but so what? A month ago, an old congregant bellied up to Merle after a service to protest the way her figures cheapened the grounds: "I'd as soon put old jalopies out front, with their prices soaped on their windows." (He'd already protested to me, with results not to his liking.)

Merle asked Adamson how many children he'd lost. He said he was a bachelor. "Doesn't answer the question," Merle said. That confused him. He said he'd *never* had any children. Merle told him to have one and then lose that one before opening his mouth again. That wasn't fair, or loving, and it tightened the man's jaw and drove him and two more off to the Disciples of the Pentecost. But he and his hangers-on were a sour bunch, anyhow, and proudly unreliable tithers.

Another Sunday, after dinner, Merle went on a belated cleaning binge. I pitched in. We worked in Cecil and Bernal's room, more or less dismantling it. "I won't have this room a shrine," she said—frozen in time the way that we'd frozen Holly's, she meant. "Holly may come home, but the boys're gone."

"Not for good," I said.

"You expect to see them sleeping here again?" she asked.

No, I didn't. Even if the Parousia restored them to us, it wouldn't be to their cowboy bunkbeds and fitful earthly sleep. Merle got to work on clothes. I foraged in a closet and came upon a pair of boxes with detergent labels printed on them. They bulged with record albums—all dusty, all spider-webbed.

"What're these?" I asked, gripping an album jacket by one corner and sliding it out of its cardboard storage box. The sleeve had a five-sided hole punched in the corner I'd eased it up by, all the way through the front and the back covers so that it missed the vinyl disk between them. I stooped. Every jacket in the box had such a corner hole, as if a snake with one five-sided fang had pierced them.

"Records," said Merle, scarcely giving them a look. "Old LPs."

"I mean the holes."

She stopped sorting jeans. "Those are discards. Music stores weed their stock and put the junk on sale. Cecil always checked the discard bins—to make his lawn-mowing money go further."

I flipped through the battered jackets. Not much I recognized, not much my mama would've liked. One-named folk singers, heavy-metal bands that backward-masked their lyrics, bubble-gum music, a monaural Edith Piaf, country-rock groups that had disbanded before Cecil's birth, little that'd repay a respectful listen.

"Cecil bought these? He listened to them?"

"He and Bernal both. Not to the records, though—to tapes they'd made of them. At bedtime they put the tapes in Cecil's player so they could fall asleep to music."

"They put all these albums on tape?"

"Yeah." Merle had finished the jeans and started in on flannel shirts.

"Why didn't they just chuck the records? Or sell 'em back to record stores?"

"*Discards*, Rogers. The stores are glad to be shut of them. Cecil thought maybe we'd want them. 'Daddy liked the Beatles,' he'd say. 'And the Byrds, and the Mama and the Papas.' He was waiting for you to come back around—him and Bernal both."

"I was around," I said, not guarding my words, "more than you were."

Then, feeling what I'd done, I braced for the counterattack. Merle sat down on Cecil's lower bunk. She let her upper body topple into the stack of flannel shirts beside her. "*I* knew what these records were," she said.

"I'll throw them out," I said through the pinch of unfamiliar tears: "Okay?"

"Sure. Toss them. Who'd ever listen to them, right? They can be discards twice."

I carried the boxes in two trips to my pickup and drove them to the nearest county Dumpster. I sailed them over its rusted side in a shingle storm of jackets, a skeet barrage of sleeveless disks.

Three weeks back, on a Monday evening, Merle and I took a ride. Passing the churchyard at Living Bread Tabernacle, we saw a crow-black Lincoln town car parked slantwise under the pecan trees.

An old guy in checkered pants and a Banlon shirt ("Another goofy golfer," Merle said) was pulling up her most recent cutout—a straw-haired boy with a cane pole in his hands, a plywood bullhead swinging from its line. (Neither Cecil nor Bernal had had the patience to fish, but true-to-lifeness isn't the point of our cutouts.) I spun our pickup into the Living Bread lot and yelled out the window, "Sir, *what* are you doing?"

"The bastard's stealing it," Merle said. "Anyone with sense can see that."

The man stopped. We'd nabbed him—not quite red-handed because the cutout had too much polyurethane on it for paint to stain his hands—but clearly "in the act." I leapt out to confront him.

"Don't hit me," the old man said, backing away.

"I'm the pastor here, and I don't hit old men. I try not to hit anybody. Why're you taking it?"

"I like it. If it's yours, I'll pay you for it."

Merle stood beside me. "I made that for my sons. You can't afford it."

Merle's presence, along with what she'd said, blasted some of the sand out of the old bird. "Oh, I'm so sorry," he said. "Forgive me. My name's Samuel Halterman. I'll put it back."

After nearly tripping on the plot curb behind him, he walked slew-footed toward our sons' headstones, his trouser cuffs flapping in a new breeze. Although he'd pulled the figure up himself, he couldn't reposition it, so I helped him, using a mallet from the truck. Afterward, the three of us sat down at a concrete picnic table between the tabernacle and the graveyard.

"I wanted it for my wife," Samuel Halterman said. "To go with the ducks."

"Where is she?" Merle asked.

"Dead like your boys, Mrs. Tilghmon. We always used this road to drive between our house and West Georgia Medical Center. There were shorter ways—faster ways, at least—but Neva took this route to and from her chemo to see anything new you'd done. It always gave her a lift. Honest to God."

"Where's her body?"

"Cremated, Mrs. Tilghmon. I scattered her off Dowdell's Knob, as she wanted."

"Please, Mr. Halterman, take the fisherboy."

"Merle, we just got it planted good again."

"I'll put a used figure over there," Merle said, nodding at the graveyard, "until I've finished something new."

"I planned to send you a money order," Halterman said. "It would have been anonymous, but it would've come. Ah, crazy. What have *I* got to mark? Is that why I wanted it?"

Merle urged her fisherboy on Halterman, but he wouldn't take it, which was fine. I'd've had to yank it up, put it in his trunk, and tie the lid down with rope. And even the brief absence of a cutout near the boys' graves would have niggled hard at Merle, a hook in her mouth, a goad to bigger and better plywood markers.

Our chance meeting with Halterman, as he tried to pull off his thievery, worked no magic on Merle. It is making and setting up memorials—as she has felt in her bones all along—that redeems her grief. Nowadays, the smoke gusting off her, often rolling in glimmering dark billows, seems like the smoke rising forever from the ruins of Babylon. That smoke speaks of Babylon's earthly fall, but also predicts the coming of the City of God. I preach that, I preach it hard—but the only place I find it working in my life is in the charcoal haze uncurling again from Merle's face and hair.

"What're you doing?" I asked a day or two ago as she sat hunched at her sewing machine in Holly's room, an onionskin pattern spread out beside her on the bed. "Giving up on your markers?"

"No," she said. "It's a wardrobe for Holly, something new and pretty for when she comes back."

"Merle, who says she's coming back?"

"She'll come. And when she does, that'll be your Living Bread coming again, and Cecil and Bernal, and maybe even you too."

"Hey now," I said.

"Leave me to it. If you're looking to help, there's a sheet of plywood on the table, ready to cut."

OTHER ARMS REACH OUT TO ME

When
  I
    first carried my violin into Bright Bower Hospice, I imagined myself a rare female musician-for-hire boarding a deathship. Mrs. Choate, the director, had offered me small session fees to play for the residents, and over the holidays I hoped to make five hundred dollars, even if I must shut my eyes while playing.

The hospice looked like a ship. Bright Bower, a five-sided building clad in battleship-gray vinyl, floated atop a small hill. Inside: hardwood floors and clean white bulkheads. It should have calmed rather than unsettled me. Spruce trees hung with blue and silver balls stood in the parlors at the heart of every four-room enclave, and the piped-in music ran not to Muzak but to brassily orchestrated Christmas carols. Still, you could get lost in the corridor between its suites and the inner pentagon of offices and nurses' stations, and the floor seemed to tilt under me like the deck of a wave-buffeted schooner.

"Steady," said Roberta Choate, a large woman with off-blonde hair in a top-heavy beehive. Her knees protruded from under the hem of her purple woolen skirt like dented grapefruits. "You okay with this, Mrs. Moody?"

"Yessum," I said. "I've played lots of sets at Loretta Hickok."

Right across Myrtle Street from Bright Bower, Loretta Hickok offered assisted-living care for the aged and the disabled. After hearing my Beethoven program for the residents at Hickok over Thanksgiving, Mrs. Choate had asked me to pull a Yuletide stint at Bright Bower. I suspected that my hiring had more to do with her friendship with my aunt, Opal Wheaton, than with my violin skills.

"Her husband Talbot left her to work on a shrimper out of Tybee Island," I could hear Aunt Opal saying. *"And with a six-year-old and a toddler, Dreama could use some help, Roberta."* I loathed that sort of charity, but how could I turn down a job resulting from my aunt's acquaintance with a local bigwig? I heard myself say, "And the folks there liked my performances." If they weren't deaf, comatose, or crazy, I refrained from adding aloud.

"Well," Mrs. Choate said, "playing for the dying may feel a bit different."

"Why? Some of Hickok's patients are dying. You can tell by looking at them."

"Our clientele at Bright Bower *know* they're dying. Not one expects to leave here under his or her own power."

"Then they need music therapy even more than the people at Hickok do." I saw music therapy as my calling.

"Our rooms have TVs, CD players, and VCRs, Mrs. Moody. Our clients can see or hear almost anything they want—*if* they can see and hear."

"Still, they might prefer a warm human being bringing their music to them."

Mrs. Choate took my arm. "Are *you* warm, dear?"

I glanced down. I had dressed in heavy black slacks, a black sweater with vertical cords like oversize chain links, and a pair of black calf-leather boots. With my spiky hair and pale skin, I looked like a sexless stand-in for Death. Barney Fife, seeing me, would have run to Sheriff Andy crying out that I had a machine-gun in my violin case. Self-consciously, I wiped a hand down my slacks.

"Should I have worn something else?"

"No, no!" Mrs. Choate laughed and led me along the corridor to a high-ceilinged parlor on which the doors of four rooms—two to each side, facing one another—stood ajar. The gas-burning logs in the fireplace flickered cozily, but a handsome middle-aged couple on the plush sofa before the hearth clung to each other as if freezing. Mrs. Choate introduced them as the Zwiebels. The husband's eighty-year-old father lay in one of the four rooms in the ultimate stages of total systemic failure. Mrs. Choate asked me to stand next to the fire and play for this couple, as well as for old Mr. Zwiebel and other persons dying in his enclave.

I uncased my brindle violin—the only thing of value Talbot had ever given me, not counting our kids, Zack and Brittany—and lifted it to my chin. I placed my chin on the Kun rest that I had scrimped to buy and launched into a Haydn minuet. The red-eyed Zwiebels gaped at me as if I had just stepped off a flying saucer, and Mrs. Choate gave me a mouth-only smile.

When I finished, Mrs. Zwiebel said, "Lovely," and asked me to play something, well, "sadder."

I thought, Do you want me to raise your spirits or wreck them?

But as snowflakes tumbled past the window, I coaxed from my violin a tender rendition of the Bach-Gounod *Ave Maria*. At its end, the younger Mr. Zwiebel blew his nose into a monogrammed handkerchief, and he and Mrs. Zwiebel applauded me softly, using only their fingertips.

"Music hath charms," said Mrs. Choate, now really smiling.

I thought, Yeth, it hath. Encouraged, I asked, "May I enter one of their rooms to play?"

"That depends on what the guests want. And on how brave you feel."

Mrs. Choate and I strolled to the next enclave. Here, even with a fire sputtering on the hearth, the parlor rang with an eerie vacancy.

Mrs. Choate said, "Right now only one of these four rooms has an occupant, and Mr. F. Simms Ledgister seldom, if ever, has a visitor other than a young man from his gravel-hauling business. Mr. Ledgister likes his door shut. Two of the residents in this enclave died last month, and he's paid us a generous sum to keep the room next to his empty."

"Is that legal?" Despite the blown heat in the parlor, I shivered like a Chihuahua with parvovirus.

"Yes, so long as folks who want hospice care can get it. It's also good business. A top-of-the-line place like Bright Bower costs caboodles to run. So we take help from any reputable quarter, Mrs. Moody."

"Did Mr. Ledgister get *rich* running gravel trucks?"

"I guess so. But Bright Bower doesn't cater only to the rich. We serve all of West-Central Georgia."

I tried to imagine a homeless street person in one of these rooms—in particular, a broomstick-skinny woman who for years had pushed her crippled son around Tocqueville in a shopping cart. I couldn't see either that woman or her wretched boy in Bright Bower; in fact, I couldn't imagine myself on the premises, not as a patient. Since Talbot's alleged defection to the Georgia coast—no one really knew where he'd gone—I had supported Zack and Brittany as a teacher's aide, a part-time music therapist at Loretta Hickok, and a violin tutor to an eight-year-old who never practiced. Daily child-care ate up my earnings, though, and the alms that Aunt Opal crumpled into my hand usually went for plumbing fixes or car repairs. Short of dying, a stay in this place would have seemed as blissful to me as a Tybee Island vacation.

"Would you like to meet Mr. Ledgister?" Mrs. Choate asked.

"What's he dying from?"

Mrs. Choate raised an eyebrow. "Does it matter?"

I raised an eyebrow of my own. "Is it a secret?"

"Cancer, I guess. I'm not his doctor."

"Does he *want* me to play for him?"

"Well, let's see." Mrs. Choate pushed me into the tweedy dusk of Mr. Ledgister's room. A television screen in a tall console of ebony plastic faced the cranked-up bed. A VHS tape about Ireland flickered on the screen, flooding emerald rays of light into the gloom.

At once, a slender male figure in designer jeans and a plaid jacket leapt to his feet from a chair beside the bed. His wire-rimmed glasses, whose lenses rippled green, gave him the expression of a starving owlet. His nervousness suggested that we'd caught him getting ready to inject the old man with something, possibly strychnine.

"Hello," he squeaked.

"Turn that off," said Mr. Ledgister from the bed, waving a claw, and his jumpy visitor pointed a remote, making both the picture on the screen and its gloom-mitigating green light fade to gray. "Now *what* in holy hell do y'all want?" Mr. Ledgister had a long skull, a long nose, hair so wispy that it looked arson-ready, a naturally greasy mouth, and wattles like a lizard's. "Speak up, Mrs. Choate."

"Sir, this is Dreama Moody, a wonderful violinist and the niece of a close friend of mine."

Mr. Ledgister nodded at the young man near his bed. "Well, this is Agile Gathers, paymaster of Ledgister Rock and Gravel and bungle-footed errand boy. He doesn't really do much to live up to his name."

When Agile Gathers ducked his head, as if unused to prolonged human contact, Mr. Ledgister said, "Take this morning's tapes back to where you got them and bring me back some fresh ones."

Mr. Gathers, a toady *par excellence*, picked up the frail rectangular packets of the scattered tapes, crammed them into a valise, and banged out the door.

"Wouldn't you like to hear Mrs. Moody play?" Mrs. Choate asked Mr.

Ledgister. "She has scads of talent."

"Not really," the old man said. "I'd like to talk to her alone."

"Sir?" said Mrs. Choate.

"Leave us. And don't eavesdrop. I won't eat her up like a goddamn biscuit."

Mrs. Choate flushed scarlet and lifted a pudgy hand. Then she exited, easing the door to with an abashedly gentle click.

"Relax, Mrs. Moody," Mr. Ledgister said. "Is your first name really Dreama? I've heard stupider, but only amongst Nigras."

I sucked in a breath. The old man's room returned a faint reek, like a snakehouse or a summertime poultry yard.

"Let me see your damned fiddle."

"Violin."

"Looks like a fiddle to me."

"I won't say Stradivari made it, sir, but only the ignorant call it a fiddle." I held it up, like a chef showing off an apricot-sauce-glazed flounder. When Mr. Ledgister merely grinned at my insult, I asked, "What would you like to hear?"

"Nothing," Mr. Ledgister said. "I can't abide music. Good or bad, highbrow or low, I can't abide it."

My eyes must have goggled. "You're kidding."

"It all sounds like jackhammers or catfights to me. But you do have a very pretty fiddle . . . for an instrument of torture." Mr. Ledgister's liver-spotted arms sprawled on his coverlet like unrolled entrails.

Even Poe's over-delicate Roderick Usher from "The Fall of the House of Usher" could stand the sounds of *stringed* instruments.

I said, "You talk without wincing, sir. And you watch hundreds of tapes. Surely some of them feature background music."

"Ordinary talking doesn't affect me, and Agile *pre*-views my tapes—to make sure they don't have marches or explosions. Some of them he has an engineer out to Dataplant mess with—you know, to drop out the unbearable patches."

"That must cost a sparkly penny."

Mr. Ledgister smirked. "As Agile always reminds me, I'm worth it."

To kill Mr. Ledgister, a doctor would have first had to perform a smugectomy on the old goat. "If I can't play for you, sir, I'd better go."

"Wait. One thing would help me listen to your fiddle without my nerves going all haywire—one and only one."

I hung before Mr. Ledgister like Odysseus on his mast. "What's that?"

"You should play for me nekkid."

My entire head felt like the top of a hot thermometer. "I'll pretend you never said that." And I reached for the door's sculpted handle.

"Five hundred in cash," Mr. Ledgister said quickly. "Half on our handshake, half on you doing what I've asked."

"Why not just order Mr. Gathers to fetch you a whole pack of soft-porn videos?"

"Listen, Dreama. This isn't really about sex. I've seen all the smutty films a man my age could ever hope to hot himself up by."

"Then please tell me what it *is* about."

Mr. Ledgister hissed like an iguana: "*Closenessss.*"

"So pay Mr. Gathers to strip naked and act out some charades. That'll keep you from having to endure the agony of my violin playing."

"*Lisssen,*" Mr. Ledgister continued. "I'm not a faggot. I fought at Iwo Jima. I married four times. I sired nine children—six of them boys. So this is really just about man-woman *closenessss.*"

"Closenessss?" I hissed back.

"A dying old fart who's buried four wives and gone ornery to boot can't hope to get closeness without paying for it. It's damned disgusting, I say!"

"And why should you, please tell me that?" This time I actually left, but unlike Mrs. Choate, I slammed the door.

Over the next week, I played three hours a day for all the occupants of Bright Bower, except Mr. Ledgister. I played "Vocalese" by Rachmaninoff, "Sonatina" by Clementi, "Eleanor Rigby" by Lennon and McCartney, lots of Vivaldi, "The Brook" by Schubert, "Old Folks at Home" by Stephen Foster, "Amazing Grace," "Softly and Tenderly" and "In the Garden" from the *Cokesbury Hymnal*, sections of *Appalachian Spring*, and so on. Mrs. Choate praised not only my playing but also my selections, my dedication, my stamina.

I often saw Agile Gathers toting his valise to or from the parking lot, his sallow face deep inside his turned-up plaid collar. I asked Eunice Thrum, the nurse who usually dealt with Mr. Ledgister, what all these videos *meant*. I couldn't credit that a dying man would have such a hunger for watching television, even if he did avoid silly network fare like sitcoms and soap operas. Didn't he have a better use for his time, like making peace with his family?

"No," said Nurse Thrum. "Nobody but Mr. Gathers ever visits him."

"Not even his kids and grandkids?"

"Honey, they must live in Tahiti. I haven't laid my eyeball on a one of them." At that precise moment, Agile Gathers came plodding down the corridor. Nurse Thrum clothes-lined him with her forearm. "Hold it. Show Mrs. Moody just what you've got in your case."

Promptly, Agile Gathers swung his valise onto the counter and sprang its catches. It held a couple dozen tapes: a dog-training primer, a history of the World War II battles on Peleliu and Okinawa, a documentary about the Brooklyn Bridge, another on the rise and fall of American vaudeville, an introduction to Islam, and BBC adaptations of novels by Jane Austen, Charles Dickens, Wilkie Collins, and Anthony Trollope—a crazy salad of tapes, although several, including the vaudeville video—must surely chime and shake with music.

"I don't get this," I told Mr. Gathers.

"Mr. Ledgister thinks no one should stop learning until they drop dead."

Nurse Thrum agreed. "He watches educational junk like this all the time—like he's cramming for Heaven's entrance exam."

"This isn't the stuff he's likely to get asked about," I said.

"Watch your fingers," Mr. Gathers said. "I have to go." He dropped the valise's lid, snapped it shut, and swung it off the counter, almost toppling with it before catching himself and careening out into the bleak asphalt lot.

I walked behind him to my car, which squatted in the cold close to his. As Mr. Gathers opened his trunk to stow the valise, I turned my ignition key and pedaled the gas. The ignition clicked, the engine went *rrrrr-rrrr-rrr*, and icy silence ensued. If I didn't get home shortly, Aunt Opal and her boyfriend Dexter Fletcher, today's babysitters, would no doubt strangle Zack and Brittany. I turned my ignition again. When it refused even to ratchet, I laid my cheek on the steering wheel and cried.

"Need some help?" Standing beside my hood with jumper cables, Mr. Gathers looked like a brush-arbor deacon juggling timber rattlers.

"Oh thank you," I mouthed. "Thank you."

But his engine-boosting try failed, and Mr. Gathers traipsed back inside to call a towing service. I saw money draining from my account like oil from a busted crankcase: Brittany needed cough medicine, Zack went through shoes like an oysterman shucking oysters, and I still had Christmas gifts to buy.

Steering-wheel plastic creased my cheek.

Mr. Gathers trudged out again from Bright Bower. When I rolled my window down, he told me a garage was sending a truck. He relayed its likely cost and added that I might need a new alternator. Then, as if a Gorgon with jumper cables for hair had frozen him to the asphalt, he lingered.

"What?" I snapped. "What else?"

"Mr. Ledgister asked me to tell you that the deal he offered still goes—if you take a notion to do it."

"What deal, Mr. Gathers?"

"I have no idea. He said *you'd* understand."

The tow truck arrived, hitched up my car, and yanked it out into Myrtle Street. I rode in the cab, which stank of old beer and older oil, with a guy in a green T-shirt and a hunting cap with earflaps. All the way back to the garage, my oblivious rescuer hummed a Ray Stevens novelty song.

The next afternoon I drove to Bright Bower in Dexter Fletcher's pickup. I stalked inside wearing black velvet high heels and a burgundy coat buttoned from the throat all the way down to my shins. I loitered outside Mr. Ledgister's enclave until Nurse Thrum emerged from the old man's room, nodded, and shuffled past me into the main corridor. The sound system was trumpeting a tinny "Joy to the World."

I entered the sitting parlor, knocked on Mr. Ledgister's door, and eased into the flickering gloom. I stopped in front of the TV, my heart throbbing like a hurt cuttlefish. Ballpark noises—a galloping organ hurrah, a baseball cracking like a walnut—sounded at my back, followed by the schmaltzy voiceover of an invisible he-man narrator. Then a clicker muted the set, and Mr. Gathers sprang up at his boss's bedside, gaping at me like a mental deficient.

"Give Dreama two hundred and fifty dollars, Agile," said Mr. Ledgister.

Mr. Gathers produced a bulging wallet, pinched three bills from it, and reached them across the foot of the cranked-up bed toward me. I grasped them and slid them into a pocket on my long woolen coat.

"Take out the same amount again, Agile. Wait in the lobby. If Dreama tells you the password when she shows up out there, give it to her."

Head down, Mr. Gathers departed.

"Maybe I should have held out for more money," I said.

"That's an awful damned lot if you don't *do* anything. Of course, there's nothing to keep you from coming back again."

A stormy Irish seascape hung on the wall to my right. I hadn't really noticed it before. Its colors roiled and twisted surreally, maybe because I had a headache. I put my violin case across the bottom of the bed and fumbled it open. My fingers felt as brittle as icicles, but I unbuttoned every button on my coat and dropped it to the floor in a starched-looking pyramid. Thank God, warm air whooshed up from the floor vents and the room's tweedy gloom served as a make-do cover-up. I pulled out my violin and turned sideways to show as modest a profile as I possibly could.

So, of course, Mr. Ledgister snapped on his reading light.

"Thanks for wearing heels, Dreama. I'm pleased to see those wavy stretch marks of yours too."

"Please shut up. If you don't, I'll put my coat back on and leave."

"No, you won't—not if you want Agile to pay you."

With my left arm supporting my violin and concealing my breast, I teased out the opening of an aria from Handel's opera *Semele*, "Where'er You Walk."

"Not that highfalutin tripe!" Mr. Ledgister said.

A ripple of irritation, or maybe just a chill, wriggled from my nape to the small of my back, gooseflesh popping out all over me.

"For God's sake, woman, play something else!"

My bow merely whispering, I played "Georgia on My Mind." In my imagination, Ray Charles's bluesy voice crooned its lyric to my accompaniment.

"Oh," said Mr. Ledgister. "Oh." He talked over Ray's ghostly voice, *"Other arms reach out to me,"* humming the words he couldn't remember, his face ecstatically horsy, his voice a faint wail. He never shut his eyes, though— never looked away—and when I finished, he said, "Now come here for the password." I reached for my coat. "No, ma'am, you must come as you are."

Shivering, I obeyed. I had obliged the manipulative old bastard to this point. Why endanger my payoff? Everybody whored now and again: Preachers did revivals at other preachers' churches. "Unbuyable" American film actors did hemorrhoid-suppository ads in Japan. Me, I crossed my arms over my chest and lowered my head, not my vulnerable torso, to Mr. Ledgister, who let me hang beside him for several seconds before telling me his stupid password.

Buttoned up in my coat again, I strolled to the lobby, where Mr. Gathers sat on a hassock with a dog-eared copy of *Fortune*.

"Simoleons," I said.

Mr. Gathers laid his magazine aside and paid me the second two hundred and fifty dollars.

With this money I paid for car repairs. I bought Brittany her expensive antibiotic. At the Wal-Mart on Carrollton Highway, I scouted gifts for everybody on my Christmas list, exulting that I could afford them.

Now I understood—a little—how the women in those so-called gentleman's clubs in Atlanta could flaunt their bodies in front of conventioneers, tourists, and other strange males. Some probably liked to self-exhibit, but others had kids to feed and bills to pay. Playing violin naked for a dying man, even one with a piggish leer, qualified as a kind of charity: It showed kindness to "one of the least of these." Between the discount videos and the packaged candies, I felt a surge of tenderness for Mr. Ledgister, and of quiet awe at my own gallantry. Why *not* visit the old coot again? Why *not* squeeze tribute from him for resuscitating his humanity? I could only do us both good.

After shopping, I drove to Jalopy Jack's, a hotdog eatery downtown, and sat at a stool at one of its facing counters.

Placards on the walls said, among other things:

SMALL BOTTLED COKE—60C

FREE ADVICE—WORTH WHAT YOU PAY FOR IT

JJ'S GRILLED EGG SANDWICH—AVAILABLE ALL DAY

OUR LEMON SQUIRT WILL PUT THE HURT ON YOUR THIRST

TENNIS RACKETS RESTRUNG—ASK JALOPY JACK.

Six workers in Jalopy Jack polo shirts and mustard-stained aprons steamed buns and assembled orders in the pit between counters. As they worked, I nibbled at a hotdog with spicy tomato relish and sucked the ice in a lemon-squirt to cool its burn. The patron next to me rolled several coins across the counter and left.

"Hello," squeaked Agile Gathers, claiming the other man's stool.

"Hello." I turned to him. "Funny you should come along. I was just about to head over to Bright Bower for my afternoon sets."

"And to drop in on Mr. Ledgister?"

I could hardly tell Mr. Gathers that he had no business asking this question, but it still felt pushy of him. "I might," I said. "Why do you ask?"

He leaned in so close that, alert to my own tomato-relish breath, I leaned away. "I think you should know," he whispered, "that Mr. Ledgister occupies his place in Bright Bower under false pretenses."

Almost before I could blink, he added, still *sotto voce*, "Mrs. Moody, my boss isn't actually sick. He bought his room there and the other three around it with some of the proceeds from a big lottery payout. That sum, along with his stock portfolios and annual profits from Ledgister Rock & Gravel, rank him among the fifty richest folks in the state of Georgia."

"I thought the filthy letch had cancer!"

"No, Mrs. Moody, he doesn't."

"Then some other horrible disease?"

"No, ma'am—unless you'd count greed and old age."

"Then why would he check into a hospice? Just to watch one egghead video after another? That makes *no* sense. And why have you told me this?"

My questions took Agile Gathers aback, but after tucking in his pointed chin, he said, "Mrs. Moody, I think the place feels a tad like family to him." Blushing, he added, "I told you the other because, uh, I really thought I ought."

So I went again to Mr. Ledgister's counterfeit death chamber and walked in on a grainy tape about the Great Depression. I planked my violin case down on the foot of his bed. It must have hit a toe because he yelped and one knee jerked up, making a teepee of his coverlet. I took my bow from its case and prodded Mr. Ledgister with it, poking his throat and then scribbling its tip across his chest.

"Damn it!" His eyes had widened in alarm. "Stop that!"

"You lied to me, Mr. Ledgister—straight through your phony teeth." I poked him a frightening one in the bottom lip.

"I lie to everyone." He slapped feebly at the bow. "But that money you toted off from here was real enough, wasn't it, you clumsy little slut?"

"Real or not, I despise you. Everybody does. That includes Agile Gathers, Nurse Thrum, and all your kids and grandkids."

"Just shut it, Missy."

"I won't. It's easier for a camel to pass through a needle eye than for a rich son of a bitch to enter heaven."

He gave me a bleak buzzard leer. "You've got a hot line to St. Peter, do you?"

"You've faked dying to snatch sympathy from people with good reasons to hate you. Actually, though, you've already gone to hell. Only Agile visits and the only voices you hear jabber on the soundtracks of boring video tapes." I poked him again—expertly.

"This one's not boring at all. I lived through the Depression, and now I'm learning how it happened and what it did to us. It's what you call self-uplift, Missy—never-ending, death-defying self-uplift!"

"For what, you silly bastard? For *what*?" I threw my bow at the wall. It ricocheted from the roiling seascape to the floor. Then I tore the coverlet down Mr. Ledgister's body to my violin case, and he lay in his gown in the wretched near-nakedness of his grayness and frailty. The gown hid him no better than did his cobwebby skin.

Then he convulsed. His eye fuses blew, and his bottom lip scrolled out. His hands twitched at his sides, his fingers frost-white and talon-like, and I knew at once what had happened. After blinking in panic, I crossed myself like a Catholic and intoned, "Hail, Mary, full of grace—good riddance—rest in peace."

I retrieved my bow and violin caddy and strode to a monitoring station to tell a nurse what a machine had just confirmed, that another Bright Bower Hospice resident had made his inevitable final crossing.

With Zack and Brittany asleep, I returned to my living room. I shut every interior door, drew my curtains, turned up the heat, and stripped to my skivvies. In the middle of the room, I tapped my brindle fingerboard and began to play.

"*Other arms reach out to me,*" I crooned to myself, my eyes open but sightless. In this reverie, it was not my ex-husband who came galloping through the waves of an Atlantic seascape to rescue me—no, not my vanished ex, but the bumbling paymaster of Ledgister Rock & Gravel. My bow snagged, but

I kept my eyes open. I trembled as if freezing. Meanwhile, a phantom Agile Gathers splashed toward me in navy-blue baggies with enormous white magnolia blossoms stamped on their fabric.

Dear God, I thought, spare me another such blunder.

To keep Agile from arriving, I moved in midstroke from "Georgia on My Mind" to *Ave Maria*, and this music clad me from head to toe, robing me, for a time, against the reproachful silence of the night.

How
BEAUTIFUL
WITH
BANNERS

Even
   when

        he doesn't need to, my dad loads clothes into the Kenmore, dumps the resulting clump into a plastic basket, puts the basket in Guy's old Radio Flyer wagon, and wrests the wagon out back to banner the carousel clothesline that he put up on finding out how much emphasis the folks here in Zalmon place on hanging out a wash.

"Let me help," I say even though Christmas, home from Athens, did not actually recommend itself to me as a chance to (pardon the localism) *laundry-banner.*

"Therapy," Dad says. "I can do it."

Maybe. Hiking in the Little Grand Canyon in October, he jumped from a clayey ledge into a ravine and snapped a vertebra in his lower back. Two months later, he had recovered enough to begin puttering around his rock garden again, but he couldn't do his job at DyeTrak without frequent bouts of eyeball-popping pain. As a result, he took early retirement.

Pulling the Radio Flyer, Dad reminds me of Boris Karloff in *The Mummy,* doing that touchingly spooky glide-shuffle of his—except Ronald Garrett glide-shuffles with a kid's wagon across our browned-off lawn in full view of neighbors and random townies driving by in their pickups and parboiled clunkers. It hurts to watch him, to see the local yokels cast amused glances his way as he toils to create a bannering worthy of their regard with sodden underwear and khakis.

I follow him out to the carousel, six horizontal pentagons of bright plastic cord on different airy strata. I bend to get a work shirt. Dad cracks the back of my hand with a backhand of his own. We both massage our stings—

I, aggrieved, openly; Dad covertly, yakking to hide his annoyance:

"You don't know how to do this, Pierce. You also think it's stupid."

"I don't think *bannering's* stupid," I say. "I think pretending it's art is stupid."

Guy, my older brother, sticks his thin, comely face out his second-story dormer. "Lay off him, Pierce. It's a hallowed Zalmonellaville tradition."

"As in 'Wasting away in Zalmonellaville'? As in 'We're all like to come down with zalmonella'?"

"Stop it," Dad says.

"You've heard the poultry trucks grind through," Guy calls out. "You know the dangers."

"Cluck cluck," I cluck. "Cluck cluck."

We've got the patter down. It's vaudeville, pure shtick given a scant modicum of respectability by the fact that Guy and I have spent months away from home as students, with no chance, for over a quarter, to indulge in such lunacy. But even from thirty yards off, the half-moons under Guy's eyes give him the look of a dissipated ghoul.

Disgusted, Dad growls in his turkey-wattled throat.

Guy and I never expected to move from Wichita to Georgia, but Dye-Trak offered Dad a big raise if he left Kansas to manage its southeastern headquarters here, and so we arrived three years ago, clueless Kansans, refugees from the Air Capital of the World, beef-fed transplants to a realm of turpentine pines, birddogs, and BBQ joints. So Guy's still got wheat fields in his eyes, and I haven't yet plumbed the protocols governing the use of *you-all*, much less the scary depths of laundry bannering.

"Dad, I'm sorry," I say. "Come on. Let me help."

"You don't know how. You're a ten-thumbed piker."

Dad loves it that I have no bannering talent, because he hates it that I outperform Guy academically in Athens. Also, I excel in card games, play half-a-dozen musical instruments, and vocalize in lean phrasings reminiscent of our late mother's. Although Dad takes pride in my accomplishments, he resents the ease with which I earn them. Guy struggles like a galley slave at almost everything.

"You could get him a footstool!" Guy shouts.

I look up. Guy's face and shoulders protrude from his dormer like a loose-limbed scarecrow's.

"The footstool! From the garage!"

"Oh," I manage, for once slower on the uptake than Guy, for once a total klutz. "Right." I bid farewell to Dad to fetch his collapsible metal footstool from the booby-trapped clutter in the garage.

When I get back, he's already hung a khaki shirt, three pairs of knee-length navy socks, and a nylon jogging jacket. But if this work represents a creative breakthrough, I can't tell what sort. My look betrays that opinion.

"I'm not through," Dad says. "Set the stool down. No, damn it! Over *here!*"

I obey.

Guy vanishes from the bedroom window. Music drifts out, something exquisitely godawful by Nirvana or Nine Inch Nails.

What's Guy doing up there? Trying to study? Playing air guitar? Reading some of Dad's old sci-fi paperbacks, with special Yuletide attention to James Tiptree, Jr., Philip K. Dick, and that half-forgotten ghetto intellectual, James Blish? Who knows? Guy, left alone, becomes a melancholy recluse, and damn all the textbooks, punk rock, and sci-fi claiming even a loose grip on an Unimpeachable Answer to It All.

Up on the footstool, Dad drapes his topmost pentagon with towels and washrags. They form a blue and brown curtain above the stuff already arranged below them. Again, I can't see that he has made anything remarkable, even when a gust of wind stirs through and sets the whole congeries flapping.

Dad suspects as much. A hand on his lower back, he comes gingerly down for a fresh view and a summing up.

"It's lousy." He cocks his head. "Mediocre, in fact."

"They'll dry," I say. "And, hey, you didn't spend years putting it up." (Does Dad think he's a primitive genius, the Howard Finster of laundry bannerers?)

"I need more stuff. Another load or two would help. Go in and fill up the washer, Pierce."

"Sir?"

"College boys used to stagger home with *bags* of laundry. *I* did. My buddies did. What's wrong with you and Guy?"

Before I can respond, he yells, "Hey, Number One Son, how much laundry did you bring home?"

Passing his open dormer, Guy hears only by chance: the yowls from his CD player could drown an artillery barrage. "*Sir?*" Hacked, Dad repeats his question, and Guy says, "None. I came with what I'm wearing. And a change."

"Criminy!" Dad says. "You pack like a monk. I know you've got clothes money. I send it—that, tuition, and a lavish plenty for gadding about."

"Thanks," Guy says. Dully. Automatically.

"I've brought some stuff," I say. "Hold on. I'll go start a load."

It takes forty minutes to wash the dirty laundry I've toted home in my duffel. Dad insists on unloading the Kenmore, putting Guy's Radio Flyer to work again, and jolting out back to finish his display. *Display* is his word. Even after three years as a citizen of Zalmon (albeit one who spends more time in Athens), to me it's still just *hanging out the wash*. But Dad banners religiously, even though back in Wichita he would not have hung out a wash (exposed to inclement weather, not to mention possible ridicule) for a brand-new set of Snap-On wrenches.

I climb the stairs to Guy's room and let myself in. From his window, I can see Dad struggling to create his display—also other clotheslines, other *displays*. The one at the Baumans', two houses south, consists entirely of em-broidered lace handkerchiefs, lace antimacassars, nearly translucent ankle stockings, and a dozen ivory facecloths with satin trim. Guy has some high-powered binoculars on his window seat. I use them to scope out the Bau-mans' effort. Through them, the snowflake figures in the antimacassars show as intricate as magnified flies' wings. At three houses down, the Stowes', every item on the lines ripples purple, lavender, or violet, and I know that in winter in Kansas, it would all hang as stiff as two-ply cardboard.

"You came with one change of clothes?" I say.

Guy now has an old Doors album on, turned down enough to make talk possible. "Day after tomorrow, I'm going back to Athens."

"What about Christmas?"

"I'll come home again."

"Lots of driving. Lots of wear and tear. Besides which, Guy me lad"—I say *Guy* in the French way, to rhyme with *key*—"you're gonna break Papa's heart."

"Ha! I *remind* him of heartbreak." A pity-party grenade, which Guy lobs to frag me with memories, *his* memories, images that reposition Mom in the auto crash that Guy caused north of Cottonwood driving on his learner's permit, passing on a yellow line in a frog-strangling downpour, taking as a dare her warning that he couldn't get around that pokey Sonoma before the unfolding curve disclosed the headlamps of an oncoming truck cab. Which, devastatingly, it did.

"No," I say. "You're Number One Son." In both birth order and paternal regard, this is an indisputable truth.

"Yeah, well, I have to go back."

"Why?"

"Who do we know in Zalmon? What's to *do*, especially if you don't get off on either bannering or Dad's musty sci-fi?"

"I'm here. Dad's here. You can restock on paperbacks at the Stop N Swap on Railroad."

"Lila Duggit's about to dump me. I need to stop her."

"Hasn't she gone home too?"

Guy and I have our own cars, friends, and allegiances. He lives east of Athens, in a doublewide off Turkey Pond Drive; I share rent and living space with Brandon Ely in a house near the city airport. In Athens we rarely see each other, and the distance between our residences doesn't figure very much in our lack of contact.

"Lila clerks at Lerner's," Guy says. "She won't drive home to Dalton until Christmas Eve. I've got to stop her from cutting me loose."

"Do yourself a favor. Let her."

I turn the field glasses around.

Guy slumps at his desk clicking a computer mouse, tossing widening Technicolor spirals across the face of his monitor. Through the binoculars, he appears as distant twins of himself. You'd need a pair of tweezers to pluck him out.

"Pierce, do me a favor—just lay off."

I lower the 'nocs. "Take a look at what Dad's doing."

Groaning in protest, Guy slouches to the window. We both peer out.

Dad sees us. "What junk you've brought me!" he yells and, still on his footstool, spreads out one of my T-shirts so that we can read its legend: *Shakespeare Eats Bacon*. "All class!" he rants. "All class!"

His bannering hasn't gone well, even with my laundry as an additional resource. Sweatpants. Tattered jeans. The duffel bag in which I hauled it all home. Dad double-pins a white sock. He yanks my sweatpants from the carousel's central pentagon and flings them down. He dismounts the stool, kicks the basket before him to the house, and limps inside before reemerging to shout up at me:

"Why do you buy such crap? How can you wear it?"

Bang! Crash! Dad reenters, clumps to the kitchen.

Guy and I view his handiwork. The Baumans and the Stowes have fashioned clothesline masterpieces, at least in comparison to Dad's insipid pennantry.

"He'll never get one of those rainbow tokens the Bannerers Guild hands out," Guy says. That we agree on.

I galumph downstairs and try to jolly Dad into a frame of mind that will enable me—us—to coexist with him.

Just as I begin to microwave three prepackaged meals for dinner, Hester Yount, a widow just past fifty, shows up to drop off a Christmas gift. Miss Hettie is a low-burning flame of Dad's. She pays two unmarried, middle-aged blacks (who stroll Zalmon in search of cigarette butts, aluminum cans, and beer bottles with semipotable dregs) to cut the mistletoe out of her plum trees, the kudzu out of her elms, and the creepers from her muscadine vines. Everyone calls this couple Joseph and Mary. Before Dad hurt himself, Miss Hettie occasionally coaxed him to perform these tasks.

"Ah," she says as I let her in. "The Tarleton Twins, home from the hostilities."

"Just school, Miss Hettie. And we're not twins."

"But handsome as those boys nonetheless. And school, if I remember aright, can often be a battlefield."

"Yessum, I guess." I've always thought Miss Hettie a handsome woman, but she looks a decade older than her age, as if early widowhood, balky automobiles, the weird peregrinations of Joseph and Mary, and several successive spring tornadoes have plucked away at her youth. The first time I saw her—me, a Kansan, and no fan of *Gone with the Wind*—I pegged Miss Hettie as a Georgia cliché, a superannuated Suthren belle to outvie the breed. Usually, pathetically, she fulfills the stereotype.

Dad, shuffling in, brightens. He shows Miss Hettie to a chair, offers her a "toddy" (warm bourbon with a sugar cube in it), and hollers up at Guy to trot down and greet our visitor. At Dad's request, I crank up a Mannheim Steamroller CD—to *beseason*, as he says, Miss Hettie's call. She lays her gift on the coffee table. About cigar-box size, the package is a shimmering burgundy gold.

When Guy—barefoot and sullen, his Flying Rat Toli Club T-shirt falling almost to the knees of his chinos—finally comes down, the dazzle in our parlor halts him on the bottom step.

"Ah," Miss Hettie says, "now y'all can open my gift—even if it's a tad more for Ronnie," patting Dad's knee, "than his two charming boys."

"It isn't Christmas yet," Dad protests. "And I don't have a blasted thing for you."

Miss Hettie shakes her head. "Delaying gratification isn't my strong suit, and I didn't expect you to. Goodness, I didn't *want* you to."

Guy nears the coffee table, his chin tucked hard against the stretched crew neck of his shirt. Dad undoes the flaps wrapping our gift and slips the black enamel box out of the loosened paper onto the table.

"I bought the box," Miss Hettie says, "but I *made* what's in it."

The box's lid slides in parallel grooves at the tops of its two longest sides. Dad presses with his thumb, nudges the lid over a quarter-inch, and then pushes it all the way open, revealing a set of what I first take for fancy, ceramic chess pieces. Actually, as Guy and I realize when Dad removes one and holds it up, the enamel box contains handcrafted clothespins.

Miss Hettie rocks back a little. "Now, I know you handsome young fellas can't imagine what earthly good such items are apt to do you, or you them, but even if you give over their use to a wife or significant other or just store them away in the attic, one day they'll be worth plenty."

"I believe it," Dad says.

"These clothespins evoke Zalmon. They qualify, even from my old-money hands, as folk art, and I trust Ronnie will leave them to y'all as part of your inheritance."

Poker-faced, Guy says, "I'll take the fish."

Miss Hettie has made her clothespins in phantasmagoric fish and animal shapes, each a gem of painted, glazed, and fired potter's clay. The "mouths" of the varmints serve as the clip ends. Dad lays them out. I finger ponies, trout, octopuses, seahorses, dolphins, spaniels, penguins, even manatees. They gleam like chloroformed scarabs.

"In truth," Miss Hettie says, "I plan to make another set so each of you boys can eventually have one."

"Hettie, that won't be"—*necessary* is probably what Dad meant to say, but of a sudden he fathoms the implications of that remark. "Won't that be a lot of work?"

"I enjoy it, or I wouldn't do it. And I think the world of all three of you."

"Even if Pierce thinks bannering's lame? Even if Guy"—Dad grabs Guy's ripped T-shirt—"dresses like a bum?"

Calmly, Guy removes Dad's hand.

Miss Hettie says, "Boys will be boys." She squints at Guy's library-basement pallor. "You should get out in the sun more, though."

"Yeah," I tell him. "And laundry-banner."

Our mother, Claire Pierce Garrett, is buried in Sedgewick County, Kansas. I don't guess that Guy or I expect to have a plot in that cemetery, but we've always assumed (or so I assume) that Dad would one day lie down in the grave next to hers. That disposition of his remains, however, daily grows more doubtful. He likes Zalmon—the climate, the bass fishing, the bird hunting, the laundry bannering. If he remarries, whether Hester Yount or another local, the likelihood of his returning to Wichita will drop dramatically, and Guy recognizes and laments his reduced odds of returning home as a member of the Ronald Garrett household.

After dinner, for which Miss Hettie doesn't stay, I knock on Guy's door again. If I don't go to him now, on this trip we won't connect again at all. I rap ten or twelve times before he grudgingly calls, "Yeah, yeah. It's open."

When I enter, Guy has a toli stick in either hand. He is tossing a hard wicker ball from one thong-fashioned cup to the other, like a juggler with grotesque prosthetic devices. If he drops the ball, he scoops it up—with the cup on the stick end, not with his hands—and resumes juggling. The only light comes from his computer screen, where the face of a helmeted Mayan warrior pulses in bronze and indigo. This warrior glares at us with arcane severity.

"I'm afraid I've flunked my classes," Guy says.

"All of them?"

"Three, I think."

"You're taking forty-five hours. That's three classes."

"Okay. All of them."

A slow amusement grips me. "Why? You love anthropology. You've got a *talent* for it."

"My classes seem pointless. Besides, I hate measurements, bones, middens—all the depressing kipple of the human past."

"Change majors. You don't have to be an anthropologist."

"I do. It's my calling."

We laugh at this altogether unexplainable inside joke.

"Do an ethnography on Zalmon," I say, "with a chapter on laundry bannering and all its attendant rituals."

"And another on husband-hunting former debutantes?"

"Sure. It's best-seller stuff."

"No, it's just more kipple. Pierce, I don't belong here."

"So where do you belong?"

"Some other planet. Some other dimension. Wichita."

I have a sudden willed vision. The toli sticks in Guy's hands mutate into digging tools, and he stoops beside a grave near a cottonwood stand to excavate it. This image passes, and in the backwash from his computer screen, Guy stares at me with bemused contempt—the very expression on his pixel-built Mayan.

Before noon, Guy packs up his '84 Audi, hops in, keys the ignition, and bids Dad and me goodbye.

"This is ridiculous," Dad says. "It's Christmas. You're making a two-and-a-half-hour trip for nothing."

"No, sir, not for nothing."

"On a less than cost-effective wild hair, then. You think I'm made out of money? I'm retired, Guy, and on disability."

"Love you two." Guy waves, and shoots the Audi some gas. "See y'all soon." He varooms away, leaving tread dents in the edge of the lawn.

I have to face Zalmon pretty much alone. Guy has trapped me. How can I leave when Dad expects at least one of us home over the break? All my friends from high school—as if I had that many, tiptoeing my way into town as a senior—have found day jobs elsewhere or jaunted off to their grandparents' houses in other towns, other states, other mindsets. As for Dad, he's got football to watch, pecans to pick out, Miss Hettie to worry over. He must wonder how a corporate manager of his can-do ilk ever sired an anthropology wonk like Guy and a would-be session player like me. I sit next to Dad before another televised game, his gazillionth, and pray for relief.

Miss Hettie brings it. "Ronnie, your boy doesn't give rip about that nonsense."

"It's a free country," Dad says, waving her in. "He could read. Scrub floors. Take a walk."

"Come on," Miss Hettie says to me. "I'll tour you."

What kind of tour? But Miss Hettie's invitation, even lacking specifics, has an almost sexy allure.

"Sure," I say.

And so Miss Hettie takes me off in her hearselike Lincoln, and I see what I have seen on other such cruises through town—Victorian houses intermixed with clapboard hybrids and lots of eccentrically displayed laundry.

People in Zalmon fly laundry the way people in other towns flaunt Old Glory on President's Day, Memorial Day, Independence Day, Labor Day, Veterans Day. Men as well as women hang out washes, bachelors as well as husbands, kids hardly tall enough to reach a clothesline as well as teenagers at eye level with their work. Socks and undies serve as pennants, shirts as party flags, bed sheets as undulant sails. As a result, our town provokes an occasional cutesy-pie article in the Atlanta papers or in travel magazines. In the early 1970s, even *National Geographic* did Zalmon. You can see the color photos in the trophy case at our local library.

It's too bad, but most Zalmonites exhausted their genius for aesthetic freshness long ago. So we pass yards in which bannerers have hung their clothes upside-down (pants by the cuffs, shirts by the tails), or in mix-and-match color blocks, or with small dark items set against immense pale quilts. Some bannerers have raised or lowered their lines or set them out in multi-level cat's-cradles. More than one house boasts lines draped with Christmas bulbs. Switched on at twilight, they glitter like sequins on velvet or float in the wind like fireflies.

"You see why I love this town?" Miss Hettie says.

"Yessum."

"Stop in at my house for a toddy?"

"Sure. I'm still not twenty-one, though."

"My me," Miss Hettie snorts her pet expression. "So what?"

At her sprawling ranch-style—no magnolia trees or Grecian columns out front—she gives me a strong one, stiff and sweet. We sit in her kitchen at an antique pub table. In her window hangs one of the seven rainbow tokens that the Bannerers Guild has awarded her over the years. This token consists of a painted metal arc from which hang silver-plated charms symbolizing garments or line; it is no more than five inches from tip to tip. I sit gaping at it, impressed because Miss Hettie has six others almost exactly like it and my dad would kill for just one.

"I got that the winter after Kyle died," she says. "My most recent." She glances at me, shrugs.

"What did you do—create, I mean—to get it?"

"You really want to know?"

"Yessum." To my own mild surprise, I really do.

"It snowed that year. Only rarely do we get a snow. It reminded me of something. I fetched my satin wedding dress out of the attic and pinned it dead center on my line. It shone against the snow. Whoever was judging that month, well, that person made a truly generous call. And so you behold my final rainbow."

"Maybe not your final one."

"Maybe not," she agrees. "Fifty-one seems less old to me every day and life just a series of—" She stops.

"Of what?"

"You know, of ever more outlandish shocks."

No snow, but rain: a cold, depressing, general downpour. I imagine Guy lounging in the bathtub under his doublewide's skylight, listening as the raindrops pummel down. His roommate, Jeff Palino, has returned to Tennessee, and Lila Duggit . . . what has Lila said?

And how did Guy finally do in his "pointless" classes?

Without Dad's knowledge, I telephone Athens and get this message:

"You have reached the number you have reached. If it's the right one, talk to us after the beep."

Guy's message, but Jeff's recitation.

The machine beeps.

I say, "Hope you've kept your head above water during the monsoons. C'mon, Guy, give us a call."

No call, either an hour later, or five. But, of course, healthy students on break don't return to their college towns to soak for hours in a bath. They go back to party. So too, presumably, would Guy.

Dad says, "A really lousy day for bannering."

"Lousy. It's impossible."

Half delightedly, half sheepishly, he cackles. His knight has captured my queen. "Wow. This is weather Betty Furness invented the electric dryer for."

"Who?"

"Never mind. Just heed the board."

In three more moves, I blunder into checkmate. I win at cards, Dad at chess—that's the bargain. But today, losing to Dad feels irrelevant. My nerve ends dance, bacon on a griddle, a metabolic echo of the rain on the streets.

The phone rings. Dad and I jump for it. Dad wins. To Dad's surprise, Miss Hettie asks for me. "Hey, Pierce," she says, "how you'd like to get out?"

Dad's chagrin and suspicion spur me to say yes. I drive over to Miss Hettie's. With my Georgia Bulldog umbrella, I make my way inside and give her a shivery peck on the cheek. She has plans. She wants to banner. Like the snow of her widow year, the rain has inspired her. She needs help, though, and I am the assistant she's enlisted. We telephone around.

"Raingear," she says. "Right. Yes. Absolutely."

Then, phantoms in the quicksilver rain, we go from door to door collecting the pledged garments, namely a chaotic mix of raincoats—yellow crossing-guard slickers, plastic chemises with clear hoods, army-green firefighting gear, satin-finished navy-blue topcoats, oilskin half-jackets, ankle-length macs, and so on. We stagger like looters under our booty. Once back in Miss Hettie's yard, we hang the raincoats out, our own included, arranging and rearranging until the ground under us has turned to tobacco juice and our arms groan in their sockets. When we get everything as we want it, the lines tug at their crossbars, virtually twanging.

"You know, Pierce, I think maybe this conceit's a first. An original."

Although my feet have nearly fused with the mud, I turn to scrutinize our—no, Miss Hettie's—bannering.

"Well?" she says.

I turn back to her. She lifts her eyebrows and then her arms. The rain illuminates her splendidly.

"Maybe," I say, unabashedly admiring her figure.

When I come traipsing in, Dad demands that I call Guy in Athens. I reach the answering machine—not Jeff's voice now, but Guy's:

"'Overhead, the banners of the rings flew changelessly, as though they had seen nothing—or perhaps . . . everything, siftings upon siftings in oblivion, until nothing remained of the banners but their own mirrored beauty.'"

Tinnily, the machine beeps.

"What the hell's that?" Dad takes the receiver from me and cradles it. "Doped-up, artsy-fartsy rock poetry?"

"The end of an old sci-fi story," I say. "James Blish, I think."

Dad doesn't recall Blish. As ardent an enthusiast as he once was, sci-fi writers all blur for him today.

He says, "That's fitting. He sounds out of it. Off-planet." I can only agree. "Drive me up there, Pierce. Now."

Which is how, nearly three hours later, we bump onto Turkey Pond Drive and up the muddy hill to Jeff and Guy's doublewide. Out of my car, we stride down to the police cruisers and EMS wagon parked about sixty yards below the drive itself.

There we find Lila Duggit standing near the fishpond. When I take her aside, she whispers, red-eyed, "Guy drowned himself out there because of me. Please, Pierce, don't tell your daddy it wasn't an accident."

"Sure, Lila, sure."

Of course, the truth—if not the whole truth—will come out, no matter what.

Guy's plus-sized landlord huddles with a deputy from the county sheriff's office, and blue lights strobe through the pines. The body has already been retrieved, by means that I avoid learning.

Dad cuts in and takes Lila's hand as if to kiss it. She places her other palm to her mouth and vents a complicated hiccup of grief or guilt or both.

"Water to water," Dad says. "He really hated rain."

"Sir?"

"Shhh." Dad lays a finger across his lips. "Shhh."

Early the next morning, with the landlord's blessing, we rummage through Guy's belongings, including some clothes that he wore as a boy (a Cub Scout uniform, a T-shirt from a Methodist summer camp) and some stuff so unlike him (a tweed jacket, lemon-lime Spandex cycling shorts) that I can't envision him wearing them. Neither Dad nor I ever saw him tricked out thus.

We transport his gear in my car and Guy's Audi back to Zalmon.

The funeral, a day later, draws a modest crowd, but Miss Hettie sits beside Dad and me during the graveside portion of the service, under a mortuary awning that shields us from the pale sun rather than a late-December rain. If Guy hated rain—until two days ago, news to me—the weather grants him a mocking reprieve.

Another day passes, and Miss Hettie suggests a route to solace that Dad readily accedes to, namely, laundering Guy's clothes and bannering them in all their unsettling diversity across the backyard. Dad, Miss Hettie, and I work side by side at this task, then Dad takes photos, and Miss Hettie sends out word that whoever helps us take down this wash may select an item or two from among the garments composing it. Guy would have loved the idea of this no-strings potlatch.

Indeed, more townsfolk come to the dismantling than attended the funeral—but, as Miss Hettie says, people will be people, and life today is a series of ever more outlandish shocks.

THE
RUSSIAN
AGENT

When

    Charlie

        Riddle spied a limousine nosing into the Burger Barn parking lot and half-rose to determine where it might park, he sloshed a chocolate milkshake onto his copy of *The Brothers Karamazov.*

"Christ." Riddle blotted the creamy-brown stain with a napkin.

At least he had not soiled the pulp-paper publication that he had received from Moscow four years ago.

Raskolnikov featured several mystery stories in Russian, in Cyrillic characters, and a cover depicting a set of rickety stairs mounting to the door of a fleabag apartment. Its editor had enclosed a letter praising Riddle as a writer "in the spirit of Dostoevsky" and asking permission to reprint his Edgar-winning story "Diary of a Dead Man" in the next issue. "I offer no payment," this stranger had written, "but a fine Russian construal of your story and two contributor copies. Maybe you will also take comfort from a crowd of exciting new readers."

Riddle could not imagine *Raskolnikov* getting into the hands of more than twelve of the editor's friends, but he had agreed to the reprint request and soon forgotten about the matter. Then, two evenings earlier, John Baywater, an eighty-year-old Miami-based writer who still wrote one old-fashioned private-eye novel a year, had telephoned to ask Riddle if the name Volodya Dukhobov meant anything to him. Well, no. The moniker suggested a vodka or a Balkan political movement, and Riddle wondered if Baywater hoped to sucker him into a time-consuming collaboration. He'd itched inside his suspicions like a psoriasis victim in a moldy bear suit.

"Volodya's a Russian litry man," Baywater said in his creepiest Southern accent. "He flew in to visit me three days ago. Now he'd like to see you."

"Let me talk to him."

"He ast me to talk for him, Charlie." (*Ast*, for Christ's sake.) Baywater explained that Dukhobov planned to visit several of his American friends while touring the eastern United States on his way to New York City and a flight home to Russia. Baywater made sure to add that *he* had done his duty by the fella.

Riddle's suspicions grew itchier. "Do you *like* this guy?"

"He has a dry charm. Ony thing is, he's worn me out." (*Ony.*)

"Does he smoke?"

"The ony Rooskies who don't have diaper rash or asthma, Charlie."

"Lydia's allergic to tobacco smoke." In the parlor, Riddle's wife Lydia banged out "We've a Story to Tell to the Nations" like raucous jellyroll blues.

"He steps outside to do it," Baywater said. "But he thinks us Americans awfully damned fussy about health-related stuff."

Riddle had laughed. "Really? One of the folks who gave us all Chernobyl?"

Now, in the Burger Barn at the Perry exit off I-75, he peered out at Baywater's ivory-colored sedan and its mysterious smoke-gray windows. He had agreed to meet Dukhobov here and to drive him back to Mountboro. Amazingly, Baywater's chauffeur pulled the old man's ritzy limo into the slot next to Riddle's beat-up yellow Pinto station wagon. It blazed beside his vehicle like a bonfire next to a candle nub.

Soon three people, none of them Baywater, got out: a chauffeur with a white-blond ponytail, a pudgy woman in a gold pantsuit, and a slender young man wearing purple sunglasses and a brown fake-leather jacket. Riddle pegged this man as Dukhobov, perhaps because his glasses' lenses resembled balalaika picks, or maybe because, like a mountain climber sticking his face into an oxygen mask, he cupped his hands and lit up a cigarette. Smoke trailed away from him dreamily, like clouds in time-lapse photography. Steeling himself, Riddle walked out to the parking lot.

Dukhobov immediately approached. "Charles Riddle?" His smile formed a gentle scar. "You look like yourself, yet different from the man on your book covers."

"That's an old photo," Riddle said, shaking Dukhobov's small hand. "I don't allow my photo on my dust jackets anymore."

"Too bad. You are still an attractive man."

Still? "Too many women wrote me mash notes." Riddle intended a joke, but Dukhobov's smile vanished like a pressure-whitened thumb slowly regaining its color.

"Wahl, wahl, wahl," he said.

The blond chauffeur and the pant-suited woman helped Baywater from the car and led him over to Riddle and Dukhobov. Baywater took a drag from Dukhobov's cigarette, squinting at Riddle as if the surf noise from the expressway might awaken him to Riddle's identity. Nothing happened, though, and Riddle realized that Baywater, after who knows how many hours of coaching, had drawn a humiliating blank—humiliating for both Riddle and him.

"Charlie Riddle," the pantsuited woman said. "He's here to pick up Volodya, sir. Then we'll drive on to our symposium in Virginia."

"Riddle!" Baywater cried. "Liked yore last book a lot, I sholy did." He glanced at his chauffeur. "Get me a Whopper, Eddie."

"They have Wagon Wheels here, sir, not Whoppers."

"Mox nix," said Baywater irritably, and Eddie wandered off to fetch the burger. "Charlie," Baywater said, "keep an eye on our good friend Ivan here."

"Volodya," Dukhobov said. "Call me Volodya."

"Gotcha." Baywater's gaze drifted from the Russian to his female assistant and then to Riddle again. "Volodya here's going to open up Roosha as a top-flight market for beaucoups of American writers, Charlie. Mark my words."

"You say too much too kind," Dukhobov said.

In the parking lot, Riddle recalled that after his telephone talk with Baywater, he had visited the parlor to talk to Lydia. "How would you feel about playing host to a guest from Russia?" he had asked. Lydia looked briefly puzzled, then smiled and dove headlong into the love theme from the movie *Doctor Zhivago*, which he had never before conceived as a polka.

"Let's go," he told Dukhobov. "Whether we're heirs of Dostoevsky or Spillane, if we keep standing here, someone will run over us."

Driving to Mountboro, Riddle began thinking of Dukhobov as Volodya, because he had asked Riddle to call him that and because he spoke tenderly of his wife and young daughter in Moscow. Then Volodya talked of the peril—the uncertainty—of a literary career in the New Russia. He hardly *stopped* talking, always in a smoky Slavic brogue that exhausted Riddle, who now understood how Baywater could say that Volodya had worn him out. Eventually, as if picking up on Riddle's weariness, he *did* shut up, and the April peach orchards in their lavender pinafores rippled past the station wagon like animated computer graphics. Volodya grimaced at the gnarled trees, the blossoms, the velvety green corridors connecting them.

"Sorry we have so far to go," said Riddle, conscious of his failures as host and guide. "Our country has a tendency to sprawl."

"So you think your country has a monotony on bigness?"

"No. I just know how tired *I* get after several hours in a car."

Volodya pointed his chin at the salmon-and-mulberry vista through the windshield, at its hazy foliage and camel-backed ridges. "Russia spreads even bigger." Well. Volodya wanted to measure dicks, to inform the smug American that, even as a fading superpower, his country had resources beyond those of the puerile, money-grubbing West. Heedless of Riddle's annoyance, he took his copy of *The Brothers Karamazov* off the dashboard. "Ah, Dostoevsky. Have you only now begun to read his most sublime novel?"

"No. I first read it as a college student."

"What makes you read it again? A crisis of faith?"

"No," Riddle said carefully. "My wife gave it to me. This translation allegedly restores some of the original's unique comedy."

"Comedy?"

"So the translators claim, one a native Russian."

"Wahl, wahl, wahl." Volodya returned the novel, its binding smudged, to the dash. Riddle wondered why he'd brought it. Clearly, Volodya saw it as an affectation—"Look, I read your Fyodor the way some folks read Conan Doyle!"—or as a hokey way to establish rapport. Besides, for that, he had brought *Raskolnikov*, his passenger's *samizdat* mystery magazine. But Volodya had recognized him without his having to hold up *Raskolnikov* like a chauffeur brandishing a name placard at the airport, and Riddle resented him—how weird was that?—for *not* needing the magazine. Perhaps Volodya, once inside their house, would metamorphose into the Man Who Came to Dinner and squat there like a tenant in a rent-controlled apartment, defiantly chain-smoking.

"Do you love movies?" Volodya suddenly asked. "American film noir?"

"Sure. Who doesn't?"

"Do you know our cinema? The revolutionary films of *glasnost*?"

"No. Unfortunately, Georgians don't go in much for foreign films."

"Ah, but you speak of *American* Georgians. The Georgians of our old Soviet Union created very exciting work. They knew film history and also had great political courage." He launched into a monologue about *fin de Soviet* cinema and the intrepid Georgian filmmaker Tengiz Abuladze, whom another great Georgian—not Jimmy Carter, but Eduard Shevardnadze—had encouraged to proceed with his anti-Stalinist picture *Repentance*. Riddle got lost in this spiel, but focused again when Volodya spoke about the dynamiting of Moscow's Cathedral of the Savior in the 1930s. Apparently, a clip of this controversial event figured in *Repentance*, which the public had seen only because of the political spring of *glasnost*.

"Wait," Riddle said. "Did this Georgian director—?"

"Abuladze."

"Right. Did Abuladze approve or disapprove of the cathedral's destruction?"

"Disapproved. Nobody could have said such a thing under Brezhnev or any of the other little Stalins. Do you know the famous last line of *Repentance*?"

"No." How could I? Riddle thought. He'd never seen the film and hardly expected to find it among the grade-D opuses at his local video store.

"*What good is a road that doesn't lead to a church?* In the nineteen-eighties, astonishing words, Mr. Riddle, truly astonishing."

"Charlie," Riddle said grudgingly. But this surprising discussion of a Soviet film affirming religious freedom comforted him a little. Volodya would spend the next two and a half days in Mountboro before going to Nashville to visit mystery novelist Jack Deacon, an itinerary that placed Volodya in his home on Friday evening when he and Lydia hosted a home-fellowship study.

What would Volodya think of this group?

And what would their friends think of the presumably atheistic Russian planked down amidst them?

But as Riddle drove, Volodya talked and talked, and Riddle's brain, laboring to decipher his accent, dieseled like the Pinto's balky engine.

Lydia welcomed Volodya as if he had just returned from a Soyuz mission. "You must be bushed," she said. "Totally drained." Riddle felt that *he* had a proprietary interest in those adjectives, but kept his mouth shut. Volodya was charmed. He raised Lydia's hand as if to kiss it then let it go and stepped away. His eyes, however, scrambled up and down Lydia's body like eager army recruits on a rope ladder.

Lydia provisioned Volodya with towels and toiletries, showed him the guestroom, and led him to the kitchen. He observed as she scrubbed three baking potatoes, plopped three broccoli stalks into a steamer, and shredded greens for a salad. Under their visitor's gaze, Riddle rubbed garlic salt into three enormous steaks.

"Who *else* will eat with us?" Volodya asked.

At the table, Lydia thanked God for bringing Volodya safely across the sea to America and then from Miami to Mountboro. As she blessed the food, Volodya glanced about as if surveying the kitchen for future reference. Then she passed Volodya the salad. He accepted some, cut his steak into fussy strips, and abruptly sat back.

"You don't feel well," Lydia guessed.

"Olga, Maria, and I could persist a week on what you've given me." Olga was his wife and Maria his three-year-old daughter. He had already shown them photos.

"Would you like something lighter? Chicken soup, maybe?"

"For tomorrow, some fruit please—an apple, if I could, or a banana."

"Certainly. We'll buy some. But what about tonight?"

"Only some tea." Volodya stood. "Please let *me* to make it, for tea I brew to the diffusion of perfection." With Lydia's help, he found tea bags, filled a kettle, laid out mugs. "Olga says no one makes tea so well. You must do the steps just so—dit, dit, dit."

Riddle started to say, *I understand Georgia Tech has just commissioned a doctoral program in tea brewing,* but refrained. He felt both replete and empty. Why hadn't Lydia asked after *his* physical and mental comfort? The juvenility of his cavils—one must show visitors hospitality—annoyed Riddle, but Volodya had planted a petty resentment in him. He had a deadline soon, and driving to Perry had cost him a day's work.

When the kettle boiled, Volodya stood up again. "Do you have a jar, Mrs. Riddle, and some bread? Also, perhaps, some raisins?"

"Bread?" said Riddle. "You still have food on your plate."

"Not to eat. To make for you kvass, a kind of sauce for vegetables."

"I thought kvass was liquor," Riddle said. "Something like Russian sake."

"Kvass isn't so alcoholic," Volodya said. "Only an angel or a little carp could get drunk on kvass."

Lydia found an empty mayonnaise jar, a loaf of wheat bread, and a box of raisins. Volodya folded two slices of bread into the jar, flooded them with tap water, dropped two raisins into the mix, screwed down the lid, and set the jar aside. "Tomorrow we'll have kvass—to eat with vegetables." He mimed spooning vegetables, doubtlessly stewed beets or cabbage. "Or maybe to drink."

Riddle caught Lydia's eye. In the morning he expected to find broken glass in the gypsum board and odd spatters on the walls and ceiling. Lydia mouthed *Relax, it's okay.* His lightheadedness intensified, and he could almost imagine himself swooning. Gravity seemed on the verge of repeal. The kettle sang. Volodya poured boiling water into an ugly gray teapot and turned off the stove eye.

"Six minutes and perfect tea. Good for the stomach, also the nerves."

"Better give Charlie two cups." Lydia cleared the table.

Volodya watched as if she were modeling not only her slacks-and-sweater outfit, but also her housekeeping techniques. Esteem suffused his face, a kind of glory.

Riddle said, "Volodya, how will you get to Jack Deacon's place in Nashville?"

"I trust that when I have stayed my time, something good will happen."

"Why don't you call Jack and make arrangements?" Lydia asked Riddle.

He did not want to call Jack Deacon. Twelve years ago, in a review in the Sunday *Atlanta Journal-Constitution*, Jack had dismissed his third mystery novel, *The Elevation of the Host*, as "formally impeccable but emotionally vacuous." Jack had never behaved less than civilly in person, but Riddle still suspected that his colleague regarded him as a lightweight . . . or an imposter.

"Can't it wait, Lydia? I'm not feeling all that chipper."

But Volodya wanted to leave on Saturday, the day after tomorrow, and Lydia insisted that Riddle call. He stumbled to the wall phone and jabbed his finger into its outdated rotary dial. He caught Deacon watching an ice-hockey game on TV and tersely discussed with him the logistics of transferring Volodya from Mountboro to Nashville—by bus, the cheapest and easiest way. After ringing off, Riddle found that Volodya had no money. He seemed to think that his serial hosts could swap him amongst themselves with giant slingshots. He had no notion of incidental expenses or any plans to pay his own way.

His smug helplessness goaded Lydia to ask, "Volodya, do you believe in God?"

"The Oversoul, I think—but not in a humanlike figure with a long white beard and a heavenly robe . . . Pardon me. Do my words offend?"

"Oh, no," Lydia said. "I'd say you have more faith than many church-goers."

Faith in the milk of human kindness, Riddle thought, which all too soon curdles or runs dry. His indignation built. He'd have to buy Volodya a bus ticket, provide him lunch money, drive him to the bus station in Tocqueville.

"How do you like my tea?" Volodya asked Lydia.

"Excellent," she said. Lying, of course, for she seldom drank anything other than water, and Volodya's tea was bitter as old licorice.

At breakfast, Riddle found a brand-new issue of *Raskolnikov* beside his plate, its tan cover depicting a silhouetted male figure with an upraised ax. Riddle's "Diary of a Dead Man" occupied its first nine pages. He pored over the Cyrillic letters of Volodya's translation as if they were spry Pentecostal flames. Lydia found a thin reed scroll, which, when, shaken out, disclosed the face of a fat-cheeked cat with Betty Boop eyes.

Lydia laughed, but Riddle thought it cheap and jejune. "An ax murderer for me," he said. "But, for you, a Cossack rendition of Sylvester the Cat."

"Charlie! Imagine trying to pack gifts for ten or twelve different house-holds."

"At least his damned kvass didn't explode."

As they ate, Volodya sauntered in wearing yesterday's slacks and a gray drip-dry shirt stamped with yellow fleurs-de-lis. His wet hair glistened. When he sat down, Lydia praised her scroll and Riddle thanked him for the new issue of *Raskolnikov*.

"No finer Russian version of your story can ever exist," Volodya said. "Unless you learn Russian and do your own translation."

Bullshit, thought Riddle, but the flattery softened him. After breakfast, he drove Volodya seventeen miles up the highway to Tocqueville. The cin-derblock bus station, between a shabby body shop and a ghetto of tin storage units, did not appear to demoralize Volodya, who took in every detail with the jaded nonchalance of someone familiar with squalor. Riddle explained that the bus business had fallen on hard times. Most Americans preferred to drive or fly.

"Of course," Volodya said.

Riddle bought his ticket and drove him to the Kroger on Commerce. Army-green Dumpsters bracketed the store, swirls of motor oil shone in the curbside rainwater, and a seagull hovered over a blowing snack wrapper before veering off and alighting on a cart-return corral. The seagull astonished Riddle. Tocqueville lay hundreds of miles from any ocean, over twenty from West Point Lake or the Chattahoochee River.

Volodya nodded at the seagull. "It does not belong here either, eh?"

They prowled the supermarket's hallucination-bright aisles. Volodya, who must have shopped with Baywater's chauffeur in Miami, did not *ooh* and *ah*, but made note of everything—cans of mandarin oranges, cartons of lime sherbet, frozen-enchilada dinners, a virtual armory of shieldlike pizza pans. Following Lydia's list, Riddle picked up bread, chocolate chips, sugar, butter, flour, and apples.

"Do you Rooskies still stand in line for toilet paper?" he needled Volodya.

Volodya thought for a moment. "Only post-Soviet *apparatchiki* use it anymore, so spiritual have our people become."

Clever, Riddle thought. Irritated, he took his items to an open express lane, which *did* excite Volodya. In Moscow, the number of items one wished to buy had no relation to the time one stood in line. Volodya thought this express-lane idea "brilliant." A plump but pretty checker bagged Riddle's purchases. She listened to Volodya's every word, tugging her green smock down on one side to disguise a meaty hip.

Riddle turned to Volodya. "I almost forgot. Did *you* want anything?"

"These." Some cigarettes in an impulse rack. "*Fewer Additives, More Flavors.*"

"That's bilge, Volodya. Egregious Madison Avenue hype." If Riddle bought him cigarettes, Lydia would look at him as if he had kneecapped a paraplegic. Undismayed, Volodya handed the pack to the checker.

"Hello," she said softly. "You really from Roosha?"

"Of course." Volodya stared hard at the young woman, who kept her head down while scanning the cigarettes. "Here." He took his sunglasses from his shirt pocket and handed them to her. "A token of remembrance." The checker, blushing, accepted them. She had an improbable crush on Volodya, and Volodya obviously thought that all young American women regarded frail Russian men as rock stars.

In the parking lot, Riddle demanded, "What was *that* all about?"

"I don't understand."

"Do you miss your wife so much?"

"No. I have a strong—what do you call it?—prejudgeness against fat people."

"*Prejudice?*"

"Yes. Standing in line, I wondered if American food stores hire fat persons, do its liquor stores hire alcoholics? This thought—this *prejudice*—shamed me."

"So you gave her your sunglasses *out of guilt.*"

"Ah. You understand."

"No. No, I don't"

Volodya rubbed his shoe over some oil on the asphalt. "I compared that young woman to Lydia. In America, I've seen no woman more beautiful than your wife, Charlie. I speak even more of her temper than of her body."

Dumbfounded, Riddle walked briskly toward the Pinto wagon.

"Wait," Volodya called. "I think you have forgotten the bananas."

Riddle halted and looked into his bag. He *had* forgotten the bananas, the first item on Lydia's list. He pivoted, marched up to Volodya, and slammed the plastic bag into his gut. "Get in the car. I'll buy the bananas. You can't give that moony checker your shirt if you succumb to another sudden pang of guilt."

Back in the store, Riddle headed for the produce. Clumped like giant brown slugs, the bananas festered on two upturned harvest baskets. He had never seen uglier bananas. Their putrid sweetness embalmed the air. He pulled out the blackest-skinned bunch and carried it up front to the same checker.

"Eieuuu," she said. "You sure you want those?"

"Indeed I am."

"Take them. I couldn't possibly charge you."

Riddle exited before a manager could veto her generosity.

A scrawny seagull perched on the Pinto's hood, staring through the windshield at Volodya, who stared back at it from the shotgun seat. Riddle lifted the grocery sack and yelled, "Beat it!" The seagull spiraled off over the parking lot, and Riddle jumped in to scold Volodya for not chasing it off himself.

"You can't get their mulberry-colored shit off the metal," he said. "Not even with a chisel."

"Sorry," said Volodya, smiling cryptically. "We were having a talk."

Right, thought Riddle. In English, Russian, or Seagull? He maneuvered out of the lot and gunned for the highway, where they cruised toward Mountboro in a silence that Riddle thought awkward, even though he refused to break it. At length, Volodya lifted the bag of bananas and sniffed it. Then he extracted the bunch and held it like a decomposing chandelier, a dispenser of rot rather than light.

"These are the bananas?"

"Sure. Have one."

"They don't look like bananas."

"No? What do they look like?"

Volodya studied the obscene drupes. "Big curved cigars."

"Well, feel free to have a smoke."

Less than halfway home, Riddle repented of his surliness. If they continued on to Mountboro, Lydia would not be there to greet them. Every Friday morning, she took a group of preschoolers to an area nursing home to sing for the residents.

"We've got time," Riddle said. "Care to do some sight-seeing?"

"Please," Volodya said.

At the next turnoff, Riddle yanked the Pinto onto a road whose sign a garland of kudzu obscured. Which road was it? Smoky Road? Lickskillet? He had no idea. Despite two decades in Lydia's hometown, he still hadn't explored all its surrounding countryside. Well, he and Volodya could *both* do some sightseeing. The Pinto rattled along the narrow road—past hollows, clearings, groves, dry inlets, homesteads. Sunlight fell like a shifting yellow wave on the asphalt, and the station wagon tilted and swung. Volodya looked at everything. Even without a memo pad in his lap, he seemed to be jotting down all that he observed, and Riddle thought, *Good.*

Abruptly, the road ran out at a glade of sycamores and red oaks. A shotgun church with a lopsided steeple and a crumbling porch huddled in this glade. Worshippers had to park in the mulch under the trees or at the edges of the dead-end semicircle fronting the churchyard. On a mound to Riddle's left squatted a yellow-plastic sign, its black plastic letters trumpeting SCEPTER-OUT-OF-ISRAEL TABERNACLE. It amazed Riddle that every word on the sign was spelled correctly. A message in smaller letters floated beneath this title, but the Pinto bumped past before he could read it. "Crap."

He killed the engine. "We've dead-ended. I thought this road would take us somewhere."

"Please. Recall Abuladze's *Repentance*. *'What good is a road that doesn't lead to a church?'* And this church is very pretty."

"I've never seen *Repentance*," Riddle told Volodya. "How could I *recall* it?"

"Probably you couldn't."

The light coming through the oak and sycamore trees projected shifting puzzle pieces onto both men's faces. There was only one way to go—back to the highway and south to Mountboro. Riddle cranked the Pinto's engine and turned it around. Passing the signboard again, he decoded the message under the church's name: *Where Will You Spend Eternity — Smoking or Nonsmoking?* Volodya read this question and guffawed. For the rest of their drive, he talked without letup, mostly about his plans to agent Riddle's work in Russia and to make Riddle a household word among the persecuted but discriminating intelligentsia.

Not long after Lydia got home, a chill blue rain began to fall, darkening the town and attaching veils of water to every eave. Lydia suggested that Riddle retreat upstairs to write until dinner. "Go ahead. Volodya won't melt without your attentions."

"*Man serves the family as head, but woman as the neck*," Volodya told Riddle. "*As the neck turns, so turns the head.* Obey your wife."

"Listen," Lydia said. "Volodya's been eyeing your video collection. A couple of movies will keep him happy until we eat."

"Okay!" Volodya grinned like a decapitated possum.

Riddle helped him select a pair of competent film noirs, both from the late 1940s, and showed him how to work the tape player. Then, upstairs in his office, he sat idly as rain bludgeoned the shingles on the porch roof. Twice his desk telephone rang. Lydia answered it downstairs, but Riddle, listening in, heard two members of their study group say that the weather made it impossible for them to come this evening. How could he work? He *couldn't* work. He needed to review this evening's New Testament lesson and crib some insights from a commentary. The members who had just cancelled took up most of their meetings' conversational slack, and he could hardly expect the Parrishes, or Ron Boutwell, or twenty-year-old Kristal Wellborn, who came only because she worshipped Lydia, to jump in and help him out.

At dinner, Volodya burbled about the videos he'd seen: a kinky Richard Widmark thriller, *Kiss of Death*, and an early Burt Lancaster film, *The Killers*. Such artistry! Such anxiety! Such camera work! Such unsettling background music! The noisy downpour had only heightened his appreciation of these "masterpieces."

At twenty till seven, even before they'd finished eating, Ron Boutwell, a heavyset African-American computer programmer, tramped in with a Tupperware bowl of melon balls that he had prepared himself. (The melon balls looked bruised and deflated.) Riddle introduced Volodya to Ron and then drew Volodya aside to assure him that neither he nor Lydia would take it amiss if Volodya chose to opt out of their Bible study.

"Oh, no. I'll do as my hosts do." He lifted a palm-sized recording device. "Would you object if I taped the meeting?"

"What for?" Riddle asked.

"As a remembrance. And so that Olga may hear and study her English."

The Parrishes arrived. Introducing them to Volodya, Riddle noted how much they resembled clean-cut parents in an Eisenhower-era TV sitcom. Kristal Wellborn arrived. She sported white eye shadow, a short beige corduroy chemise, and pantyhose the color of kaolin. Volodya kissed her hand, a startling gallantry that made her giggle.

After dessert in the kitchen, the group repaired to the parlor and circled chairs on the area rug in front of the TV. Volodya turned on his tape recorder, which whirred faintly throughout the study. This evening the group focused on the eleventh chapter of the Letter to the Hebrews, and Riddle asked everyone to name the chapter's key verse and to explain his or her reasons for selecting it.

Sheila Parrish spoke up: "The sixth verse: *'But without faith no one may know God.'* Because it's true, Charlie, it's just *so* true."

"Amen," said Kristal Wellborn. "Amen."

Volodya held his small recorder toward Sheila. "But how may a person lacking faith acquire it, Mrs. Parrish? Especially if it must come as a gift?" Sheila and her husband Nick regarded him as if they had never before imagined such a puzzler, and Riddle wished that he could demanifest their Russian guest—indeed, everyone present but Lydia—with a finger snap. The silence in the book-stuffed room lengthened.

"Visit the sick," Lydia told Volodya. "Wash the feet of the homeless."

"Gross!" said Kristal. A typical bit of Wellborn exegesis.

Riddle led everyone through the roll call of faith heroes clotting the remainder of the chapter: Abraham, Sarah, Isaac, Jacob, and so on. An odd queasiness—a familiar lightheadedness—seized him. Maybe some of Ron's melon balls had fermented. The blurry ache in his gut sharpened, but he finished his survey by croaking *"that only with us should they reach perfection."*

Perfection.

In his sudden illness, Riddle had reached a perfect sort of agony, but he hid it—heroically, he hoped—as inimical to their study. "And what does that mean, everybody? *That only with us should they reach perfection?"*

Ron shifted his middle-linebacker haunches. "That Old and New Testament people get blended in Christ, like in a beautiful omelet."

The Parrishes considered this interpretation. Kristal crossed her legs, flashing a crescent of stockinged thigh. Riddle's agony intensified.

Volodya leaned forward. "I agree with Ron. The end of this letter reminds me of the end of a fine old science-fiction novel. The essence of humanity—a glowing stream of souls—merges in outer space with the souls of other God-tending species."

"*Childhood's End*," Ron said. "Great book."

"Yes," Volodya said. "A great sky storm occurs when the souls merge. But in no other way can humankind evolve beyond itself to . . . to perfection."

Nick folded his arms. "I don't buy that. Evolution's a secular-humanist doctrine. It's counter-Biblical."

Riddle tumbled from his chair. The desolating pain in his gut made him fear that he was dying. He sucked back his tongue and curled up like a frying sausage link. Kristal cried, *"Ohmygod, ohmygod."* Lydia knelt beside him, smoothing his hair and whispering, *"Easy, Charlie."* His bodily pain diffused and vanished, but anguish and something like heartbreak kept him pinned to the floor. Ron said, *"Dial nine-one-one."* Nick offered to drive him to the emergency room in Tocqueville. Volodya—at long last—switched off his tape recorder. With Lydia's help, Riddle unkinked and struggled upright. Waves of relief and chagrin combed over him. His lips felt as cold as if a malign demon had rubbed them with a blade of dry ice. Nick asked, *"Hey, man, what happened?"*

"A stitch in my side from sitting so long. If I could just lie down—"

The home-fellowship group broke up. Its members departed. Lydia walked Riddle upstairs to their bedroom, helped him undress, and tucked him in like a feverish child. The scroll of the silly cartoon cat that Volodya had given her hung on their wall over the light switch. Riddle drifted off while staring at it.

He woke up to find the other half of the bed empty and the digital readout on the clock radio glowing *11:40*. Lydia seldom retired later than eleven and usually far earlier. Only housework kept her up till midnight, and tomorrow, Saturday, held nothing more eventful than Volodya's departure by bus. Riddle slipped on his pants and tiptoed down the stairs barefoot. In the dark foyer, he peered through the dining room at the closed kitchen door. Anxiety-ridden, he let himself out the front door, eased down the steps under a sky roiling with moonlit clouds, and minced through the wet grass on the south side of the house. The kitchen porch creaked when he pulled himself up on it to peer through the sweaty window of the Dutch door. Lydia and Volodya sat nose to nose at the table. Lowball glasses shone at their elbows. A trencher of banana bread steamed between them. Riddle hit his forehead on the glass, Volodya glanced up at him, Riddle ducked, footsteps sounded. Thinking his sheepishness absurd, Riddle stood again.

The door flew open. Volodya struck him in the heart with his open hand. Riddle sprawled backward onto the grass. His head bounced, a shower of sparks short-circuited his consciousness, night slammed down.

A sweet-sharp smell. A change in posture from horizontal to upright. Riddle was sitting at the kitchen table staring into a bread-stuffed jar.

"Charlie, what were you *doing*?"

"Forgive me," Volodya said. "I thought you were a burglar." He grimaced and accidentally sloshed the contents of the jar.

"What's that . . . *smell*?" Riddle said.

"My kvass. It's good. Lydia and I were sipping it with her lovely bread."

Riddle clutched his temples. Lydia pulled his hands down and told him *not* to go back to sleep. If he did, he might drift into a coma. He needed to sit up—with Volodya and her, if Volodya didn't mind—for at least another hour.

"I don't mind," Volodya said. "To go to bed here is to miss something, maybe."

"Eat some banana bread," Lydia told Riddle.

"And try some kvass," Volodya said. "It tastes better than it smells."

Still groggy, still befuddled, Riddle ate and drank to humor them.

The next day, he drove Volodya to the bus station, where the Russian clutched not only his cardboard suitcase but also a paper bag full of banana bread. A handler took the suitcase and pushed it into a wide bin under the fume-blackened skirts of the bus, which chuffed like a locomotive in its dock. Volodya ground a cigarette underfoot and boarded it. Midway up the steps, he turned and looked down on Riddle. "Do you know the saying, *In words a cathedral organ, in deeds a kopeck whistle*?"

"No," said Riddle, squinting up.

"For you and Lydia, I must change it: *'In deeds a symphony orchestra,'* I would say." He saluted and vanished into the bus's maw.

The bus pulled out, backfiring. Oily billows of smoke burst from its tail-pipe. The billows spread across the road between the auto body shop and a row of shaggy mimosa trees, staining the day and drifting back toward the station like a judgment. Most of those who had come to see off the bus's passengers retreated, but Riddle let the smoke lap and cloak him. His eyes and nostrils burned. Then the smoke tattered and curled away. With a sudden clairvoyance, Riddle saw Volodya arriving in Nashville—and in every other town along the Greyhound's route—and stepping down from his bus like a missionary, a secret agent of a credo that he did not even profess.

Stung, Riddle fished out a handkerchief and wiped it angrily at the fiery grit in his eyes.

DOGGEDLY
WOOING
MADONNA

Dear

   Ms.

     Ciccone,

It being Tuesday and my after-hour remedial work here at St. Elmo's some differential equations (at which I stink), I did a mental checkout and decided to propose to you. My name is Prentice Metcalf, so some of the kids call me Prentz. What a yoking, Lady M and Prentz.

You Jane, so to speak, and me Tarzan.

As I started to write you, Barb Trager yanked me out of my resolve by virtue of her looks, and by their vice as well, I guess. She trailed a smell prettier than most, here in Father Billy Jay's mobile unit, and, in a series of provocative steps, hip-shot herself from desk to desk seeking help or dishing the biz.

But Barb dates Eddie Sebeok, captain of St. Elmo's head-to-head academic squad, and I didn't want to snake the only whiz in school to nail at the buzzer, for an upset win, a 250-point bonus question, even had I the charisma to snake her—which, I fear, Barb's old-fashioned loyalty to Ed renders, well, highly unlikely.

So, Ms. C., I've picked not Barb, but you, the Material Girl, to propose to. As I write, at the tag end of November, you're just a year shy of two decades older than me, but so what? Barb's out of the question.

So, like a virgin, that leaves *you*: a long-in-the-tooth, rap-out-the-truth Italian and French-Canadian RC girl. Divorced. From that spacey surfer in *Fast Times at Ridgemont High*, Mr. Penn. Sullied by the breakup, the nasty-mouth, the conversion of your undies, and others', into gone-ballistic evening wear. Performance art for the MTV set. Some'd say such guff—but not me, who *liked* the way you dissed Kevin Costner with that gag-me retch. And the way you posed in the total crinkle-butt for a book called *S*x* that I couldn't afford and still haven't even seen. When Marilyn stood over the grate in that old flick of hers, her skirts blew up. Yours, I take it, blew right off. But did you give an upside-down Mohawk clip how far you'd spook the boojies? No. (Ding.) (Dang.) (Wow.)

I see you as the epitome of experience, wealth, and heroic unflappableness. Your entire evidentiary body, your corpus delectable and multimediate, tells me so . . . even if I'm your opposite in nearly every existential way.

I don't know jack, unless it's book—or maybe cable-borne. I do have a way with words, but not with VCRs, cars, can openers, babies, firearms, T-squares, hypotenuses, unputtied windows, shotgunned egrets, sleeping-bag zippers, or pruning shears. My dad never has any money, and even though I put the crispy jackets on the chicken at our own Finger Lickin Fried (my one nonliterary skill), neither do I. And, up against adversity, I flap like a chicken in the grasp of a would-be FLF neck-wringer.

In my threadbare Sunday threads, though, I'm nigh on to presentable.

Nearlybout suave.

So will you marry me, Madonna Louise Veronica Ciccone?

Rest easy on this point: I don't want a pfennig of your pfilthy lucre. I will draft to your specifications, not merely sign, a prenuptial agreement ceding all my most-beloved earthly property—my Button Fly 501 Blues, a navy and scarlet long-sleeve shirt from Structure, my Kenny G *Breathless* tape, a cheesy plastic softball trophy, a dog-eared set of Ray Bradbury paperbacks (one of which cost 35¢, new) that Aunt Vi gave my mother, and so on—to you, Ms. Ciccone, in the likely event that I piss you off and our marriage collapses . . . as so many showbiz/commoner hitch-ups seem prone to do. I don't want your money, your fame, or the right to bask in its backwash. And I don't even mount this proposal assuming that mounting you, or maybe the reverse, on our sweaty yabba-dabba moneyhoon will lift me to—install me in—Nerd Nirvana. Because, no offense, I don't find you all that s*xy, my taste in female beauty running, Barb Trager aside, more to the urchinesque: Winona Ryder, like.

So, you must be wondering, what prompts me to propose? Why should you agree to wed a pimply nobody who doesn't even own one Madonna CD, video, or gilt designer condom? Sticky question, that.

A: Because, better than any other guy you've bumped into yet (even Snowman Sean), I will cherish, validate, esteem, and love you for yourself—

the inside person out of which all your public/private selves take form. And I ask in return only this: the same. No more, no less: this for that, tit for tat, a reciprocal reciprocity.

Another question you may have is, How will this ever work, this union of Bengal tigress and scrinch-eyed alley cat? Can't work. Won't work. Sridiculous. Yes, except that I stand as tall as you do, with pelage as fine, even if I growl on paper or computer screen while you do so right out in public. So if your opposite, I'm also your equal. Deferential, though; ever mindful of my youngness and puerility.

Q: Will you marry me? (No joke. No jive.)

Say yes.

Answer me yes oh say yes you will say Yes.

I send you this proposal seven times—in care of your record company, in care of a fellow at the Atlanta newspapers, in care of a geek who claims he's met you, in care of New Yawk Paris LA and Detroit. In care of my caring.

Say Yes.

Doggedly and sempiternally yours,
Prentice (Prentz) Metcalf

Playing study-hall monitor, Father Billy Jay sits up front carving a cantaloupe into a jack-o'-lantern, not quite for Halloween, which has fled, or for Christmas, which hasn't come yet, but to spook us stupes with fruitful visions of the sempiternally damned.

Skag Patton and Joy Roving play video poker by the duct-taped panel on the eastern wall. Everybody else whistles the Hallelujah chorus with long breaks between notes. (You have to be a savvy old hand hereabouts or a freak with a jammed internal chronology to recognize it. Me, I'm the former. I exult on each note and finish my letter at a triumphantly belated *–JAH!)*

Mrs. Hewitt wanders over and puts her hand on my shoulder. She has to baby-sit us, as Father Billy Jay's aide, as part of a practicum or something leading to a degree in counseling from our community college. She's got almost ten more years on her than my own mother does, but tunes in better than most of the school's salaried schleps, including the melon sculptor up front. She's really just off-beautiful, for a grownup on the downhill skids to fifty.

Prentice, she sez, you should be doing math. What's that—a letter?

I hand it up to her. When she tilts her head, I nod *Go on* and she lays it back down and reads through it, her fuzzy cardigan buffing my ear.

You want to marry Madonna?

Silence from this shrewd dude.

Come on.

Yessum. I really do.

And you plan to send this proposal to the object of your, ah, affections?

Lust.

That's not what you say here. You claim the chastest sort of devotion—spiritual, almost.

Yeah.

"Doggedly and sempiternally yours"? You think that's going to woo her, kiddo?

Sure. Of course.

Well. Your prose may impress her, if she reads it, but don't get your hopes up. This *won't* do what you want it to.

Yeah? What's wrong with it?

There's nothing about *you* per se—except you can write, which the letter itself more or less proves.

There's a lot about me, if you read it close.

Okay. You're sixteen, lousy in math, a drudge for Finger Lickin Fried, generous but not rich. And so on.

A lot. More than that.

Tell her about your mother. And more about your dad.

Why?

It'll steer her to Yes.

Bullcrap.

If you do it, I'll mail it for you. And your follow-up letter. Cross my heart. Tomorrow.

Fine. Tomorrow. There's plenty of time.

How do you know? Tomorrow she could run off and marry some hot-shot celeb.

Who?

I don't know. Clinton's lawyer. That Stipe guy in R.E.M. Sean Penn again.

Then even your first letter'd be too late, wouldn't it? So pen a follow-up. Two letters are better than one.

She tweaks my rat-tail, which I don't mind, and takes up my letter like it's the Declaration of Independence—to post to Ms. Ciccone, maybe with a drop of sealing wax (like Madonna's own facial mole) on the overflap. Then she moves to Joy and Skag, to unplug them and cram their noses back into a social studies lesson.

Get to work, she sez. Now. While you still have the scent of cantaloupe to inspire you.

Later, before Dad gets home from his eight-to-fiver at the metalworks, I mop the kitchen and, as the Lysol evaporates, sit down to write my follow-up:

Dear M:

A woman I trust—an advisor, a counselor, a confidante—urges me to say more about my family. Okay. I have one parent at home, Dad, and no sibs to fuss over or with.

Dad shapes wrought iron, wrighting raw metallic wrongs into benches, balcony rails, and spiral staircases, like superbig helixes—helices?—of petrified DNA. He wants me to have the house clean when he gets home, from tub to topmold. So if you marry me, you'll have a dab hand at many domestic drudgeries, even window washing. I don't, like some homemakers, pull the blinds and strip to my Ichabodish self to do these swabbings, but I would, if you wanted me to—either one, or both.

Theoretically, you see, Dad wants the house clean for his "dates." Practically speaking, he doesn't have any. He gets home from the metalworks, grabs his gear, and beats it over to the health club, where he works out a couple hours and takes a sauna. Then he hits the sports bar where they keep the TVs tuned to a cable station with girls in Spandex (shades of the Blonde Ambition tour) pumping aerobically, elbows out, elbows in, to like "Into the Groove" or "Express Yourself" and loads up big-time on Heineken Dark, to make up for fluids lost weight-lifting and sweltering in a hot-rock ripple bath. He maybe eats a scrambled dog.

He gets home, or doesn't, around the bong of midnight, now totally pugnacious. He checks out the house for dust on the mantels, grime on the bathroom grout, legs-up roaches under the sink. Finding a few, he yanks me from my sleep (less gently than Barb Trager interrupts my fugues) and dances me around like a slam-pit raver. I have scars to prove it, this deep red one inflicted after an inquiry from a DFACS lady.

I don't fight back. I stand as tall as my dad, but weigh forty pounds less. If my story bestirs you to pity, fold it five ways and you-know. Half the kids I hang with get slapped or catch the daily dis lip. Should you want to spend a little sympathy on me, lay it on the fact that my mama left Dad to join the Army. She trained at Fort Benning then whirled away with the first batch of troops ordered from Fort Stuart to Operation Desert Shield. Today, Uncle Sugar has the former Mrs. Metcalf at a supply unit in Germany, where she keeps folks supplied. She writes me a letter every month or so, none as hot or newsy as mine to you. So, Ms. Ciccone, even though my mama didn't die when I was l'il, like yours did, I *feel your pain.*

Ow. All this stuff has made me remember something: I have a skill: I can wield a camcorder. You know, in *Truth or Dare* where Warren Beatty tells this guy examining your throat, "She doesn't want to live off-camera much less talk [there]"? If we hitch, I promise to record our every waking moment, except for time to rest up from lens toting and to stand down from reality to become our observer/historian.

My videos, of course, will skew the reality under scrutiny, but I offer this praise: It appears to me, from research, that you sabotage the Heisenberg Uncertainty Principle by being the same in view (maybe) as out of it. If we hitch, I'll learn, during camcorder breaks, if this particular praise should stand or topple.

Another thing: You have a nastymouth. If we hitch, please watch it. Or would you, for reasons only God Herself savvies, regard heeding *this* request as "compromising [your] artistic integrity"? Dogs sniff one another's butts and wallow in nightsoil, but you descend from a long line of human beings, including an angelic mother who winces every time you grab your private self pubically [sick] or rudely blurt some smart-alicia Anglo-Saxon slang. Hey. Just because I've got standards, don't call me bluenose or suppose I'd brown-nose by compromising my integrity. Listen:

> *"To fart, to fart, 'tis no disgrace,*
> *For it gives the body ease.*
> *It warms the blankets on cold winter nights*
> *And suffocates all the fleas."*

Now *that's* cute. But sometimes your in-the-face vulgarity siphons away some of your glamour, like a black hole funneling light into its anal-retentive sump.

Be imaginative, unpredictable, and strong, sure—but, Jesus, galchick, give over the nastymouth when its sole point is to make innocents uneasy, or to discombobulate your daddy, who seems like an okay guy, or to prove you're on top of the whole glitterati crop. Show some class. On the other hand, don't change just for me. I don't know jack, even if I can run a camcorder. It's just that you cuss like *my* dad, a bad-smelling, stuck-up creep, and I sorta wish you didn't.

What's wrong with saying a show's "neat"? I mean, Costner, observing the gentleman's code, didn't *slam* your performance. What would you have done if he'd said "Bitchin'"? Or "Far out"? Or "Groovy"? Or "On the entertainment Richter scale, a booty-shakin 9.8"? Or "Hey, you peroxided hank, you really made the groundlings squirm tonight, baby"? Would you have liked it a whole lot more if he'd slapped you around and outed a Beretta when your bodyguards moved in?

I guess what I'm saying is, The world confuses me. So do you. Which is partly why I admire you and promise to cherish, validate, esteem, and love you for yourself. Sometimes love, I think, can shunt confusion onto a sidetrack so damned long it rusts into a mellow acceptance of all the crap around us. Maybe.

So: answer in the affirmative say you will say yes my sweet Prentz baby Yes.

Doggedly if perplexedly yours,
Prentice

Mrs. Hewitt reads my follow-up, her graceful olive hands on my shoulders.

Oh my.

What?

First, you praised her for doing a gag-retch when Costner called her show neat. Here you scold her for it.

Yeah?

Do you admire what you inwardly disapprove of? Or inwardly disapprove of what you admire?

Look, I *confess* to her I'm confused. I tell her so.

Do you really think a woman who swears like a stevedore, and doesn't give a see-through fig leaf if you like it, will appreciate your, uh, snippy self-righteousness?

"Papa Don't Preach"?

Exactly.

Maybe not. You mail my other letter?

Of course.

Mail this one too.

After Mrs. Hewitt takes it, Barb Trager bumps into her. Sorry, Barb sez. Saw your little powwow. Couldn't help wondering about it.

Meaning? Mrs. Hewitt sez.

Prentz wants Madonna to marry him? He's written her like a *proposal*?

Barbara, it's none of your concern.

Well, I think it's . . . neat, your helping him. I mean, I thought once about sending Christian Slater a letter, with like a picture of me in it, but—

A Polaroid! yells Skag Patton. A shot that didn't have to make it through Kodak's developing rooms!

Everyone but Mrs. Hewitt and Father Billy Jay laughs, even Barb herself.

Enough! Father Billy Jay barks. If you all don't start doing your work, I'm going to keep everybody here another half-hour.

Yeah. Like he enjoys alternative St. Elmo's as much as the inmates do.

A bad week. I scald my elbow at Finger Lickin Fried. Dad doesn't come home Thursday night. When he does get home, he drags me from bed, knocks me into the water heater, makes me fix him coffee, a cheese omelet with taters, onions, and Worcestershire sauce, and a pitcher of OJ. Bleary-eyed, he scoffs and slurps. I read the paper. A blurb in Peach Buzz sez Madonna's putting the move on a 15-year-old boy, a football jock and model, spending big bucks on him in tony department stores.

The guy's mom, Peach Buzz sez, "is not amused."

Much later, in remedial, Mrs. Hewitt doesn't show. Father Billy Jay, answering a question from Gabe Wardlaw, sez her husband had a stroke or something. Mrs. Hewitt is at his bedside on the ICU floor at St. Francis.

A teacher peeks in and sez, Mr. Hewitt just died.

Skag Patton stands up and, with Father B. J.'s okay, leads us in prayer. Nobody can do any work, though, with the result that the father turns us out twenty minutes early. I never knew Mr. Hewitt. I feel no grief for him, only over the hurricane debris that will blow through Mrs. Hewitt's heart now that he's bought it.

Outside, it's raining. I walk along the sidewalk watching gravel float up in its cracks and pecan leaves stick to it like ragged Day-Glo decals. In her rain slicker, Joy Roving reaches out and wetly brushes my arm.

Mrs. Hewitt'll be okay, Prentz. She's a counselor. She can handle bad shit.

Like she's buried three husbands already?

That's not what I meant. You're—

I hustle on, leaving Joy there rain-soaked and pissed.

Dad takes the Dodge Dakota to Eufala for the weekend, to do some camping and fishing. In Saturday's paper, Peach Buzz reports that the tabloid rumors about Madonna's 15-year-old boyfriend have all the truth, thank God, of a UFO sighting. First bright spot in my week. Even if the kid sez he only talked to Madonna like twice real briefly and she struck him as a "deeply sad soul."

Poor little rich girl; poor little *muchacha rica*.

¿Quien es esta niña?

I spend my weekend studying math or writing my Chosen One fresh letters of proposal. Each is a *cri de coeur* of heartfelt regard.

Also, at a nearby pharmacy, I pay for a card for Mrs. Hewitt. I take it home, write a message, sign it, and carry it to a mailbox for pickup and delivery. Nobody close to me has died yet, but, hey, I *know* bereavement. It kicks you then gradually lets your air out then aches in you like some sort of internal wind- or sunburn. You can't reach it to coat with lotion. Finally it stiffens into a prickly underrind.

Maybe.

On Sunday evening, after I've put in a 7-hour shift at Finger Lickin Fried, my dad drifts in smelling like mildewed khaki, live bait, and scraped fish scales. He toasts me with a can of Schlitz and sits down without showering to watch Jessica Angela Fletcher Lansbury unscramble a homicide.

A week goes by. Two. Three. I pepper Ms. Ciccone with six-page proposals, all honorable, all sincere. She never replies, but she's only a few hundred miles cattywampus to me in decadent Gotham.

She's not such a big-deal singer/dancer/actress/mediaqueen after all.

Mrs. Hewitt returns in late January. I don't see her much because I've hoisted myself by my loafer tassels out of remedial. Anyway, she still has this odd off-beautiful look, bleakly undercut, like the sandman's daubed her eyeballs with glue, or held a blow dryer to her hair for weeks on end, or hung up all her dresses on crooked hangers. (Or all of the above.) Plus, the light under her skin has faded; her throat has a sorrowful slack.

I go to her one Thursday in the cafeteria. Sorry bout your husband, Mrs. Hewitt.

Thanks, Prentice. Your card was sweet. It helped.

Well, you know, good.

Still wooing your Material Girl?

But I don't want to talk about that, it embarrasses me more than death-gab. News of my fixation has swept St. Elmo's, and I can't walk twelve feet without catching a rib. (On my locker one day, I find this grease-pencil message: MADONNA AND PRENTZ, SUPERDUMB DUO.) So I edge away to an empty table next to the Jesus mural over by the trophy cases.

Prentice Metcalf! a female voice cries from the counter at Freddy Stetka's Finger Lickin Fried. *Hey, my Prentz, where the fuckinhell are you?*

What now? Thelma Brown sez.

I peek through the pass-through over our boiling chicken dip and spy Madonna herself in leopard-spotted Spandex pants and a quilted silver jacket with a fur-lined hood! She stands on the counter's patron side, squinting through mirror lenses tinted gunmetal blue and tapping one gold ballet slipper. Somebody—Gabe Wardlaw? A bodyguard?—aims a camcorder at me, catching my amazement for posterity.

At the curb, beyond the speckled plate-glass, a limo as long as Italy. White. Sleek. Shimmery. It shines right next to a dilapidated, low-slung Impala and a jacked-up 4-by-4 pickup with a gleaming chrome rollbar.

Come out, my Prentz! Come out!

Git yosef on out there, Thelma sez. But don't you dare run off on us, neither.

I wipe my hands on a towel and go out front.

Gabe Wardlaw, who has just taped St. Elmo's cagers against the boys from Pacelli, still has his camcorder. Ms. Ciccone's bodyguards, meanwhile, have sidled into FLF's boxy dining room to check it out and smash any paparazzi about to exploit their boss's presence in Mountboro.

You Prentice Metcalf? she sez. The self-styled Prentz. My dogged long-distance wooer.

It puts my hackles up to hear her talk—not from the abrupt February out-of-the-chill thrill of it, but instead from weird deep-dish anger that this mythical person has invaded my place of employment. I knock Gabe's camcorder off his shoulder and square up like John Garfield in *Body and Soul*. Gabe tries to hit me in the nose, but one of my beloved's jumpsuited goons puts him in a half nelson and wrestles him outside. A second fellow in a lavender nylon jumpsuit, with an ivory yoke and green piping down the pants, retrieves the camcorder, which still works, and resumes Gabe's taping.

You write a real kick-ass letter, Mr. Metcalf.

What're you doing here?

She shrugs and rubbernecks. Checking out the goods in your stinkin' little meat market. I thought you wanted to marry me. A lot.

I didn't ask you to come *here*.

She's passing through, sez the camcorder guy. To a concert down in Albany.

You've proposed in about 12 encyclopedia volumes' worth of letters. Now tell me in 25 words or less why I should favor you with my fuckin hand.

I'd like to kick her in the shin, but I don't. To cherish, validate, esteem, and love you. Just for yourself.

Dear God, he's got it by rote. Instead of for what? My ass? My limo?

Yeah. For yourself. The quintessential you under the glamdazzle and crap.

Spare me, boy. The real me percolates up into the stuff you think I'm under.

I have no answer for that. Madonna's bodyguards—I count 5, including the fella who just bounced Gabe—have emptied FLF's dining room of customers, by reimbursing them for their chicken plates and urging them outside into the neon mizzle. When the gawkers have gone, the camcorder guy pushes me into the dining room, over to a corner table. Madonna sits there too, and the camcorder guy steps back to record the tag end of our tryst.

No, she sez. I won't marry you.

Who ast you? I'd like to say, but I've asked her maybe a trillion vermilion times, in writing, and she's got the goods somewhere: blackmail bait.

Now don't go jut-jawed and bug-eyed on me, my sweet Prentz, *s'il vous plait*, sez the Mother of Od.

You don't belong here. This is where *I* work. This screws up Thelma and Lucy George, it overloads 'em bad.

You write a fuckin' lot sweeter than you talk. She lights a cigarette, scissors her legs, puffs some smoke. Maybe you write a better game than you play.

You don't own this place. You can't just herd people out. You can't just impose yourself like this.

Au contraire. But it's okay if the intrusion's epistolary, right? E-piss-o-lary.

What do you want? If she has no plans to marry me, why has she swung through our backwater little Mountboro at all?

I want to adopt you.

I've got parents already.

Yeah? Where's your mother? Germany, right? A fraulein in khaki and tarnished brass?

Polished brass. Don't get on her case.

"Cherish, validate, esteem, and love." Oh, yeah. Truth or dare, boy-o?

That rocks me back. I gape dry-mouthed.

Come on: truth or dare?

Truth, I say.

You don't love me. Even a prima Madonna like me can figure that. So. Do you *like* me?

Sure, I blurt. Yeah.

My God. She drops her head, shakes it, giggles. What a lying little prick you are.

My anger has run out. She has me pegged: I don't even like her. A blush climbs my throat and face like mercury climbing a thermometer.

Okay, Eric, she tells the camcorder guy. We're out of this stupid pit stop of a town. She stands, drops her cig, stubs it with a slippered toe, crosses toward the counter, looks back over her shoulder. Keep writing, Prentice Metcalf. Just never deign to make a public appearance.

The white limo backs from Finger Lickin Fried's lot onto Highway 27, and the only woman I've ever asked to marry me vanishes in a blur of taillights and radiant rain.

When Gabe Wardlaw reenters, he's carrying his camcorder. He pokes it right in my blotchy face.

Well, Metcalf, he sez. I take it you blew it.

Later, at home, my dad passed out on the living-room sofa, I round up notebook, paper, a pen, one self-adhesive U.S. postal stamp, and an envelope. I write:

Dear Whitney,

I think about this salutation to another media superstar, then cross it out, and start again:

Dear Mrs. Hewitt,

Uh-oh. I'd have to move away to make our new relationship go, and how many kids have even celebrated long-distance paramours spawned via mere pen and ink? If she wrote me back, though . . .

If she wrote me back, damn, how neat.

BABY
LOVE

At thirty-seven, Briggs Captor became the sole guardian of his infant daughter, Adelaide. This transformation occurred when the right front tire of his wife Irene's sedan shredded on I-285, near Atlanta, and an 18-wheeler ploughed into her Toyota as it limped across four lanes of traffic toward an off-ramp lined with violets.

In her padded baby seat, Adelaide—or Addie, as her parents called her—hurtled out the car's sprung rear door into a bed of these flowers but survived, a tiny astronaut splashing down in her space capsule. A piece of metal pierced her earlobe, daubing it and her jaw with scarlet flecks. Otherwise, she had not a scratch, and Briggs, miles away, entered in ignorance the country of single fatherhood.

Irene's mangled Avalon burst into flames. A week later, a socially inept friend sent Briggs a video of the car burning on the bypass, and he watched this tape over and over, haggard in his fixity of purpose, until Ted Chutney, a better friend, popped the tape out and ash-canned it. But the image of Irene's car on fire stayed in Briggs's memory, a picture of iconic loss that often manifested as he lay in bed or hunched before his TV set eyeballing infomercials.

Briggs retired from his job as a calamity analyst to care for Addie. (Few people had grasped what he did, even when he explained it as "performing autopsies on stillborn construction projects.") He did not *need* to work. He had profitable equities, Irene's will kicked in, and he had long wanted to break from his sole business associate, a workaholic attorney-cum-engineer.

In huaraches, khaki shorts, and his red Georgia Bulldog jersey, Briggs pushed Addie about town in a stroller. Soon, everyone in Mountboro knew about Addie and her widower daddy. Residents hailed them. They chucked Addie's chin. They invited Briggs to dinner, offered to babysit, lauded him for his devotion.

"May I call you when she poops?" Briggs asked.

Addie's melon head and big fawn-eyed face tickled him. She looked at once like photographs of the chanteuse Edith Piaf and a portrait of that model of imperial neotony, Napoleon Bonaparte. Her large head had caused Irene to labor for nineteen hours before authorizing a C-section. Then Addie had emerged "timely ripped," as Irene later put it, a purple and yellow nematode.

Now, Briggs spooned vegetables into Addie from fist-sized jars. He haggled at yard sales for wooden puzzles, snap-crotch jumpers, and rubber dolls. He clutched her to his chest as talk radio lulled them to sleep every night. In crib or bed, Addie sprawled like a small human empire. Briggs did not care. He slept well, exiling the nightmares that had haunted him since that pyre on I-285 to another reality, one now inaccessible.

Part of him thrilled to Mountboro's acclaim. *"What a guy." "You don't see many single men* truly *caring for a baby." "Never thought he had it in him."* But another part cringed, for what actually fired him like new sparkplugs, was Addie—cooing, crotchety, or grinning like an idiot savant. He loved her fiercely, as in their courting days he had loved her prematurely cremated mama.

Some evenings Briggs carried Addie to The Inlet, a bar on the highway, where he held her on his lap, nursed a beer, and shot the breeze with Walker Prine. In the neon-lit haze, he schmoozed with store clerks, grease monkeys, potheads, and GBI drug agents in laughably oldfangled hippie disguises.

"This is no place for a kid," Walker said.

"It's hardly a place for a grownup." Briggs pulled on his beer, and Addie reached for the bottle.

Another patron said, "Give her a sip, Briggs."

"Not on your life. You don't give infants booze."

Leigh-Anne Cowper sauntered over in a gust of schnapps and formaldehyde and leaned into Briggs. Walker called her Morticia (not to her face) because she worked in a funeral parlor and had a strong whiff of carnality—or mortality—about her. Divorced, childless, and fast approaching forty, she swung her peroxided hair and her comely body as a teenager might.

"If you're fretting over Addie's health," Leigh-Anne said, "look." She waved her hand. Smoke eddied in blue volutes.

"God, you're right." Briggs paid for his beer.

"Bring her to my place. I don't smoke."

"A shame," Walker said. "If I worked where you do, I'd carry a pine torch."

Briggs left before a gender-blind slugfest ensued.

In his two-story house, where he now felt like a BB in a rain barrel, Briggs carried Addie upstairs. Recently she'd begun to talk. "Bey-bey," she said, straining in his arms. "*Bey-BEY!*"

In the sewing room, he carried her to a glass-faced cabinet in which Irene had displayed her own and her late mother's dolls: Madame Alexanders, Barbies, Dutch and Finnish models, even threadbare Raggedy Anns. Addie pointed to a doll no bigger than a beanbag, dressed in dotted gingham. Briggs gave it to her, and she clasped it in an elbow crook. Addie often held it as she dozed on his belly, the gray-blue television screen their nightlight. During the day, Briggs often made her laugh by lifting the doll and crooning, "*Bey-bey, Bey-Baaay, Bey-BAAAY!*" Sometimes she chuckled until she choked, crazy for his Little Richard impersonation.

Her adulation intoxicated him. Despite his croaky voice, he tried other songs: "Light My Fire," "Baby Love," "The Star-Spangled Banner," a pseudo-cockney number that his father, a Vietnam veteran, had trotted out when he wanted to embarrass Briggs's mother:

> "*I came to town to see*
> *That old tattooed lydy.*
> *Tattooed from head to knee,*
> *She was a sight to see.*"

The song listed the lady's tattoos topographically, from the Royal Flying Corps on her jaw to the Union Jack on her back to the gods of wine that wreathed her spine to a fleet of battleships circumnavigating her hips. It ended, although never soon enough for the longsuffering Mrs. Captor,

"And over her left kidney
Was a bird's-eye view of Sidney,
But what I liked best
Was upon her chest
My little home in Waikiki."

Singing, Briggs scrunched up his face like Popeye's and protracted *Waiki-ki's* last two syllables. Addie watched as if committing each line to memory.

A few months past Irene's death, after she began to say *light* and *dog* and *Barney*, Addie coined a name for Briggs: *Baba*. He had hoped she might call him *Daddy* or *Papa*, but once she hit on Baba, she never abandoned it. In Russian the word meant *Grandma* and in English *rum cake*, but Addie applied it to Briggs. If he praised her—"You look sweet in that jumper, kiddo"—she always said, "Tank you, Baba," and he genuflected before her in his heart.

Dirty diapers Briggs changed easily. Viruses, infected ears, bellyaches, and colic took more out of him. If her nose ran, Addie wiped mucus over her face and up into her hair and Briggs erupted, "Jesus, do you want to make *me* sick too?"

But when Addie matter-of-factly replied, "Baba mad," he repented. "Baba's not mad, punkin. Baba's scared."

A few months on, Briggs's best friend Craig Gale e-mailed news that he and his German fiancée planned to marry that June in Heidelberg. Briggs told Ted Chutney, and one day near the frozen-food case in the local IGA, Leigh-Anne Cowper marched up and asked Briggs if he meant to take Addie to the wedding.

"Sure. Why not?"

"By yourself? With no help?"

"I've got no help to speak of here." Briggs cocked his head. "Does Addie look puny or neglected to you?"

"I could go as her nanny."

"Leigh-Anne, I can't afford—"

"I'd pay my way. I'd like to see Europe and help you with the rug rat."

Briggs gazed into his cart at microwave-ready pizzas and TV dinners.

"Strictly business," she either cautioned or assured him. "No hanky-pan-ky. I get my own room wherever we go."

So Briggs agreed. "Just keep it quiet. Or Ted and Walker will splash it all over Mountboro like yard-sale paint."

In her shopping-cart seat, Addie held her arms up. "Leah go too," she said.

They flew Lufthansa in a Boeing jumbo jet packed with passengers, in-cluding a golden retriever puppy. Addie, facing backward in her car seat, eyed the puppy warily. Leigh-Anne sat apart from them, as if traveling alone.

"Puppy get me," Addie said.

"No," Briggs said. "He looks about as ferocious as cotton candy."

"It's weird how your kid has to sit facing us," the man next to Briggs said. "She stares at us, we stare at her."

"It's a safety regulation."

"As if sitting backward would help her if we drop into the Pacific."

"Who knows? She was in that very seat when an 18-wheeler wiped out my wife. Irene was crushed like a bug, but the kid survived."

The other man shut up.

They landed in Frankfurt, rented a blue Renault, and drove to Heidel-berg, where they found Craig and his fiancée Gisela Riess talking to Gisela's mother in Gisela's sixth-floor apartment on Bergheimerstrasse.

None of them knew what to make of Leigh-Anne, who had changed from jeans into a gold-lamé gown and glossy black heels. The wedding was a week away. Because they still had arrangements to make, Craig told Briggs to follow his ideal itinerary—to travel in Belgium and France before returning to Heidelberg. Meanwhile, Gisela and her mother passed Addie back and forth like a rare cantaloupe.

"You must leave this one with us," Gisela said.

"Oh no," Briggs said. "This one's my life."

Leigh-Anne framed a brittle smile.

They spent the night in separate rooms and departed the following morning for Trier, reputedly the oldest city in Germany, the site of historic Roman landmarks. In the Renault, passing fields of sunflowers, Briggs asked

Leigh-Anne why she had donned her showy wedding outfit.

"I wanted to impress them."

"You did, but in the opposite way from what you hoped."

Leigh-Anne mulled this silently.

In her car seat, Addie threw Cheerios and squirmed like a torture victim. "Out," she wailed. "Addie get out." They'd hardly driven an hour, but she sounded oppressed and miserable.

"Calm her down," Briggs said. "Earn your keep."

"I've paid my way. *You* calm her down."

But Leigh-Anne rummaged up a *Schnulli*—a pacifier—and slipped it into Addie's mouth. She also gave the child a doll and stroked her hair until she fell asleep.

"Thanks," Briggs said.

"Up yours," Leigh-Anne said.

In Trier, they ate at the Roemergrill on Simeonstrasse, stared over the city from the top of the lofty Roman gate, and walked the cathedral's aisles like penitents. Addie, wearing a floppy lavender hat, jogged in Briggs's backpack. Leigh-Anne's face looked less horsy than usual. She smelled not of formaldehyde, but of a sweet amalgam of apple juice, White Shoulders, and sweat.

A day later, in Brussels, they realized that they had only travelers' checks and deutsche marks, no Belgian francs. They had arrived in the city with no prior familiarity and evaporating reservoirs of patience. Brussels spread to the horizons, traffic bleated, and the people—especially in the Asian barrios, before Briggs asked for help—seemed to regard them with either indifference or outright loathing.

When they failed to locate the train station (so they could change their travelers' checks), Briggs wheeled their Renault through defiles clogged with taxis, pushcarts, and canvas-draped trucks. He refused to ask for directions again, so they recursively doubled back or idled in infuriating jams.

"Briggs, Addie's hungry and you're getting us nowhere."

He zipped through a turnabout on a wide boulevard and hit the brakes before a big tan building with overflowing trashcans along its sidewalk. The sun dangling over them like an evil gong, they hiked across four lanes of traffic to a music store. The clerk spoke broken English and pointed them down

a street that Briggs feared would end at a Turkish enclave they had already
visited. Ahead, behind barricades shingled with handbills and adorned with
sausage-like graffiti, lay the Brussels train station. He seized Leigh-Anne's
arm and led her by a dingy reflecting pool into the station's fluorescent maw.
At a booth near the food court, he traded for Belgium francs. Leigh-Anne,
who'd left her passport in the car, asked him for a small loan.

"Never mind," Briggs said. "Sit over there and feed Addie"—he nodded
at some metal tables—"and I'll fetch us something." In the air conditioning,
his mood modulated, softened. The court sold pizza, hamburgers, fried fish,
and Chinese food, but he headed to a stand specializing in pita sandwiches.

Nearby, a squat professorial-looking man in a tweed jacket buttonholed
Leigh-Anne and tickled Addie. His crimson mouth framed an O. His eyebrows waltzed. His brown umbrella waggled behind him, a lewd appendage.

A harmless coot, Briggs decided, as he ordered sandwiches and lemon-
ades. Then, with a cardboard food caddy, he approached the dining area.

As if from nowhere, the old man manifested before him in a boxer's pose.
His umbrella clattered to the floor like a musket. *"Ha!"*

"Ha! yourself," Briggs replied.

"You're an American?"

"Yes," Briggs said. "We're from Georgia."

"Ah. Georgia." The old man jabbed at him energetically, always stopping
his fist just shy of Briggs's belt buckle. He must have thought this funny.

"Atlanta hosted the 'ninety-six Olympics," Briggs told him.

"Pickup trucks, black people, Johnny Reb." The old man feinted at him.
"I know America. I taught in *Chicago.*"

"You're a professor?"

"A professor and a boxer. If my students got unruly, I knocked them out."

Briggs's stomach flopped. "Then you probably liked the Olympic box-
ing."

"Pfaugh. Black brawlers, only black brawlers. I like the gymnastics of the
girls—the sexy half-moons of their asses."

"Have a nice day somewhere else." Briggs tried to sidestep the professor, who turned with him, chin pointed and fists cocked—a threat more of
embarrassment than of physical injury.

"I *loved* Chicago," the professor said. "I loved the sluts in my classes." He
thrust his crotch forward. "The ones who got good grades I screwed. If *they*
wanted As, they screwed *me.*" Briggs edged behind a column, but the profes-

sor leapt into his path again. "Fuck Georgia!" he cried demonically. "Fuck Atlanta!"

"Leave off, old man." Briggs set the food tray on a table and pivoted. "You *really* don't want to mess with me today."

The professor retrieved his umbrella and twirled it in Briggs's face. "Listen, you, I'll call the police."

"*You'll* call the police?"

"Give me that baby. I'll show her how really smart girls make good grades." His umbrella went transparent. Beyond its taut fabric, light-shot architectures bloomed within the train station.

Outraged, Briggs stalked the professor, visible now through the fabric as a frail hobgoblin.

Leigh-Anne, holding Addie, caught the old guy's elbow.

"Go away before something bad happens." She released him and raised her palm to Briggs as a plea or a warning.

"Fuck Georgia," the professor said. "Fuck *you*." He collapsed his umbrella and marched out of the station, a boxer taking a unanimous decision. Briggs stared after him incredulously. Leigh-Anne led him to their table, telling him in calming tones that the old man was "sick, like those homeless schizos in Atlanta." They sampled their pita-bread sandwiches, travesties of pineapple, meat gobs, and sauce. Leigh-Anne threw hers away, but Briggs obliviously chewed his.

Addie said, "Sing Baba's Song."

Briggs did not feel like singing. Addie leaned toward him from Leigh-Anne's arms and pinched his cheeks between her hands: "Sing Baba's Song." Lacking all enthusiasm, he tried "Light My Fire," "Baby Love," and "The Star-Spangled Banner." Addie frowned and repeated, "Sing Baba's Song." At last he sang "That Old Tattooed Lydy." Addie listened as if to the world's most soothing lullaby.

"That's terrible," Leigh-Anne said. "Really terrible." Briggs shrugged. Leigh-Anne laughed. They all laughed.

They left Brussels and drove to Bruges to see Michelangelo's *Mary and Child* in one of its churches. They arrived during a soccer tournament and retreated to Oostkamp, where they took cheap rooms at the Het Shaack Hotel. Leigh-Anne wanted to return to Bruges for the Michelangelo and stay the next night there. Most of the soccer fans would have left by then. The day after, they could drive to Paris.

"Paris?" Briggs said. "Total pandemonium all over again."

"You can't visit Europe without seeing Paris."

"Listen, the French dislike Americans. If you don't know the lingo, they *despise* you." At a buffet-style restaurant in Strasbourg several years ago, the staff had stood by as Irene and he tried to determine which line to enter, where to get utensils, and whom to pay. He could not imagine Americans treating foreign visitors that way.

"You must mean rich foreigners," Leigh-Anne said. "We treat poor foreigners as badly as anyone."

Two days later, Briggs, Leigh-Anne, and Addie schussed down Highway A-1 through a cobwebby rain. Under charcoal skies, the fields shimmered green. Although Briggs had never visited this part of France before, it felt almost friendly. Still, fear of a replay of their traffic disaster in Brussels made him uneasy.

"Let's park in Chantilly and ride the train into Paris," Leigh-Anne said, poring over a map. "That way, no big-city traffic."

Briggs said, "Can you even *do* that?"

"This is Europe. In Europe, people ride trains. Let's stop in Chantilly and see."

They stopped. In the visitor center, a young woman told Briggs that Leigh-Anne's plan made total sense. She made reservations for them at a hotel on the Rue de St. Denis that a British couple in Bruges had suggested as cheap and clean. They bought a full-day parking permit and parked in front of the train depot. In the incessant gauzy rain, they consolidated items for one night into three small bags and stepped inside for round-trip suburban-line tickets and metro-access passes.

Then they gawked in alarm at the changing overhead rail schedule. To whom did they give their tickets? Where did they board? Once in Paris, how did they travel to the Gare de Châtelet—Les Halles? In her backpack, Addie twisted Briggs's ears as if trying to tune in a radio station, then yanked her body backward, nearly toppling him.

"*Addie!*" Briggs caught himself.

A handsome Latino man stepped up and took Addie's hand. "Such a charming child." He kissed her fingers. "May I assist you?"

The man hailed from Uruguay, but taught classical guitar in Paris. He told them that they must notch their tickets or risk expulsion from the train, possibly even arrest. He led them onto the platform and into a double-decker passenger car.

In thirty minutes, this car pulled into the Gare du Nord in Paris. Just as Briggs sensed the onset of a new panic attack, the man reappeared and led them through a crush of commuters to the train to the Châtelet—Les Halles. Then he vanished again, and Addie's face shone in the car's window glass when the rocketing tunnel wall turned it into a haunted mirror.

It was an easy walk—the rain had ceased—to the Rue de St. Denis and their hotel. As they hiked, Briggs told Leigh-Anne that they owed their good fortune, the intercession of the Uruguayan man, all to Addie. She had bewitched him.

"Addie's pure gold," Leigh-Anne said, "but *she* didn't figure out using Chantilly as a steppingstone to Paris."

At the Hotel de la Vallée, a walkup to a series of close-packed rooms, they found that the Egyptian desk clerk had let one of their rooms to another guest. Briggs protested that they had reservations. The clerk shrugged.

"I'm sorry. Another person has already paid."

Briggs and Leigh-Anne conferred.

They could share a room for one night. The issue of observing middle-class proprieties seemed moot in Paris, even if they intended to observe them.

They had expected a tiny room, but this one stunned them. It reminded Briggs of a walk-in closet. The door abutted the thin bed, which abutted the wall. The room had a sink, a dowel for hang-ups, a bidet, and a third-story window. At this window he gazed down on a sex shop, the words BOTIQUE ERO-TIQUE ablaze in neon. A thuggish-looking crowd loitered on the wet cobbles.

"We're in a red-light district," Briggs said, laughing. "I can tell Ted that in Paris I slept with two beautiful females at once."

They ate at a nondescript Italian restaurant on the Rue de Rivoli. Rain had begun to fall again, gently. Still afoot, they went in search of the Louvre. On a concrete island at a red light, a laughing young woman, a true fashion-model type, approached Addie in her backpack and rubbed noses with her.

"Forgive me," she said in English, looking up. "I could *not* resist."

Waiting for the light, they talked. Learning that they were going to the Louvre, the woman said, "Then you must go the *other* way." They thanked her and, marching off, arrived in time not only to enter the museum through the glass pyramid but also to visit two of its four wings before its closing.

Briggs took photographs of Leigh-Anne holding Addie in front of *The Raft of the Medusa*, the *Mona Lisa*, and the *Venus de Milo*. Then uniformed guards ushered everyone out.

Walking in the rain across the courtyard, Briggs said, "Addie saved us again. If that pretty French gal hadn't seen her and set us straight, we'd have never made it to the museum tonight."

At their hotel, a toilet stall balanced halfway up the staircase between their floor and the next. It reminded Briggs of airline toilets, except that it had no sink and he could see out its tiny portal to an old brick apartment building.

When he returned to their room, Leigh-Anne wore a flannel nightgown and Addie lay out on the bed gratifyingly zonked.

"You take the outside," Leigh-Anne said. "We'll let Addie have the wall."

They killed the light and lay down, Briggs in his burgundy boxers. He had no fear of lying beside Leigh-Anne because he had matured *beyond* sex. Astonishingly, then, her *nearness* had such power that he had to face away.

"You're a lucky man, Briggs." Her whisper warmed his nape.

"My wife died in a car crash."

Leigh-Anne squeezed his collarbone, but did not speak.

"Tell me *how* I'm lucky."

"You fathered a sweet kid. You have no money worries. Ninety-nine percent of the world's people would trade places with you."

"You think?"

"Sure. Give Bill Gates five minutes to ponder it and even he'd probably make the switch."

"Because I'm lying next to *you*?"

"I don't think that much of myself. And—"

"And what?"

"I can't have children. A quack in Atlanta helped me *not* to have one, and now I can't, ever." She touched him between his shoulder blades. "We could do it, you know." Her hand crept over his flank and found what it sought.

Briggs slid off the bed and stalked to the window looking out over the BOTIQUE EROTIQUE. "And let Addie see us rutting like dogs?"

"It happens, Briggs—not everybody owns a house with five bedrooms and only two tenants."

"It'd terrify her. She'd probably think we were trying to devour each other."

"She's sleeping, and you've got more horns on you than a cattle ranch."

"Knock it off, Morticia." Immediately, Briggs rued Walker's slur.

Leigh-Anne climbed over him, gathered up her slippers and carryall, and left their room. Addie sprawled like empire. Light snores issued from her like faraway harmonica notes. Briggs followed Leigh-Anne, leaving the door ajar, and glanced up and down the stairwell. She sat above him on the step outside the WC. Even from the landing he could detect the blood in her eyes.

"What're you doing, Leigh-Anne?"

"I'm going to step into this changing room and dress. Then I'm leaving."

"Where will you go? It's almost midnight."

"I don't know. Barcelona, maybe, or Prague—pick a city."

"The rest of your stuff's up in Chantilly. You may need it." When she declined to reply, Briggs said, "Leigh-Anne—"

Her eyes winked copper. "Go back to Addie. She could wake any minute, *Baba*." When she entered the precarious toilet, its OCCUPIED sign flashed on.

In the morning, Addie said, "Where Leah?"

Briggs had shaved and pulled together their belongings. He turned and looked at Addie. "From now on, kiddo, it's just you and me."

Holding Addie and two bags, he checked out, walked down the steps, and futilely surveyed the street for Leigh-Anne.

At the Châtelet—Les Halles, he bought a carnet, a packet of ten metro tickets, and rode with Addie to the Charles de Gaulle exit, where he climbed aboveground to see the Arc d' Triomphe. There, amidst pigeons and pavement, it loomed—a big neoclassical deal. You could hike down to a tunnel, walk beneath the traffic circle, and pay to climb to the top, but Briggs, weirdly forlorn, asked Addie if they could skip it.

Absolutely, she said. *For God's sake, Baba, please yourself.*

Except for one, Briggs gave his leftover subway tickets to a stranger and hauled Addie to the subway station for the return trip to the Gare du Nord. There they ordered a chicken-salad sandwich on a gallery overlooking a dozen or more suburban train bays. Twenty minutes later, they boarded the train to Chantilly and sat in the upper level of a nonsmoking car. A young man in a tattered grey jersey stopped in the aisle and mounted a stirring appeal in French on behalf of the poor. A well-dressed Parisian who had been talking with Briggs in English pretended not to understand, but Addie put her palm on Briggs's cheek and said, *Give him fifty francs, Baba.* When he did, their stingy seatmate fell silent the rest of the way to Chantilly.

They retrieved the Renault, and Briggs snugged Addie into her car seat. After a stop for gasoline, they drove to Soissons, from Soissons to Reims, and so on eastward on autobahn-like surfaces toward Strasbourg. An hour passed, then two, then three, and still they bore on toward that city, which an Englishman at a rest stop told them was rife with Arab-immigrant crime.

Facing backward in her seat, Addie said, *What will Craig and Gisela say when we return to Heidelberg without Leigh-Anne?*

"Who cares?" Briggs said.

Evening neared, but the light persisted like an amorous hand. When Addie fussed, Briggs dropped her special doll in her lap. He sang to her. He coasted off the highway into a rest area with dog-walking areas and fast-food facilities. He changed her diaper and let her totter about a windy meadow as if its gravity had properties alien to her. He found her *Schnulli.* Despite her protests, he strapped her back into her seat. She keened around the pacifier like a heartbroken ghost.

"Addie, hush!"

Trying to regain the autobahn, Briggs swerved to the shoulder when a truck cab pulling two canvas-sided trailers whooshed past with an air-horn blast. Addie screamed, and Briggs pummeled the wheel, outraged by his own inattention and her terror. Moving again, they rode another hour, reached Strasbourg, and parked on a split boulevard. After a long search, carrying Addie every step, Briggs found a fifth-floor room in the Vendome Hotel, across the plaza from the railway station. The woman at the desk spoke bantering English, as often to Addie as to him, and when he asked where he could park overnight, she suggested the underground garage on the remodeled street out front.

"Don't leave your car aboveground," she said. "There've been burnings."

Briggs paid with a credit card and hauled Addie outside to drive the Renault into the subterranean car park. This floodlit cavern swallowed them hungrily. Its yellow-grey light, smelling faintly of char, drifted like smoke.

Get me out of this plastic animal trap, Addie said.

Briggs undid the clasps and pulled her out. She kissed him under the eye. The grotto's urinous light thickened. After a dozen steps, Briggs halted and gazed about like a robot. An engine growled to life in the cavern, and Briggs set Addie down. She seized his pant leg. Tires squealed at a far exit and keened stridulously away. Briggs walked Addie to a concrete alcove where patrons paid for their parking. Here, groaning, he sat on the curb. Addie eased down beside him. He laid a hand on her nape, but then, as if someone had thrown a switch, altogether ceased to move.

"Baba," Addie said. "Get up, Baba." She peered up at him. "Baba, get up." She climbed into his lap and laid her head against his chest.

Footsteps approached—many footsteps, a small hostile army coming through the subterranean garage toward them.

"Sing," Addie said. "Sing Baba's Song." She made him close his fingers around her doll. "Sing, Baba."

In his frailest voice, Briggs robotically obeyed.

CHANGE
OF
LIFE

On
   that
      September morning, NellJean suffered her first hot flash. Gazing at a TV monitor in the Atlanta airport, she believed the heat a surge of hormonal sympathy for the victims of the twin-tower assaults. When a huge Fabergé egg of flame burst near the top of the second tower, her flush seemed part of a horror-fueled chain reaction, which leapt from person to person throughout Hartsfield International.

NellJean had just returned from a weekend in North Dakota, where she had tried to persuade Andy Greaves, a collector of larval amphibians for the Northern Wildlife Research Center, to save their long-distance affair. If he took a biology professorship at Byron Reece College of the Piedmont, where she worked as director of alumni relations, their love light would click on again, to incandesce forever. Georgia had more frogs than both Dakotas together (not to mention toads, salamanders, and newts), but Andy didn't want to move. He loved *Rana pipiens*, the Northern Leopard Frog, more than he loved NellJean Hopkins, her autumnal beauty notwithstanding. In fact, her autumnal beauty had worked against her.

And so she watched TV with the other passengers, some slack-jawed, some so angry that they both wept and swore. The fireballs erupting on screen erupted in her, a series of stunning shudders and blushes. Of course, she was shuddering and blushing *for others*—at least until she suppressed these reactions and hurried off to baggage claim on high heels and adrenaline.

*

Five semesters ago, NellJean's husband of thirty years, a doctor of comparative religion, had left her. A student named Sofia Kuebler had ensorcelled him with street-urchin eyes and a svelte meerkat body. Daniel had proposed to this daughter of a German printing-press baron and then invited his own daughter, her spouse, and his ex-wife to the nuptials in Atlanta's German consulate. Out of pity for the bride and respect for herself, NellJean had not attended.

Now the new Hopkinses lived only a mile from campus, and NellJean ran into Daniel or Sofia several times a week. She always greeted them, dropped her voice, and, under her breath, called her successor *Trofia*. The couple never quite understood if she had insulted them. Told by phone of this petty tactic, NellJean's daughter Molly rebuked her (even though Molly had once called Daniel a "slimeball cradle thief"), but NellJean refused to stop saying Trofia. And, lately, the new Mrs. Hopkins had begun crossing the street to avoid her.

NellJean had first met Andy Greaves when he flew in from Bismarck for a conference of amphibian specialists in the Mark Trail Science Center in Nugget. That shindig had begun two weeks after her divorce, and she had endeared herself to Andy—a bearded wraith with the look of an iconic Russian saint—by arranging for him and two of his biologist pals to skydive onto an intramural soccer field. In a Kermit-green jumpsuit and a frog-belly-white harness, Andy had fallen like a rebel angel till his 'chute yanked him up and he swung to earth. As he dragged his silks toward her, a film-idol smile transfigured his homely face.

After that weekend, they dated seven more times. Once, Andy drove down with a buddy for a frog function in Savannah, and stopped to see her going and coming. Three times, he flew down alone. They either cuddled in a bed-and-breakfast in Dahlonega or cohabited like old marrieds in the house that she had retained in her divorce settlement. Twice she flew to Bismarck and visited Andy in Jamestown. Amphibians and skydiving aside, they had similar interests: photography, bad sci-fi movies, Japanese literature, and slow late-night lovemaking.

In Dixie or the Dakotas, no one lifted an eyebrow when Andy squired NellJean around. At fifty-two, she had ten full years on her beau. But if she snapped enough frog pictures, saw plenty of old flying-saucer flicks, read lots of Yukio Mishima, and siphoned off stupendous joules of his energy in bed, surely Andy would propose.

Once, drained but edgy, he had asked, "NellJean, do you still cycle?"

"Just to the post office and back. The last time I did Bicycle Ride Across Georgia was a decade ago. Molly and I conquered it together."

Andy said, "I meant, do you still have your period?"

"I still alternate light months and heavy months, but sometimes I skip a month or two. If I could skip six or seven, I'd feel liberated."

"Sounds like your cycles have entered the anovulatory stage."

"Whoa. I thought you specialized in frogs, not women's health."

Andy persisted: "You can probably still become pregnant, but of course there's no guarantee."

"I guarantee I won't. The last thing a gal my age needs is a baby out of wedlock. It's the last thing I need, period." A brief pause. "Oops."

Andy's next remark raked like a tractor harrow: *"If we marry, I want a child."*

"Hey, becoming a mother again appeals to me about as much as . . . as wearing a chastity belt."

And so, still professing to love her, Andy had broken it off. He could not forego children without resenting her. Although he'd let her visit him in North Dakota, perhaps assuming that she would agree to adopt, nothing had really changed, and their affair had ended.

NellJean fell in love with Andy Greaves not because she *needed* a partner, but because, without even trying to, Andy had played upon her long-suppressed romantic impulses. In his everyday dealings with others, especially women, he behaved artlessly. You thought of him as a brother, a eunuch, or a preoccupied wildlife-biology wonk. This impression fell to shambles when he took you to a secluded place—yours, his, a walled-in campus nook—and seduced you. His *technique*, a word ascribing more ulteriority than he probably possessed, featured shy glances and more notice of your yen to talk than you were used to (at least since Daniel's calculated courtship), and a plainspoken account of his history or a confession of his ardor. Then he made love, the sort that transformed a bed under an office lamp into a sleeping bag under the moon. In fact, Andy seemed the too-good-to-be-true child of a bashful evangel and a feisty Alabama backdoor man. He certainly *wasn't* your brother.

Although only forty-two, Andy had studied late to become a wildlife research biologist, after stints as a high-school science teacher in Wichita and then, having burned out there, as the night manager of a fast-food franchise in Bismarck. He resembled what NellJean imagined a science teacher or a fast-food manager must look like, if that person hailed from Paraguay or the Celebes. On the street, Andy drew no more attention than a nondescript CPA; nearer to hand, his olive skin, violet eyes, and thin goatee provoked glances of reassessment. Then the onlooker relaxed. True, in North Dakota or the North Georgia mountains, he seemed a scosh feral, but not in a threatening way. Maybe he'd had relatives who were boat people.

Andy *did* have a private tragedy to recount, which NellJean cajoled from him early on. At nineteen, at Wichita State University, Andy had met a woman seven years his elder: an adjunct history professor named Dori Trout. She *ensorcelled* Andy—the word NellJean used to explain Sofia's misappropriation of her husband. Within a month of their first date, Andy bought Dori a ring and asked to meet her folks, who lived in Los Angeles—to him, a land as fabulous as Paraguay—to make an old-fashioned plea for her hand. Dori counter-proposed that he move into her flat and cache the ring in a safety-deposit box until *she* was ready to marry. Then she waxed large, bore a son, and kicked Andy out.

At twenty, he found himself bewitched, ditched, and woebegone.

"Dori used me as a baby maker. My fee was room, board, and sex until she knew she was pregnant."

Worse followed. Dori asked Andy to come to the infant's christening—she had named him Travis Anthony Trout—but, later, would not let him see the boy. Andy could not tell his hard-shell parents what had happened, and his youth and ignorance of the law kept him from applying for visitation rights. Then Dori moved back to California without telling him, and he learned Travis's whereabouts only because Dori's sister, who frowned on Dori's ruse, called from Oakland one evening to give him the address. He borrowed a dilapidated car and drove two days to an oak-tented bungalow above the bay. Here, an unshaven man in ragged shorts blackened his eye and threatened to call the cops if Andy kept "stalking" them. Bruised and demoralized, Andy crawled back into the borrowed car and meandered home.

His assailant, Vince Palladino, later married Dori, but Dori did not take his name, nor would she let him adopt Travis. She informed Vince that Andy had virtually raped her (whatever *virtually* meant in such a case), but that Travis's *real father* was a political-science professor of Mensa-grade braininess who had provided Dori high-octane milt for her artificial insemination.

Andy's every birthday card to Travis came back unopened, and when he called the Trout-Palladino house, Vince grimly listed the tortures that Andy could expect if they ever met in person. Andy soon stopped phoning, but every March, Travis's birth month, grueling pangs racked his chest, and he went to ground like a wintering toad. How could Vince's promised excruciations ever match these? Although Andy ate little, he lost what he ate. He lay in the dark as if the hope with which light might seed him would rot before it germinated.

Then Dori's sister moved to Ireland, Vince and Dori abandoned California, and Andy almost forgot what so sickened him every March. But his *body* remembered, and every year he huddled alone until long after Easter.

"What happened to Travis?" NellJean asked.

Home from Dublin, Dori's sister traced Andy to North Dakota, and called to tell him the date and place of Travis's high-school graduation, plus a number at which Andy could reach the young man. Andy called. Sounding much like Vince, Travis lambasted his father as a date-rapist, a stalker, a burnout, a burger chef, and, with amused disdain, a "frogman."

When Andy said, "Actually I'm your daddy," Travis said, "Actually you're a liar. Don't ever call me again."

For a week this toxin writhed in Andy's system. Then he inexplicably stopped hurting. On a whim and a dare he began to skydive, and four ensuing Marches growled in and bleated out without one debilitating twinge.

After the terrorist attacks, anthrax in the mails.

NellJean dropped into a funk as deep as Nugget's reservoir. She slept thrashingly and craved oddball foods: chili-cheese dogs, spicy tomato relish, Honey Buns, raspberry yogurt, beef jerky. Headaches savaged her like microscopic skull-bound mako sharks. She wept for no reason or snarled like a dyspeptic pit bull. Folks *besides* Trofia Hopkins crossed the street to avoid her.

Uncharacteristically, she played the vamp. Ten days after the attacks, she patted a teaching assistant's khaki-clad heinie. A recent graduate of Byron Reece, Yancey Eaker turned to her and said, "That's sexual harassment, Mrs. Hopkins."

"No," NellJean said. "Honest-to-God men regard a copped feel, if a female cops it, as something else entirely."

Yancey's eyes darted about like panicked minnows. "Like what?"

"Foreplay, usually. They *never* regard it as sexual harassment."

And that evening, Yancey drove to her house on Kimball Mountain in a pickup truck flying tiny American flags on its gunwales. She opened the door with a wineglass in hand and her Welsh corgi, J. H., at her feet. Yancey, clutching a gym bag, blinked against the sheen of the den's libidinous pink walls. The corgi nosed his crotch, stamping a wet spot on the khaki. "Stop that, J. H."

Lowering the bag, Yancey sidled in. "Why do you call him J. H.?"

"He's the canine reincarnation of Jim Henson." Detecting bafflement, she added, "The man who invented the Muppets." Yancey gawked. "I initialized the name because I like initials."

From his bag, Yancey produced a bottle of Wild Turkey, a pack of playing cards, an "erotic" video, and two army-surplus gas masks.

"Gas masks?" NellJean said.

"In the event of a chemical or biological attack."

"*Really?*"

After filling two shot glasses and watching Yancey's movie, they drank through five games of gin rummy and a strip-poker session. When NellJean got Yancey down to gym socks and boxers, he tossed in his cards because he had divested her of only a clip-on earring, which did not qualify as clothing. It was decorative, not modesty sustaining, and its removal signified her lack of seriousness.

NellJean's breasts, neck, face, and scalp glowed with stovetop heat. Without losing a poker hand, she shed her blouse and camisole and strode about fanning herself with her fingers. Yancey seized her and carried her into a bedroom, where whiskey or second thoughts unmanned him, and he lay next to her murmuring, "Sorry."

NellJean did not mind. In this perilous season, she *liked* having Yancey there. Soon he began to snore. But sleep stalled for NellJean, who attributed her alertness—drolly, she figured—to a bad case of Osamnia. When sleep did come, she dreamt of tanks, barbed wire, and bomb craters. Albino frogs rained on bone-white mountains. Wraiths in striped bed sheets trudged this terrain holding blank maps and empty scrolls. When one figure reached out to touch her, she started.

A naked man in a gas mask stood over her. "S-s-sorry," he said, as if whistling into a pipe. "You were sn-sn-snoring."

NellJean bolted upright and stared at the interloper. "Get out, Yancy." And when he merely gaped: "GET OUT!"

With the U.S. bombing of terrorist training camps, her malaise intensified. More hot flashes and sleeplessness. More itches, anxiety, and heart palpitations.

The country had also gone bonkers. Flags flew everywhere. Billboards hyping a radio station featured Osama bin Laden in the gun sight of a rifle. UNITED WE STAND, cried a marquee outside a fast-food joint: TRIPLE-DECKER BURGER SPECIAL, $4.79. On TV, firefighters and police officers wept, famous athletes discounted their talents, and the President gave speeches in intelligible English. Wal-Mart sold bags of chocolates in mixed red, white, and blue shells; on each bag, two tricorne-wearing chocolates gimped along playing a drum and a fife—patriotic candy, imagine that.

Eating it, NellJean recalled that she loved Andy Greaves, who wanted a child. Was his desire so strange? Years ago Dori Trout had absconded with his only son. Much later, Travis had done his damnedest to shatter any hope of reconciliation. It amazed her that Andy had not altogether written off the idea of fatherhood. But he hadn't. And so he had ended their fling, but only after confirming that *she* would not start motherhood over so late. In what did his unforgivable delusion consist—imagining her in a role in which she could not imagine herself?

J. H. sat at NellJean's feet eyeing her candy. Animals, she decided, made okay companions, but piss-poor kids.

After work on the first Monday in November, a married history professor named Lloyd Silcox came on to NellJean. Lloyd had a head like a llama's (pointed ears, shaggy hair, prehensile lips) and a body molded by barbell lifting to the sleek muscularity of an Oscar statuette. After admitting that his wife and two children had gone to visit her folks in Tennessee, he asked NellJean over for dinner as an antidote to his loneliness. It wasn't loneliness niggling at the professor but unrequited libido.

Recent events had flensed NellJean's self-esteem to a skeleton, and *she* ached for company. "Sure. Let's go." And then she blushed . . . not from embarrassment, but from a body-engulfing hot flash.

In Lloyd's ranch-style house, at his kitchen counter, NellJean remarked the llama-like mobility of his lips as he made a stir-fry. When he fetched a

bottle of Wild Turkey and told her to pour two walloping drinks, he confirmed her hunch that Yancey had told Lloyd of his "conquest." So when
NellJean poured, sheets of amber sluiced everywhere.

"Whoa," Lloyd said. "I don't bite."

"My shakiness has nothing to do with you. I'm going through the
change."

"Maybe you could use some ERT—estrogen replacement therapy."

NellJean said, "I'd call that an ill-advised short-term fix for the natural
processes of aging. And, say, perhaps *you* could use a pharmaceutical therapy
for your defective fidelity gene," language that merely made the reprobate
smile.

Eating, they talked about the war on terrorism, which Lloyd called "ERT
for a geopolitical climacteric." Every smart bomb that American warplanes
hurled at strategic Afghani targets was a dose of estradiol to that nation's frail
body politic; every strike against radical-Islamic money-launderers, a shot of
tamoxifen to the cancer-creating cells of menopausal chaos.

"You've just mixed metaphors," NellJean said.

"So I've mixed metaphors. I am large. I contain hobgoblins. Consistency
is the mind candy of little multitudes."

At 8:30 p.m., Lloyd escorted NellJean into his back yard to see a play
fort that he and his wife Isabel had bought for their kids. It had monkey bars
with red-cedar dowels, chain-hung ramps and bridges, a helical slide, and a
rustic open turret into which they clambered. No rain had fallen in weeks.
Stars trembled like the eyestalks of thirsty garden slugs. Then the sky did
something really *weird*. Colors streamed like throbbing sheets of oil. Reds
predominated, but spikes of green, blue, and purple pulsed within the broad-
est sheet. NellJean seized Lloyd's arm. His face shone splotchy and pale. He
hurried out of the play fort and raced inside.

The operator told Lloyd that they had just witnessed a rare manifesta-
tion, at this latitude, of the aurora borealis, or Northern Lights. No terrorists
had struck. No jetliner had exploded in midair. Instead, a huge solar flare on
Sunday had created meteorological conditions amenable to the aurora.

"Boy, did I get that wrong." Lloyd kissed NellJean's forehead. "Would
you still like to . . .?"

Not really, but she could not say so. She could, though, refuse to lie with
him in Isabel's bed. And she did. She made Lloyd open out the sofa bed in
the family room, wallpapered throughout in dizzy-making vertical stripes.

Alone in that ugly playpen, she disrobed and wrapped herself in a sheet whose horizontal blue-and-white stripes bound her like so many fabric bars.

At length, Lloyd entered. "Jesus, NellJean, what's this?"

Under the sheet, her headache raged like a neurological aurora. Naked, Lloyd slipped in beside her. She flipped the sheet over his head, binding him to her like an embalmed Egyptian king. She felt less like his lover than like an item of posthumous property on a voyage into the afterlife.

"Kiss me," Lloyd said.

She draped her arm over his hip. "Don't move."

"You're burning up. Let me toss the sheet back."

"No. Just hold me."

Lloyd, who may have resented her bossiness, neither raped nor evicted her. Finally, he slept, and NellJean fled their linen prison, from which his legs stuck out like those of a mutant frog. In the master bedroom, she daubed two words on a soiled index card with a magenta lipstick. Then, in the walk-about closet, she pinned this card to a stylish Sunday dress: LLOYD CHEATS. When Isabel found it, what kind of replacement therapy would *she* need?

One week later, an Airbus A300 departing La Guardia Airport crashed into a residential area, killing eight people on the ground and over 250 passengers. When NPR reported this news, NellJean slumped at her desk waging psychosomatic war against nausea. The next day she played hooky.

Thereafter NellJean cocooned, even at work. She did her business via telephone or computer, ate lunch at her desk, and returned to Kimball Mountain and her bed. Even the green mountain and the soft-voiced sycamores could not offset the disquiet poisoning her joy.

Halfway through the month, NellJean willed herself to get up early—not to see anyone or to call Molly, but to do energetic aerobics to old Doors songs like "Light My Fire," "Twentieth Century Fox," and "Take It as It Comes." Once, she peered out her patio doors and counted thirty shooting stars in less than three minutes. They terrified her. *Any* celestial brightness terrified her, as it had to nowadays—but, this time, she espied nothing more fell than a spasm of the Leonid meteor shower.

*

On Thanksgiving, Molly arrived from South Georgia with the genius-in-the-making that sonograms had shown would grow into NellJean's grandson, Ryan Lescaze, Jr. Molly had driven four hours, bringing a holiday meal in tinfoil-clad casserole dishes stacked like ingots in an Igloo cooler. Free of morning sickness, she stalked in and got to work. Within an hour—all praise to microwave technology—they were eating.

"So what's happening with your frogman?" Molly asked afterward.

NellJean recited the story of her breakup with Andy and its sequel since Molly's last update, but left out her embarrassing bedroom adventures.

"If Ryan gets killed overseas and something happens to me, would you raise Ryan Junior?" Molly asked.

"Sure." But would she have asked if she'd known of her fuckups and instability?

Molly laced her fingers over her belly. "Think about what you've agreed to, but in relation to your frogman."

"Grandparents shouldn't have to raise young children."

"It happens. And you tell me that Andy would gladly adopt, and a school-age kid as soon as he would a baby."

"Yeah, but—"

"No yeah-buts. Andy's parachute brought him down from a higher place than a Cessna. Call him, Mama. Use my cell phone."

Molly deflected her every cavil—from the late hour to the unlikelihood of finding Andy home on a holiday. But because her cell would not work indoors, NellJean stepped outside and, in a chilly purple fog, clutched the phone's bent paw.

Andy said, *"Hello."* NellJean said her name, and Andy told her he was awaiting an important call. "I can't explain tonight. But I'll get back in touch ASAP."

Even by Sunday morning, as Molly prepared to leave, Andy still had not called.

In the driveway at the rear of her van, Molly gave NellJean a shoebox. "Mama, I got these for you at a library sale. Four books for a dollar."

NellJean peered into the box. "Guess that's what a divorced mama's worth these days, a buck?" She could not make out their titles.

*

Three days later, NellJean walked uptown for lunch. On a bench on the central green, a young woman in black jeans and a lavender sweater moped. Rocking fore and aft, Trofia—no, *Sofia*—clutched her own shoulders, heedless of NellJean's approach. Although NellJean wanted to scuttle past, she eased down next to Sofia, who turned to her and blurted,

"Everyone shows the flag. Everyone cheers the bombings. No one thinks of the babies or the hate that keeps building."

"I do."

But clearly this young German woman—for historical reasons a despiser of any show of unbalanced nationalism—felt like a stranger in a strange land. "Even Daniel puts out the flag. I don't belong here anymore. And I don't want my children growing up here. What mother could love such self-centered patriots?" Tears wet her cheeks, but when NellJean reached to comfort her, Sofia shook her head. "Can you imagine how I feel?"

Without irony, NellJean said, "Yes. I think I can." They talked for so long that she failed to eat lunch. "Come see me, Sofia." NellJean stood to return to her office. "Any time you like, please visit."

She squelched the impulse to add, *You know where I live.*

That evening she found the box of books that Molly had given her. The books included a biography of Rebecca West, John O'Hara's *Appointment in Samara*, a memoir of suicidal depression by William Styron (*Darkness Visible*), and, weirdest of all, a book of poems, *June 30ᵗʰ, June 30ᵗʰ*, by Richard Brautigan, a counterculture hero of NellJean's wild young womanhood. But in 1984, at age forty-nine, he had committed suicide—with a shotgun, in bleak emulation of Hemingway.

That night NellJean read the Brautigan. As Molly well knew, she had loved his early novels (especially *The Abortion: A Historical Romance, 1966*), and these seventy-seven short poems looked as if they'd need the least brainwork. Brautigan had written them in Japan in the spring of 1976. The sing-song title *June 30ᵗʰ, June 30ᵗʰ* alluded to his departure from the islands on that day.

One poem brought NellJean up short. She arose from the couch and hurried to her office. There she wrote Andy an e-mail message, noting that in "Japan Minus Frogs," Brautigan reports searching his English-Japanese dictionary and finding no listing for the word *frog*.

"*His poem ends*, 'Does that mean Japan has no frogs?' *Well,*" she typed, "*does it?*" She signed her message, "*Love, NellJean,*" and hit Send.

The bombing went on in Afghanistan, the FBI and the CDC continued tracking the source of the anthrax spores in letters posted to members of Congress, and NellJean eyed, but could not bring herself to read, *Darkness Visible.* Then, on the day that the Afghani Taliban either surrendered Kandahar or fled from it in tatterdemalion droves, this email arrived in her inbox:

"Japan has frogs aplenty. The haiku masters Basho (1644-1694), Yosa Buson (1716-1783), and Kobayashi Issa (1763-1827) all wrote poems apostrophizing or alluding to frogs. Granted, nuclear fallout after World War II, industrial pollution, and acid rain have impacted Japan's frog populations, causing diebacks and sickening mutations, but outright extinction isn't in the cards.

"An amphibian specialist on a site I checked today makes a 'confident minimum estimate' of 10 billion frogs on the Japanese archipelago. Stack them on top of each other and clap your hands so that they all jump five centimeters—not quite two inches—at once, and the topmost frog will bump his head on the moon.

"Although I like rhyming poems better than I do haiku or Brautigan, life without NellJean Hopkins isn't much fun.

"What if I came to see you for Christmas?"

Andy urged her not to deny his request on the compelling but misleading basis of his silence since her Thanksgiving call.

On that same evening, Dori Trout's sister—with whom he hadn't spoken since his son forbade him further contact—told Andy from New York City that Travis had died on the ninety-third floor of the north tower of the World Trade Center. As a new trader in the Agencies Department of Austin-Antilles Management, Travis had started working there only three weeks earlier. A search team found his body the day of Dori's sister's call. As soon as Andy received this news, he drove to Bismarck and flew to New York to attend a family memorial service.

"You have a right to come," Dori's sister had told him. "But I couldn't blame you if you didn't."

"At the service," Andy's message went on, *"Dori said, 'Keep your mouth shut about you-know-what,' but she invited me to sit behind her and her folks, and to come to a reception at their hotel. There I spoke with a pair of Travis's luckier Austin-Antilles colleagues, who mistook me for an uncle. They called him a polite, smart, witty kid who could crack you up just by lifting an eyebrow.*

"Vince Palladino did not beat the shit out of me. He died a year ago in an SUV

crackup in Tennessee, on a visit to Travis at Vanderbilt. The younger of Travis's
friends insisted on hosting me in his home for two days and showing me around
the city. When I got back to Jamestown this afternoon, your no-frogs-in-Japan
e-mail popped up.

  "What do you say, NellJean? May I come?"

Airport security in Bismarck stopped Andy for three baggage checks before allowing him to board. When he asked if security had profiled him— stopped him on the basis of appearance—the officer said, "Either we do this here or downtown." So Andy opened his suitcase and stepped back.

His visit to Nugget lasted until New Year's Day, and he and NellJean talked more than they ever had. When Andy left, he seemed sorry to go.

In March he returned to take NellJean camping near Brasstown Bald, the tallest mountain in Georgia. They pitched a tent by a nameless lake and slept in goose-down bags in the pre-Easter chill.

On the second morning, NellJean awoke to find Andy's bag rolled and his boots missing. A fist squeezed her heart. Then the tent flap popped inward and Andy ducked in carrying a clear plastic freezer bag.

"This is what I'm giving you instead of a ring. I had rotten luck the only other time I gave a woman a ring."

He held out the bag. Whip-tailed creatures like fishy spermatozoa swam in its two inches of dingy water. NellJean lifted the bag and peered at it searchingly. The creatures inside it were tadpoles.

No
PICNIC

Every

time

    I stepped into Worthy Pratt's room in the Loretta Hickok Elder Care
Center, Mister Worthy scrunched his face as if I'd dragged in a foul odor.

"Hey, Mister Worthy," I'd say. "What's shaking?"

"Nothing, Shadrach, nothing." His nostrils shone red, and his eyes pled
for me to get in quick and out quicker.

I called him Mister. He called me Shadrach. Loretta Hickok liked its
residents on a first-name basis with staff, even with Head Nurse Shadrach
Hinter, so SHADRACH was stitched over the breast pocket of all my scrubs.
Besides, as a child of the Jim Crow era, that old paleface was never going to
call me Mister.

But my main measure of Worthy Pratt—a man of snooty privilege who
too often stood aloof—fell apart like boiled cabbage when I saw him josh-
ing around with other coloreds. When Nurse Leda Gregson joked with
him, he laughed easy enough. And Joe Cheek, the midnight-blackest of us,
never had a problem because Mister Worthy got off on his deep-muscle
back rubs.

"It's not blacks Mister Worthy shies from," Leda told me. "It's you."

"Leda," I said, "I turn the old coot. I feed him. I ease him into fresh pee-
jays just like a mama would."

"Yeah, but he don't want you to. You *afflict* him."

I never let Mister Worthy's dislike rattle me. I had meds to give, charts
to update, housekeepers to dispatch, and kinfolk to calm down. I worked
Loretta Hickok six years before he came, the five years of his residency, and
a year after he passed. So his shying off from me never truly got me down.

But I did often puzzle over it.

"Forget it," Leda said. "It's a mystery."

Mister Worthy, a widower, came to Loretta Hickok at age seventy-seven, after a stroke. His only daughter lived in Atlanta and visited once a month. She had a high-stress stock-market job, an angry ex, and a shut-mouth girl name of Evelyn, who always came with her and always wore black, like a full-out teenage Goth.

On one visit, though, Evelyn gave Mister Worthy a cap with an emblem of Buzz, Georgia Tech's yellow-jacket mascot, right over its bill. He put on that cap and seldom took it off. He read the *Journal-Constitution* wearing it, watched TV wearing it, limped to the john wearing it, and tried to sleep wearing it. His roomie, Seth Tyler, swore if *he* had a noggin like Mister Worthy's, he'd've worn a cap too.

Mister Worthy flat worshiped that cap. When he got down, he fretted bout it. If he mislaid it, he tottered to the nurses' station to get somebody—anybody but me—to help him look for it. Tall, with hardly no gut at all, he'd look so woebegone that Leda would mosey back to his room to help him search and often found it under the funny papers or stuffed inside a pillow-case. He'd stick it back on and flop into a chair, his cap-worry gone but every other spur to the fidgets still a-gigging him. Once, when I snatched at that cap playful-like, he hollered and slapped me with it like a madman—till Joe Cheek stepped in and pulled me away.

After that, I kept a closer eye on Mister Worthy's meds. Dr. Titus, who did rounds on Tuesdays, had prescribed Ludiomil—but too much for too long. *I* suggested dropping the dosage or pulling the old son off it. Once, the damned stuff kept him from peeing for nine straight hours. He needed some other drug. Praise Hippocrates, Dr. Titus heard me and switched to a substitute that offered relief without angering Mister Worthy's heart or blocking his whiz-works.

He still got antsy if he misplaced his cap, still drifted into trances, and still shied off from me. So I let the other nurses give him his meds, and he actually got better. I just had to track him from a distance.

Before his drug switch, Mister Worthy told *Reader's Digest* anecdotes and one-liners from late-night TV. He liked jokes with a racy twist or se-nile oldsters in them. He told them to everybody—men or women, black or white, upright or bedridden. He took high joy from the punch lines, but seemed mostly free of malice. *After* his drug switch, Mister Worthy mixed up his jokes with personal stories, which he also told to everybody. Sometimes he shuffled into the rec room and sort of morphine-dripped his stories into the wheelchair-bound ladies watching *Oprah*, often with the sound turned off.

Sometimes I listened in:

"Before my wife got ill, we hiked the Mountboro Trail and came upon a big circle of toadstools. *'A fairy ring!'* Mildred said. *'Jump in with me!'* I wouldn't. So she stuck her tongue out, stepped into it alone, and crossed her fingers beside her neck. Then she made a wish. She thought the first person to see and hop into a fairy ring would get their wish, every time."

Sally Drexel, one of the old gals in front of the TV, smiled at Mister Worthy like he'd just played *Ave Maria* on the violin.

"Later I asked Mildred just what she'd wished for," Mister Worthy went on. "*To win the lottery,* she said. Two weeks later a letter from the Georgia Lottery showed up, with a check for eight dollars and thirteen cents. *I should've wished to win big,* Mildred said. *You must* always *wish to win big.* A month later she took sick. Seven weeks later, she died."

What a crap load, I thought. The Lottery only pays off in whole dollars.

"What did you do with your windfall?" Miss Sally asked him anyway.

"Mildred said we should go to McDonald's. But I called some friends and asked them with us to a very nice place, a Taste of Cilantro. That way, Mildred's eight dollars and thirteen cents covered our tip."

"Bravo!" Miss Sally said.

After that, I pulled many extra shifts, horsed around with the night housekeeping crew, and visited the ladies holding stitch-and-bitch sessions in the dining room. At one stitch-and-bitch, a woman waved me over.

"Shadrach," she said, "Sally's failing. I can tell—her smell's gone off."

Three nights later, Miss Sally shrieked aloud. I hurried to her room and found her half-sitting up, smote with holy terror. A Georgia Tech cap sat crushed on her night table. When I touched her, Miss Sally opened her mouth and regurged blood. I felt like I'd run into a flamethrower. Leda and Ernestine Traylor rushed in.

"Change your scrubs," Leda said. "We got this."

"Yes, we do," Ernestine said, "but it won't be no picnic."

I took off my shirt and stormed out bare-chested, my bloody scrub looped round my forearm. In the hall, Mister Worthy almost slipped trying to get out of my way—then gawped at me like he would a pit bull with slobbery jaws.

I gawped back. Miss Sally had died and Mister Worthy had him another hard bout of grieving ahead. I banged into the john, flung down my shirt, and put my forehead to an ice-cold tile.

Two weeks on, the old man's daughter, Miss Claudia, and *her* daughter, Evelyn, came to visit. Passing them near the nurses' station, I nodded real polite.

Soon after, Evelyn sashayed into the staff lounge. She wore a short black skirt, purple fingernails, and lipstick like dirty-white candle wax. I sprawled on a leatherette settee listening through headphones to Nina Simone. To snag my notice, Evelyn waved her little black purse.

"Shadrach," she said, cocking her hip.

I removed my headphones and sat up. "This room is staff-only, Evelyn."

"Give me a sec." She flopped down beside me, showing more white thigh than black vinyl skirt, pulled an old postcard out of her purse, stuck it under my nose. "What do you make of this?"

I took that postcard and stood.

Its old brown photo gave me a full-body shock. A young black man, stripped naked, stood shackled in a flatbed truck. His cuffed hands hid his privates, but whip marks streaked his legs and sides. Around him grinned a gaggle of white men and boys, but *he* stared straight at the camera. His face agitated me more than his nakedness or those scary smirking white men.

"Mama says it's uncanny—how much you two favor."

"Where'd you get this?" I shook the card at Evelyn.

"Come down to Grandpa's room. He wants to talk to you."

As we trudged to Mister Worthy's room, I studied the card.

A handwritten scrawl on its back said: *"Tocqueville, Georgia, July 17, 1927. He raped & killed Harmon Burgesses dghter. Corrine, 8 yr old, begged for her life offering a nickel in return. Give this to W., who surely remembers that day. Aunt Julia."* Smudged white triangles at the card's corners told me that Evelyn or her mama had eased it out of a photo album.

Miss Claudia met us and pointed me to the only real easy chair in the room. I took it because Mister Worthy was sitting in bed in a slick satin robe like a boxer would wear. Somebody'd trimmed his sideburns and also the U of hair round the back of his head that made him look like a monk. Mister Worthy's roomie, Mister Seth, had gone off to a fish house with his family so we had the room to ourselves.

Mister Worthy nodded at the card. "Did that surprise you?"

I just stared at him.

"I saw that fellow hung," he said. "I was eight, the same as Corrine Burgess, his victim. That morning, my father—Walter Elias Pratt—carried my mother, my little sister Elsie, and me to a field beside Drowning Boy Creek. We packed a basket, got into our Ford, and rode out to join the wagons and motorcars pulling in."

Mister Worthy glanced at his granddaughter.

"Go on, Grandpa," Evelyn said. "Tell it. There were kids there younger than I am—you, for instance."

"Four men, including three friends of my father's, had taken that boy from his jailers in Tocqueville. In fact, the jailers just handed him over. In the lea by Drowning Boy Creek, he was already beaten up like that, but now people spat on him and bounced pine knots off his back.

"A man cried, *'Decency demands that women and small children stay here while we do what we must!'* A woman shouted, *'Just let us see him when it's done!'*"

Jesus, I thought. What else could I think?

"Mister Walter said because I was tall for my age, I could go too. His friends put the Negro in a truck and drove him through a creek-side sycamore copse into the sun. Then they did what you see there—disrobed and whipped him. They stood him up so a runty photographer could take pictures. He asked for cooperation, and everyone obliged, passing him equipment and such like."

Mister Worthy kept glancing off away from me, but he *also* kept talking:

"The Negro said Mr. Burgess often hired him to do chores, but that Mr. Burgess had also lied. *Lied*, he said. Well, he yelped when the whips bit into him, but he never whimpered. He swore he'd never touched the girl and he asked for mercy, but he never begged. After a time, he stood steady as a judge and held that deep-red to-hell-with-y'all eye on every one of us."

A terrible fury seized me. "But you *still* watched him hang!"

"I wanted to return to Mother and Elsie, but Father said a true Pratt would watch the hanging and afterward recall it with honor."

"That's just gross," Evelyn told him.

"The hanging occurred on Drowning Boy Creek Bridge, a quarter mile below the meadow. They jounced him from the bridge a couple times to make sure his neck broke. Then they drew him up, bundled him in a quilt for decency's sake, and slung him off the bridge again so the women and kids could troop down there for a look-see."

Evelyn shook her head in disbelief. I liked her for that.

Miss Claudia never moved, her eyes downcast. Once, long ago, her father had watched the lynching of a young black man, but instead of recalling it, with or without honor, he'd sawed away at the memory until he'd almost cut it out. But seeing me every day and running into me bare-chested and bloody outside Miss Sally's room had stuck it back together, piece by piece—to the point he'd sent Miss Claudia rummaging through a photo album of his folks' for the postcard now between my fingers. Maybe he figured he was apologizing to me in some high-white, privileged way.

I stuck the card in my pocket and, without speaking or looking back, stalked out of that old man's room.

Jarvis, my wife, said, "That was a sorry way to leave out, Shadrach."

"I've got no power—and no wish—to forgive that old coot's family, or him, their deviltry," I answered back.

Jarvis set down two plates of leftovers, gave thanks, and spun a spaghetti noodle onto her fork. It hung there like a rope.

"Baby, he was eight. His daddy made him go."

"He had a lifetime to screw his head on straight, but all he ever did was drum for Hotpoint stoves, lip-read the news, and tell silly jokes." I slid the postcard across the table and tapped the victim in its photograph. "I look like this young blood bout like a rooster does a refrigerator."

Jarvis pulled her chair around and held the card where we both could study it. "O, Shad, you *do* look like him. You do." And, sorry for that sad truth, she touched her temple to mine.

*

Back at Loretta Hickok, I started doing stuff for Mister Worthy again. He let me do it without flinch or encouragement, as if doing *me* a favor. Up till the day he died, he and I never talked bout how he'd taken me for my own blood kin hung decades ago for a horror he'd had no hand in.

Jarvis and I did not attend Mister Worthy's funeral, but several months on, at the throwing of his ashes, Evelyn gave me his Georgia Tech cap. I keep it in the kitchen in a hardware drawer. Sometimes, when I need a nail or a socket wrench, I drag it out, and the stench in its musty felt stands me in the flatbed of a 1920s truck I've never in this life set foot in. It always takes me a while to come unstuck from such freeze-ups and to grab on again to where I truly stand.

FREE

As

the

noon siren began to wail, Bartley climbed down from his Dakota pickup into the parking lot of Talmadge State Prison. Shaking his head in disgust, he waded through the heat fumes undulating over the pavement toward the blockhouse granting entry to the prison. Loops of razor wire topped the chain-link, and the glister of August sun on metal made Bartley squint. He joined a sinewy old man in khaki shorts and two middle-aged women in summer dresses waiting outside the blockhouse.

At an interior window, a female guard perched on a stool picking cashews out of a tin of nuts. She felt the visitors' gaze upon her, got down, passed through an inside door, and shoved open the outer blockhouse door.

"You can't come in yet. They're still doing the lockdown count."

"Shoulda been done an hour ago," the old man said.

The guard glanced at his sunburnt chicken legs. "Well, it wasn't. And *nobody* gets in wearing shorts." She rolled her eyes, and the door shut with a liquid click.

The man muttered inaudibly. He spat. The older of the women lifted her flabby arms. "Calm down," she said, but his muttering got louder and mushier.

"Go to Wal-Mart," Bartley said. "Buy a lightweight warm-up suit. Wear the pants inside. After your visit, take them back for a refund."

"You ever done that?" the man asked.

"Sure," Bartley replied. "It was either that or drive a hundred miles home and another hundred back."

The old man's entire party perked up. A superstore lay less than two miles from the prison, just off Rakestraw Road. They thanked Bartley, shuffled over to a battered green station wagon, and drove off.

Bartley turned to a huge stenciled sign on the blockhouse fence: blue lettering on cracked white paint. The old man and his female entourage had obviously spent next to no time scrutinizing its **Rules for Visitors**. (Bartley had made the same ignorant shorts mistake on *his first* visit.) You couldn't enter the prison unless 1) your name appeared on a manifest of Approved Visitors, 2) you were Properly Attired, 3) you were *not* Under the Influence of Alcohol or Drugs, and 4) you left every Potentially Hazardous Item in your possession in your vehicle or in safe keeping in the blockhouse.

Potentially Hazardous Items included watches, pens, keys, paperclips, combs, brushes, compacts, lipstick tubes, rings with ornate settings, charm bracelets, necklaces with pendants, cell phones, and handguns. No, handguns hadn't *really* made this list, but only because somebody in the system had recognized such a stipulation as an insult even to the intelligence of hoodlums and dolts.

Behave, Bartley warned himself.

But he *was* behaving. He had brought only his driver's license (for the photo ID), his ignition key (for the ride home), and a Ziploc bag of coins (for the vending machines in the visitors' room). When you got downstairs, you could embrace your loved one—if the inmate qualified—only at the beginning and end of your visit. Two months earlier, he had seen the fat baby-faced guard, Hottle, threaten a tattooed Hispanic prisoner fondling his lithe Capri-pants-wearing girlfriend with both expulsion from the visitors' room *and* a bad-behavior report.

Of course, Bartley and his brother never hugged and thus had little to fear from Hottle or any other guard. But he and Carlo did occasionally let their gazes drift to the touchy-feely folk among them. Women who traced their beloveds' wrists with a painted fingernail. Cons who cupped their significant others' chins, or leaned forward to sweet-talk or brush noses. Carlo, thank God, wanted nothing like that from Bartley. Carlo just wanted Bartley to feed him.

The prison cafeteria never served on weekends. Inmates without visitors fended for themselves, using personal-account credits to buy snacks or ramen noodles from the commissary. Carlo sometimes prepared noodles on a hotplate in the dayroom of his cellblock, Building C. So Bartley—*Bill* to intimate family—was not unwelcome when he joined the change-gang of parents, wives, kids, and friends bearing snack bags filled with quarters.

Bartley had his bag in hand. He hefted it. It astonished him that TSP forbade ballpoint pens (potential shivs), paperclips (likely eye-gougers), and lipstick tubes (bomb-concealing suppositories?), but did not object to visitors entering with bags of *coins*: saps with which, working together, they could coldcock a whole platoon of guards. Profit over fortification. Lucre over locks. Hey, maybe an enterprising prison official should get the state to install slot machines downstairs....

Earlier that morning, Bartley's wife Micki had accompanied him from the kennels to his pickup, tugged along by the three borzois—Russian wolfhounds—that she always exorbitantly coddled, well beyond her indulgence of any other kenneled dog. Even the names she'd stuck on these ethereal-looking hounds—the offspring, Bartley sometimes thought, of a big blonde weasel and a lecherous seraph—underscored the depth of her subjugation to them: *Nikolai, Fyodor,* and *Yevgeni.*

If these dogs did nothing else, they kept Micki busy and svelte, as did Mountboro Kennels themselves. Fyodor, a rare hip-dysplasia sufferer among borzois, limped ahead of Bartley, often halting to lick his wrist, but when moving together, the dogs pulled so hard their slender heads threatened to pop off.

At the pickup Micki made them sit, agitated and panting, a trio of regal captives. Behind them, in the kennels, her weekend boarders leapt against the fence barking, just as much inmates as the men at Talmadge State Prison and the brother whom he must visit. Still, the dogs were far less captive to the kennels than was Micki, who could never travel anywhere without hiring a stand-in.

"Don't stay all day," she cautioned Bartley.

"You know I won't." He was only doing his brotherly duty—reluctantly.

"He'll try to keep you through both damn sessions. Which is weird, because he doesn't even like you."

"He enjoys the intellectual stimulation."

"He enjoys the grub your quarters buy," Micki corrected him.

"*And* the stimulating talk."

"Right: 'How bout Smoltz's last outing, Carlo?' 'No, Bill, how bout my new cheesecake calendar?'"

"Goodbye, Micki." He kissed her on the forehead, gripping Fyodor with both hands to avoid another sticky wrist laving.

"He can't leave, so he does all in his power to keep you there too."

"Goodbye. Again." Bartley had decided to leave early to make morning visitation and to get out gracefully by noon.

Ah, the best-laid plans of cons and kin. It was as the Bible said: No one boasting of next year's profit really knew that he would survive the day. . . .

Other visitors joined Bartley outside the blockhouse, some of whom he knew. He nodded or muttered hello. Eventually, the old man and the two women showed up again, but Bartley ignored them, regretting that on his way over from Mountboro he had gotten caught behind a prison detail picking up trash. Funny: *those* jailbirds had kept him from getting into Talmadge before morning lockdown—before lunch, in fact. He had been visiting Carlo every month or six weeks for three years, which felt to him no longer than an Ice Age, no more bothersome than an IRS audit.

Carlo, of course, scoffed at *his* sense of an imposed burden. Carlo had his own gripes. Jail time *crept* by. Everyone—except Bill, he admitted—had forgotten him. His lawyer, Marshal Trotman, never called or filed to shorten his sentence with parole or a nonviolent offender's early-out. Carlo's ex-wife lived in a rehab center in Florida, and Derek, their only son, twenty-three and long estranged, had just reported for duty in Iraq. So Bartley had no call to lament *his* alleged bondage to Carlo, the *real* sufferer here—no call at all.

A male guard handed Bartley a clipboard with a sign-in sheet, which he wearily filled out: name, relationship to inmate, vehicle model and year, tag number, arrival time, etc. When a pair of morning visitors exited the blockhouse, the female guard waved him in, took his keys and driver's license, and palmed him a circular metal chit with which to redeem them. He then entered a chain-link holding area and waited for her to buzz open the big inner gate. Here, his palms always grew clammy, no matter how hot the day, and his nerves felt stripped, peeled of insulation.

When the gate popped, he strode along a zinnia-lined walk to the prison, entered, turned right, and passed through another airlock, but a smaller one whose opposing doors whirred open and shut in push-pull synchrony. From this box, Bartley trotted down some echoey steps to the antechamber of the visitation room.

He gave the guard at the door his brother's name and looked out across the people already present, parties of four in pale-green folding chairs, two to a side at a low green stool on which visitors set coins and inmates placed snacks. The guard passed Carlo's name to another guard and waved Bartley to an empty island among the archipelago of chairs. Bartley picked his way through a foot-clogged aisle to sit amidst burglars, holdup men, bunco artists, blackmailers, car thieves, rapists, murderers, and their loving human support systems.

To join him, Carlo still had to trudge up from Building C.

The smells of Cheetos, microwaved pizza, scorched hot wings, and stale popcorn permeated the area. Bartley crossed his ankles under his chair and rocked on its edge. He hated this place, not because he feared its occupants, but because talking with Carlo for two hours (the minimum humane duration of a stop-by, given his drive time and Carlo's appetite) was painful. They had little in common but their childhoods, and their folks had died in the early 1990s, Papa of a stroke and Mama of Alzheimer's. Carlo had majored in business and jumped into investment banking, while Bartley had worked as a reporter for the *Atlanta Constitution*, often visiting the wrong government officials for interviews, too often missing assigned deadlines.

For the past eighteen years, though, Bartley had taught high school English in Mountboro, whose residents thought him a minor celebrity because he wrote a column, "@ My Wit's End," for the weekly *Hothlepoya County Messenger*. Carlo, however, had seldom treated Bartley even as a *relative*, regarding him as a slacker with no ambition or business sense. Despite living less than thirty miles apart, they had rarely socialized. A lucky thing, then, their folks had died before Carlo, a victim of country-club tastes and several bad stock investments, got five years for criminal fraud after bilking an elderly client of half her savings in a clumsy embezzlement scheme.

If not already immune, the elder Bartley would have died of mortification. In Mountboro, their surname stood for industry and achievement, good humor and probity. How, without those virtues, could they have run Bartley's Cash & Credit Grocery on Railroad Street for forty-six years?

A mug shot of Carlo had appeared on the front pages of the *Hothlepoya County Messenger* and the *Tocqueville Daily Crier*. In it, Carlo's long face looked like a grizzled horse's. A childhood scar over one eye suggested a knife wound. His well-trimmed hair resembled—Bartley could not reckon how—

an army barber's buzz cut. Worse, his blue eyes had a sociopathic cast—surely the camera's fault, for Carlo had never used drugs or alcohol. If a jury hadn't sent him up, that mug shot would have, and if not the mug shot, then Carlo's haughty replies on the stand. (He had insisted on testifying.) Carlo never grasped just how poorly his patrician lack of remorse played to the jury. In fact, Micki, once a tepid advocate for Carlo, bailed after his first appearance in the dock, and she had *never* visited him in prison.

Bartley wished that she had come today: she knew how to keep a conversation going. But their fraternal incompatibility irked her. Twice after their parents' deaths, when Carlo came to dinner, Micki soon retreated to the kitchen to make brownies or load the dishwasher. Bartley didn't blame her. He and Carlo could never talk sports because Carlo hated games. Politics were verboten because they disagreed about the president's competence, the necessity of invading Iraq, and a gazillion other issues. They could not discuss movies or TV because Carlo never watched them. Books failed to suit because Carlo read only electronics catalogues and financial newsletters. Even their overlapping boyhoods posed a problem because one of them always dredged up a slight or cruelty that still rankled. They had similar musical tastes (1950s and 1960s rock 'n' roll), but nature, pets, religion, food, travel, and fashion prompted either arguments or mutual numbness. Expensive cars, state-of-the-art gadgets, and corporate takeovers *did* interest Carlo, but Bartley yawned even at their casual mention.

Jokes: they both liked jokes, comic strips, e-mails full of silly nostalgia and sillier wordplay. And every Monday afternoon, whatever else he planned to do, Bartley sorted through a fresh stack of printouts and clippings, selected the funniest, crammed them into a long white envelope with a few hasty personal remarks on a Post-it note, and mailed it to Carlo. He did this religiously, to honor their parents and, hell, to fulfill Jesus' charge to comfort the prisoner. And so he'd become a joke distributor, folding all sorts of material into a weekly epistolary grab bag.

Here Carlo came, visible now through a slit-window, climbing the slope from his dormitory. (Carlo called Bldg C his *dormitory*, and the African-American bank robber and accidental killer who shared his pod his *roommate*.) His white hair gave him the look of a no-nonsense army major, but the vertical lines alongside his lips bespoke his strain and bitterness. He had a cut on his left jaw and a flesh-tone Band-Aid on his temple. The Band-Aid showed because his skin was the color of library paste, not of calf leather. His uniform—white with blue trim at collar and pockets—and his shiny black shoes accented his military look. Then he passed out of view.

Guards named Shadburn and Hottle patted down Carlo at the prisoners' entrance, Hottle in Carlo's face and Shadburn clearly chagrined by Hottle's over-the-top manner. When they finally passed Carlo through, he limped over and stuck out a pale hand.

"I'll bet I should see the other guy." Bartley instantly regretted his snark.

"You *can't* see him. The bastard tried to nelly-boy me." Lovely verb, Bartley thought. "The *screws*"—Carlo mocking his own pulp-fiction slang—"slapped him in solitary."

"God, I'm sorry. Did he—hurt you?"

"Bruised my tailbone." Carlo hurried to add, "I hit the dayroom wall and slid straight down it."

"Did you provoke him?"

"Besides walking by in this delectable body?" Bartley sat down, and so did Carlo. "Hell, no. The fucking shine's crazy."

Bartley flushed. "Was it your roommate?"

"Bloodworth? Bloodworth's just everyday crazy. Slater's a gorilla pervert, your typical oversexed, low-IQ Mau Mau."

"For God's sake, Carlo, hold it down."

Carlo smirked.

"And what do you mean, 'typical'? What about Bloodworth?"

"What *about* Bloodworth? He's a nice guy for a goddamn jailbird."

"Jailbird aside," Bartley said, "he doesn't fit your smug racist stereotype."

Carlo snorted in a way sadly familiar. "Somehow or other they *all* fit my 'smug racist stereotype.' If they don't, I just expand it, Bill."

"Jesus."

"Okay, let me try that again: 'I just expand it, *Jesus*.'"

Make allowances, Bartley told himself. Aloud, he said, "Should I leave?"

"Spend some of those quarters on me." Nodding at the Ziploc bag on the stool.

Only visitors could use the vending machines against two of the room's flat-gray walls. "Sure. What would you like?"

"Two Dr. Peppers and some hot wings."

Bartley visited the machines, waited six or seven minutes at the only microwave, and worked his way back. Carlo, who had sat primly erect during his absence, received his offerings with a grunt.

"I see Miss Micki didn't make it—again."

Bartley started to explain—again—Micki's responsibilities at the kennels.

"I disgust her," Carlo said.

"She just can't abide the two of us together."

"Let her come alone." Unsettlingly, Carlo smirked again.

"Fat chance."

Carlo demolished the hot wings, even sucking their bones. To clean his sauce-stained lips and fingers, he turned the napkins Bartley had brought into an incarnadine pile. He kept his uniform spotless, though, and slugged down a second can of Dr. Pepper as if to reward himself.

Bartley carried the refuse to a trash barrel and returned with a slice of pizza, a bag of pork skins, a Snickers bar, a bottle of lime Gatorade, and more napkins. Heedless of his supplier, Carlo fell to again.

Another inmate's four- or five-year-old boy saw the bag of quarters on their stool and sidled over with the clear intent of snatching it and carrying it back to Daddy. Carlo pointed the tip of his pizza at the kid: "Don't even think it, Sambo." The boy frowned and retreated.

"How to win friends and influence people," Bartley said.

"Another thief in the making—like sire, like son."

"That doesn't always hold true," Bartley said, ironically.

Carlo peered at him with blue-eyed loathing, and Bartley, feeling at sea in dark waters, lifted his hands in surrender. Carlo gobbled and drank, and time dragged by as if wrapped in waterlogged sailcloth. Bartley despondently eyed the clock over a vending machine.

Eventually he said, "You hear about the strip club that opened in Mecca?"

Carlo stopped eating. His eyes crinkled in expectation.

"It features full-facial nudity."

Carlo grinned. "Good one." He then resumed chewing.

The guard named Hottle waded into a section of the visitation room near the hot-wings machine. "Get off that man's lap," he told a prepubescent girl clinging like lichen to her daddy. "And pull down your skirt."

A balding black inmate said, "Hey, that's my daughter—barely thirteen."

"If you mean her legs, *barely*'s the right word. You know the rules, Waddell."

The girl climbed out of Waddell's lap and sat in the ample lap of her scowling mother.

"Asshole," Carlo said.

"Hottle or Waddell?" Bartley asked.

"Hottle."

"And *not* the black guy?"

"With the black guy, it goes without saying."

"Wow. Do you and the other Aryans in here have your own after-hours Ku Klux Klan operation?"

Carlo looked at him obliquely. "What we have in here, besides these visits, is chapel services and counseling sessions." He nodded over his shoulder at a high blond footlocker against the rear wall. Raised oaken letters near its top spelled out the motto **In Remembrance of Me**. "The chaplain's white, but he's a closeted agnostic and a fucking dork to boot. Someone should fillet the son of a bitch."

Bartley leaned forward. "You weren't raised this way, Carlo."

"In prison? Amid street scum and cretinous government fuckups? How in sweet Jesus' name did you figure *that* out?" Bartley tightened his jaw. "Look," Carlo said. "Go home. Stop visiting me. Stop sending me 'Zits' and 'Get Fuzzy' strips and all those lame goddamned Internet jokes. I'm not the same man I was three years ago. I'm a bitter and resentful cynic. Cut me loose before the bacteria infect you too."

Don't tell him, Bartley thought, that *a bitter and resentful cynic* described him at least ten years *before* his imprisonment. So Bartley grimaced instead.

"I said cut me loose. Go home. Make our divorce final. We'll both do better."

"You're my brother. I came to visit you."

"Really, Bill, you came to quiet your gnawing conscience."

"Think what you like. I'm staying."

"Yeah? Well, so am I—as if I had a choice." Carlo crossed his legs and sipped his lime Gatorade as if nursing a mai tai.

Visitors and inmates shifted in and out. A low drone dominated the room, with spikes of laughter or exclamation. Bartley, hands fisted in his lap, tried to match names and crimes with the inmates' faces even as he monitored their comings and goings. At three, the guards would chase everyone out, no exceptions. But *he* would leave at 2:30, having satisfied honor and propriety, and maybe even eased his guilt.

Still, he had over an hour to go and Carlo was pretending that he didn't exist, humming an unidentifiable song: the Gatorade he was sipping baffled its melody. At length, Carlo swallowed. "God, I'm going crazy in here."

"The assembly room?"

"The Talmadge Co-rectal Institute. Except it's a prison now, not a correctional futility." He rocked on his stool's edge. "In any case, Trotman does nothing. Trotman, the bastard, says, '*Rot, man!*' And so I rot."

Bartley held his peace, and Carlo started humming again, but more distinctly because he had no Gatorade in his mouth.

Then he began to sing, deliberately widening his eyes and mincing the words: "*Twinkle, twinkle, little star. / How I wonder what you are. / Up above—*"

"A nursery song."

Carlo stopped singing and said, "Prison has reduced me to this."

"Prison?"

"Sure. A man who once made caboodles for his investors now sings '*Up above the world so high, / Like a diamond in the sky*' over and over. It's insane."

"You stole. You *admitted* stealing."

"I *embezzled*, Bill. And rotting in here, how can I make restitution to the bitch I scammed."

Carlo's humming grew louder as he rocked more aggressively. Other prisoners and their visitors took note.

Bartley touched Carlo's knee. "Easy."

"*Like a diamond in the sky*. Like a *diamond* in the sky. On the Fourth of July, I could see fireworks out my pod window. Countless sparkling gems over the lake at the tail end of Independence Day and I'm rotting in the same pod as Joshua Bloodworth, a pot-smoking, Bible-believing homicidal spook. *Like a diamond in the sky*, my rosy red ass!" Humming, he rocked even harder.

This time Bartley tapped his knee. "Hey."

"*What!*" Carlo barked.

"*A-B-C-D, E-F-G,*'" Bartley sang. "*H-I-J-K, L-M-N-O-P, / Q-R-S, T-U-V, / W-X, Y-and-Z. / Now I've sung my ABCs. / Next time won't you sing with me?*" When he finished, Carlo gawped at him. "The melody," Bartley divulged—"is the same as the tune to 'Twinkle, Twinkle, Little Star.'"

"Bullshit."

"No, a little-known fact. If you sing yours and I sing mine, we'll be doing a lovely little nursery-rhyme duet."

"Don't shit me, Bill. I get enough guff in here from strangers."

"If you sing and let me join you, you'll hear how the melodies coincide."

Carlo set down the Gatorade bottle. "I'm rotting," he said, "from my teeth to my toenails." But he began to sing "Twinkle, Twinkle, Little Star" softly, *belligerently* even, and Bartley, in a brittle tenor, sang the alphabet song. They finished on almost the same note—like practiced lovers, Bartley thought.

"Do you see?" he asked. "Did you hear?"

Sidelong, Carlo eyed the inmates and visitors looking at them. "They don't sound any more alike than a penny whistle and a pig's fart," he said. "Your melody threw mine off." He was lying, but he had the false tact to add, "Or vice versa."

Twenty minutes before Bartley could leave, but he declined to mention that "Baa-Baa, Black Sheep" floated on the same tune as the other two rhymes. Carlo would regard that assertion as an evil attempt to altogether untie his mind from reality.

But Carlo broke the lengthening silence: "You know that old folk song 'Stewball Was a Racehorse'?"

"Yeah," Bartley said.

"I think John Lennon stole its tune for his Christmas song—part of it, anyway. And George Harrison filched the tune for 'My Sweet Lord' from 'He's So Fine,' an old Chiffons' hit."

"What's your point?"

"Lots of songs sound alike. Lennon stole. Harrison stole. But it didn't put either of them in prison. They had connections."

"They're both dead," Bartley noted.

"You think a man in prison is living?"

That ended the conversation. Bartley and Carlo sat, roiling inside—like pressure cookers lacking release valves.

For six weeks Bartley kept mailing jokes to Carlo; no one could accuse him of a lack of loyalty or thoroughness. He would stay the course and win the laurel. God would smile. Then, on an October Saturday long ago marked on his calendar, he drove to the prison again, arriving before ten so he could visit Carlo, depart by noon, and return home to help Micki in the kennels.

Carlo came into the visitation room doing a Charlie Chaplin walk and wearing an idiot grin. He told Bartley that a state legislator—*not* Trotman, *not* his attorney—had interceded for five nonviolent offenders at TSP, and for two dozen more at other Georgia prisons, to secure them early-outs. The lawmaker called this intercession "opening a release valve." Overcrowding in the state penal system made thinning inmate populations a necessity, and in two weeks Carlo would walk out a beneficiary of that need.

"Do you know the first thing I plan to do, outside?"

"Take a counter job at McDonald's?"

"Go to Trotman's and ring his doorbell. When he lets me in, I'll whiz all over his wingtips." Carlo awaited approval. He had devised this plan in utter seriousness.

"Trotman might press charges for assault, bro', and—*boom!*—there goes your nonviolent-offender status."

"Nah. Trotman's a weenie. He'll take it because he deserves it."

Carlo talked effusively between bites of cheese sandwich and slugs of Mountain Dew. The caffeine and the endorphins from his psychological high fueled his talk. He slandered guards, inmates, counselors, doctors, and all the blacks among these groups—all with impressive bursts of venom. His color had come back. The dark marionette lines beside his mouth had faded to mere pale threads.

Back in Mountboro, Bartley found Micki in the kennels and told her the news. She was filling food dispensers and hosing down the pens. Stepping through the muck and spray, he announced that he had decided to take Carlo's advice and cut his brother loose. His sentence would end with Carlo's, and Bartley would do all in his power to avoid further entanglements. Micki said that was "very George Washington" of him and swamped his feet with a stinging hose blast.

"I'll get you for that!" Bartley said, hopping on one foot and then the other.

Micki threatened a burst to his chest. *"Baa-baa, black sheep,"* she sang. *"Have you any wool?"* She agilely avoided his pursuit.

"All right," Bartley said, surrendering. "How can I help?"

"Take Fyodor out," she said, indicating her favorite among the three borzois that had access to the house. "Poor guy's fidgety and blue."

Bartley crossed to Fyodor's pen, caught him by the collar, and hooked a leash to it. He led the limping hound down the run to the rear gate, opened it on a grassy paddock of pecan trees and dogwoods, and led the dog out into it.

In the paddock Bartley knelt, unsnapped the leash, and let Fyodor run, a feat that the borzoi performed on three legs, heedless of his hip dysplasia until some obstacle in the pasture—a rock, a half-buried bottle—threw him off stride and sent him yelping onto his flank. He flopped a time or two before lying still, his head inquisitively raised and his tail apologetically thumping.

Micki appeared beside Bartley. "Bill, I didn't mean for you to let him go without you. My God, look at him."

"He's okay. He just hit a bump."

"And went down hard. If you'd kept him on the leash—"

"Stop, okay?"

Bartley tramped through the grass, scooped up the dog in his arms, and labored back toward the kennels. A knot formed in his gut, a familiar and unrelenting lack of ease that he knew he would never shake. Sunlight ricocheted off the chain-link, though, and in its intermittent dazzle Micki stood laughing at him. He stopped and adjusted his grip on the borzoi. Then, grinning like a halfwit, he resumed struggling toward his wife and the faint fecal reek of Mountboro Kennels.

RATTLE- SNAKES AND MEN

Several

Aprils

ago, a tornado blew Reed, our daughter Celeste, and me out of our house in northern Arkansas. Three friends in our hill town died. A dozen others suffered injuries or property losses that funneled havoc into their lives too. Even though Reed and I worked—Reed as an auto mechanic, I as an aide in the county library—we had no money to rebuild and no reason to stick around once we sorted out the scramble the twister had made of our belongings and minds.

Dusty Shallowpit, an army friend who had kept in touch since his and Reed's final tour in Australia, called us every other day through June. At last, his voice twanging through our cell-phone speaker, Dusty offered us a low-cost rental house in Wriggly, his hometown in Georgia's southern pine flats, along with jobs that he swore would stand us Godfreys up on our feet again.

"Soon enough, Reed, you'll make manager at Shallowpit Feed & Seed, but you got to *start* in equipment repair."

"What about Wylene?" Reed asked, glancing at me.

"She can feed her artsy side by grooming dogs and her outdoorsiness doing guide stuff at the wildlife refuge." And Celeste, who'd just finished first grade, would do just fine, he predicted, because "kids her age are so danged adoptable."

"A-*dapt*-able," I said at Reed's ear, clearly irritated.

"Right," Dusty said. "Your kid's already got a family. Anyways, you all should come. You'll like it here."

I doubted that—at least he hadn't said we'd "love" it—but three days later we rented a trailer, ball-clamped it to our pickup, crammed it full, and drove to Wriggly, way down in Nokuse County, in grueling Dixieland-in-July heat.

I knew right off we'd really goofed, but our two-bedroom brick tract house had its charms, namely a red-cedar privacy fence, a rock garden that the last tenants had kept up nicely, and a slat-framed glider under a sprawling fig tree. I would have liked some grass, fescue or such, but Nokuse County has sandy soil and, blessedly, we wouldn't have to do a lot of yard work harassed by gnats.

How I learned our move was a mistake, maybe even crazy, happened our fourth day in Wriggly when Dusty Shallowpit and his father, Jasper, knocked at the door after Reed's first ten-hour shift at the Feed & Seed and I discovered Shallowpit père on the front stoop holding a long hole-filled box by a leather hand strap. Celeste ducked under my crossed arms to peer through the screen at our visitors, while I gaped at them in dimwit wonder.

"What's in the box?" Celeste pushed open the screen to reach for it.

Before I could pull her back, Dusty seized the box from his dad and retreated to the sidewalk. Jasper Shallowpit was caught between pique at his son and concern for his three new tenants. He flushed purple and wiped his palms on his khaki trousers.

I laid my hand on Celeste's collar bone.

From the tiny kitchen, Reed hollered, *"Who is it?"* And when I'd told him: *"Let 'em in, Wylene! Let 'em in!"*

Soon all five of us—three Godfreys and two representatives of the hamlet's second largest employer—stood in the outflow of our window-lodged AC unit with sweat drying on our brows and napes.

Reed dabbed his lips with a limp paper napkin, while my arms locked our squirming daughter in place before me.

"What's in the box?" Celeste insisted.

Mr. Shallowpit snatched the box back from his son, bowed his bald head to her, and spoke directly to Celeste, though he meant his speech for all of us:

"First, let me formally welcome you all to Nokuse County and to Wriggly, its county seat. I should've stopped by earlier. Second, as your landlord and the current chairperson of the Nokuse Rattlesnake Alliance, I've come—*we've* come—to give you"—he lifted the box a few inches—"this young *Cro-*

talus adamanteus, a variety we call the 'lozenge-spot': a pretty little tutelary starter serpent."

I couldn't speak. Then I laughed. Then I blurted, "That's really funny, sir. Thanks for the giggle." What else could I have said? The doofus was our landlord—Reed's plenty potent new boss.

"He ain't joking," Dusty said. "It's a BioQuirked watch-snake, a baby rattler, your all-for-free, native-to-the-Greater-Southeast threshold sentry."

I pulled Celeste closer. "But we don't want it."

"Thank you, Mr. Shallowpit," Reed said, reaching for the leather strap to accept the snake-carry. "We truly appreciate your generous gift."

"Reed, we've got a child. Where would we put it? How would we feed it?"

A pit viper, I thought: *A pit viper?*

"You don't get it, Wye," Dusty said, clearly peeved at me.

The elder Shallowpit inclined his head to me as he had to Celeste, this time focusing on *my* face. "The Nokuse Rattlesnake Alliance has a long, illustrious history, Mrs. Godfrey. Every year for fifty years, we've hosted Nokuse County's Rattlesnake Rodeo and Roundup here in Wriggly. *Crotalus adamanteus* has played an enormous role in both the economy of our region and the shaping of our identity as Nokuseans."

"Forgive me, sir, but so what?"

"Wylene," Reed said.

Mr. Shallowpit's naked face made a fist.

"Sir," I said, "what does all that have to do with giving us a venomous *snake*?"

"It's been a county law down here nearlybout forever, Wye," Dusty said.

I shot question marks back and forth between both Shallowpits.

Daddy Jasper's face unclenched. He opened his slippery hands in what he must have figured a kindly appeal. "Everybody in the county has *got* to own a rattlesnake," he said. "It's a ordinance every city council in every town in our county, however little or big, signed on to on a well-remembered day back some sixty years ago, Mrs. Godfrey."

Reed said, "Sir, you can call her Wylene."

I gave Reed the stink-eye but simmered my tongue to silence.

Mister Jasper heeded Reed: "Wylene, our whole pine-flats society just wouldn't exist without rattlesnakes and what they do for us."

"Or turpentine," Dusty said. "Don't forget turpentine."

Irked, Dusty's father flat-out ignored his son: "Our forerunners decreed that every home, business, and every guvment building, except the town hall and county courthouse, must make space for their own *Crotalus adamanteus*. In fact, to flout that ordinance is to spit in the all-seeing eye of Lady Justice herself."

"She's blindfolded," I told Jasper Shallowpit.

"What?" he said. *"What?"*

"You *can't* spit in a blindfolded person's eye, not so it really matters."

"Listen, Wylene, Nokuse County is a very special place. We love our crotalids here. They protect us. They contribute to our economy. They amuse us. They validate us as folks in tune with our reptilian as well as our human natures. Terden BioQuirked Creations is our biggest employer. We brought you this baby"—nodding toward the snake-carry—"as a sign of our concern for your family's welfare and as a down-home welcome to our ways."

Although I crossed my arms over her scrawny chest, Celeste slipped free and dashed into her bedroom.

For several reasons, I had not asked our visitors to sit. The curtain-free living room boasted only two chairs, each with a cardboard box in it stuffed full of winter clothes or pre-owned car-repair manuals. We'd unboxed and stowed almost everything else, but, inside, the house resembled a barracks for elves, and we Godfreys squatters. Reed lifted the holey box to remind me again of our housewarming gift.

"Where am I going to put a rattlesnake?" I asked all three men.

"In here," Celeste called. "There's a place for it beside my bed."

The Shallowpits guffawed—a trombone and a kazoo, respectively—but Reed raised his eyebrows at me half in plea, half in warning.

"Over my dead body," I called back to Celeste.

"Easy." Dusty sniggered. "You just might get your wish."

I stormed into the bedroom, the men all following, and found Celeste kneeling by an empty aquarium I'd all but forgotten. Maybe I'd thought for forty seconds about cleaning it up and dropping a few minnows and angelfish into it, but those forty seconds I'd lost amid a host of more urgent settling-in matters and never recalled until now.

"See there," Shallowpit père said. "Your problem solved."

And for the men, even Reed, it was. In Reed's thinking, the Shallow-pits had saved us the expense of buying a snake to comply with a hallowed county ordinance. All we need do was accept their gifts—of the rattler, the aquarium, and an injection-molded plastic hide-box (still in the snake-carry) that we would set in the aquarium for its brand-new tenant to slither into to conceal itself from our basilisk human gazes. And all would be well, all would be well, all would be mystically and moronically well.

Well, to *hell* with that shit.

"Put the tank outside," I said. "Celeste and that ugly critter"—which, to that point, I hadn't even glimpsed—"are *not* sleeping in the same room."

Celeste began to wail.

"Hold on, Wye," Dusty said. "You'all've got to keep your threshold sentry beside your place of residence's main entrance."

"Right," Reed said. "We'll put it by the front door."

I was fuming, but Dusty toted the aquarium from Celeste's room and set it down in the living room near the front door. Then he lifted our gift-snake from its box, squeezed it behind its spade-like head, and held its lozenge-spotted rust-brown body over the aquarium floor. By a wrist twist and a bit of luck, he let go of it without getting bit, for it seemed intent on striking his freckled forearm or a smudged pane of glass in the fish tank. Kneeling beside that tank, Dusty drew hypnotic fingertip circles before the watch-snake. As he did, a soft moleskin pouch under his arm poked out to one side and then the other in gently random bulges. I glanced at the elder Shallowpit to detect if he wore a similar pouch, but if he did, his sports jacket hid it. Even so, I suspected—felt sure, in fact—that both men were carrying herpetological heat.

Then Dusty began talking about our snake and how we all must feed it once, soon, to set its imprinting "biostats" for each person living in our house. That would make it our "special protector." Terden BioQuirked Creations, Inc., had used gene quirking and amino-acid infusions to augment the vomeronasal organ on the roof of our crotalid's mouth and hence to allow it to bond with all the "souls" in our house by our specific body temps and odors. With this imprinting and a like sensitivity to the telltale anxiety of strangers come for evil purposes (based on *their* body temps, reeks, and dicey mannerisms), these rattlesnakes—whether you called them "security paladins" or "threshold sentries"—would almost always bite and slay any unwanted intruder.

"The best defense against a crook with a carry-snake," Dusty told us, "is a household with a certified and imprinted TBQC rattler." He noted that each such snake rattled its rattle only for its household's residents. By genetic design, it *avoided* rattling its rattle for intruders, the more reliably to strike and to kill the evil sons of bitches.

Although Dusty explained a lot more about these BioQuirked "creations," Celeste came howling into the living room as he spoke. She howled when I shushed her and howled when I took her back to her room. I told her to hush and stay in her bed. She stayed in her bed (so long as I sat on it beside her), but did not quiet until, at long last, she drifted into a whimper-punctuated sleep.

By that time, the Shallowpits had blessedly taken their leave.

Heading to our bedroom, to which Reed had already retired, I saw that Dusty or his dad had put a lid on our slithery protector's tank, securing it with clamps and bungee cords. So we were all safe for the night, if home invaders didn't burst in, rape, torture, and behead us all between now and sunup. I didn't care. The Shallowpits worried me more than did our young viper. But I *did* care that Reed lay facing away from me, rigidly mute, as if I had shamed him before his new bosses-cum-landlords.

I draped an arm over Reed's back and ran my finger over the scar of the arrowhead wound he'd suffered under his heart in Operation Outback in southwestern Queensland. He caught my hand, roughly, and held it. After a while, though, he raised it to his lips and kissed it. Such a blessing: he didn't hate me.

"We can't live day to day with a snake in our house," I whispered.

"The people here do."

"All of them?"

"It's the law, Wylene."

"Is it a law for them to tote rattlers around with them in little moleskin bags?"

"I don't think so."

"Maybe you should find out."

"If it were mandatory, Wye, Dusty would have told me my first day at work. He's got too much invested in me—in *us*—to let me get arrested and locked up."

"Yeah, well, I think he and his daddy carry *personal* security paladins."

Reed sighed heavily and let his higher shoulder slump. "Of course they do."

"Do they tote them even at work?"

"Most Nokuse Countians do, I'm afraid."

"Most? Do you mean everybody?"

"Nearly every man does. It's like wearing a beard is to a grown Muslim male. I don't think many women carry them, even as gewgaws for their outfits."

I couldn't help it: I laughed derisively. "It sounds as if the dudes around Wriggly are all in little-cock compensatory mode."

"Don't go all multisyllabic and shrink-minded on me. I wouldn't know."

I got mad. "Toting a snake everywhere a person goes puts the wearer and everybody else around *him*—I use the pronoun on purpose—at great risk. It all stinks to heaven of fear and fetishism."

"Wye, give me a break."

I crawled over his distractingly sexy shoulder, nibbled a while on his eyebrow, and stared him right in the eye.

"It's crazy. We've got a deadly serpent in our house, and these yokels pack them around like warlocks with their creepy familiars, tutelary totem creatures."

"Wye, I'm beat. You're making my brain ache."

"How many people in this loony burg die every year of snakebites?"

"Only bad guys and dumb asses—felons and fools."

"Hey, even beat, you alliterated. But I don't believe it. Accidents happen. Nasty acts of greed and sad ones of self-aggression occur."

"You heard Dusty. TBC augments its snakes with biostats, or something like that, to make 'em safe to be around if you're their owners."

"Good old Dusty—he's taught you a lot."

"Yeah, good old Dusty. Still, forgive me for saying so, Wye, but if assholes came any bigger than Dusty's daddy, the most profitable businesses on planet Earth would make toilet paper. Now please let me get some sleep."

Reluctantly, I did.

As things turned out, we didn't have to worry about what to feed our new "pet." Shallowpit Feed & Seed had a reptile-chow enterprise in Nokuse County consisting of imported white lab rats and home-grown rice rats, bobwhite quails, and marsh rabbits. Dusty made sure that a part of Reed's monthly pay went to feed our new adder, the amount depending on the fare that Reed toted home for Vype.

Vype was the name Celeste called the critter after Reed said that she could *not* baptize it Wriggly because too many other threshold sentries in town surely bore that name already. *I*, however, suggested the witty gothic spelling for her *next* favorite choice.

As per Dusty's advice, Reed and I fed Vype first, to make sure it quickly imprinted us as its family. Then Reed focused on getting Celeste to take a turn, so that we could uncover our tank and benefit from the security and peace of mind that a free and functional watch-snake would provide our household.

But I feared that tenderhearted Celeste would find feeding Vype its live dinners too upsetting. I never thought she'd volunteer for the job, and I told Reed that, even in Wriggly, only a piss-poor parent would let a second-grader feed a pit viper.

Reed begged to differ

He lectured me that Celeste completely got the naturalness of gorging and being engorged. Feeding Vype would teach her more than just the "in-put-and-outgo rhythms" of all earthbound life cycles. It would also teach her caring—"Not for its terrified prey!" I put in quickly—as well as adult respon-sibility. "She's a kid," I argued. "And we're supposed to guarantee her safety."

"Too much guaranteeing her safety will turn her into a *permanent* child. She's got to face the world as it is."

"Not yet, she doesn't."

"We're not guaranteeing her safety if we don't allow Vype to imprint on her as one of his household wards."

So, initially, Reed fed Vype its scared-shitless rats and its run-amok quail chicks. But he let Celeste watch, and Celeste *did* watch, and although she was taken aback at first by this transfixing drama (sometimes picking up a white rat and stroking it to calm it), soon she had evolved into a rational observer with a scientific sympathy for both eater and eaten.

Within days, she asked for permission to lower a prey animal or bird into the tank, using a miniature dumbwaiter in a harness of strings. Like a puppet master, Celeste did this skillfully, with no fear at all and, afterward, no gross victory whoops. Then, finally, we took the lid off Vype's tank so that, now, our BioQuirked serpent could properly carry out its role as our security paladin.

Dusty had sworn I could satisfy my "artsy side" and my "outdoorsiness" by grooming dogs or by serving as a wildlife guide in the swamp forty miles south of Wriggly. But most of our hamlet's canines were redbone or blue-tick hounds that needed grooming no more than did Jasper Shallowpit's razor-nicked noggin. And because I didn't want to commute eighty miles every day in our about-to-die pickup, I stayed in town decorating our boxy house and fitfully looking for work.

I found rugs for our scratched pine floors, thrift-shop chairs for the living room, and items among our own belongings for wall hangings. I nailed three of Reed's machine-turned army crossbows in an arrangement above our TV.

On another wall, I hung a big photo display of the 23rd Bowmen's Brigade helping to defend Brisbane, Queensland. It pleased him, I think. In fact, he asked Dusty over to see my handiwork and ignored his favorite TV shows, *Aussie Archer* and *Knife Music*, as they guzzled beer, pointed out slain or surviving comrades in the photos, and reminisced with hale-fellow-well-whiffled sloppiness.

Meantime, even though Vype had coiled up in his utility hide and snakes may be deaf, Celeste read a fairy tale to him, and I perused help-wanted ads in the *Nokuse County Sentinel*. One said, *"Archery instructor for adults & children at RV camp: experience a must. Ditto: having good teaching skills & own equipment."* The ad listed two telephone numbers, one for daytime calls and one for evenings up until 10 p.m.

In Reed's and my bedroom, I called the second number. Reed had often taken me bow hunting, and some of our happiest outings in Arkansas had involved energy-bar picnics and archery expeditions in secluded Ozark glens. I explained all this to the owner of the RV camp, a guy named Newall Alpo, who asked me to come out for a face-to-face interview the following morning.

I had never known anybody with the surname of a brand of dog food, and when I met Newall Alpo in person, I didn't know how to take him. He had a well-oiled 1930s-style pompadour, an ugly snakeskin vest, oddly wide hips, and a brusque, smug manner. Further, he wore a snake on his person, an adult *Crotalus adamanteus*, hanging about his ample waist in the belt loops of his trousers. The snake appeared drugged. Its triangular head stuck out just where a belt buckle would have gleamed, had Mr. Alpo worn a belt instead of a rattlesnake. And although I tried not to let this weird sartorial accessory distract or discomfit me, I didn't fully succeed.

But Mr. Alpo liked my replies to his questions and what I showed him of my archery skills, and when I left his RV camp, I had a job I could walk to and his assurance that I'd get off early enough every day to take care of my daughter after school. Landing this job seemed to me the most hopeful thing that had occurred to us since our arrival in Georgia. It not only pleased Reed: it delighted him. As for Celeste, she begged me to let her come to one of my practices later in the week.

This she did back out at the camp's archery range, standing safely behind me. Each time I emptied a quiver, she scampered to the bales to wrench my arrows out and fetch them back. "You're just like William Tell!" she cried. "Shoot an apple off my head!"

I threw down my bow and shook the goulash out of her. "Maybe I can and maybe I can't, but I'll never even *try* to do that! Don't ever ask me again!" I pushed her away so that she staggered back a few steps and fell.

Immediately, Mr. Alpo waddled up and asked what the hell was going on. (Had I just tossed my first piece of Wriggly good luck onto its funeral pyre?)

Celeste stood and brushed off her dress. "I back talked to Mama, sir. She's told me not to, lots of times, but I . . . I . . . I did it again."

Sizzles of shame shot from my cheekbones and brow.

Mr. Alpo scowled at Celeste. "Always mind your parents. Always."

"Yes sir."

He swung his scowl toward me. "None of that shit with my campers, Mrs. Godfrey. You got that?"

I pulled Celeste to me. "Yes sir, I do."

"It's good nobody else hereabouts saw what I saw." Then Mr. Alpo stalked away, gripping his snakeskin vest by its lapels while his watch-snake writhed in his belt loops like a baleful hula hoop.

Still, I loved the job, especially in the early fall when the RV camp had *beaucoups* of campers clamoring for archery lessons. Fairly frequently, Newall Alpo loaned me out to other tourist concerns in Wriggly, a canoeing outfitter, or a special event in the wildlife refuge, but never so late in the day that I could not catch a ride home before Celeste got out of school. That and my new income made the arrangement seem a perfect helping of grace.

But Nokuse County wasn't perfect. I'd missed the annual Rattlesnake Roundup & Rodeo held in March, an event that featured prizes for those wranglers who caught the most native un-BioQuirked diamondbacks and later killed them with hatchet chops behind their heads. As sidelights to the annual roundup, there were also rattlesnake races, training in how to treat rattler bites, and venom-milking shows.

Some of the events to which Newall Alpo "sub-let" me focused on these secondary activities. They occurred throughout the year at city schools or in outdoor venues set aside by civic groups, often on weekends so that Celeste and Reed could see me in action. I was always a diversion from the fore-grounded snakiness of everything else going on: the sale of snakeskin vests, wallets, and slippers; of rattler-related videos, coiled-snake ashtrays, and fake plastic, plush, or rubber crotalids; and even of food items consisting of fried, fricasseed, or grilled rattlesnake—*et cetera, ad nauseam.*

A hot Friday night, mid September: Dusty Shallowpit asked us to a football game against Brunswick High in which his son Doug would play. By coincidence, Mr. Alpo had arranged with Doug's head coach for me to work at this game during halftime showing our cheerleaders how to use bows and arrows to burst big Mylar balloons representing the four best players on the Brunswick Pirates. We'd shoot in the eastern end zone where our novice archers could not endanger anyone else attending. Earlier, of course, I'd as-sumed that our arrows would stand for the metaphorical fangs of our Nokuse County *Diamondbacks.* Or our Nokuse County *Rattlers.* But I was wrong.

As a halftime performer and a guest of the Shallowpits, I got into the stadium free, as did Reed. We perched not quite halfway up the poured-concrete tiers, near the fifty-yard line, awaiting kickoff in the steamy dusk. Celeste was going to a movie with a friend from school, and Reed and I were enjoying, sort of, our first real date in Wriggly.

To our right, someone in a furry black bear costume cavorted in front of both the band and the student sections. Talking with our hosts, I paid little heed. Eventually, though, I began to wonder why this cavorter had dressed up like a bear. When I asked this question aloud, Hallie Shallowpit said, "A bear's the official mascot of Nokuse County High School."

"Not a rattlesnake?"

Dusty said, "Wye, how could a kid dress like a rattlesnake? You'd have to stuff three students in a long hoop-braced tube and then they'd all have to grab one another's shoes and wriggle this way and that on the ground."

Reed laughed heartily at this picture . . . or at me.

My dander rose. "One kid could be a rattlesnake if you used a sliver of imagination and a nickel's worth of design sense," I said. "It wouldn't even be that hard."

"Wye, our mascot's a black bear," Hallie said again.

"Yeah, but everyone here's so rattlesnake crazy it seems a no-brainer."

Dusty explained that *Nokuse* was a Muscogee-Creek word for "bear," specifically the black bear, which had thriven hereabouts back in the 1800s. Most of these bears, he told us, had long since retreated northward to more heavily treed regions. I said I bet they'd done it because diamondbacks were a damn sight tougher than the absconding bears.

"Even so," Dusty said, "bears still got them a stake in our tradition too."

Squeezing my knee, Reed whispered, "You've just defended the diamondback. You always surprise me, kiddo."

I shoved his hand off my knee.

Doug Shallowpit, a chunky boy who didn't much favor either of his folks, played guard on the Bears' offensive line, but he kept getting hammered by the Pirates' hefty but fleet-afoot pass rushers. The game proceeded sloppily, and, about six minutes into the second quarter, Doug got slammed again. He crumpled to the turf and just lay there.

Dusty yelled, "O my God!" and he and Hallie stood. The Bears' coach and a student trainer hurried out to tend to Doug, who still did not uncoil. Then an olive-skinned woman in designer jeans and a white peasant blouse trotted across the field, a brown-and-ocher scarf streaming silkily behind her. She stooped beside Doug.

"Who's that?" Reed asked.

"Lakshmi Chakraborti," Dusty huffed. "*Doctor* Lakshmi Chakraborti."

Understandably, he and Hallie left us to descend to the field and to hurry across it to their son. Eventually, a motorized cart removed Doug and his folks to the eastern end zone, and the Shallowpits did not return. Reed and I wondered whether to look for them or to stay in our places until they came back.

A minute or so later, a man from a lower row of our concrete tier stopped us on a nearby stairway. A wide-faced man of fifty-five or so, he introduced himself as D. V. Purina and said that Dusty and Hallie were going with their son to a hospital in Waycross because Wriggly, a town with a population of a thousand or fewer, did not have one. I had already known that, so it had pleased me to learn that the woman seeing to Doug was in fact a bona fide doctor.

D. V. Purina—a second local surname echoing that of a pet food!—added that Doug had suffered an ankle break and that his parents hoped we would stay to see the rest of the game. If we liked, he'd drive us home afterward. I didn't like that idea much because he had a live crotalid coiled in one of his jacket pockets. In fact, it had propped its head on the pocket's upper edge. To Reed's chagrin, I asked D. V. Purina, what his initials stood for.

"Viper Disciple," he said.

"Mr. Purina," I said, quasi-coquettishly, "that would make your initials V. D. instead of D. V., so please tell me the truth."

Grinning, he said he'd flip-flopped his first two initials to avoid having them suggest "venereal disease"—wouldn't I have done the same?—and returned to his seat over by the band's clarinet section. We returned to our seats on the Shallowpits' favorite tier.

At halftime, Brunswick's band played well. The Wriggly band followed. It marched out of sync while badly reprising vaguely familiar ancient rock tunes, but the band members' parents and pals stomped and cheered like madmen anyway.

Then I went out to direct four giggling cheerleaders in a bow-and-arrow shoot of the Mylar-balloon Pirates bobbing in the end zone like buoys on a hurricane swell. It took ten minutes, and the pops these Pirates made when they burst were fewer and harder to hear, even from where I stood, than the hits that the human Pirates inflicted on our boys in either of the first two quarters.

We would have gladly walked home, but D. V. Purina found us, led us to his snazzy SUV, which boasted snakeskin seats, and dropped us off at our house. Before we told him goodbye, I commented that perhaps our squad would have played better as Diamondbacks than as Bears, better as Rattlers than as Bruins.

"I've always thought that." He handed each of us a business card:

D. V. Purina
Attorney at Law & Coroner
Pastor, Take-Up-Serpents House
Nokuse County, Georgia

Later we learned that, as a student, he'd been a star running back on the Bears and, a few years later, a wrangler with three consecutive victories in the annual county Rattlesnake Roundup.

As for Doug Shallowpit, he had surgery in Waycross on Saturday. Two days later, he came home to Wriggly sporting a newfangled style of ankle cast. He and Dusty mourned the fact that his season had ended, but Hallie confessed to me her secret relief.

A few days later, Celeste awoke with stomach pains. I sent her to school anyway. When she came home still complaining, I made her an appointment at the Wriggly medical clinic with Dr. Chakraborti.

In its split waiting area, which only a few decades ago had seated whites on one side and blacks on the other, we peered at the art on the walls: reproductions of work by Henri Rousseau, Norman Rockwell, and a startling one of a nude young woman charming a cobra. We also glanced at the people waiting alongside us, and I realized that most blacks, however many had once resided in Nokuse County, had long since left it. Dr. Chakraborti might now be the darkest-skinned person in town. I'd suspected as much, just as I'd known that Wriggly lacked a real hospital, but, filling out a patient-information form for Celeste, a cold adder of apprehension snaked down my spine.

"*Celeste Godfrey,*" the receptionist called.

Dr. Chakraborti did not keep us waiting forever in the examination room, and, upon entering, shook Celeste's hand as well as mine. Good: she had her priorities straight. She also had a no-nonsense demeanor and a dry humor that softened her directness when she asked Celeste, not me, about her problem.

When she got down to business, she brushed Celeste's hair back, checked her throat using a tongue depressor, and palpated her stomach and flanks. After this examination, she told Celeste to get dressed again and led me into the hall by my elbow.

Alone with Dr. Chakraborti, I asked, "What's wrong with her?"

"How do you mean, Mrs. Godfrey—as your daughter or as a scared young person?" Her question took me aback, but did not put me off.

"The second of course, but the first too . . . if you know."

"Beyond my medical training, I don't know much. But I discover a great deal."

"What have you discovered about Celeste?"

"She could have a virus or early intestinal cramps, but I *sense* that she's suffering from anxiety, possibly a school phobia."

"Why do you sense that?"

"Other children in town have psychosomatic pains akin to Celeste's."

This was news to me, but hardly a dumfounding surprise.

"Do you have a rattlesnake in your home, Mrs. Godfrey?"

"It's a law here. So, yes—yes, we do." My defensiveness alarmed me, but I couldn't shut up: "Celeste calls it Vype. She reads aloud to Vype. She feeds Vype. She's totally okay with Vype, I assure you."

"I'm sure she *thinks* she is, just as I'm sure she'd very much *like* to be."

"I'd like to be okay with Vype, too."

"But you're not?"

"Of course I'm not. How could I be? How could anyone?"

"I've been in Nokuse County a bit over a month, and three children under twelve have *died* of rattlesnake bites, one here in town just a day or so ago."

"I've heard nothing of this."

"At the behest of the Rattlesnake Alliance, local authorities conceal the information from the general public. Moreover, a county law mandates the suppression of death notices for anybody killed by snakebites."

"Whatever happened to the First Amendment?"

"We're in Nokuse County, the Realm of the Raving Rattlesnake Wranglers. Surely, you saw the Paul Desiré Trouillebert in our waiting room."

"I'm sorry—*what?*"

"I'm talking about a painting, of a woman and a serpent."

"Oh, right. The woman in it's nude, right?"

"Yes, that's the painting."

"I actually like it, doctor, but it seems shockingly *naked* . . . in many disturbing ways, especially in a doctor's office."

"Mrs. Enots, my receptionist, tells me that a year ago a member of the Alliance came in and hung it where you saw it. Then he insisted that it stay there."

"But it's an Oriental scene, and the serpent in it's a cobra, *not* a rattler."

"It's still a snake-loving male's ultimate wet dream."

"Yeah," I glumly conceded. "You're probably right."

"I've taken it down and shut it up in a closet at least four times since my arrival, but Jessica—Mrs. Enots—always finds it again and puts it back up. She says we're safer with it on the wall."

"I can believe that, too."

"I'm sorry, Mrs. Godfrey. I've taken us pretty far afield, haven't I?"

"No problem—but how did a woman of your background wind up in a godforsaken little backwater like Wriggly?"

She told me that a program in India and a similar one in the U.S. had supported her move to our under-served county. They gave her a scholarship for additional training at the medical school in Augusta and loan-repayment aid if she practiced two years in a rural area. But they'd provided few clues about what lay in store for her.

At that point, Celeste emerged from the examination room, dressed.

"Doctor," I said, "I saw you at Friday's game helping an injured player."

"Oh yes, young Mr. Shallowpit. I discovered his problem and sent him to Waycross for surgery—not a very satisfactory use of my hard-earned skills."

"But helpful: *essential* for anybody who happens to live here."

"*I'm* here now." Celeste held out her arms to prove it.

Dr. Chakraborti leaned over and kissed her sweetly on the forehead.

"Why, yes, so you are. I'm prescribing something for your stomach pain and maybe something else as well."

"What 'something else'?" I asked.

"I thought a tranquilizer, but she's far too young, and I don't want to hurt her. Nor do I wish to incur a malpractice suit."

I winced at this pronouncement.

"Steady." Dr. Chakraborti turned back to Celeste. "If you'd care for a lollipop, go see Mrs. Enots. She'll bestow one on you—like a medal, no doubt."

Celeste ambled down the corridor, her fingertips brushing the wall. Dr. Chakraborti gazed after her with undisguised fondness.

"Doctors have their peculiar wild-hair notions, too," she said. "Good ones—and I'm a good one—don't act on them." She added that Celeste had sensed my anxiety and adopted it as her own: a secret act of filial concern for whatever was now troubling me. "Would you like me to prescribe *you* a tranquilizer?" she asked.

One of the kids who had died of a rattler bite had gone to school with Celeste. At a parent-teacher meeting three days after we saw Dr. Chakraborti, I got this word from the mothers of two of Celeste's classmates.

These women claimed that the tutelary rattler of the boy's family had bitten him as he slept. But his daddy, a member of Take-Up-Serpents House and the Nokuse Rattlesnake Alliance, denied this assertion and did not take him for an antivenin treatment. Both Dad and Mom claimed that a fever had seized the boy and that they'd thought aspirin and cold compresses would banish it. When this did not happen, they drove him to Waycross for a definitive diagnosis, but on the way he died. This story had big holes in it, but the boy was irretrievably gone, and Celeste slid more deeply into her upsetting funk.

You can't easily hide the death of a school-aged child, and this family did not manage to. Publicly, his parents said the boy had died of a rare and virulent form of meningitis. His memorial service, a few days after news of his death ran through town like a flashflood, drew many mourners, young and old. Celeste asked Reed and me if she could go. Bleakly cheered by her interest, we accompanied her to the event, which wrapped everyone there in a cosmic despondency.

The next day, a skinny young stranger walked all around Wriggly handing out flyers or sticking them under the wipers of parked cars. The flyers said that at least three children had fallen victim to rattlesnake bites over the past month and that several adults in the pine flats north of town had suffered bites that had made them deathly ill or, in the case of one victim, killed her—though her husband refused to admit that their threshold sentry had so much as flicked its tongue at her.

Mr. Alpo caught the skinny stranger slipping a flyer into the door handle of an RV in his camp, braced him against it, and read the flyer. It ended by urging every citizen to turn in their tutelary rattlesnakes to a state veterinarian who would come to town shortly to examine and possibly even defang them.

Because Mr. Alpo had thrust a dropped flyer into my hands, I knew their common message. Further, I knew that each one bore this signature: *Lakshmi Chakraborti, MD, GP, RCG (Rural Care Giver)*.

And our skinny flyer supplier, given dire warning, wisely hightailed it.

Uh-oh, I thought: Uh-oh indeed.

Two days later, I returned to Dr. Chakraborti with Celeste to see about her lingering apathy and depression. We sat in the waiting room paging through old magazines, sneaking glances at the naked snake charmer as I tried to fathom my reluctance to take Vype out back and decapitate him.

The clinic door opened, and Jasper Shallowpit stuck his head in and whistled shrilly. Mrs. Enots whistled back in a less shrill tone, apparently acknowledging that he and his pals had arrived just when expected—by Mrs. Enots, if by nobody else.

The door then banged entirely open, and, along with Jasper and Dusty Shallowpit, three more mostly ugly men burst in: D. V. Purina, Newall Alpo, and Tug Terden, a grizzled country-western rocker who allegedly owned more rattlesnakes in Nokuse County than any other native-born citizen.

In his shaggy mid-sixties, Terden was also the heir to and the figurehead CEO of Terden BioQuirked Creations and hence a major source of funding to institutions, festivals, associations, and alliances dependent on both native rattlers and the BioQuirked kinds. I had heard of Tug Terden years ago, for a record called "Snake-Bit Klooxer" and for several well-publicized arrests for indecent exposure at various undersold concerts. But, until moving to Georgia, I had never known that he hailed from Wriggly or that he derived such clout from its most notorious "bio product."

All five men burst in shouting, "Lakshmi! Lakshmi! *Lakshmi!*" Celeste screamed, and two or three other patients also stood, I among them, as they toppled end tables and yanked cheap reproductions by Rousseau, Rockwell, and Warhol from the walls, but left *The Nude Snake Charmer* hanging. But, even as distraught as I was, I figured that Terden had taught his fellow marauders all he knew about staging disruptive chaos.

"Mr. Terden!" I shouted. And: *"Mr. Alpo! Mr. Purina! Mr. Shallowpit! Dusty!"*

All five men paused in their wilding to gawk at me.

"Wylene," Dusty's father said, "take Celeste and get the hell out of here."

"No sir, I will not."

"You better," Mr. Alpo said. "You all could get hurt damned nastily." The snake in his belt loops did its signature peristaltic horizontal dance.

"Go ahead and fire me," I said. "We're staying."

"Why?" demanded Mr. Shallowpit, or possibly, "Wye!"

"To witness and testify to your vile punk vandalism!"

Dusty looked nonplussed, sheepish even, but Tug Terden sidled over and stuck his drug-drawn mug so near to mine that I could smell the whiskey in his pores.

"Look," he said. "I'd never hurt this little chicky of yours—not here, anyways—but, you buttinski Ozark hoor, *you're* fair game."

Lakshmi Chakraborti stepped into the waiting room. "Mrs. Godfrey is not your prey, Mr. Terden. Or, I shouldn't have to remind you, anybody else's."

Dusty pulled Terden aside to menace me: "Wye, if you throw in with her to make us put down or defang our rattlers, you'll pay!"

"Tell me how, Dusty: You gonna sic your trouser-snake Wriggly on me?"

Now a cayenne-pepper red, he lifted a white-knuckled fist.

Dr. Chakraborti said, "You have no credible reason to pay this clinic such an unruly visit. Get out, all of you. And don't leave without Mrs. Enots. She's fired."

"What?" Mrs. Enots said. "Why?"

"Because you're Newall Alpo's sister, Jessica, and you never told me."

"What difference does that make?" Mrs. Enots asked.

"That nude over there belongs to Mr. Alpo, and from Day One you've colluded with him to keep that inappropriate image on our clinic's walls."

"Hang on a sec," D. V. Purina said. "Stop passing out flyers threatening our rights to own and handle serpents. Stop asking your patients intrusive questions about their threshold sentries. And what the hell's 'inappropriate' about a snake?"

I held up my cell phone. "Should I call the police, ma'am?"

Before Doctor Lakshmi could respond, Terden eased over to her, grabbed her throat with one raw hand, and banged her head against the door behind her. I hit the number for the police department in my cell listings just as he took a rattler from the thigh-pocket on his camo pants and thrust its wicked head into the doctor's face.

Queasily, I thought, He could've done that to *me*.

"You'll soon be one badly snake-bit quack," he told Doctor Lakshmi.

D. V. Purina grabbed Terden and flipped the rattler free of his grip. "You're abusing that snake, Tug." It had now begun to coil about on the linoleum as if either stunned or galvanized. "We've made our point," Mr. Purina said. "Let's haul our grits out of here." He seized the twisting rattler, folded it back into his pocket, and dragged Terden away from the doctor. He and his pals led Jessica Enots, their spy, toward the office door, Dusty glaring back at me venomously. As they left, Mr. Alpo stopped, lifted *The Nude Snake Charmer* from its brackets, and carried it out with him.

The door slammed shut, and all I could think was that we had survived a potentially deadly assault of rattlesnakes and men. Two patients who'd endured it with us broke down, one in tears, the other in discreet gibbering.

*

Dr. Chakraborti did not back off, and because she didn't, the Nokuse Rattlesnake Alliance invoked its assets all the harder: zealous supporters, deeply ingrained rattlesnake fetishism, well-established local law, a culture of machismo entitlement, abiding economic interests and incentives—*et cetera, ad nauseam.*

Doctor Lakshmi continued to preach to local mothers, appealing to the instincts of life-preservation that the Rattlesnake Alliance had also staked out, albeit differently. She and her followers stressed nurturing and sustaining life, the Alliance its lordship over natural and BioQuirked creation and also its members' right to proactive self-defense.

Doctor Lakshmi's approach appealed more strongly to me, but many women sided with their men because they disliked being labeled ultra-fems. Others had livelihoods based on raising and selling either rattlesnakes or their prey, on making rattlesnake novelties and clothing; or on hawking security systems dependent on Tug Terden's BioQuirked threshold sentries.

Very few men sided with Doctor Lakshmi.

I worked on Reed. "Do you know what your friends the Shallowpits and their crew want local law to do now?"

Unhappily, Reed shook his head.

"To mandate two rattlers for every three human beings in a household! To authorize living pit vipers even in the public schools!"

"Shit." Reed looked down in palpable chagrin.

"Doctor Lakshmi says a baby that recently supposedly died of SIDS has—"

"Died of what?"

"SIDS: sudden infant death syndrome; crib death. Some say it happens from infants sleeping on their stomachs. Some say it's—"

"Okay, okay. Hasn't that SIDS crap been passé almost forever?"

"I guess, but some Nokuseans use it as a cover for babies that die of crotalid bites. Our coroner, Mr. Purina, regularly reports snakebite deaths as SIDS-related. If an adult dies of a snake bite, he blames either a heart attack or a stroke. *You'd* be stricken by the number of *women* who die of these two 'causes,' especially in homes cited for domestic disturbances and likely abuse."

"Who told you all this crap?" Reed asked.

"Doctor Lakshmi."

"Jesus, she's overstepping herself—that's all private info."

"I don't believe that, and if it *is* legally private, it shouldn't be. We're talking public health here, mister."

"Bullshit," Reed murmured.

"Right back at you. Think on this: Your friends the Shallowpits would rather lie than admit that one of their precious pit vipers has murdered a baby."

"*Murdered?* Snakes lack consciences. They don't murder—they kill."

"Dead is dead if it's your child. The *Shallowpits* have consciences, don't they? How can they swallow all the Alliance's cynical and transparent lies?"

"They grew up here. It's their livelihood, partly—also their culture."

"To watch their kids and other family members die? And to think they're addressing the issue by asking every citizen to harbor even more venomous snakes?"

Reed pursed his lips. "Wylene, they're *BioQuirked.*"

"You know, if it took a normal adult human male nine months to have an orgasm, maybe he'd finally get it."

Reed's eyes widened in horror. "*What?*"

"What do guys invest in creating a kid—two minutes of drool-accompanied pelvic thrusts? If it took you three quarters *of a year* to get your ashes hauled, maybe you'd feel a tad more committed to the resulting kid and wouldn't start so many damned wars or shrug off your own and other peoples' kids' premature deaths as if they had no more significance than a swatted housefly's."

After several beats, Reed said, "I sort of resent that, Wye."

"Adults who can't handle life's fatal realities have no right to resent the truth." Those words spoken, I stomped away fearing they'd had no effect whatsoever.

War broke out, raged or sputtered, and whelped its casualties.

At an official meeting in Take-Up-Serpents House, the Rattlesnake Alliance and our Wriggly city councilpersons—most of whom were *members* of the former group—approved a resolution requiring that households of more than three persons adopt two pit vipers as guardians, with another serpent for every three additional persons. It also insisted that every classroom in the city's public schools purchase a "pedagogical security paladin" from Terden BioQuirked Creations, Inc.

After this in-your-face local victory, the Alliance took these proposals to every town council in Nokuse and petitioned for their adoption. Despite some organized opposition, every council voted to do as asked. Two town councils stipulated that the snakes fulfilling a protective function must be "deadly native, i.e., North American, pit vipers." This clause permitted households to catch or buy copperheads and cottonmouth water moccasins, not merely native or bioengineered American rattlesnakes, as threshold sentries and living pocket protectors. It did so even if their lack of BioQuirking made them more unpredictable and thus more dangerous than TBQC crotalids— which rattled politely for their owners' benefits but for nearly everyone else maintained a deadly dead-eye-dick silence.

Tug Terden opposed this clause, but by this point the extremists among these outlier Alliance members had the upper hand and prevailed. (Extremists? How does an extremist define *extremist*? I saw them as self-righteous lunatics or psychopaths.) Still, BioQuirked sales teams began going door to door with young rattler specimens as starter or pedagogical serpents. They had warrants to search each house to ascertain if they had the needed number of security paladins for all their human residents.

Doctor Lakshmi and I, along with many women and a few men (although not yet Reed), protested these mandates, picketing TBQC, Shallowpit Feed & Seed, the businesses of those making snake-related novelties, and even the homes of non-Alliance city councilors who had cravenly or corruptly yielded to every damned Alliance demand.

We were heckled, harassed, beaten, and snake-bit, even as two of our persecutors were lethally poisoned by their own carry-snakes in two separate assaults on us. Our foes' rattlers, despite BioQuirking, often struck randomly in such melees, just as a sane person would expect. I read the deaths and injuries to our enemies as Poetic Justice (God forgive me), but in most of *their* cases, access to antivenin prevented deaths.

By contrast, we were *denied* antivenin treatments. Hence, we always donned high-topped leather boots and thick clothing for our protests. Of course, I felt sorry for the wives and children of the men who had fallen victim to what I couldn't help calling "benevolent vipery," but it served the jerks right.

Didn't it?

*

Life dragged on, like a satiated serpent seeking a spot to digest a big meal. Our protests occurred less frequently. Newall Alpo had long since fired me, and when I applied for the receptionist job at the Wriggly clinic, an anonymous committee nixed my application and gave the post to Hallie Shallowpit. In addition, Mr. Alpo, D. V. Purina, the Shallowpits, and a host of others continued to revile Dr. Chakraborti and her allies, me included, as outlaws, traitors, and saboteurs of Nokuse County culture.

VIPERS SAVE LIVES, Morrison LePieu, the lobotomized chairman of the board of Terden BioQuirked Creations, liked to say, and anyone disagreeing was an alarmist idiot. To me, that motto made about as much sense as Orwell's fictitious slogans WAR IS PEACE, SLAVERY IS FREEDOM, and IGNORANCE IS STRENGTH. When a rumor began circulating that Tug Terden had approached the Irish government about supplying it with BioQuirked rattlers as stealth defenses against some militant separatists (because, after all, VIPERS SAVE LIVES), Reed clutched his head in histrionic agony and cried in his worst Irish accent, *"Has the whole damned world gone buckfuck then?"*

Unfortunately, Celeste did not improve, and because her classmates had targeted her as the spawn of both troublemakers and traitors, I pulled her out of school and taught her at home. Further, Dusty told Reed that if I did not stop agitating for Doctor Lakshmi's agenda, he'd fire Reed, as painful as he, Dusty, would find doing so.

Reed, either manning up or losing his grip (if not both together), replied, "Fire me, Dusty," and when Dusty did, we Godfreys found ourselves income-less in a house that Jasper Shallowpit said we must vacate in two weeks.

That evening I shot arrows into as many sun-bleached planks in our privacy fence as I could. Drenched in sweat and so blurry-eyed that the whole bonkers world looked watery, I said to myself, *"What do we do now? Where do we go?"*

That night Celeste overheard Reed and me talking—about Wriggly, its inhabitants, and our current dilemma. I found her outside our door and walked her back to her room. Again cynically channeling Julian of Norwich, I told her that everything, every single thing, would be well, yes, all would be well, yada yada yada.

The next morning, looking zombie-like over her Cream of Sawdust, Celeste let her spoon fall and slumped sidelong before Reed or I could catch her. Reed scooped her up and carried her back to her bed. A thorough examination revealed that she'd neither bumped her head nor bruised any part of her lower body. We checked her out for Vype's bite marks and found nothing worrisome. We rarely let Vype out of his tank anymore, but Celeste still doted on him, and we could *not* watch her every moment. But because we'd inspected her for bites, we now had not a clue what had prompted her swoon.

I called Doctor Lakshmi at the clinic, and Hallie told me, coldly, that she had not yet come in. I more or less believed her, but maybe Hallie didn't give a keratin rattle what befell *any* of us backstabbing Godfreys nowadays.

Then Hallie said, "I'll tell her you called, Wye, as soon as she gets in." She sounded no warmer speaking these words, but she did what she said she'd do, for in less than an hour Doctor Lakshmi made a house call on us.

"It's more of the same," she told Reed and me.

"Meaning what?" Reed asked.

"Suppressed immune system, extreme depression, and total withdrawal as a form of subconscious escape and self-protection."

I asked, "What should we do?"

"Get her out of here. Take her back to Arkansas. Relocate to Alaska."

"Are those our only options?"

"Import a gazillion king snakes or mongooses and let them wipe out every rattler in the region." She shook her shiny but unkempt tresses as if to dislodge a sleeping asp within them. Then, knowing that she had *not* encouraged us, she referred us to a child psychologist in Waycross. This sad concession to our hopelessness broke my heart.

"Oh, Doctor Lakshmi!"

She grimaced in apology, and we hugged like long-lost sisters reuniting. Reed stood to one side fidgeting, like the father of a terminally ill child . . . as maybe he was. Well, no—no, he wasn't.

Doctor Lakshmi returned later that day to give us a prescription that she'd filled in town: pills for Celeste's stomach, others to buffer her depression. She and I sat for a while in the glider on our stone patio out back, staring at the fletched ends of the arrows protruding from plank after plank in our privacy fence.

"How do you plan to get all those out?" Doctor Lakshmi asked me.

"Maybe," I said, "I'll just let Dusty snatch them out with his teeth."

The next day, Doctor Lakshmi told us, she'd take a leave of absence—

with a PA, or physician's assistant, from Brunswick as a fill-in—and drive to Atlanta to ask officials at the Center for Disease Control for help in halting the preventable epidemic of snakebite injuries and deaths in Nokuse County:

"It's criminal and the state should intervene," she would tell them. Us she would tell, "In my absence, Godfreys, you must hold your heads up, take care of Celeste, and, yes, *keep the faith*."

Somehow or other, Dr. Lakshmi Chakraborti took her concerns not only to the CDC, which rebuffed her (owing to the discovery in Iowa of a veteran of the Australian war infected by bacterium with global-epidemic potential), but also to representatives of the *Atlanta Constitution* and three of the city's local TV news teams. None of these organizations—apparently—had Rattlesnake Alliance sympathizers in their executive hierarchies, and so Doctor Lakshmi was able to speak to both print and broadcast reporters. She conferred with them about falsified medical reports from Nokuse County and about the snakebite deaths that its well-established coroner, D. V. Purina, had attributed, questionably, to other causes.

Segments of these interviews aired on TV in Atlanta and environs and, amazingly, in Wriggly via a satellite service that we subscribed to. I say "amazingly" because censors at the Atlanta-based stations generally redacted from the feeds to our area any and all commentary critical of the crotalid-related industries in South Georgia.

"What do you want to happen?" one reporter asked Doctor Lakshmi.

"Real improvement in the lives of the citizens of the county in which I've worked these past few months."

"Are *you* a citizen of that county?"

"Only in a technical sense—I'm fulfilling an obligation I incurred while earning my medical degrees in Augusta."

"You've raised serious concerns about the integrity of a county official."

"I've told the truth. Clearly, this coroner is protecting Terden BioQuirked Creations, the culture of herpetological excess that reigns there, and also people making tons of money from these interests' dangerous activities."

"Uh-oh," I said sidelong to Reed.

"No shit," he replied.

Later, when everything was over, we learned that somebody in Nokuse County had contacted Governor Bixby Wheeler, a smoothly corrupt South

Georgia boy, to tell him that a "buttinski foreign hoor" had gone on TV to besmirch the proud names and the economy-driving livelihoods of thousands of law-abiding Nokuse Countians. And she was doing so—*"Irresponsibly!"*—at the expense of those very citizens.

When Dr. Chakraborti returned to Wriggly three days after these interview snippets aired, she found a group of vigilantes boarding up her clinic. Several patients had queued up outside to watch, as had many other people, all initially unbelieving. This time, the vigilantes did not include even one of the five Alliance big shots who had disapproved of the flyers she had paid an "out-of-town mercenary" to pass out.

No, this group consisted of four or five younger males who looked as if they denned every night with rattlers. All had face-only smiles you'd expect to find on Halloween masks, and their carry-snakes had come along as hatbands, epaulets, belts, or slippery pocket riders. Their activities in front of the clinic pissed off rather than scared Doctor Lakshmi.

"Stop!" she ordered them. "Tear down those boards."

Instead, said my informant, they seized her, duct-taped her mouth shut, laid her on the sidewalk atop a big sheet of plywood, bungee-corded her to it, and poured blackstrap molasses over her from tins they had brought along with their clinic-closing tools. Doctor Lakshmi fought this indignity, lurching futilely from side to side and struggling to scream through her duct-tape gag.

She had no help, though, and the vigilantes had their sick premeditated way.

"If I'd been there with quiver and bow," I told my informant, "I'd've shot each of those douche bags straight through an eye—*thwap! thwap! thwap!*"

"No, the layout of the buildings wouldn't have let you. Even if you'd been shooting from a rooftop across the street, all the spectators would've posed problems. If you'd been on a street or a sidewalk, you might've hit one, maybe two, of her attackers, but those guys pack throwing stars as well as snakes, and they'd've hit you with a *shuriken*, or closed on you and pulled you down before you could hit more than one of them. Only a fool would have tried it, Miss Wylene."

"You're giving those damned sons of incest too damned much credit."

"No, ma'am, you're giving them too little. They're fanatics. They practice all the time. They're fallible, but they're also good enough to bean you with a *shuriken* and slap a snake on you to deliver the *coup de grace*."

My informant went on to say that the Alliance vigilantes then broke open five or six goose-down pillows and shook their feathers all over Dr. Chakraborti—a modified tar-and-feathering that led even usually decent people in the mob to laugh, point gleefully at the victim, and revel in the high-and-mighty doctor's humiliation. I just could not get this behavior, but my informant said there had been plenty of other witnesses and that it all had "gone down" just as he was describing it.

Next, he went on, the triumphant clinic closers had lifted Doctor Lakshmi's plywood bier and carried it above their heads through the streets like a shoddy float in a two-bit Mardi Gras procession. My informant knew where they were taking it, but he, unfortunately, could not follow them there—at least not yet.

"Where?" I demanded. "Where did they take her?"

To one of the warehouses of Shallowpit's Feed & Seed, my informant replied. When they arrived, they put her plywood pallet atop a bank of plastic-wrapped hay bales. Helpless in her bonds, sweltering in oozy syrup, she lay beneath a swaying electric lantern in a vaulted niche of the warehouse. Then they left, locked the building, and scattered. They wanted Doctor Lakshmi to suffer. And she did. Insects—mosquitoes, horseflies, and blurry-winged millers—tormented her. Rats came to taste the molasses and maybe her flesh, and, after the rats, the warehouse's security paladins, rattlesnakes all, emerged to eat the bloated rats and poison the brutalized woman.

"That last stuff never happened," I said by way of protest.

"No—no, ma'am, it didn't."

It didn't happen because, later, my informant crept up to the warehouse, made a way in, and with a Finnish Army knife, kitchen tongs, olive oil, and many other small serviceable items, freed Doctor Lakshmi from her bonds.

He then guided her to a shower stall in the old structure, gave her soap and a curry brush, privacy for her ablutions, and, later still, a tee shirt, a pair of jeans, and some tennis shoes to replace her own spoiled clothing. He also handed her keys to a doubtfully reliable pickup on the premises and advised her to use it to carry her out of town. And she used it for just that purpose while my informant limped home and crawled into his bed as if he had never, at least on that night, stirred from it.

*

"You're talking about Doug," Reed said as we drove *our* pickup away from Nokuse County as fast as possible—with a trailer attached and the freight of all our problems heavy on our minds, but weightless on the truck's spavined frame.

"I am. He swore me to secrecy, Reed, until we were out of town, but he couldn't let me go without easing my mind about Doctor Lakshmi."

"My God, the nerve of the boy."

"He's a really good kid."

"I guess so, but Dusty would shit a brick."

"Hallie wouldn't. She must've done something right or Doug would have turned out just as sadly adder-pated as his daddy."

In fact, Doug's actions that night, and also later, enabled Doctor Lakshmi to travel to Washington, D.C., to confer with a female senator from Georgia who sent U.S. Marshals to Wriggly. They arrested D. V. Purina and each of the five vigilantes in the feather-boarding of Doctor Lakshmi.

Cell-phone videos of their assault not only easily identified the culprits, but also ran on national and state newscasts, with simultaneous Internet showings, many of which went viral. The videos created a tsunami of outrage that further embarrassed local officials and the furious leaders of the Rattlesnake Alliance. They could not condone what their young thugs had done, but neither did they wish to condemn their actions. And, by denial and demurral, they scoffed and did not condemn them.

Reed glanced sidelong. "I'm sorry I ever brought you down here, Wye."

"One way or the other, we all pass through this territory eventually."

We rode listening to the hum of our threadbare tires. Celeste snoozed on the bench seat between us. Her health, mental and physical, had measurably improved just in the past week, and she had not fallen prey to any apparent separation anxiety from leaving our rental house, Wriggly, or our snaky companion, Vype. In fact, I had set Vype free in the exhausted turpentine flats behind our fence, and he had quickly slithered away.

Shallowpit Feed & Seed, Terden BioQuirked Creations, and the Rattlesnake Alliance all remained in business, and Bixby Wheeler was reelected in the gubernatorial race that fall. But a spotlight had shone on all Nokuse County and its bizarre mores, and it continued to shine upon them.

Doctor Lakshmi had not yet returned to town—many people wiser than I knew that it was unsafe for her to return—but she now had friends in higher places than our gold-domed Capitol. Also, I had her cell number and her email addresses, as she had mine, and the world seemed far less venom-filled than it had mere days ago.

As we cruised away from Wriggly, Reed said, "I can't get over Dusty's kid."

"The boy knows a real human being when he meets one. Doctor Lakshmi qualifies." After a moment, I added, "So does his mother."

"Sunuvagun," Reed said: *"Sunuvagun."*

I had never heard that expression before, but the way Reed inflected it, it had an affectionate, even upbeat lilt that kindled in me a scrappy hope. I asked him where he had heard it and what it meant.

"It's old Koorie army slang. Dusty once said he thought it meant something like—you know, like *'Will miracles never cease?'"*

The next day we entered Great Smoky Mountains National Park in Tennessee—for we had traveled north—and took time to drive through Cades Cove. Celeste jerked upright on our pickup's bench seat to peer through our bug-spattered windshield into a glen carpeted with grass and studded with oaks. In this glen, a black bear and two cubs seized our attention. One cub sat on a limb high above their watchful mama, but the other romped all about her through lush spears of emerald green.

And for the first time that year, I felt almost as if I had come home, even as I also knew that one day we'd return to Nokuse County to meet with Doctor Lakshmi again and to atone for our failures there—not with its BioQuirked rattlers, but with the men whom those snakes had so easily and thoroughly beguiled.

ABOUT
THE
AUTHOR

Michael Bishop is the award-winning author of *No Enemy But Time* and several other acclaimed novels, including *Ancient of Days* and *Brittle Innings*, and also such story collections as *At the City Limits of Fate* and *Brighten to Incandescence*. He lives in Pine Mountain, Georgia, with his wife, Jeri, a retired elementary school counselor, who is now an avid gardener and an occasional yoga practitioner.

ALSO BY
Michael Bishop

BRITTLE INNINGS

In 1943, at the height of World War II, the Highbridge Hellbenders of the the class-C Chattahoochee Valley League deep in Georgia acquire a 17-year-old shortstop from Oklahoma named Danny Boles. Jumbo Hank Clerval, a mysterious giant, and the mute Danny Boles strike up an improbable friendship that culminates in a host of haunting discoveries in both the simmering South and the wind-swept Aleutian Islands. Hailed by critics as a contender for the Great American Novel laurel, *Brittle Innings* evokes a bygone era of worldwide conflict and homeland unity.

ANCIENT OF DAYS

What if a living specimen of *Homo habilis* appeared in the pecan grove of a female artist living in Georgia? What if she reached out to her ex-husband, a restaurant owner in the small town of Beulah Fork, to help her establish the creature's precise identity? A rare combination of science fiction, noir mystery, and comedy of manners, *Ancient of Days* will challenge you as have few other novels.

COUNT GEIGER'S BLUES

While skinny-dipping in a pool polluted with radioactive waste, Xavier Thaxton, arts editor at a major Southern daily, is afflicted with superpowers all his own and becomes that which he most scorns. A radiation-induced ailment, the Philistine Syndrome, forces him to assume the persona of comic-book hero Count Geiger to allay its career- and indeed life-threatening symptoms. This novel of intellectual heft and self-spoofing kitsch is a take on superheroes like no other: a rollicking foray into high and low culture that mines the vicissitudes and tragedies of everyday life for serious belly laughs and bona fide heartbreak.

WHO MADE STEVIE CRYE?

Mary Stevenson Crye, a recently widowed young mother known as Stevie depends on a balky PDE Exceleriter for her free-lance writing. Then the PDE Exceleriter goes noisily on the fritz, and so many other things begin to go wrong as a result, including her machine's insistence on typing segments of her everyday life as she either lives or hallucinates it. A novel of the American south, an alternately tender and scathing parody of twentieth-century horror novels, and an involving account of one woman's battle to maintain her sanity.

PHILIP K. DICK IS DEAD, ALAS

In this heartfelt science-fiction homage, Philip K. Dick dies in 1982 in Santa Ana, California, during the fourth term of the repressive imperial presidency of Richard Milrose Nixon. Soon thereafter, stripped of his memory, Dick turns up in the office of Lia Bonner, a young psychotherapist in Warm Springs, Georgia. Ultimately, Dick manifests at Von Braunville, the American moon base, as a key figure in a gonzo conspiracy to trigger a "redemptive shift" of world-changing scope.

A FUNERAL FOR THE EYES OF FIRE

Seth Latimer, a human member of a family of clones, finds himself marooned on Gla Taus with no way home unless he joins a mission to a neighboring world to negotiate the transfer of a minority population from one planet to the other. Diplomacy devolves into brutal expediency against a background of complex gender and religious polarization. Alien settings and cultures are lovingly woven into this story of passionate individuals caught up in the sweep of history toward tragedy, change, and eventual renewal.

JOEL-BROCK THE BRAVE AND THE VALOROUS SMALLS

Joel-Brock Lollis's family has vanished into the labyrinthine Sporangium below a curious Georgia emporium, Big Box Bonanzas. Glimpses of an older J-B Lollis of the Atlanta Braves on a BBB television suggest that Joel-Brock may never get back his parents and sister. Joel-Brock and the Valorous Smalls forge their way into the mushroom realm to change that possible future.

from Fairwood Press & Kudzu Planet Productions
www.fairwoodpress.com

CPSIA information can be obtained
at www.ICGtesting.com
Printed in the USA
LVOW12s0417090817

544325LV00003B/295/P